THE SKY THRONE

CHRIS LEDBETTER

Month9Books

Published by Month9Books, Raleigh, NC 27609
Cover design by Najla Qamber Designs

Month9Books

To my father who put my first book about Greek mythology in my hands when I was five years old.

THE SKY
THRONE

CHAPTER ONE

Since the moment I started at Eastern Crete Lower Academy two years ago, I'd felt like such an outcast. The guys, mostly Potamoi and sons of Headmasters Okeanos and Tethys, never regarded me as an equal. I didn't even warrant bullying. It's like I never even existed. If only I'd known how visible I'd become in the coming days.

I always got picked last for swim team and crew in physical fitness class. I actually was the third best wrestler overall in school and peerless in javelin throwing due to superior training from my guardians, the Kouretes. When Eastern Crete competed in the Mediterranean Invitational Games against academies from Phoenicia, Egypt, and Libya, I placed first in the javelin event, beating Gurzil from Libya who was the reigning champion from years past. I even won my weight class, *the lightest class there was*, in wrestling by beating Melqart from Phoenicia. But none of that mattered.

I was still invisible.

I loved science class. The lessons where we studied energy and matter were like fresh spring water to a parched throat. But the rest of my classes bored me to tears. We had language arts, music, and math in the mornings. Physical fitness, agriculture, and science took up our afternoons. I wouldn't say I was intellectually ahead of them, because, hey, that'd be conceited. But my mother prepared me well, with all the goat tending and such. And she always said when I came home from classes each night that they just didn't know how to teach me on my level.

So, I was forced to make my own fun. No one would probably notice anyway.

After the big Invitational Games win, I was posted up at the school's entry columns with my best friend, Anytos, watching the Oceanids as they arrived for classes one morning. Sisters to the Potamoi, the Oceanids were the sea nymph daughters of our headmasters. Okeanos and Tethys, aside from being our school administrators, were also Elder Deities of the vast ocean, which is why we at Eastern Crete dominated all water sports. Swimming. Cliff diving. Crew. We bested all comers. But not me. I dove and swam exactly the same ... like an anvil.

The Oceanids descended upon the campus from their barracks like a wave crashing against the shore. Telesto, the most beautiful sea nymph by several stadia, smiled at me for the first time since I'd been going to the school. Okay, it wasn't a full smile. The corner of her lip twitched upward as she flipped her wavy, aquamarine hair over her shoulder and glanced past me. But that counts, right?

I backhanded Anytos in the chest. "You saw that. That's my opening. If I don't make my move, she'll be gone to the upper school next year."

"Pssht, she is *beyond the Mediterranean* beautiful. Completely unattainable."

"Did you see that come hither stare she flashed me?"

"Looked more like indigestion."

"You are as wrong as you are false. Cover my back. I'm moving in."

I crossed the courtyard in a flash and caught Telesto's arm as she reached the weather-beaten front door to the main school hall. "Telesto, you look as if the sun radiates from you."

She paused and leaned back against the doorframe. "You're just saying that because I wore my yellow tunic today."

"You shine with such brilliance; you should wear yellow every day."

She folded a strand or two of stunning teal hair behind her ear and twirled the ends. "But what happens when I wear my purple tunic?"

"A tunic hasn't been invented that could dampen your beauty."

She giggled and turned away from me for a moment. "Zeus, is it?"

I nodded, surprised she even knew my name.

"You're the one who pulled that massive prank on my mother, Headmaster Tethys, aren't you?"

Oh, that's how she knew me. Not invisible after all. I bowed. "I am him. He is me. One and the same."

"Crazy. She was so mad." She shook her head, stifling a smile. "As far as I can tell, language arts must be your favorite subject. Your tongue is spectacularly sharp-witted."

"Not really. But I am feeling a little inspired right now."

Several strands of her hair fell to cover half her face. "Are you going to the bonfire at the beach tomorrow night?"

"I wasn't invite—"

Several of Telesto's broad-shouldered, dark-haired brothers bumped into me from behind. "Those are uncharted waters, boy. Careful now," One of them called over his shoulder. Those were the first words they'd ever spoken to me.

Telesto rolled her eyes. "Pay them no mind. They're harmless. You were saying?"

"Those bonfires are an Oceanids and Potamoi thing? It's kind of a secret club that you have to be born into, right? Being brothers and sisters, children of Headmasters Okeanos and Tethys... young water deities in training… masters of rivers and streams…"

"I guess. But you should come out any way. It's all night, under the stars. Eating, drinking, stargazing… What's better than that?"

Gazing into her mesmerizing, iridescent eyes, my mouth fired before I could stop it. "Kissing you under the stars. That's better."

"Sprint much? You're a fast mover."

"I just go after what I want."

"Well … " A pink tint rose on her high cheek bones. "We shall see. But first you have to show up." Her lips twitched gain. "I have to go to class. See you tomorrow?" She disappeared inside the school hall.

I turned to Tos with a pterodactyl-eating grin on my face. He shook his head and smiled.

The boring part of my daily routine was set to commence. School. Classes. Ugh. I wished the school day was already over so I could just go to games practice. As Tos and I walked to first period, I was struck by the overwhelming urge to liven my day up just a bit.

"Tos, I have a good one. You with me?"

"Oh heavens. Is it what I think it is?"

"I feel the need … the need to prank!"

Tos shook his head. "My pranking days are over."

"Come on. Just one more. Promise it's the last one."

He glared at me.

I explained the entire idea to him. "It'll be after language arts, all right? It's going to be good."

After class, Tos and I waited until all other students had left. He took his position at the door to make sure no one came in. I approached Professor Ceto at the front of the room. Tablets and scrolls decorated the top of her desk.

"Professor, do you have strong hands?"

Her intelligent eyes narrowed. "Sure, I do. Why?"

"I bet you a homework pass that you can't balance a goblet on the back of your hand."

Her forehead wrinkled.

"Place your hand on the desk, palm down," I said.

She complied.

I filled her water goblet and placed it on the back of her hand.

She smiled. "See. No problem at all."

I picked up the goblet. "Now place your other hand on top of this one."

She sighed. "Why? Is that supposed to be harder? So, if I fail, you get a homework pass, yes? If I complete the task, what do I get?"

"It's a surprise."

"Go ahead, then," she said, placing her left hand atop her right. "Get on with it."

Barely able to contain my giddiness, I balanced the full water goblet on the top of her two hands.

"See," she said with triumph in her voice. "I did it. Where's my surprise?"

"All right then, I'll see you next week. Have a good weekend." I walked quickly to the door.

"What? Wait, I can't move my hands without spilling water all over my scrolls."

Tos opened the door and we both rounded the corner in a flash.

We were halfway to period two music when I heard an unholy roar across campus.

"ZEUS!"

Tos and I laughed our behinds off and slapped hands as we passed a solitary blueish post in the center of the courtyard. No one knew much about it or who designed it. But its presence was striking.

Upon reaching music class, Tos and I took our positions near the kithara and lyre. Our teacher, Professor Leucosia and several more students entered and we prepared for instruction. Leucosia had the most beautiful singing voice. Simply spellbinding. Sometimes, I felt light-headed when she'd sing along with our accompaniment.

Shortly after arriving in class, Headmasters Okeanos and Tethys shadowed the doorway to our room. The expression on Tethys' face could have killed a wild boar at forty paces.

"Zeus, Anytos, we need you to step outside right now." Tethys said. Her eyes mirrored the Aegean during a storm.

I looked at Tos. My heart rate quickened to a pace I'd only felt after running sprints. Slowly, I rose to my feet. This couldn't have been good.

We walked over to Okeanos. I had to crane my neck just to see the Headmaster's eyes. His biceps were bigger than my head, despite silvery blue hair atop his head and an aged, wrinkly face.

His somber and deliberate voice rumbled. "You are hereby expelled from Eastern Crete Lower Academy. This infraction and expulsion will go on your master record. You may apply again next term."

"Why? What did I do to deserve this?"

Professor Tethys stepped forward to grab my arm. "Your little pranks have gotten you in deeper water than you can swim in, young man. You obviously need some time to think about how you can be a better contributor to the educational system."

"No. You can't expel me. Please!" I clasped my hands in front of my face. "My mother will kill me!"

"Not our concern." Okeanos folded his gigantic arms. His voice rumbled again. "You must learn to be a better student. A better citizen."

"But they were just pranks," I pleaded.

"Yes. And this is the seventh such prank we've endured at your hands. And since Anytos helped you, he shall accompany you home." Tethys pointed east toward Mount Ida, the highest peak on Crete. "You have until the sun chariot reaches its zenith to leave campus." She gazed upward. "By the looks of things, your time's nearly at an end."

CHAPTER TWO

I hung my head. Anytos glared at me. His gaze screamed all the words he didn't say. On our walk home, we passed the bobbing ships in the harbor port, and the dry dock where most of the Kouretes, my guardians, built seafaring vessels. Aristaeus headed the watercraft and open sea navigation program to post graduate students who didn't get invited to the upper academy. He also coached for some of the events at the games, mainly crew. But that was a thinly veiled recruiting push for rowers to eventually man the oars on his long distance, open water vessels that visited foreign lands.

My school, or rather the school I just got expelled from, was part of the Olympus Academic District, which included six other lower schools around the Mediterranean and Aegean. The Nereids, daughters of Elder Deities Nereus and Doris, went to schools on the islands Euboea, Samos, and Limnos. Eastern Crete Lower Academy, despite its name, actually sat at the central northern edge of the island, attached to a harbor. There used to be a Western Crete on the far northwest corner of the long crooked finger of our island. But that school closed and the students were split between Eastern Crete and Kithira, which is an island off the bottom tip of the mainland to our north. Actually, all of the island lower schools and the mainland of Hellas were north from us.

All lower schools fed Mount Olympus Preparatory Academy and Othrys Hall Academy, yet only the most elite pupils who graduated with honors from a lower school were invited to attend the great mountain school, Mount Olympus Prep, on the mainland. I was sure Telesto was a lock to move on. Since my expulsion, however, my chances of making it that far had been reduced to somewhere between slim and none.

Anytos exhaled loudly through his nose every couple of steps during the entire walk back to our goat drawn chariot. He never spoke a word during the entire ride home, made even longer by the silence. And let's be real, goats just weren't that fast to begin with.

My mother, Amalthea, stood in a field near my cave home, tending our goats when we arrived. Her smile embraced me. "How was your day?"

Had I been alone, I would've told her nothing about what had happened at school. I mean, I might've mentioned it eventually. But having Tos standing next to me with this horrendously sad expression forced my hand. I sulked, hating that I had gotten my friend in trouble as well. I only wanted to have a little fun.

"I ... uh ... " I began and then sighed. "Well, we actually were ... uh ... sort of expelled from school today."

Mom's eyes flashed fire as she glared at me. "I don't have time for your antics, Zeus! I have a goat farm to run." Her hands flew skyward. "What do you mean ... expelled?"

Anytos eased away from us toward the cave that we both called home. He left me there to explain the entire ordeal to Mom. The disappointment on Amalthea's olive-toned face hurt the most. The dimple on her smile had been erased, replaced by a furrowed brow. She listened and then very calmly told me I was on punishment and that I was to finish watching the goats for the remainder of the day and then shovel their dung. Tending goats was like watching the sun crawl across the sky. It made watching grass grow seem like a party. Shoveling goat patties was even worse. I nearly vomited numerous times.

Amalthea used to teach agriculture at Eastern Crete. When she retired, she became a prize-winning goat farmer, breeding goats to be shipped to every lower school in the Olympus Academic District for use in agriculture classes. The Kouretes lived nearby. When they weren't building ships, they provided security and protection for Amalthea's goat empire. Mom expected me to take over the goat farm. Anytos stood next in line to inherit the goat security operation. He could have had both, as far as I was concerned. He didn't have to worry about me fighting him for either dungtastic job, no offense. I had grander plans in mind.

Σ

The following day after goat tending chores from sunrise to sunset, I bathed and then collapsed, exhausted, into a deep sleep on my bed inside the cave. I woke in the middle of the night with a start that almost made my heart leap from my chest for beating so hard. I shook Tos' shoulder.

He finally opened his eyes. "What in the underworld do you want?" he whispered.

I put my finger to my lips and pointed to outside the cave. "I have to show you something."

"Wha—"

"Shhh!" I glanced around the semi-darkness. The torches at the cave entrance cast just enough light inside that I could see that no one was stirring. I tugged on Tos' tunic and then rose to my feet atop sleep-weary legs. Tos followed. We snuck outside the cave, careful not to alert anyone.

I whispered again, "We have to get to the bonfire."

"The what?"

"Just before we were expelled, Telesto invited us to a bonfire at the beach tonight. It's an all-night affair."

"Are you crazy? I'm not going anywhere with you in the middle of the night."

"Please. I need this. You do too. This is the first invitation we've ever gotten to an Oceanids party. Trust me; there'll be enough girls and food for you too."

"That's not my concern." He sighed. "*You* just got *me* kicked out of school. *You* are on punishment. And now *you* want me to get in more trouble? No, thank you."

"It's not more trouble. Is the water goblet always half empty for you?"

Tos narrowed his eyes at me.

"Okay, bad joke." I glanced around to the cave entry to see if anyone had heard us. "Look, I'm going. You can stay here if you want." I rose to my feet.

"Telesto must've singed a few brain cells when you were flirting with her earlier. You have completely lost all logical thought."

"Who needs logical thought when sea nymphs beckon? So you're in?"

Tos shook his head. "I can't let you go by yourself. Who knows what trouble you'd get into without me."

"Great, we'll be back before sunrise and then act like we're getting ready for goat duty."

"Goat duty is your bag. When we return, I'm taking my hind parts back to bed."

I gripped his hand. "I'm glad you're talking to me again."

"Shut up before I change my mind."

We stole ... no, *borrowed* a chariot and one goat. Luckily the goat was half-asleep. By the time it began bleating, we'd traveled several stadia away. We turned the chariot northward. The beachfront spread out before us at the base of the cliff that overlooked the harbor port near school.

When we arrived, crackling fire already stretched into the night sky. Flames leapt high above our heads. At least a hundred people dotted the beach, unless I didn't pay close enough attention in math class and my estimating skills were off. Some of the guys threw a circular disc back and forth. Others threw spears at a ringed target. Girls danced in groups while others played lyres and flutes. The waves provided percussion for their efforts.

After I asked several people if they'd seen Telesto, and received either blank stares or sneers, Tos pulled me aside.

"You look as desperate as a fish flopping around, struggling for air." He clapped me on the back. "I told you we shouldn't have come. It's just like school, only darker outside. It's not like we were winning any popularity contests."

"Confidence is everything. Act like you belong, and you will."

"Sure, because that's worked for the last two years at Eastern?" He sighed "I only came along to keep you from getting in more trouble. I have accepted my lot in life. Goat security is my future. That, and boat building. I'm a Kourete, and that's all we've ever done. I'm never getting called up to the big school. You at least had a chance. Until you blew it."

"Goat security and protection, huh? You calling me a goat, now?"

"If the hoof fits, brother … "

I rolled my head and neck several times, finally realizing the near pointlessness of searching for Telesto, a drop of water in the sea of Oceanids and Potamoi. I took my sandals off and walked toward the water's edge. The drum and hiss of the waves on the shore soothed already frayed nerves.

I turned to Tos. "See? Isn't this nice?"

He looked at me as if I were talking a foreign language. "So you mean to tell me I woke up from a deep sleep, snuck out of our home, stole a chariot *and* a goat, and traveled many stadia in the dark … just to stick my toes in surf?"

I had to admit, he had a point.

A soft voice sailed up behind me like the sweetest musical note. "Zeus, I thought you were going to leave me hanging tonight."

I turned to see Telesto, an absolute vision of loveliness. Warmth flushed through me.

"I heard about your expulsion and figured the stars just weren't aligned for us," Telesto continued.

"I must admit … " I began. "I was soundly wrapped in the comfort of sleep. It took every ounce of strength I had just to open my eyes. Tos here had to remind me about the party. Otherwise … "

Telesto narrowed her eyes. "You're such a bad liar. I bet you dragged your friend here kicking and screaming."

"Yes and yes," Tos responded.

Telesto laughed, and then turned to slide her arm around another girl she'd brought. "Tos, I brought a friend of mine. Her name is Eos."

Anytos and Eos shook hands. The gleam in his eyes told me everything I needed to know. He was as struck as a harpooned whale. They walked off down the beach. My job there was done.

I returned my attention to Telesto. But, I tried to play it cool. Or at least cooler. Tos had been right. My skin had itched with the sense of helplessness when I couldn't find her. But all was right in the world after all.

"Something's different about you," I said waving my forefinger in front of her.

"It's the hair," she said without missing a beat. Her mass of aquamarine hair was pinned atop her head in a wild nest. Seashell earrings dangled from her ears. "Bonfire night isn't about being cute; it's about living life to the fullest."

"I couldn't agree more. That's exactly what I told Tos."

Telesto held my gaze. Her voice softened. "Thanks for coming out. And thank you for approaching me at school. I wondered if you would ever step up and talk to me. I don't bite. At least not at first." A wicked grin creased her cheeks.

I took a bold chance and slid my hand over hers. She didn't move away. That was the moment I knew we'd get on fabulously. I relaxed on the beach beside pearl-skinned Telesto. We talked for what seemed like forever. Until what was once a sky full of stars, now featured a sole defiant sparkle. After a full night of getting to know each other, she rose from lying on her back to resting on her elbows.

"What's next for you, Zeus? What will become of you?"

That was difficult, given my current status at school. So I deflected. "You first."

She laughed and sat all the way up with her legs crossed. "I'm expected to graduate from upper academy. I'll probably end up at Othrys Hall like most of my older siblings. I heard it's near impossible to get into Mount Olympus Prep anymore." She took a deep breath. "And then I want to come back and teach. Or maybe teach at the schools on Limnos or Samos out in the Aegean. Now stop fooling around. Where's your life headed?"

I stared at the lonesome star in the sky as if it held the answers I sought. It didn't. I sighed hard. "I hope to get *off* this island, truthfully. Maybe hunt dragons on the mainland. I could make good money, you know?"

"You sound just like some of my brothers, those crazy flapadoodles! They think there's some mysterious beast at the bottom of the Aegean that they can kill and become instantly wealthy. Boys and their dreams."

"Mom wants me to take over the goat empire she's built. But the goat herding thing just isn't my bag."

"What about school?"

I drew out the next word into a two-syllable construction. "Yeah ... That's the thing. I first need to make it through lower school."

In front of us, a gradually dying fire gave way to the pre-dawn glow in the sky as Anytos and Eos returned.

"You kids have fun?" I asked Tos.

He gave Eos a quick hug as the surf washed up around their ankles and then ambled over to stand next to me. A smile dimpled his cheeks, which he quickly stowed away. He kicked my feet. "Zeus, look at the sky. We need to go."

CHAPTER THREE

I had to admit that he was right. We'd been out way longer than other times I'd dragged him out. In my defense, no matter how long we'd stayed out before, we always made it back on time. Except this time, we were both already on punishment.

"Wait … " I held my finger in the air, and then turned back to Telesto.

She rifled her fingers through my hair. "Tonight was fun. We should do it again sometime."

I flashed a grin. "See you tomorrow?"

She purred, "Maybe—"

Tos jogged to the top of a dune. "Seriously, we don't have much time. Remember Amalthea's mantra: The Sun sees what the Moon disregards."

I pulled Telesto to her feet and stared into her iridescent eyes. We threaded fingers as our lips met. She tasted like the sea, salty and untamed. She turned and walked down the beach into the surf. She waded out and dove into a cresting wave. Her legs morphed into a fishtail as soon as the seawater reached her hips. As I turned, I knew the surf was already washing her footprints away.

I sighed, trudging back up the darkened beach, digging my toes in the sand with each step. We definitely needed to get back to the cave before Mom and the Kouretes woke up.

"Don't you ever get tired of goat herding?" I asked Tos once we reached the chariot.

"That's what we do, Zeus."

"It's as dreary as watching the moon crawl across the sky; death by boredom." I said. "They do nothing but graze and sleep." I'd always felt like I could do more. *Be* more than a goat herder. Something inside of me clawed for the extraordinary. I couldn't be a teacher without schooling. Teacher, farmer, or livestock herder … those were the only options on Crete. Telesto clearly wanted me to be more than I was. She was quite unimpressed with my dragon hunter idea. I had to face that I'd likely never leave Crete.

Tos turned to me and huffed. "The Kouretes are going to be volcanic if we don't get back before they wake. Not to mention Amalthea," he said. "I never should've let you talk me into going to that bonfire."

I laughed. "Yeah, 'cause you had *such* a terrible time."

"That's beside the point." Tos straightened his tunic. "Are you ready?"

I waved my arm in front of my chest. "After you—"

I stepped onto the chariot after Tos. With a whip of the reins, we shot off, heading south down the trail back to Mount Ida, which sat almost perfectly in the middle of the island. I knew the mountain's position because Amalthea made me map the entire thing before heading to Eastern lower school. Our chariot raced so fast, we took curves on one wheel.

"Faster, you blasted goat!" I yelled. "Yah!"

Ahead, Ida's elevation beckoned. My mother's dark silhouette emerged from the cave's shadow. Damn! We hadn't made it back in time. Amalthea waved her staff in the air.

I glanced over my shoulder as we pulled into place. The sun's orb rose faster than usual, pushing through beautiful crimson and gold cloud bands. Darkness to light in a split-second.

Tos turned and almost pulled my arm almost from its socket. "That's not normal. Hurry!"

We sprinted the final stretch around several of the Kouretes, now awake. Aristeaus blew a horn to summon the remainder of them.

We drew closer to the cave. My mother stood and pivoted toward the sun. The sky brightened from blue to intense yellow in several heartbeats. Beginning as a golden disc, the sun grew in size and intensity until the entire sky filled with orange fire. I shielded my eyes against the searing heat, but dark spots swam in my vision like tadpoles.

"What's going on? I realize I was late coming home, but this is ridiculous."

"Hyperion is descending! Get in the cave. Now!"

CHAPTER FOUR

A malthea yelled something else just as we ran through the cave's entrance, but I couldn't tell what. My breath caught in my throat. I headed back into the brightness and scorching heat. My face stung like being inches away from bonfire flames.

Tos' fingertips dug into my arms to pull me back. "Don't—"

"I'm not leaving my mother out there!" I jerked my arm from his grasp, and then grabbed my battle helmet from inside the cave, the one I owned but never used. I rushed into the clearing, gripping my spear and shield as well. Tos' footsteps—as I knew they would—followed closely behind me.

I searched the horizon for my mother, finally finding her scampering down the hill around trees that shriveled under the intense heat. Goats scattered in front of her, some falling motionless to the ground. I wondered why the temperature didn't affect me the same way. The Kouretes had already taken up battle stances in the wilting high grasses, shields folded across their chests, spears ready to throw. My mother tossed her walking stick aside and scurried back behind them.

"Get back in the cave!" she said. Her eyes widened as she caught sight of me, with Tos not too far behind. Her wrinkled and severe face resembled a fig left in the sun too long. She gazed over my shoulder. "Anytos, I thought I told yo—"

The ground quaked beneath our feet as a roaring explosion throbbed through my ears. A mountain of a man emerged from the gargantuan fireball. His soot black chariot pulled by four enormous stallions the color of sunset descended slowly to the ground. His onyx hued helmet, breastplate, greaves, and battle skirt swallowed light, not reflecting it.

Hyperion.

I stood slack-jawed, never having witnessed Elder Deity magic before. In fact, I wasn't sure it even existed until that moment. Teachers never exhibited it. Okeanos either. I thought it simply whispers that hissed around campfires. Stories told to maintain order.

My chest heaved like I was hyperventilating. Fighting for every breath, I gripped my shield and spear tighter. Perspiration trickled down my forehead and into my eyes.

Hyperion bellowed, "Where's the boy you're harboring?" Flames leapt off his muscular, dark brown arms and legs. The air around him refracted and shimmied like a mirage.

"What boy?" my mother answered, shielding her eyes.

"The Oracles foretold of a boy who is not of Potamoi blood on this island who shall meet an untimely death, unless he surrenders himself to me." Hyperion stared at Amalthea and straightened his breastplate. "Where is he right now? Patience is not my strongest quality."

Before I could form words, Tos pushed his way around the Kouretes. "I'm the only boy here who meets that description," he said. "What business have you with me?"

"Surrender or be taken," Hyperion roared.

"I've wronged no Elder Deities." He drove his spear into the ground. "I am not the boy you're looking for."

"The Oracles do not lie." Hyperion nodded his head forward. "Take him." Two young men with shoulder length blond hair jumped off the back of the chariot. Muscles rippled beneath their shiny, black armor.

My mother inhaled sharply through her teeth. Her head twitched sideways like she wanted to check over her shoulder at me, but she stopped.

"I'm not going anywhere." Tos grabbed his spear and stood his ground.

"He must be the one!" Hyperion pointed at Tos. "If he won't come willingly, then just kill him so I can return this chariot to the sky."

My eyes bulged beneath my helmet. I gasped, wanting to call to Tos. Had we done something to anger the Elder Deities? All I did was a silly prank. Oh, and kiss Okeanos' daughter. I edged closer to the Kouretes and blended in with them, ready for anything.

The Kouretes charged past Tos toward the chariot. Hyperion's horses reared up and breathed fire on them, halting their progress. With shields raised, the tribe could draw no closer than twenty paces to the towering chargers or the young men.

Tos and I retreated to protect Amalthea. The Kouretes launched their javelins. Hyperion swept his hand in the air dismissively. All twelve spears flew off course. I gaped at the display of power.

One of Hyperion's attendants stepped forward and threw a long, black spear toward us. It sailed over the heads of the Kouretes before they could block it. I barely had enough time to reach my mother. Scrambling to fold my shield in front of her, I knocked the spear off course. The spearhead groaned against the shield, diverted course, and then lodged into Tos' chest with an immortal thud.

"Anytos! No!" All the air in my lungs expelled.

My best friend flew backward several feet from the force of the impact. A sharp pain sliced through me like I'd also been hit. I ran to him.

He wheezed, "I'm sorry I failed you, Zeus. Protect Amalthea—"

I stood just in time to see the second of Hyperion's attendants release his spear. I pushed my mother aside but the weapon *veered* toward her. I watched helplessly as the javelin's tip sank into her shoulder. The force spun her halfway around.

My mother belted out a skin-crawling yell before crumpling to the ground. Anger heated the blood surging through me. I grabbed the obsidian spear shaft that stood erect from Tos' chest. It reflected no light, oddly. In fact, the shaft absorbed any available light. I yanked with all my strength to dislodge it.

I whipped around to return fire, cocking my arm back like the Kouretes had taught me. I set to deliver the most crippling blow I could. But the spear was forcefully torn away from my grip. Hyperion held out his hand and the spear flew straight to his palm.

Hyperion laughed from deep in his belly. "He clearly *wasn't* the boy we're looking for. He died far too easily." The deity turned his attention back to me and the other Kouretes. "I *will* return to this island to continue my search. Or Kronos will. And you don't want *him* to come down here."

I narrowed my eyes and glared through the slits. My arms shook with fury as the young men mounted the chariot. With several whips of the fiery reins, Hyperion returned his chariot to the sky.

I rushed to back Tos' side. "Come on man. Get up. Wake up. Say something. Anything." I removed his helmet. He offered no response. Blood gushed from his horrific chest wound. I grabbed him and looked around frantically. "Somebody help me!"

I grasped his hand and pulled him close. A dull ache pulsed in my chest at the same location of his wound. His spirit embraced me as confirmation of what I feared. The Kouretes scrambled to help but it was too late. I pounded my fist on the ground, breathing in short bursts. My teeth hurt from clenching them so tightly.

One of the Kouretes pulled me off Anytos. "Let him go. He was gone as soon as the spear hit him," he said. "Go tend to Amalthea."

More Kouretes carried Anytos to the cave. I turned to my mother, who lay on her side, curled into a ball, but still breathing. Her tears dampened the soil, and blood pooled at her wound. But, at least I had hope for her.

"Please, Gaia, Earth Mother of all beings, please make my mother whole again." I crouched close to the ground. Her back arched when I worked to remove the weapon. I set the spear on the ground, and then the strangest thing happened. The spear became a shaft of dark smoke, which drifted away on the wind, leaving a sulphuric odor behind.

I shook my head. "What the—?"

Aristaeus, leader of the Kouretes, brought me a towel and some water. He stood tall over me like a tree. His sinewy, muscular frame shaded me from the remains of the burning sun.

"Did you just see that?" I asked him. "The spear vanished into the air. What kind of weapon does that?"

"Deity magic is unparalleled." His lips drew to a tight line. His gaze intensified. "But more importantly, look what *you* have done!"

I stared upward at his expressionless face. His skin was tight and stiff like goat's leather.

"Why did you return home so late *this time?*" Aristaeus yelled. "You got kicked out of school. You dragged Anytos to who knows where. And now your carelessness got him killed!"

My voice cracked. "It was an accident. I swear. We just wanted to go to this bonfire with my school mates."

I didn't need his lecture. Shame wrapped around my shoulders like an iron cloak.

My mother groaned as I rolled her toward me. "Easy … " I whispered, pressing the towel against her wound and pouring water over her cracked lips. She opened her eyes slowly and coughed.

"You're not safe here anymore," she whispered. Then she fell unconscious.

CHAPTER FIVE

I snapped my head toward the sky. The sun was again where it should've been, like it had never descended. The distance between darkness and light was a split-second, my mother once told me. A sliver of space. The breadth of a strand of hair. However, I hadn't known what she'd meant until today.

I wished I didn't still.

While the Kouretes hauled Anytos into our home and searched for wayward spears, Aristaeus carried my mother inside. She lay motionless along a wall. I swept the wispy curtain of dark brown hair away from her eyes. Her shallow breaths gave me hope that she'd be all right. I clenched my jaw and rubbed my arms to curb the sudden shivers wracking my body.

My mother lay so peacefully. I dripped more water over her lips. A spring of new sadness welled up as I extended my hand toward her. My fingers trembled against her olive-toned skin, pressing her cheek where her dimple would've been.

My voice quaked. "Mother—"

Aristaeus called out to me, his skin drawn tightly over his boney face. "You *will* stay inside! You hear me?"

As if I would go anywhere after what just happened. I rolled my eyes, wanting to yell at them. *Anything* but having to face my responsibility in what had become the darkest day of my life.

I walked to Anytos and knelt beside him. I stared at his closed eyelids, my throat constricting, wishing he was simply asleep and would wake at any moment. "I'm sorry. I should've listened to yo—"

Aristaeus approached and I couldn't hold back my anger. "Why didn't you protect us?" I snapped, standing upright and bracing myself for retaliation.

"Protect you? You mean drag your ass back from wherever you went despite being on punishment? Is that what you mean?" He scoffed. The Kouretes moved in behind him at the sound of commotion. "*You* got Anytos killed." He pointed his gnarled finger at me. "Your carelessness. Your disregard for rules. Your disregard for family. Your poor shieldsmanship—"

"My shield," I yelled, "saved my mother's life. More than you can say!"

"And killed Anytos." Aristaeus paused. His eyes sliced through me. "You never think of anyone but yourself. Ever since the Elders dropped you off as an infant, you've burdened us, in one way or another." After several breaths, he spoke evenly. Almost a whisper. "You're leaving tonight."

"Come again?" I stepped backward.

"Hyperion *will* return. And I can't risk anymore lives." Aristaeus sighed. "You've been here far too long as it is. You must find and reconnect with your *real* mother."

His words stung. Disbelief clogged my throat. "*Wha—*"

"Amalthea is not your birth mother."

I opened my mouth to speak, to protest, but words failed to form. My stomach wrenched.

"She raised you, yes. But another woman gave birth to you.

Perhaps you'll find her one day."

"Liar!" Brimming at the edge of my eyelid, a tear formed, trembled, and fell. Then another. I fought to contain them, but the day's events left me standing on shaky ground.

He shook his head. "If only I were ... "

Memories flashed through my brain, threaded together like a tapestry, threatening to unravel at any moment. What in my life had been real? Certainly my friendship with Tos had been. A person can't fake that kind of authenticity.

But Amalthea? She may not have always coddled me, but she was always there to encourage and teach me. I never felt unloved. And yet ... this entire portion of my life had been a lie. I walked over to her. Anger laced through me. I wanted to yell and ask her all the questions in the world. Every query began with a "why," with a few "hows" thrown in for good measure. I had no idea who my "mother" was anymore. I had even less of one as to who I was.

I clenched my teeth and turned to Aristaeus. "The Sun Deity descends upon us and two sheep-for-brains with deadly aim assault us. And, now ... *now* you tell me she's not my real mother!"

"It's deeper than either of us can fathom," Aristaeus said. "Rhea warned us this could happen, that Kronos might look for you one day."

"Who are these people and what do they have to do with Hyperion?"

"We sail tonight. You'd better get some rest." Aristaeus walked away, leaving me simmering in a pool of frustration. My glare turned to a scowl. I paced, wearing a path in the soil.

Despite all of the lies, perhaps my allegiance should still lie with Amalthea. After all, she did raise me. Which was more than my *real* mother ever did. Whomever she was ... she was definitely going to get an earful when I found her.

The Kouretes built a small pyre for Anytos outside the cave. They believed the ceremonial cremation of the body would allow Tos' soul to rest. I couldn't even bring myself to look at it. I could barely breathe through my thick and swollen nostrils. My legs refused to walk in Tos' direction. Instead I walked to the underground spring to clean myself and put on a new tunic.

I hurled my bloodied tunic against the wall of the cave. But the memories of Tos and the time we spent together swept through me anyway, like a river whose dam had broken.

Aristaeus called me outside. My steps were uneven as I begrudgingly approached the pyre with my friend's body on top. I covered my mouth with my hand and closed my eyes.

"Take this," Aristaeus said.

He extended a torch toward me, urging me to grasp it. I couldn't. My hand refused to move.

"Take it!" he demanded. "This was all your fault. You're not killing him. He's already dead. You're simply releasing him. Send him to peace. You owe him that much."

Pressure built at the bridge of my nose. Each tear that gathered felt like salt in an open wound. The torch's light prismed into a kaleidoscope of colors through my tears. I climbed onto the pyre, grabbed Tos, and held him close one last time. My heart weighed heavy like the mud bricks we used to build forts with. Guilt, self-doubt, regret, and sorrow kept slamming into my chest. What could I have done differently? That spear had my name on it. All I wanted was to start the whole day over.

My hand trembled when I took the torch. I turned away from the pyre as I let the torch drop from my hand onto the pyre. I returned to the cave and put my head between my knees.

"Here's the plan." Aristaeus approached again. "When night falls, we'll sail until you reach your new home, Mount Olympus. We'll be your personal escorts until you reach the shores beneath the big mountain. Then, hopefully someone from the Academy will greet you. If not, you'll be on your own."

"So, you're sending me to Mount Olympus Prep? But I haven't

finished lower school yet. I just got kicked ou—"

His voice reverbed in a deep solemn manner. "Yes. I know."

"What about my mothe—, I mean Amalthea?" I asked. I stammered over the words as they clogged my throat. I pulled at the neck of my tunic and rubbed my sweaty palms on my legs. "I am not leaving her."

"She'll be all right. Time is all she needs. After all, they weren't after her."

"But—"

Suddenly, Amalthea whispered through the air, "Zeus."

I rushed to her side. "You're awake." I embraced her, careful not to press the wound. Warmth filled my chest. Every question I had rushed my brain, competing to be voiced.

"Zeus ... y-you must get to Olympus," she whispered.

"I can't leave you. Not in this condition," I said.

"You endanger us all now," she whispered. "You have to—"

Aristaeus knelt beside her. "We're steps ahead of you, Amalthea. Hyperion must retire his chariot at day's end. We leave tonight." He turned to me. "Once you get to Olympus, you'll find the answers to all your questions. Hopefully."

CHAPTER SIX

I hated being uprooted. My stomach cramped in consideration of all that I'd lost the previous day. My best friend. My mother. My home. Life as I'd known it. I definitely wanted to leave Crete, but not *this* way. I refused to live the rest of my life ducking to avoid capture all the time. One day, I wouldn't have to hide. If it was the last thing I ever did, I'd become powerful enough that I wouldn't have to hide anymore. From anyone.

I wanted things to return to normal somehow.

No descending suns and disappearing spears.

Just two boys chasing some nymphs.

We set out from the harbor port under cover of night in one of the boats Amalthea used to ship goats to Aegean schools. The moon and stars guided us. Through the next several days, Aristaeus and the Kouretes rowed me to my new home with urgency and amazing speed. Sails and a powerful tailwind helped as well. We made several stops to drop off goats, eat, and wash up.

Every day we stopped at a different island. I drank in the new lands with wide eyes. Different schools. Nereids instead of Oceanids. Finally though, we approached an unfamiliar shore where a mountain rose majestically in the distance and stretched into the clouds. Our ship lurched to a stop after it ground onto the sand.

Waves drummed the shore around us. Clouds rolled overhead, skimming off the mountain. I filled my lungs with thick, salty air. After climbing over the side of the ship, I removed my sandals. The gritty sand between my toes brought a shred of serenity. I glanced back toward the ship. The Kouretes stared at me blankly. Aristaeus nudged me from behind.

Twenty paces away, two stout columns stretched from an untouched sandy expanse into the low-hanging clouds, guarding a narrow path through a grove of trees. I gazed at the peculiar etchings that encircled the mammoth cylinders.

"All right. What now?" I sighed. My torso quivered.

I walked to either side of the columns. Then I stepped between them. As soon as my foot indented the sand on the far side, my peripheral vision registered an odd blue post standing just inside the columns. It looked oddly similar to the artistic installment back at my old school.

A flash of light blinded my eyes. Once my vision readjusted, a woman stood before me.

Tall and statuesque, she emanated power and elegance. A thin, gauzy garment draped her slender frame. Her silver-streaked, curly hair bounced as she walked toward me and tried to slip an arm around my shoulders.

I inched away.

"Do not fear me, Zeus." Her arm curled around my shoulder, causing me to immediately tense at the initial contact. Then, all of a sudden, serenity enveloped me as the woman's touch drew an odd response of familiarity.

"Welcome to Olympus. I've been expecting you."

I coughed, looking around. "But how? I didn't even know I was coming until a week ago. How do you know my name?"

"I am the head recruiter for the Academy." She brushed my hair out of my eyes. "It's my *job* to know you."

Recruiter? Academy?

"Yes. Mount Olympus Prep is actually a preparatory program for gifted and talented youth whom I've hand selected. And we selected you a long time ago."

I scrunched my face up and tilted my head in confusion. At least my heart rate had normalized.

"The Headmaster and I will attend to your queries during orientation." She peered past my shoulder with a stern gaze. "Were you followed?"

Annoyed that I was being asked more questions than being given answers, I turned around. "Not really—but, Hyperion attacked my family recently." My voice rose slightly. "I think the Elders are after me for some reason, but no one will tell me what's going on—"

"We must hurry then. Come." She whisked me away from the columns and the blue post.

I turned to look over my shoulder. The Kouretes had put out to sea again, and gently eased from my view. I wasn't sure of anything anymore, least of all, this woman. "Wait." I stopped and pulled my arm back. "How do I know I can trust you?"

She placed her hand on my shoulder. The energy that transferred, calmed me like a light misty drizzle falling within my body. "Do you feel that?" she asked.

I nodded.

"That's how you know you can trust me."

"But—"

"I don't have time to explain right now." She waved her hand and a lion appeared as if she'd simply lifted a blanket off its back. The beast threw its head back and gave a deep, throaty roar, shaking its mane. The sound reverbed through my entire body. "Get on."

I stepped backward on shaky legs at the sight of the massive cat.

She swung her leg over the lion's back and fisted her fingers in its mane. I studied her carefully. One thing was certain; the Kouretes didn't make a fuss, so this lady must've been all right. I guided my legs over the lion's bristly fur.

"Hold to my waist," she said over her shoulder.

The lion dug its paws into the sand, and then bolted off straight through the grove of olive trees and into the trough of the valley. The green of the gorge just beyond was more vibrant than anything I'd seen on Crete. Damp, woodsy aroma filled my nose as I grabbed tightly to my guide's waist. The beast raced up a well-worn path into the hills. Without warning, it gained speed, pawing aggressively at the earth, and then leapt over a wide ravine.

I dug my feet into the side of the beast, feeling myself sliding toward its tail. My eyes bulged. I held my breath as my heart rose into my throat. But the lion kept sailing through the thick air until its gigantic paws connected with earth again. Then it cut sharply and entered another narrow gorge that took a steep turn.

I exhaled what felt like three lungs worth of air and coughed.

The lion grunted its way up the sheer incline until finally coming to rest on a plateau just outside a set of immense, black gates. I caught my breath in several deep inhales, and tried to mentally push my heart from my throat back into my chest. I pried my tingly fingers from around my guide's waist and swung my leg over, stumbling a few steps atop weak knees before regaining my balance. Yellow stars danced in my vision.

The woman chuckled. "Don't worry. We can fix that."

My brow wrinkled. *Fix what*, my nausea or my frayed nerves?

"Both. Come along. Step quickly."

Had I said that aloud? Was I losing my mind? "I'm sorry, but I didn't catch your name," I said.

"I hadn't given it. Address me as Headmistress."

Address me as Headmistress, I mocked.

She cast a stern glare over her shoulder. "Nothing enters or exits your mind that I won't hear if I'm in your presence. Understand?"

I nodded my head and tried desperately to not think anything. I even tried not to breathe.

Headmistress led me to the towering gateway. Four columns flanked the black gates. In the triangle above them, a sign read, *Mount Olympus Preparatory Academeia*. I loved the strength conveyed by the structure. Such a contrast to my cave. Even Eastern Crete had nothing as impressive.

Headmistress waved her hand and the gates opened slightly. "Hurry inside. Hyperion can't touch you here."

"So this is the Mount Olympus Prep I've heard about?" I asked, wide-eyed.

"Yes." A warm smile played on her lips. "This is home. You're home now."

Now? I had a home. This was not it.

"Remember, mind your thoughts."

I clapped my palms to my temples to block out the mental invasion. Like that was really going to work.

"Come … " She grasped my hand gently, leading me through the gates. "We must get some housekeeping items out of the way."

Inside the gates stood a two-story structure. She opened the tall entry door by a brass ring that hung from a lion's mouth, and then motioned for me to enter. Scrolls hung from the dark walls. A white marble desk separated me from a huge man with wild, silvery hair. He was almost as big as Hyperion and Okeanos.

"We have a new pupil," Headmistress said. "His name is Zeus."

"Zeus, huh?" The man turned slowly to face me. His sky blue eyes flashed, cold and uninviting. His gaze raked over me severely. "I am Ouranos. *OOO-ra-nuhs*, understand?"

I nodded.

"I'm Headmaster of Mount Olympus Preparatory Academeia, or MO Prep as the youngsters call it," he said in rigid and precise baritone. "What brings you to Mount Olympus? Why are you here?"

"Uhm." I took a half step backward. My next words stuck in my throat. I eyed the Headmaster warily, unsure of what to divulge.

"Spit it out, boy. Why are you here?"

"Easy, Ouranos," Headmistress said.

Warmth from anger spread from my ears to my neck. Words leapt forth before I could censor them. "Well, a week ago I attended a bonfire and met a girl. I returned home late. Next thing I know, Hyperion spearheaded an attack on my family on Crete. My mother was wounded and my best friend is dead. *That's* why I'm here."

"Hyperion, you say." He folded his massive arms. "What business would he have with you?"

"If I knew that, I wouldn't be here, would I?"

Ouranos slammed his large hands on the marble desktop. "You may not be *here* for long with that attitude! Did you come on your own or did we send for you?"

"Ouranos, that's enough!" Headmistress stepped between us.

I wanted to yell that this entire trip wasn't even my choice, but I didn't want to upset the fig cart just yet. And I wasn't exactly sure where this line of questions was headed, so I stated the obvious. "Look, the Kouretes brought me. They said I had to come. I just want to find out why Hyperion attacked my family and avenge it."

Ouranos stroked his silvery beard. "I dare say Hyperion would never act alone." His eye muscles tensed. "Is it your assumption that someone here knows something of the attack?"

I growled through clenched teeth. "I don't know. Do you?" My back stiffened as I noticed a slight resemblance in the facial structure between Hyperion and Ouranos. "Are you who I'm looking for?"

I stepped forward, but Headmistress calmed me with the simplest touch to my shoulder blade. "Of course not, child," she soothed. "No one here knows of any Hyperion-led attacks."

I sighed. "I'm sorry."

"I can see now that I'll have to keep a close eye on you," Headmaster said. "Just keep your nose clean and there shouldn't be any trouble,"

"Don't you mean ... *won't* ... be any trouble, Ouranos?" Headmistress asked.

He glared at her while she hugged me. The energy that transferred from her embrace tingled right on the surface of my skin, and then moved through me in radiating circles. It was unlike anything I'd ever experienced. It lifted me. Not to say Amalthea's hugs didn't. But not like this.

Headmistress held me at arm's length and smiled. "You're here now, completely safe. We'll attend to all your questions in due time. For now, just relax. We are all one big family. *Nothing* will happen to you here."

My anxiety vanished, slipping through my fingers like sand. I wasn't sure how I felt about that. Anger held its own comfort.

"You have ire." Headmistress said. "That's good. We'll teach you how to harness it. Turn it into positive energy."

I had half a mind to turn around and find my way back to my *real* home. Except, they didn't exactly want me there either. I didn't have a choice. "Can I ask you a question?"

"Sure," they both chimed.

"That out of control campfire, Hyperion, said that an Oracle spoke of some boy, whom I can only assume was me. But then my guardian mentioned someone named Kronos. Where is this Oracle and who is Kronos?"

CHAPTER SEVEN

Several silent moments passed before Ouranos spoke. "I've heard of this prophecy," he said. "But I should warn you ... the Oracles speak with three tongues. You can never be sure what they intend. As for Kronos, he is of no consequence at this Academeia."

Headmistress wrapped an arm around my shoulders. I inched away but she held me fast. Her streaked hair fell over my shoulder. "I know this is a lot to process."

My voice cracked. "But you do know who Kronos is, yes? I was told I'd find all the answers to my questions once I got here."

"Yes, we know him." Her fierce blue-eyed gaze pinned me as she nodded. "And you *will* find all the answers you seek. We just need to figure out how much we can set upon your shoulders, and when."

I hesitated, and then straightened my posture. "Let me have it."

"When we deem you ready." She rubbed a circle on my back, immediately dissolving the knots that had formed there over the past few days. Headmistress glanced back at Ouranos. "I'll give him a quick tour of the campus."

CHRIS LEDBETTER

"At your living quarters," Ouranos said, "you'll find uniforms, a campus map, and a Code of Conduct. Read that well. We have rules here that exist for your safety and that of the other students. And, you'll need to see the guidance counselor for your classes."

Code of conduct? Uniforms?

"Yes. Uniforms. Simple tunics that designate you as one of our pupils." Headmistress smiled. We exited Headmaster's office and crossed a grassy square to enter a column-flanked door at the center of a large rectangular, ivy-covered building. "This Megaron structure we're in now holds classes and the eating area. But you'll get a full tour later."

I followed her across a covered wooden bridge that connected one-half of the Megaron to the other. Water dribbled slowly over rocks and pebbles in the creek below.

"Don't mind Ouranos. He always gets tense at trimester's end," Headmistress said. "Our academeia once served the whole of Hellas. All lower academies fed into these hallowed halls, including Eastern Crete, your old school."

I took a half step backward and knitted my brows. "Wait, how did you know I went to Eastern?"

"The same way I knew your name. Come on now. Keep up with me, here." She continued through several turns and doorways. "Vicious infighting fractured the faculty at MO Prep and some teachers left to found a new academeia called Othrys Hall. So I turned this school into a magnet program for a few gifted and talented students of my selection."

I wondered who the other students were, and what gifted and talented meant. I certainly was neither gifted nor talented. I couldn't even keep from getting expelled.

"Your past is of no consequence here. And we believe our program is designed to elicit the very best from all of our students. Trust me, if I didn't think you could handle our rigorous curriculum, you wouldn't be here." She sighed, bringing her hand to rest over her

36

heart. "Most of my former students were pressured by exiting faculty to leave as well. Some did. Some dropped out and returned home. In fact only five remain here, whom you'll meet soon. You're the sixth."

"Are more coming?"

A glimmer shined in her eyes. "One day."

"What does all this have to do with Kronos? Also, why did the Elder Sun Deity descend upon my mother and me?"

Headmistress stopped abruptly. Her eyes turned the color of storm clouds. Her lips tightened as she took me by the shoulders with a firm grip. "I am *so* sorry about that," she breathed, shaking her head. Her gaze held me tightly. "No one should have to endure what you have. No one. You'll discover that some of the Elders are an evil lot. Until we can get you to full strength, you must avoid them."

"Full strength?" An image of Hyperion flashed into my head, a mountain of fire and fury. "I have a debt to settle with Hyperion and his henchmen. And I need to find this Kronos person."

"I must caution you. You're not yet ready to fight them." She patted my shoulder blade. "We've yet to give you the tools. Remember, never rush to vengeance. Anger will always hog-tie strategy."

My blood temperature rose at the thought of Hyperion and Kronos. Headmistress placed her hand on my shoulder blade again. Instant calm. I suppose there were benefits to her mind reading.

"So you know a lot about these Elder Deities?"

"In short, yes. I am one. So are Ouranos and all the professors here. But as I said, some are evil. Beware of them."

Aristaeus' words returned to my ears. *Deity magic is unparalleled.*

Hyperion's ability to wave off the spears. Headmistress' ability to read minds and calm my soul. Suddenly, I remembered to shut my thoughts off from Headmistress. I wondered if I'd ever have another private thought. Headmistress cast a sidelong glance at me.

While we walked across campus, my gaze darted from the roughly-textured, vine-covered buildings to the smooth, blue dome of sky, and back to the ground. Sunlight illuminated hundreds of shades of green in the lush landscape surrounding the school. Nothing like dry and dusty Crete.

White-pebbled gravel walking paths criss-crossed the courtyards, separating the quad into grassy triangles. The energy of the place embraced me. I drew a deep breath and tried to relax.

A stone building on the far side of the yard whispered to me, calling as if with a crooked forefinger, like it had secrets to tell me. Columns lined the entire façade. I fixed my gaze on huge wooden doors at the center of the wall. A sign hung above the entryway, but at that distance I couldn't read it.

Someone behind us called out, "Good afternoon, Headmistress." The voice sang like a flute. Beautiful.

I turned and immediately had to force my mouth closed.

A gorgeous girl skipped over to us wearing a deep plum colored tunic and golden sandals with straps that wrapped around her calves. A bright fuchsia flower stuck out of her wavy, auburn hair that had been parted straight down the middle of her head.

"Where is your uniform, young lady?" Headmistress asked.

"Oh that silly thing? Don't you just love this tunic, though? I got it from The Golden Himation in the Agora." The girl twirled around and, immediately, my nose filled with notes of fresh flowers. As she spun, air lifted her tunic just enough for me to glimpse her athletic thighs.

"Hestia, whatever will I do with you? You're setting a bad example." Headmistress thumbed to me.

"Who's this?" Hestia cooed. Her hair cascaded over her shoulders like a waterfall "Do we have a new student?"

Warmth flooded my cheeks. The corners of my mouth turned upward before I had a chance to manage them.

"Indeed, we do. His name is Zeus."

"Call me Tia." She extended her hand, flashing a smile that was higher on one side than the other. "Zeus, eh? I can remember that easy. Zeus. Zeus. Zeus. Done." She gripped my hand confidently. A bronze cuff bracelet sheathed her wrist.

"Nice to meet you," I said.

"I like him already." She slid her arm inside mine. "I can show him around if you like."

"Great idea. Just make sure he ends up at the guidance counselor." Headmistress turned around. "I need to prepare for class."

Hestia led me off toward the rectangular structure and the wooden doors. "Sooo, welcome. Your first day, huh? This is a great school. Headmistress hand-picked us to be the dawn of a new revolution. You're going to love this place over here. It's our gymnasium. Do you play sports?"

"I do all right. Javelin throw. Wrestling ... "

"Wrestling, huh?" She turned to me. Her face wrinkled as she gave me a once over. "You're a bit scrawny, but Coach Pontus will fix that. He's our Calisthenics advisor as well as our intramural sports coach. We have a superlative sports program here. Wrestling in Term One, which we're in right now. War Games in Term Two. Running, throwing, and swimming in Term Three." She talked as if she were running a race, her energy, warmth, and effervescence brightening my mood.

"Am I talking too fast?"

"No, not at all."

We approached the gymnasium doors. I gazed at the sign that I couldn't read before. The words sounded in deep monotone within my mind as I read them:

HEROES ARE MADE, NOT BORN.
TRAIN LIKE A CHAMPION.

"Yep. That's our mantra around here," she said, noticing my upturned chin. And then she turned a searing glare toward me. Jovial Tia had vanished. Her celestial green eyes bored through me. "We. Don't. Lose. Here."

I returned her gaze, unsure of my next comment.

"Now then." Jovial Tia returned, her voice playful. "Let's see who's training, shall we?"

She led me through the weather-beaten, wooden doors. I'd done light training back on Crete. Running. Spear throwing. Goat roping. The scrawny comment almost offended me, until I saw a man-child in the corner of the gym floor, tossing a boulder back and forth with another male student. A *boulder*.

"The bare-chested one on the right is Poseidon. On the left in the black tunic is Hades. Don is training for the World Pantheon League wrestling championships next week."

Dark-haired Poseidon stood the larger of the two, taller and broader. Hades' sinewy, physique was highly defined. His strength compared to his size shocked me. I stood slack-jawed at how easily they tossed the huge rock. Effortless. There'd been a rock that size back on Crete that I used to *sit on*.

"Yeah, they're pretty lava-licious." She slid her arm around my shoulder. "But you'll get there. You're one of us now." She pointed to an opposite corner of the gym. "Look at those banners. The gold ones are for wrestling. Don has two and Hades has one. Ol' Shade got his before Don did. Now Don rules the roost."

I nodded.

"The blue ones are for swimming titles. Don flat out owns the water. You should see him when he swims. Magical. Rumor is that he can breathe underwater, but I don't believe it. That's just haters talking. The green banners are for War Games. We dominated the world until two years ago when Othrys Hall was formed and they beat us. Still volcanic about that."

"What's the deal with Othrys Hall?"

"It's our rival school formed with former students and teachers from MO Prep. We used to all be friends. It was us against the world. Solidarity, you know? But then the faculty splintered. And before we knew it—two schools. But now, we hate each other. It's pretty sad."

Poseidon set the boulder down with a thud that sent tremors to where we stood. He straightened his loincloth and ran his fingers through his short crop of dark hair from front to back. Glancing toward us, he grabbed an amphora jug, leaned his head back, and poured the water over himself.

Tia's arm tensed around my shoulder. She inhaled sharply and sighed. Almost purred. "I love when he does that." She shuddered against my side. "All right then. Enough of that. There's more to see."

My skin tingled from the residual closeness to her.

She wheeled me around by the shoulder and led me back out. "Just so you know," she continued, "The gym is also for Creatures Class and Calisthenics. We take fitness seriously. A sound body leads to a sound mind."

As I opened the gymnasium doors, a gust pushed past me like the opening motion had sucked it in. Three silver-haired ladies glided to the opposite edge of the quad. They appeared to be professors. Similarly dressed in white, hooded cloaks, they sang beautifully as they walked. The harmonies drifted across the yard and danced around my ears.

"Muses."

"Whoses?"

Tia laughed. "They're Muses, sisters who teach fine arts." She pointed to the sunken half-moon theatre. "You know, art, music, drama, that kind of stuff. Like I said, you're going to like it here."

I stared at how her hair parted in a straight line down the middle of her head and how the loose wavy strands fell to frame her face. "I already do like it here—"

"Eyes on the path, Zeus." A chuckle reverberated in her throat as she adjusted her cuff bracelet.

I glanced back toward the theatre structure. "What's the building behind the theatre?"

"Oh, that's the stable and barn. We have all manner of animals here. Goats. Elephants, Bulls, Stags, Lions. Professor Thalassa tends to them. And beside that is the garden conservatory where Horticulture is taught."

CHRIS LEDBETTER

"Goats, I know very well." I pause. "Lions, umm, yeah … I draw the line at them."

"I'm with you. We let Headmistress handle them. She's actually the only one who does."

"I don't think I'm too fond of elephants either—"

"Hello, Headmaster Ouranos," she sing-songed as he suddenly crossed our path.

"Ah, yes. Tia. How are you?" His robes swished with each step. "Is your project ready, young lady?"

"Almost. I'll put the finishing touches on it soon."

"Good. I've been regaling the Khaos Council with reports of your superb research on cosmic dust."

Tia's cheeks turned pink. "Thank you, professor."

"Carry on then," he called over his shoulder. He turned onto a path that wound upward through a cypress grove. A sign near the path read: *Observatory Hill.* A domed white building stood prominently high above the trees.

"Observatory? What's he observe up there? The sky?" I tried to be charming.

"Actually, yes. Interesting you should ask that. Headmaster Ouranos, or Professor O, teaches Astronomy and he rules the Sky Throne from his Observatory. That's the highest peak in the world. He controls the weather and the heavens from his Throne."

I gazed at the blue dome above us, combing over the heavens. "But it's so vast. How can he rule it all?"

She smiled warmly. "Because he was meant to, I guess." She looked into the air as if trying to remember something. Her brow wrinkled and her eyes narrowed. "'*Bestowed Upon The Bearer Of The Throne Is The Power To Rule Heavens Alone.*' I think that's how it goes. That saying is inscribed on the base of The Sky Throne. Perhaps, you'll see it one day."

"That's a mouthful."

She nodded. "Don't go close to the Throne, though. If you try to mount it, it will kill you."

CHAPTER EIGHT

When we rounded the corner of the gym, Tia pointed back toward two buildings. "The first is the Megaron. It holds general classes ... Rhetoric, Philosophy, History, Geography ... you know, boring stuff. Although, I did enjoy mapping the Underworld in Geography class."

"The Underworld ... " I echoed to myself, before my mind drifted momentarily back to Tos. I snapped back to present. "Oh hey, can I ask you something?"

"Fire away."

"Is Ouranos always such a grumpy goat?" I asked.

She returned a quizzical expression.

"It's just that he wasn't overly warm to me when I met him earlier."

Her dark eyebrows pinched. She shook her head and shrugged. "I've actually never seen him grumpy, per se," she said. "But I suppose it is a bit stressful being the Headmaster, Astronomy professor, and Sky Throne ruler. It's a good thing he has Headmistress to help him. Know what I mean?"

"One more question ... who is Kronos? I asked Headmistress and—"

Her voice dropped an octave. "We don't talk about him here. I could get in so much trouble. No doubt you've discovered that Headmistress can read our thoughts."

"Unfortunately."

Tia paused, her wide eyes darting furtively. Her voice approached a whisper. "Well, Kronos *used to be* the head coach of intramural sports here. That is, until he founded Othrys Hall to our south. Headmaster Ouranos is his father, but they have a horrible relationship. I've heard their epic arguments."

"South?"

"Yeah, it's a direction. You know ... North. South. East. West." Her hands made a cross in the air. "Where'd you come from again?"

"Ohhh, *that* south. I know what *south* is." Obviously, Tia's attractiveness was affecting my path to clear thought.

"Hey listen, forget what you just heard. I didn't tell you anything about Kronos. Deal?"

We rounded another corner to the rear of the gym.

"Now back here," she said, "we have our thermal baths. The girls' baths are here. And the boys' baths are over there." She pointed while we walked.

I loved the smooth, stone facade and the columns of the domed structures. I glimpsed a moving shadow, an indistinguishable form in the mist of the girl's bath. Soft floral scents floated from the bathhouse and swirled around me.

"Keep walking, soldier," Tia said with a chuckle. "It's probably just Hera. She's a preener. You'll meet her later."

We trekked on a path that entered a dense grove of trees. "Housing is tucked back in the woods a bit," she said. "You'll learn your way around in no time."

Down the path toward us sauntered another girl, her stride athletic and confidant. At first, the distance was too great for detail.

But as she drew closer, I became self-conscious again. The girls here were beyond breathtaking. I momentarily thought about Telesto, and all I'd left behind on Crete. Before my reflections gained strength, I was again swept into the energy of the two girls standing in front of me.

"Hey, Meter," Tia called.

"Hey, girl. Mmmm, who's this?"

Sudden heat flushed through my cheeks.

Tia turned to me. "Zeus, this is Demeter. Demeter ... Zeus."

Rimmed by dark eyeliner, Demeter's grayish-green eyes twinkled as we shook hands. Or at least I thought they twinkled. Maybe I made that up. My hand in her grasp vibrated with a slight tingle. Almost imperceptible, but it reached into me. I didn't want to break our gaze. At least not before I had to.

She released my hand, and I realized I probably shouldn't have held on as long as I did. I must have been staring too hard.

"Easy now, tiger." Tia laughed at me.

Just what I needed. Now they both probably thought I was some social outcast.

"Call me Meter." She folded her dark brown curls behind her ear. Her skin glowed as if she'd been brushed with golden dust. Leather armbands snaked around her biceps and wrists. "Well, I'm off to the quad to soak up some sun before turning in my project for Astronomy. Ugh. I had to map the heavens."

"Oh yeah?" Tia asked. "You're done already?"

"Girl, I would've much rather mapped all of Thessaly, naming each tree and flower as I went. But yes, I'm as done as I'm gonna be."

"I hear you. Oh hey, Professor O's headed up to the Observatory. I'll be up there after evening meal."

Meter turned back to me. Her cheeks radiated a golden tone. "See you around."

They certainly didn't make girls like this back on Crete. Most of the girls looked like seahorses. Except for Telesto, of course. Going to see her at that bonfire really had led to so much trouble. My blood coursed in hot torrents as memories of the attack hit me like punches to the face, each one more staggering than the last.

"Hey." Tia squared my shoulders, waving a hand in front of my face. "You all right? Your face is way too flushed. Not a good look on you. Do you always look so serious?"

I shook my head as I realized I'd been staring into space. "Sorry. I'm fine."

"If it's about Meter, let me just tell you … " Tia looked at me sternly, but nothing like the earlier glare she delivered about the sports tradition. "You can look but don't touch. We've been forbidden to become romantically involved with other students here at MO Prep."

"Why is that?"

"There are only five of us, well, now six. Ouranos is cool about it. But Headmistress says that romance distracts from educational pursuits." She rolled her eyes. "Watch out for Meter."

I arched my brows.

"If you're gonna make a move on Meter, you'd better keep it low-key. She likes to keep to herself. Oh, and watch out for Shade, too. He's a bit smashed on Meter."

A bolt of confidence rose in me. I narrowed my eyes. "What if I wanted to be low-key with you?"

"Mmm, confident much?" She smiled. "I like that. Just remember, there's a fine line between confidence and arrogance."

"Is that a yes?"

She turned away from me. "No. It's probably a bad move. Besides, I pretty much think of you as a little brother right now."

My posture sank a little. "But you do think of me—"

She grinned as we continued up the path away from the gymnasium. I turned a glance over my shoulder, half intending to get another look at Meter. We were high enough on the hillside that I could see a panoramic view of campus with the bathhouses and gymnasium in the foreground. The Megaron and other administrative buildings stood far in the background.

"To the right are the girls' cabins. To the left are the boys' bungalows. Farther up the hill is a stairwell of clouds leading to faculty housing. Let's go find your new home." She patted me on the head.

I still felt a little broken by her patting me on the head. I used to do that to goats back home. Somehow, I'd have to get past the *little brother* stigma. We passed several decorated bungalows before approaching a clearly unoccupied one. Four wooden columns supported the front façade. Above the doorway was carved the number thirteen.

"Here we go," she said. "I'll let you get acquainted with everything and I'll see you back in the Megaron Hall for evening meal. Go upstairs to the Andron." She turned to leave.

"Wait," I said. I didn't want to be left alone, so I stalled. "Where is the Megaron, again?"

"There's a map inside. Look near the desk. I'll see ya." She flashed a smile over her shoulder. The blossom in her hair bobbed as she walked away. The warmth that had been following us all afternoon left as she did and the air immediately turned brisk. Cold even. A stiff gust swept through, rustling the trees.

I opened the door and stepped into my new home, a modest, one-room building with three windows. It beat the cave any day. I trailed my hand over the grain of the wooden desk and chair. Beside them, a window overlooked a cluster of cypress and fig trees so close that I could practically pick fruit from them. I wheeled around and saw two doors with handles. *Huh.* They didn't exactly look like an entry or exit.

Wooden planks creaked beneath my feet as I crossed the room and pulled the door handles. *Ah. A closet.*

From a horizontal bar inside, hung two blue, two white, and two black tunics, along with one white cloak. My uniforms.

The fabric of the tunics felt heavy and coarse under my fingertips.

I turned them over in my hands. A bright blue 'Ω' symbol stared at me from the chest. I thought back to Tia's rich plum tunic and smiled. *Yep, definitely not in dress code.* Rebellious. I liked that.

I sat on the raised platform bed and stared ahead. The sheets wrinkled under my weight. I loved the idea of a bed with sheets and a blanket. A vision of Amalthea appeared before my weary eyes.

My heart rate increased when she spoke to me. "Do not fear your new life. I raised you the best that I could have. Your brightest days are ahead of you." Her image dissolved into a soft breeze that drifted out through the open windows.

Her voice faded slowly from my mind. It resonated even more beautifully in its fading form. I missed the softness and its steady cadence and wondered if I'd ever hear it again. I hoped she was mending quickly.

Then a memory of Tos popped into my head. One time, we'd played whack-a-rock. He'd tossed a fist-sized stone to me. All I had to do was open my stance and hit the rock with a thick branch. But, I didn't open my stance enough. I smacked the rock straight into Tos' face. Knocked him out cold and bloodied his forehead. I don't think he ever truly forgave me for that.

I sighed, dropping my head into my hands. He had sacrificed himself for me. How could I have been so selfish? He tried to warn me. I punched the bed, remembering those wicked spears, and the one that had sunk into Tos' chest. My eyes stung and rubbing them did little to soothe them. I'd have done anything to bring him back.

"You crying for your mother already?" A low voice rumbled through the room.

I looked up quickly.

Poseidon and Hades blocked the doorway. The sheer physicality of Poseidon's presence dominated the cramped confines of my cabin. Glancing around with a dismissive frown, he walked toward me, his muscles flexing with each step. "What's your name, loser?"

"Hog Nuts?" Hades jeered. His folded arms wrinkled his black tunic. A coiled mass of darker brown skin, a raised brand, protruded prominently on the bicep of his right arm. The Omega mark. Ω.

"Zeus," I said confidently. "Get out in the sun much?" I referred to Poseidon's pale skin.

"Least he's got a sense of humor, eh, Shade?"

Hades leaned against the doorframe and chuckled. The tip of his chin up to his temples formed a perfect triangle. He looked me up and down. "He's humorous all right."

"I'm Poseidon." He looked down and shoved his large hand into my personal space. The dimple on his chin twitched. "Call me Don."

My pulse raced, drumming in my temples. I stood to show I wasn't intimidated.

I squeezed his hand. "Zeus, like I said." My body heat rose so high from the tension in the moment it felt like I was once again standing in front of Hyperion. So hot I got chills.

"Firm grip. That's good. At least that means you can hold a spear. We could use another body on our War Games team next term." He thumbed over his shoulder. "That's Hades."

Hades stepped from the shadows into a shaft of late afternoon sunlight. His body wasn't as big as Poseidon's, but was definitely more defined. Black cuff bracelets wrapped around his forearms, making his arms look even bigger. His dark olive skin tone starkly contrasted with Poseidon's pale complexion.

I extended my hand to Hades.

"Everyone calls me Shade." He folded his arms again. "I don't shake hands."

I threaded my fingers together and cracked my knuckles. Nothing better to do with my hanging hand.

"Well *Spruce*," Don turned. "See you at—"

"It's Zeus. Got it? Zeus." I snapped.

He pivoted to me sharply. With piercing slate blue eyes, his icy glare pinned me. "You're *Spruce* 'till I say otherwise. As in twig." He pointed to my sternum. His square jaw tightened. "As in I could break you in half and my heart rate wouldn't increase. *Got it?*"

Shade chuckled behind him. His raven hair fell over both sides of his face, leaving only the middle third of his face visible. I immediately felt lightheaded. Or maybe it was all the hot blood rushing to my head.

As they both left the bungalow, I exhaled. I hadn't even realized that I'd been sucking in my stomach and holding my breath. What there was of it, at least. They were right about my physique, though. I would clearly need to talk to Pontus to see what kind of training I could do to make me as strong as them. And fast. I wasn't about to endure this type of harassment every day.

I lay down on my bed for a moment, only to realize I still needed to get to the guidance office to figure out which classes I needed. *Better change into a uniform, first.* I pulled off my old tattered tunic from Crete, leaving it in a pile on the floor, and grabbed a clean tunic from the closet. I slid it on as I darted out the door.

I found the guidance office door inside the Megaron Hall and knocked cautiously.

"Come in," sailed a high-pitched, frail voice from the other side.

CHAPTER NINE

I pushed open the door. An elderly lady with high, bright cheeks and a straight nose greeted me from behind a desk. Her long, silvery-white hair swept back off her face as if wind were blowing directly at her.

"Welcome, dear heart," she said. Her light gray eyes twinkled. "I am Ananke."

"Uh, hello. I, ummm, need to—"

"I know. We've expected you for longer than you could possibly know." Her smooth, rich voice danced around my ears as she handed me a scroll. "First, let me ask you ... tell me about your studies at Eastern Crete. Your records have not made it this far yet."

I wondered how much to tell her about school. It's not like I was the best student. "I held my own in language arts, math, and music. I consider myself an expert in agriculture, owing to my mother ... " I sighed. It was still difficult to reconcile that term for her. "My guardian was a goat farmer."

"Oh yes, Amalthea. We know of her."

I smiled. "Yes. And I enjoyed science class the best."

"You received high marks in these classes, I presume? I hope so."

"Mmmhmm," I lied. My breaths quickened.

"Very well then," Ananke said. "On the wall, you'll notice a list of classes in our curriculum. These are advanced, to be certain, but you wouldn't be here if Headmistress did not think you could handle the rigors. Our program builds on your previous knowledge and coursework. Look at the wall for our class list."

Blinking rapidly, I gazed at the courses: Metalworking: Weaponry and Jewelry, Shapeshifting, Horticulture, Rhetoric, Creature Creation. Philosophy. Game Theory. Leadership. Astronomy. The plethora of courses I was scheduled to take seemed endless.

"Thank you," I nodded. "Ummm, do I need to bring anything to these classes?"

She handed me a scroll. "Here is list of what you'll need on the first day of class. You'll find supplies down in the Agora of Thessaly. Ask one of the students to show you. It's near the end of the trimester right now, so you have a few days before new classes start. So there's no rush."

"Thank you again." I turned to leave, but then stopped. "What about Calisthenics? I need to get stronger quickly."

"Actually, Calisthenics is a current offering," she replied with a smile. "Follow the other students for the remainder of term. You will receive new classes at term's end. Good luck."

I managed a weak smile and left the room, closing the door behind me. Remembering Tia's directions from earlier, I searched the Megaron for the central stairwell to the upper floor. Scrolls in hand, I climbed the stairs and approached an arched entryway, over which was inscribed, The Andron.

Tables of food and drink lined a wall to my left. Silver-haired Muses sat at one table. Ouranos and Headmistress ate at another table with a burly guy I didn't recognize. Headmistress looked up and waved, smiling warmly.

A girl in a green tunic pored over the food offerings. *Sweet Gaia,* was she beautiful. Perhaps the best looking one I'd seen so far, which was saying something. How was I supposed to walk around here all day among all of these beautiful girls? At least I didn't have to worry about Tia. Little brother. Psssht. *Whatever.*

Shade and Meter talked at a far table. As I approached them, I remembered Tia's observation that Shade liked Meter, They both looked up.

"Hey," Meter said in a warm timbre that resonated in my ears.

Shade tipped his head upward. "What's up, Spruce?"

"Spruce?" Meter elbowed him. "Don't you know his name?"

"Yeah," he fired back. "Do you?"

"Stop being such an elephant's fart, Shade."

Shade's jaw tightened.

I set my scrolls down, and looked straight at Meter. "Guess I'll be tagging along to classes with you all until next term."

"Good." She smiled. "Let me know if you need someone to escort you to the Agora."

Tia's *low-key* comment came to mind. "Oh right, for supplies and such."

"And such." She wrinkled her nose. "I have to make a delivery down there to The Golden Himation anyway."

"Delivering what?" I asked.

"I have a line of Kosmetikos beauty products. They're mineral based, all natural. Really popular. Bronzer. Eyeliner. Olive oil moisturizers. Goat's milk bath soaks. You know, that kinda stuff. Anyway, let me know if you wanna go down there."

I nodded.

"I'm so hungry I could eat a rancid goat. I'm getting some more food." Shade huffed and slid his chair back. "You want anything, Demi?"

"No." The warmth left her eyes. "And you know I hate when you call me that. I'm not *half* of anything."

"I'll grab you a plate anyway."

"No, really." She glared at him. "I'm full."

"You are not. I'll pick up something." Hades skulked off.

"Fine," Meter called out. "But no meat."

I cleared my throat, suddenly confused about the Meter-Shade connection. "I guess I'll get some food too." I flashed a half-smile to Meter and ambled toward the food table.

My stomach growled. In front of me sat the most food I'd ever seen in one place in my life. Sweet and savory aromas competed to fill my nostrils. Goat meat and milk had been the bulk of my diet on Crete. Occasionally, I'd eaten seafood caught fresh by the Kouretes. And of course Amalthea always made sure my plate had vegetables.

The girl in the green tunic continued to pile food onto her plate. Figs. Olives. Grapes. Zucchini. Honey. Bread. Some kind of meat. I walked up to stand behind her, noticing the leather diadem that restrained her dark, curly locks. "What's good here?"

She turned toward me and smiled. Her dark curly hair swung over her shoulder. "I suppose you're trying to be charming," she said in a slightly raspy voice. "You must be new." Her lips remained slightly parted.

"Yeah. Just trying to figure out the lay of the land."

"It ain't me. That's for sure." She returned to filling her plate again. Then she turned back toward me, raking her green eyes over me like I had three horns growing from my forehead or something.

I looked around the room then back at her. "What did I do?"

"What are you thinking right now?"

"Pardon me?"

"She asked what you're thinking, Spruce," Shade interjected as he walked by. "She's trying to read your mind."

"Shut up, Shade," she said. "Have you found a person here who likes you yet?"

"Have you?" he shot over his shoulder.

"Guess we're just one big happy family here, huh?" I filled my plate.

She turned back to me. Her eyes softened to the color of sage. "So, what *are* you thinking?"

I smiled and popped a grape into my mouth, determined to maintain the mystery. I walked past her to grab some shaved goat meat. She followed me with her eyes, studying me as if I were some curious scroll or something.

She bit into a fig and wiped her mouth seductively. "Where you from?" she managed between chews.

I hesitated, unsure of how much to offer. "The island of Crete. You?"

"Ahh, Eastern Crete, huh? When I went to lower academy on Samos, I used to own them in running and throwing events," she answered.

"I throw a pretty mean spear myself."

"That right?" She raised her eyebrows. "You have a name?"

"Zeus." My gaze shifted from her eyes to her lips.

"Hera." She extended her hand. A brass armlet coiled around her bicep with lions' heads on the ends.

"Nice to meet you." My palm melted into her smooth grip as we shook hands. "So what's this about reading minds?"

"Don't listen to Shade. He's just mad because I can tell him what he's thinking before he says it. He's a little slow." She clenched her plate tighter. "I don't read minds. I just think faster than anyone else. It's a blessing and a curse." Her words hung in the air as she abruptly wheeled around and left the Andron, nibbling on her food.

Hmmm. Interesting. Beautiful. Intriguing. Off limits. Move on.

I returned to the table. Shade set a plate in front of Meter, who looked at him quizzically.

"You know I'm a vegetarian," Meter said. "What's all this for?"

"You need meat to keep up your strength," said Shade.

Meter flexed her bicep. "You wanna arm wrestle?"

I smiled as I took my seat. Don and Tia strolled through the door at the far end of the room, arm in arm. *Great.* My eyes rolled before I could stop them. Luckily no one saw. Tia's hair bounced as she walked. The room looked as if it had been flooded with more sunlight.

Tia joined us while Don paused to talk to Ouranos and the burly man. When Tia took her seat at our table across from me, my skin warmed, like those sunny days back on Crete. Days when life was much easier.

"Everyone has met Zeus, right?" Tia asked.

I tipped my chin upward.

"Sure," Meter said.

"Shade?"

"Yeah. We met Spruce all right."

"Who?" Tia's face wrinkled.

"Spruce." Shade pointed to me, laughing. "He's smaller than a tree branch."

"Yeah. It'd be so much funnier if you'd actually made up the name," I fired back.

"What'd you say?" Shade rose to his feet. His dark eyes glared and narrowed to slits.

The Kouretes always said to match my opponent's movements in a square off. I mirrored his intensity. The girls tensed, all eyes on me.

"Do we have a problem here?" Don's voice rumbled behind me. He placed his free hand on my shoulder. It was so heavy it almost collapsed my spine. "Gentlemen, we have much more pressing concerns." He paused, looking around at the whole group. "Like … who's up to watch some wrestling this evening?"

The tension broke and laughs circled the table.

"At Othrys?" asked Tia. "Count me out. I have to wait for sundown to finish up my Astro project."

"Meter, you game?"

"If *you're* not wrestling, Don, I don't care about it." Meter smiled, twisting the ends of her hair. I caught myself staring at her again. "Besides, that's way too many people in one hostile environment. I'll be in my cabin curled up with a nice scroll. Next week at your championships, though, I'll be there all abloom."

"Guess it's just me, Shade, and Spruce then."

"Zeus—" I interjected.

"Whatever." Don tore into his leg of lamb. When he came up for air, he added, "meet us at the Cloudwell at dusk."

I returned my attention to my grapes and olives, pondering the *offer* I'd been made; the proposal to go with the muscle-heads to some unknown place. It wasn't an actual offer. It was more like a dare. A triple-goat dare.

If I did go with them, no doubt trouble would find me. It always did. But if I stayed back, I'd never prove myself to these guys. Never become one of them.

Wait … Kronos founded Othrys. He might be there. I searched my mind for something to say.

"Did you hear me, Spruce?" Don asked after chugging semi-thick nectar from his goblet.

"Yeah, sure." I didn't look up from my plate, but the prospect of running into Kronos lifted my spirits. "Cloudwell, right?"

"Dusk, Spruce. Got it?"

"Don't be late," Shade added with a tip of his pointy chin.

I cocked an eyebrow toward Shade and resumed eating my goat meat, figs, and bread. After evening meal, I strolled to the Cloudwell after dropping off my class schedule scrolls at my bungalow. The setting sun looked as if it had exploded on the horizon. Pluming hues of yellow bent into a flaming coral fan. I *wished* the sun *had* exploded. My blood roiled with thoughts of Hyperion.

Don and Shade passed me, wearing black tunics emblazoned with that familiar 'Ω' on the chest. It occurred to me that Don had changed from his earlier white tunic at dinner. Perhaps I should've changed as well.

"You coming?" Shade shot over his shoulder.

I caught up to them. "So, why do we wear a sole Omega letter on our uniforms?"

Don stopped and turned. "Pride." With lion-like speed, he shoved his hand toward my chest and grabbed a handful of tunic right above the symbol. The force nearly crushed my lung. I inhaled sharply, trying to recapture my breath.

Don released my tunic, now wrinkled horribly. "This symbol, Omega—" He moved his forefingers around in a circle from top to bottom. "Means that we all come together as a team." He moved his fingers apart in a sharp line under the circle he'd left hanging in the air. "And keep everyone else out. We are the ultimate. The Great Omegas. Mighty Olympians."

I studied Don's face. The strength of his jaw. The intensity of his voice. The cadence of his speech. It was different from any previous interaction we'd had. As per usual, Shade stood off to the side.

"Do you *feel* what I'm sending you?" Don asked.

I nodded.

He walked off. "Good."

We snaked through the torch-lit path and arrived at the campus exit, a covered gateway guarding the edge of the mountain. In the background, for as far as I could see, the sun's last rays spilled through the valley below like lava. In the foreground, thick white clouds hovered near the sheer face of the mountain we called home.

Don and Shade showed no signs of slowing as they approached the ledge. I stopped mid stride, my limbs freezing as they stepped right off the cliff and walked straight across the cloudbank. My face wrinkled. Was something solid under the clouds?

Don and Shade began to descend the cloudbanks. As Shade turned, I could only see their upper bodies. "Come on, Spruce," he jeered. "Just step out onto the clouds. They certainly should carry *your* weight." They both chuckled.

I extended my foot and swept it through the tufted cloud. I closed my eyes, and stepped out, immediately sinking about a foot or so. My stomach rose into my throat as if I had fallen down the side of the cliff. I clutched the air and gasped involuntarily.

The cloud buoyed my weight and I exhaled slowly, taking another careful step, and then another, sinking farther and closer to the ground below each time. I soon caught up to Don and Shade, who stood next to a glowing blue post at the bottom of the Cloudwell.

"Hurry up," Don barked. "You don't know enough to teleport on your own yet, Spruce. So any time you need to go off campus, you'll need one of us or a professor. Now this ... " he pointed to the post, "is a Hurler. This is how we get around. All you have to do is think about the place you want to go, and touch the Hurler, and it will teleport you there."

I eyed the post warily, and remembered the blue post back near the columns on the beach where Headmistress first approached me. And the post back on Crete. "I can go *anywhere?*" I asked.

"As long as you've actually been there before and can conjure a vivid picture of it in your mind." Shade's voice was laced with impatience.

A grainy image of Amalthea's face materialized right before my eyes. Her olive-toned skin. Her dark curly hair. My chest warmed at the sight of her smile. I sighed, missing her deeply. Then a vision of Telesto invaded my thoughts. Her aquamarine hair and iridescent eyes. With this Hurler, I could return home anytime I wanted now.

"Snap to it, Spruce!" Don clapped his large hands in front of my face, right through Telesto's image. *Bastard.* She dissolved into the air. "Put your hand on here so we can go."

I hesitated, extending my hand, then pulling it back. My mind raced. "So, let me get this straight. I can go anywhere I want as long as I've been there before and can picture it in my mind?"

"Well, his ears work," Shade joked.

"Yeah, Spruce. And, provided the place has a Hurler, otherwise you can't get back. To go somewhere on your own, you need clearance through the Headmaster's office. Put your hand on here already."

I inched my hand overtop of the Hurler and dropped it into place, landing on the back of Shade's hand. In seconds, fire raced through my body like I'd been engulfed in flames. I closed my eyes tightly as the inside of my body liquefied. All at once, the three of us vaporized into the air.

Strangely, though I could see nothing, I heard everything. The air shooting past me. Owls hooting. The valley sighing as night draped down upon her. Then, as quickly as we'd become one with the wind, we reappeared. My body reformulated, from my hair follicles to my toenails, my hand still atop Shade's. I glanced around, my knees buckling, to see we were standing over another Hurler post. As Don and Shade strode off, I ran to the woods' edge and launched my evening meal.

CHAPTER TEN

Don turned around and laughed heartily at the sight of me clutched over. "Come on, weakling."

Great. Throwing up would go a long way toward earning their respect. Whatever had just happened to me, an odd, queasy pressure still perched near the top of my stomach, like more of my dinner wanted to come up. I struggled to suppress it.

Rubbing my quaking torso, I caught up to Don and Shade as they hiked up a steep hill. In the foreground, a circular arena dominated the landscape. In the distance, torch-lit paths snaked between well-illuminated, columned buildings. Raucous noises rose from the structure we approached. A single story of linked arches enclosed the arena. Orange torchlight flooded each archway. My eyes widened as we blended into a flurry of spectators filing through the colonnaded entry. A sign overhead announced, *Home of the Titans.*

"Stay close, Spruce! You don't wanna get lost in this crowd."

"You think Kronos will be here?" I asked.

"Who cares about him?" Shade fired back.

My heart rate sped as we stepped through the final arch into the heart of the structure. I shifted my gaze to check out the spectators as if I knew what Kronos looked like. A crowd of people were scattered randomly over the stone risers. Four huge contestants bounded around the sandy floor of the arena, preparing for the wrestling matches. I wrestled in the lightest division back home. These guys were definitely heavy weights.

Don and Shade eventually stopped and leaned against a stout column on the upper rim. They both crossed their arms, broad and intimidating. I followed suit, trying to fit in.

"Good," Don said. "They haven't started yet."

Girls pooled in gaggles of three and four. It reminded me of Eastern Crete with the sea of Oceanids. Moving. Mingling. Laughing. There were certainly more girls here than at MO Prep. Of course, even if they *did* go to my school, I wouldn't be able to pursue them romantically anyway because of that stupid rule.

One group of girls strolled, almost glided, toward us. Their long flowing chiton dresses clung to their slender frames as if they'd been custom-made. I stood straighter than before. But I didn't move. Or at least I didn't think I had. But, Don caught my shoulder. Apparently, I must have stepped in front of him.

"Watch it, Spruce."

The girls giggled. His calling me that in front of them made me want to hit him square in the jaw. My fists clenched. "Don't call me that."

Don ignored me and stepped toward the girls. He grabbed an athletic girl with dark indigo hair and crushed a kiss on her lips. Her leg lifted as she leaned into him. "You're on your own, boys," Don said, after he came up for air. He walked off with his arm draped over her shoulder. One of the other girls shot me a half-smile before walking off.

"Look," Shade said in a dry manner, "we're in hostile territory here. Let me give you the rundown. You see that bald-headed monster down in the ring?" He pointed to a wrestling contestant down on the arena floor.

I nodded, still pissed that Don had embarrassed me in front of those girls. Tos never would've done that.

"That's Menoetius, best wrestler at Othrys. They call him Money because he doesn't lose. He will absolutely eat your lunch. Steer clear of him."

I tipped my chin upward. "Mkay."

"Now look at those guys way over there. They're all brothers." Shade nodded to some guys standing across the arena opposite us. As he pointed, they looked directly at us. We were caught. The guys, three in all, began to stalk around the upper ridge toward us.

"All right. Looks like we're going to have some visitors. Quickly, the two thick necks are Epimetheus and Prometheus. Epic does whatever he's told. He has the really close shave. Notice him walking to the rear. Promo is the smartest of the bunch. Maybe too smart for his own good. He's the one with hair 'round his ears."

"And the long-haired one with the fruit fuzz on his chin?"

"Atlas. He's vicious and vindictive. He was dropped on his head as a baby."

"What? No nickname?"

Out of the corner of my eye, I noticed Shade rolling his eyes.

"Here's the deal. We don't get along too well. Never have. So just stay cool. We're in their house. If we were home, it'd be different."

The brothers marched over in their red tunics. After Shade's preamble, my nerve endings stood on end. I delivered my best nonchalant stare as they squared up to us.

"Well if it isn't the rat pack," Atlas said, rubbing his jaw that was lightly covered in facial hair. "Or is a group of rats a herd? I forget." Epic and Promo chuckled behind him.

Shade didn't move an inch. "We're just here to enjoy the matches. What do you and your peanut gallery want?"

"Rumors and resolution."

"Pardon me?" Shade shot back.

"You heard me. The Oracles in the Agora have claimed that you all will beat us handily in War Games this year. Psssht. They're obviously mistaken. Or lying," Atlas said. His straight eyebrows barely moved. "I had to laugh at such a preposterous notion."

"Oooh, that's a big word for you," Shade said with a stone-faced expression. "Besides, if the Oracle said it … must be true."

"Who's going to lead the charge? Certainly not you." He pointed at Shade. "Don's left you in his dust the last two years. Tired of living in his shadow yet?"

"Look at yourself … " Shade stepped forward. "You tired of losing to Money in wrestling every year?"

Atlas' smile straightened. "If I didn't know you so well, I'd consider that an insult." His eyes tightened and intensified. They were the oddest hue of golden brown I'd ever seen. "That's all right. Money will take care of Don in the championships next week."

"I wouldn't bet on it," I piped up, remembering the training I'd seen earlier.

All eyes shifted to me. Something inside me came to life, like the collective attention ignited an internal torch.

"Did I ask you what you thought?" Atlas stepped toward me, then edged backward. "Damn, your breath stinks!" His voice carried around the entire arena. "Did you throw up on yourself? Go chew some mint leaves or something." He held his nose while laughter cackled around him.

Embarrassment stung my cheeks and the back of my throat closed. I wanted to turn invisible.

"Great Gaia! You smell like rhino's ass." He continued his assault. "No wait … that's not fair to the rhino." More laughs rang out. Atlas squared to me again. "Look kid, I don't know you. But then again, a person of your stature would surely escape notice."

"That makes us even, doesn't it? I don't know you either." I stiffened my back and puffed out my chest. *Goat testicle.* Shade unfolded his arms and stepped in front of me. But I didn't need his help.

A crowd gathered around us, the throb of their energy pulsing at our backs. The Othrys professors must have noticed the tension, because several muscular men in red cloaks strolled over and stepped in. "Move along boys, unless you want demerits. Tartarus is lovely this time of year."

Atlas gave me one last glare, driving his hands through his shoulder length copper hair from front to back. "We're done here ... for now." He clapped his brothers on their backs and walked away.

One Othrys professor turned to us. "Don't make us send Headmaster Ouranos a message that you're over here causing trouble."

I exhaled slowly and smiled to myself. Atlas didn't want any part of me. I studied the professor's face. "You're not Kronos, are you?"

He bent down close to my face. "No I'm not, boy. But more stunts like that ... and you'll meet him faster than you'd like."

Shade yanked my arm. "Are you *trying* to get us in trouble? What did I tell you?" Shade barked. "If we'd gotten in a fight off school grounds, Don would have been DQ'ed from the championship next week. And besides that, Atlas is more dangerous than he showed you just then. A lot more."

I maintained a tight-lipped half-smile, reveling in the warmth of the energy that coursed my veins. I'd faced worse. I'd faced Hyperion. "Are you scared of them?" I looked straight into Shade's eyes. "I'm not."

"If you knew any better, you would be. And why do you keep asking about Kronos?"

"Never mind." I didn't know how much to tell Shade. I didn't really know him—or whether I could trust him—yet. I decided it was better to keep it under wraps.

As the crowd dissipated, a tall, athletic man with the obvious talent of throwing his voice to the far reaches of the arena, announced the contestants.

"From Elite Academy of Sumeria we have the Asian champion, Enlil."

The crowd applauded as the contestant jogged out. He wasn't big, but his muscles were well defined. His hands glowed as he walked to the center of the circle. The crowd gasped collectively as he slapped himself in the head and howled like a rabid wolf.

"And from our own Othrys Hall Prep ... Menoetius!"

He walked to the center of the sandy floor, flexing his muscles for the spectators. Torch light reflected off his oiled skin and bald head. He adjusted his red loincloth and clapped his hands loudly.

"Money!" the crowd chanted over and over until it reverbed in my ears.

The judge dropped his hand to begin the match and the contestants attacked and mauled one another, trying to claw their way to points of advantage.

"I'm gonna grab some food," Shade said.

"I'll tag along."

"All right, come on. But no more square offs, you hear me?"

I half nodded my head, half rolled my eyes. From our positions standing on the top ridge of the arena, we descended an aisle of stairs that divided the crowd, and then entered a torch-lined tunnel. At the far end was a large room with tables of food, much like the Andron. Guys and girls mingled, wrapped up in a dull roar of conversation.

"We can have whatever we want?" I asked.

"Sure. 'Till it's gone."

"Don didn't want any of this?"

"He's too focused on who he might have to face next week in the championship."

"Yeah? That's not the *only* face he's interested in. Who is that girl anyway?"

"You ask a lot of dumb questions."

A huge rumble of shouts and applause erupted from the arena above.

"Her name is Amphitrite," Shade said finally as we arrived at the food tables. "They've been together since before the schools split. Have you heard what happened yet? About the split, I mean."

I nodded and grabbed a fig and a handful of grapes. A new group of girls entered as I turned around. One of them ambled with uneasy steps. Her golden hair, parted over her temple, fell in waves around her face. Her friends wrapped their arms around her shoulders in what seemed like a supportive effort.

I nudged Shade and pointed at them. He chuckled, then turned and went right back to grabbing more figs. I took a step forward, but Shade caught my arm.

"You have no idea what's going on there. Don't go getting yourself in any trouble."

"Come on, man. Maybe it's not trouble. Could be anything," I reasoned.

Shade looked at me. "I can't tell yet who she is. But, she's got nothing on Meter."

"You're crazy."

He looked at me again, his eyebrow cocked.

"Besides, I thought we couldn't become involved with other stu—"

Shade brought his finger to his lips.

"You and Meter?" My face wrinkled. "But you fought like wild animals back in the Andron."

"She likes me. She just doesn't know it yet."

I returned a blank stare. My eyes drifted as a smirk turned the corner of my lips. I recalled their conversation earlier in the evening. It definitely didn't sound like she *liked him*. Delusional much?

The blonde girl's white chiton clung to her body like second skin as the girls moved into the food room. I drank in the rise and fall of her hips. Torchlight danced on her hair, creating the appearance of strands of spun gold.

I edged away from Shade and drew close to the girls, pretending to pore over the food choices.

"Pallas is lying," the blonde girl asserted, her voice choked by tears.

"So what are you going to do?" her friend asked.

"What can I do? I know why he did it. But *you-know-who* will never believe me."

I edged closer, my neck craned and my ears perked.

"Boys can be such jerks sometimes," her friend said.

"Tell me about it," I said.

All three girls turned toward me.

I cleared my throat, gaining confidence by the moment. "I'm Zeus."

"And?" the friend shot back. "Don't talk to her. She's in enough trouble as it is."

"Maybe I can help."

"Psssht. You better leave before my boyfriend comes in here," the blonde said.

"Do I look like I'm scared?" I tilted my head to the side. "Besides, if I was your boyfriend—"

Her big hazel eyes grew even bigger. Her gaze sharpened over my shoulder. I turned. Atlas approached with fire in his eyes. I hoped *he* wasn't the boyfriend. Not that I was afraid of him, but there was no reason to purposefully stir someone as volcanic as him.

Atlas bumped my shoulder hard as he walked past me to her.

Yep. He was the one. Damn! My muscles braced for conflict.

Shade called from behind me. "You ready to go?"

"Hold on." I held my index finger in the air.

"Come on," Atlas grabbed the blonde girl's arm. "You done whorin' down here?"

My heart thudded. I stepped toward them. "Let her go."

"Oh no—" Shade said. He grabbed my arm. I bristled and yanked away.

Atlas turned to me, looked back at her and thumbed to me. "What? You cheating on me with two guys now? Who's this jester?

Oh wait—" He squared his shoulders to me. "I remember you. You're the foul-odored rodent I met earlier." He looked me up and down. "There's no way you want this joker. His breath smells like goat feces. Let's go. We're leaving." He grabbed her arm, trying to pull her down the hallway but only causing her to wince.

"Let her go. I won't say it again."

"What did you—" Atlas looked around at the gathering crowd. "What did he say to me?"

Shade stepped in, exuding quiet power. I was surprised and pleased that he was backing me up. Shade glared at Atlas. "We don't want any trouble here, but if she doesn't want to leave … "

With the quickest strike I'd ever witnessed, Atlas's hand shot out and nearly collapsed my chest when it connected. I flew backward several feet over the table. Food spilled all over the floor. Laughter filled the room. Then a chant rose. *Fight. Fight. Fight.*

Sharp, spiking pain radiated through my back and chest. I looked up to see Shade squaring off with Atlas. I rose to my feet, but doubled over, coughing and struggling for breath. My vision hazed over for a moment. A crowd quickly encircled us. Don pushed through the people.

The blonde girl and her friends inched backward as Atlas focused his entire attention on Shade. "Your memory's that bad? Guess it wasn't enough that I beat you like a drum three years ago, huh?" He tore his tunic down the middle and beat his chest. "You want some more of this?"

I stood up straight and glared at Atlas. "Nice trick, mule balls." Walking back to them, I spun my leg around close to the floor, connecting with the back of Atlas' leg and toppling him backward. He hit the ground with a thud while the entire crowd gasped and laughed in muffled chuckles. He rose to his feet quicker than I'd expected.

Don reached the eye of the storm and stared Atlas down. "Three against one, punk." Don widened his muscular arms, extending them fully from his sleeveless tunic and clearly taunting Atlas.

Atlas cupped his hands around his mouth and hollered, "Whoooooo-ooooooo! Titans, Rally!"

"Time to go." Shade grabbed me. "Nice move by the way."

"What just happened?" I asked.

"He just called *all* his boys. We're only three. He's got minions," Shade said.

"This is no place to get seismic. We cannot get in a fight over here. Let's go!" Don led us back through the crowd. Epic, Promo, and some other guys dipped down into the tunnel as we exited. We rounded the corner to exit the arena's top level and then jogged back outside into the darkness.

We ran back to the Hurler. A mob formed behind us like storm clouds. I couldn't make out what they were chanting, but I knew it wasn't good. When we finally reached the Hurler, Shade and Don put their hands on the top of it, my hand following in what seemed like slow motion.

I heard a strange sound, like the air whipping. Churning. I felt something sharp puncture my back just as I placed my hand on the Hurler. My scream vaporized along with everything else.

Intense heat raced through my limbs again. My body liquefied like beads of lava, fire carried on the wind. I flew through the air and heard nothing that time. Nothing but the crackle of flames.

We reformulated at the Cloudwell. The molten spheres of my body painfully smelted back together and my muscles spasmed. Pain streaked through limbs that refused to hold me upright. I doubled over, and then crumpled to the ground.

Shade nudged me with his foot. "What in Gaia's name is wrong with you? We're home now."

I arched my back in agony. "Knife—" is all I got out before I fell unconscious.

CHAPTER ELEVEN

Clawing my way back to consciousness, I called out, "Anytos. No!" I couldn't shake Tos' dying image. The grinding scrape of the spear against the shield. The helpless heartbeat and a half before the spear sank into his chest. The split-second it took to cleave my life.

I squinted through a shaft of sunlight and shook my head. I was in somebody's bungalow. Maybe mine. I couldn't be sure. Pain pulsed through my limbs in time with my heartbeat.

The burly guy from the Andron stood over me with a damp cloth. "Zeus, I am Pontus. Are you all right? I'm glad you're awake. You must've taken a nasty spill last night."

I took the cloth and nodded. I massaged my side. "Where's the knife?"

Ouranos stood to Pontus' side with his massive arms crossed. "Of what knife do you speak? What happened to you last night?"

I sat up, removing the damp cloth from my forehead. Don pressed his lips tight. Shade brought his forefinger to his mouth.

Pontus caught me looking over his shoulder and turned. Shade quickly rustled his hands through his hair. It then fell again to frame his face, shading his eyes from analysis.

Don coughed. "Oh yeah, you did say something about a knife. Right before you passed out. But, I didn't see anything. Not even a scar."

Ouranos knelt by the bedside. His demeanor had warmed since our last meeting. "Bad blood flows like the Styx between Mount Olympus and Mount Othrys. Do be wary when you travel there."

I cleared my throat. "May I have some water?"

"Actually—" Headmistress stepped through the small crowd of people into my bungalow. "You need this." She extended a goblet. The creamy contents emitted a dull glow.

I took the goblet into my hands. "What is it?"

"It's nectar. You're one of us now. This is what you drink. Not up for discussion."

I brought it to my lips and sniffed. No odor. I swirled the semi-thick liquid around in my mouth. A burst of citrusy flavor hit my tongue, followed by a spicy kick that lingered in the back of my throat.

"There we go," Headmistress said. "If you can keep that down, you'll be all right."

I drank more and it warmed my chest cavity going down. "That was good. May I have more?" I asked.

Headmistress filled the goblet again from a painted amphora jug. "Once the nectar gets into your system, it will fix whatever happened to you on the Hurler." She glowered at Don and Shade then turned back to me. "For now, just lay back and get more rest."

Ouranos, Pontus, and Headmistress left my bungalow. I reclined on my bed and sighed. I was sure Don and Shade were going to lecture me about tangling with Atlas. But they just stared at me from various points around my room.

"Go ahead and get it over with," I said.

They stared a while longer and then burst into laughter.

"What are we gonna do with you, Spruce?" Don asked. "You know you were going after Atlas' girlfriend, right?"

"All I did was talk to a girl who was crying," I said, not opening my sore eyes.

Don snorted. "Metis is always crying about something. In any case, you won some points with me."

Shade popped his head out of my doorway and then returned. "I wouldn't go making a habit of crossing him or talking to his girl. He's a bad seed and she's trouble."

"I'll probably never see her again anyway," I said, thinking of my horrible luck with girls. I lost Telesto to poor decision making. I couldn't become involved with MO Prep girls even if I wanted. And now, I just met someone who goes to a rival school, is also off limits, and has a maniac of a boyfriend.

"I'll give you one thing." Don walked over to the doorway. "You do have a flair for the dramatic. Can you walk?"

I swung my legs over the side of the bed. As I stood, the room spun for a moment, but then my world stabilized. I took a step and exhaled.

"Good," Don said.

Thinking back to Crete, I asked, "Did you both go to the same lower academy?"

Don shook his head and sat in my desk chair backward. "I'm a proud product of Euboea Lower. Home of the mighty Seahorses!"

"And I came from the volcanic island of Limnos," Shade said.

"No mascot?"

"The Blacksmiths."

Don stood. "Let's get to morning meal. You need some food."

"Sheesh. I can't believe I've been out cold all night." I'd never experienced anything like that before.

"C'mon," Don said with a chuckle. "We have classes to go to and you have to face your first day of instruction."

After bathing in the bathhouse, I caught up with Don and Shade in the Andron. Meter walked over to me in a standard white tunic. Her grayish-green eyes brightened under dark lids as she took me in. She wrapped her arms around my shoulders.

"I'm glad you're all right," Meter whispered in my ear. When she pulled back, her eyes warmed. I melted into them. The gold flecks in her irises mesmerized me. "We were all worried about you."

"Thanks." I felt the heat of Shade's glare at my back. "I'm just glad I made it back in one piece. That Hurler was rough."

"Teleportation takes a lot out of you." She nodded toward the food table and smiled. "Go grab some food."

Hera sauntered into the room and my body turned to her like a sunflower leaning toward the sun.

"Brush with death, huh?" Hera joked as she strode toward me.

"You could say that."

"Gotta be careful on that Hurler. It gets easier though. Make sure you get some nectar."

"Thanks. I already did."

"You tagging along to classes with us today?"

I nodded.

"You'll enjoy Shapeshifting. We're going there this morning." She absent-mindedly checked the pin that held together the messy bun atop her head.

"Shapeshifting?"

A devilish grin creased Hera's cheeks. "I won't spoil it for you. Trust me, you'll like it."

Hera grabbed a plate and piled it high with grapes, figs, goat meat, and bread before leaving the room with her food. Again. I walked to the table where Meter, Shade, and Don sat.

"Hera never eats with us?" I asked, trying to spark conversation.

"Who knows what's up with that girl," Meter offered. "She always eats alone. Doesn't talk a lot, really. I'm surprised she talks to you so much. Maybe 'cause you're the new guy."

"Watch her. She's moody." Shade offered.

"Duly noted." I bit into some bread. "Anybody seen Tia?"

"Yeah, she never misses morning meal." Don said.

No sooner had the words gotten out of his mouth, than Tia breezed in. "Morning, all." Her voice sang. Her rich orange tunic matched her disposition in every way. A purple flower blossom bobbed over her right ear as she approached the table. "Rough night, Zeus?"

My gaze fell to the table. I'm certain my cheeks looked like ripe pomegranates.

"It's happened to all of us." She rifled her fingers vigorously through my hair, patted my head, and then walked to the food table.

Great Gaia! There she went with that head-patting thing again. In front of everybody.

Don cleaned his plate and nudged Shade. "You ready to go?"

"Where you headed?" I asked.

"I want to get in a few death sprints before class," Don replied. "Thanks to you, I don't know who I'm facing in the title match. We had to leave so quickly last night."

I guess that *was* my fault. "Hey, I'll make it up to you."

Don clapped me on the back. "We'll catch you later, Spruce."

Meter's face wrinkled. "What happened last night?"

I remembered Don and Shade's tight-lipped expressions in my room. I was certain that no good could come from me betraying their confidences. "Nothing. Just ran into some guy named Atlas over at the other school. What a squid-brain."

"Ahhh, yes. Atlas. He's about as stable as a three-legged throne." Meter nodded, bringing a few strands of hair forward to twirl the ends. "And that girl he's with, poor thing, she can't see him for the rascal he is."

My mind drifted back to the confrontation at Othrys Hall. "I think she can see it. She was crying about something."

"He and Metis have been on again off again since before the

schools split. She's not going anywhere." Meter paused and looked squarely into my eyes as if to read me. "And if you pursue her, you're asking for trouble."

Tia glided to the table with a plate full of fruit. "Pursue whom?"

"Metis," Meter said. "That girl has more drama than a three-act play."

"I don't know, Demeter. Maybe Zeus should go after her. Give her a better option than that wild boar, Atlas. If you can get Metis away from that toe-jam, more power to you."

Headmistress walked in and clapped her hands. "All right students, let's get going. Knowledge and skills await."

Everyone rose to their feet except Meter, who stuffed her face with the last bits of fig and barley bread on her plate. Headmistress appeared at my side and handed me a current class schedule.

"Zeus, just follow everyone else. You won't get lost."

I unrolled the scroll:

Hemera Gaia: Morning—Shapeshifting—Theatre / Afternoon—Creature Creation—Gymnasium
Hemera Nyx: Morning—Rhetoric—Megaron 112 / Afternoon—Philosophy—Megaron 210
Hemera Aether: Morning—Theatre—Theatre / Afternoon—Music—Theatre
Hemera Ourea: Morning—Geography—Megaron 110 / Evening—Astronomy—Observatory
Hemera Okeanos: Morning—Calisthenics—Gymnasium / Afternoon—Intramural Practice—TBA
Hemera Kaos: Rest
Hemera Selenes: Rest

I'm so glad I learned the days of the week at eastern Crete. Otherwise I'd be lost.

Tia looked over my shoulder. "The names for each day are the

Theon Hemerai, or Days of the Elder Deities. To give you a frame of reference, yesterday was Selenemera or Hemera Selenes." She pointed to the last day on the scroll. "Kaos and Selenes comprise the week's end. Today is Hemera Gaia or Gaimera." She took a rare breath. "But you probably knew that from lower school. Sorry, if I overstepped. I always get so excited about classes. After post graduate work, I want to teach here at MO Prep someday."

My mind drifted for half a moment back to Telesto. She wanted to teach as well. I sighed. "No worries, Tia. Your enthusiasm is quite infectious. You remind me of someone I knew back at lower academy."

Her smile beamed as she tilted her head sideways.

I followed Meter and Tia out into the courtyard. We strode toward the sunken semi-circle structure to our left where all of the students were congregating at the bottom of the risers. On the far side of the earthen floor rose a two-story building façade. A woman emerged from a distant doorway leading a shaggy mess of a goat, a proud stag, and an immense bull.

Don and Shade rumbled down the riser stairs. "We're so sorry we're late, Professor," Don said breathlessly. "You know I have the big match coming up. We were just running a few sprints before class—"

"Yes. I do know that a momentous match looms large on your horizon." She spoke in a slow, deliberate cadence, emphasizing each syllable. Her wide-set eyes narrowed to slivers as she looked down her straight nose. "Shall I regale Ouranos and Pontus with tales of your tardiness? See what their thoughts are on the matter?"

"Nooo," Don replied. Perspiration coated his hair and forehead.

"Then you'll stay after class and tend my stock. Yes?"

Don's posture slumped. "Yes, Professor."

Hmmm. The mighty Poseidon silenced by the professor.

"All right, here's what we're after today." She held the ropes that tethered her stock high in the air. Then she looked at me and flipped her tightly woven braid of white and silver hair from one shoulder to the other. "Have we someone new?"

I rose halfway from my seat. "Yes. I'm Zeus."

"Zeus, you say. Right then. Welcome to Shapeshifting class. I'm Professor Phoebe. So far this term, we've learned how to shift our bodies into inanimate objects. You can only do that for as long as you can hold your breath. However, as we learned last week and as you'll find today, you can shift into a living object for as long as you need to, or want to, including trees and flowers ... as long as the object is living. But—" She paused, tapping the tips of her fingers together, "just remember this, when you shift into something, whether it be inanimate or beast, your composition is never as strong as the original, and thus you will be a weaker form of it. If something happens and you die as the object you shifted to ... you can't shift back. Likewise if you shift into a table and the table is broken—" She dragged her thumb across her neck. "That's it. You're done."

CHAPTER TWELVE

"Zeus, since you're new ... " Professor Phoebe snapped my attention back. Her skin was pale like the moon. "There are two aspects of shapeshifting that are prohibited. The first is shifting off campus, because if something happens to you off campus while you're in an altered state, we'd never know how to find you or help you. Do you understand?"

I nodded.

"And secondly," She pointed her slender finger at me. "Shifting into another *person* is *expressly* forbidden. The ultimate unforgivable act. For obvious reasons." She paused and studied my face. I returned another nod.

"Very well then, let's get started. Divide into pairs, boy, girl. Zeus, you and Demeter come get this goat. No shifting for you today, Zeus. Just watch Demeter. She's a natural."

I clenched my teeth. "If I wanted to try, could I?" I tried not to move or even twitch one single solitary muscle in my face that would betray this verbal show of confidence. The inside of my body quaked against my will. I slammed my elbows to my sides to keep them still.

Everyone turned to look at me. Professor Phoebe's lips tightened into a line. She looked at Meter, and then brought her hand to her forehead. She massaged her temple and smoothed her hair back.

"I'll take care of him, Professor," Meter said.

"I don't think so, Demeter. Shapeshifting is quite the undertaking." Phoebe walked over. "It's all about energy and matter and—"

"I loved those lessons in lower school. I can do this." I interjected.

Professor sighed and covered her eyes momentarily in her hands. She muttered something I couldn't hear, and then glared at Meter. "All right. But no monkey shenanigans. I will keep a close eye on you two."

I had no possible idea what I was supposed to do, but if they all could do it, I'd give it my best shot. What's the worst that could happen under Professor Phoebe's watchful eye? I grabbed the goat and led it to an edge of the circular floor.

"Meter, if there's anything I know, it's goats. My guardian on Crete was a goat farmer."

"Oh, I remember when the Kouretes dropped off some goats for us on Kithira for Agriculture class."

My spirit brightened. "You knew the Kouretes?" A pang of sadness hit me.

"Who didn't? They came once a year at beginning of first term. As reliable as the moon each night." She waved her hands in front her face. "All right, we need to get to work here, goat whisperer."

I tried and failed to stifle a laugh.

Meter held my gaze. "Here's shapeshifting in a nutshell. Later, you'll be able to shift into anything you've shifted into before. Your body remembers it. But for anything new, just place your hand on the subject and accept its essence. All things have energy, some more than others. Even the wood in a table, because it once came from a living tree, right?"

I nodded and chewed on my lip.

"Then once you're full of the energy, you imagine yourself as the thing and you can shift into it. Just think hard about it. And nothing else."

"Got it." I lied. How in the Underworld would I ever be able to accept a goat's life energy?

Meter said, "I actually love shifting into trees and flowers. Sometimes, I can smell a flower's scent on my skin after I change back. You know what's beautiful about nature?"

I raised my brows.

She inhaled deeply and smiled. "Even the most beautiful flowers can have sharp thorns. Nature's all balance and symmetry." She spoke with such passion.

"All right, here we go." She placed a hand on the animal's back and closed her eyes. The goat bleated a few times and shook its mane.

She took her hand off the goat and inhaled deeply. Then right before my eyes, she slowly morphed and contorted into the goat. I gasped and stepped backward. A series of chills flushed through me as I witnessed the transformation process. By the time she was finished, I was gazing at two identical goats.

I narrowed my eyes, still unable to wrap my mind around the process. There was a *goat*, right where Meter had just stood. Beautiful Meter. Ugly goat. Smooth, radiant skin and long flowing dark auburn hair was now rough skin and a short, gray shaggy mess.

"Meter?" I uttered in an attempt to see if she was in the goat somewhere.

No response. My gaze darted around the theater floor. I wrung my hands together. How in the world would she ever change back?

I crept in front of the goat and looked squarely in its eyes. "Meter?"

"Baaaaa!"

I nearly jumped from my skin. Guess she heard me after all.

The goat contorted again. In a moment, Meter shifted out of the animal and back into herself and her white tunic. Wow. There she stood again in all her glory.

Meter stretched her arms out to her sides. "And that's how you do it."

I applauded. Words could scarcely appreciate what I'd just witnessed.

She bowed. "Thankyouverymuch."

Professor Phoebe walked over. "So, Zeus, what do you think?"

"I'm going for it."

Meter jumped in and put her arm in front of my chest. "I don't think he should try it just yet. I'm not sure he's ready."

"Zeus?" Professor Phoebe asked, swiping a strand of brilliant white hair out of her face. "Your safety is my top concern. It's all right if you don't take part. In fact, I'd rather you not."

I thought for a moment. "I'll give it my best shot."

Professor Phoebe's smile dimpled her cheeks slowly. "All right, let's see your best shot."

I walked over to the goat. It bleated when I caressed its fleece. I closed my eyes, inhaled deeply, and concentrated. "It's all energy and matter," I kept repeating to myself. "Be the goat." I placed my hand squarely on the animal's back, high, near the neck. After several moments of anxious waiting, a cold gust of wind surged into my fingers and palm. My entire hand shook as the wind streaked up my arm. Energy transferred into me, filling my body cavity slowly. Completely. Like liquid conforming to a goblet. I shivered uncontrollably.

In my mind's eye, I found myself walking through a vast plain of high grasses. A swarm of flies clouded the air before me as the stench of dung filled my nostrils.

And that quickly, my mind snapped back to the present. I looked around the theatre floor. Meter. Professor Phoebe. They all looked normal, except much taller. Then it hit me. I looked down and stumbled when I saw my cloven feet. Praise Gaia! I'd done it!

Professor Phoebe applauded. Her wide smile beamed at me. "I didn't think a newcomer could pick it up this quickly. I'm impressed."

How had I never known I had this power? I felt like running

around the theatre floor. Wait! My mind raced into hyperdrive. I didn't know how to shift back! Meter patted me on the head, and then caressed my back.

"All right, time to shift back, Zeus," Meter said.

I was stuck. I didn't know what to do. I tried to talk, but all that came out was, "Baaaa! Baaaa!"

Meter waited a little while longer, and then turned a concerned gaze at me. "Zeus? You can shif—Oh, no." She cupped her hands over her mouth. "We never told you how to shift out." Her eyes widened. Her gaze darted. "Prof!" she called out.

A sinking feeling kinked my goat stomach. I walked around in circles. Meter grabbed me and held me still. Phoebe hurried over.

Meter looked directly into my goat eyes, "Can you understand me?"

"Baaaaa!"

"Do exactly as I tell you. Picture yourself as you were just a moment ago. Visualize yourself standing here next to me. And then focus all your energy into becoming *you* again."

I closed my goat eyes and focused. I felt the calm of connecting with my own soul, like the rejuvenating happiness of seeing an old friend. Rather than cold, warmth flooded through me like sunshine and love. Every positive emotion I'd ever felt, sprang forth. Embraces from Amalthea. Telesto's kiss. Headmistress' slightest touch. Sounds around the theatre became more clear. The honeyed floral scent of Demeter filled my nostrils again. In moments, I'd returned to myself again.

Meter hugged me once I'd shifted back. "Good job. I was worried there for a moment. None of us ever picked it up that quickly, not even me. That definitely says something about you."

Professor Phoebe smiled at me and walked away to check the other groups. "Let's switch animals," she called out.

We cycled through all the animals. Each time we shapeshifted, the same nervousness and discomfort swirled in the pit of my stomach.

Without fail. Like we'd never be able to change back or something.

I turned to Meter. "I still don't understand how this works. What happens to our clothes when we shift into something?"

"Good question. Shows you're a thinker. I like that," she said. "It's like this. Everything has skin of some sort, right? With animals, our clothes become their hair, fur, scales, or whatever. Our sandals become their hooves, and so on."

By the time we'd finished shifting in and out of all of the animals, my body was fatigued to the bone. Don took away the animals and then returned.

"So, this week was easy, yes? Small, pretty simple animals. So let's recap, when might you have to shift into animals, anyone?" Phoebe asked.

Meter's hand shot up. "If you're out hunting and you need to sneak up on a stag."

"Good one." Professor responded. "Anyone else?"

No one answered. I thought about the incident at Othrys Hall. I raised my hand.

"Yes, Zeus."

"Maybe if something or someone is chasing you, you could shift to aid your escape"

"Hmmm," the professor folded her arms. "Sure. Maybe. Chased by what exactly?"

"Anything," I answered. My mind darted between images of the attack on Crete and the incident at Othrys.

"Zeus, you're an Olympian now," Professor Phoebe said in a terse, controlled manner. "So far, there's only five of you ... well, six, now. You can't afford to run every time you encounter trouble. To shapeshift to evade trouble would be cowardly. And Olympians aren't trained to be cowardly. Understand?"

I nodded. Snorts and chuckles rose up around me. I wanted to shapeshift right then. Into anything. Preferably something that could fly.

CHAPTER THIRTEEN

"Next week, we'll try larger animals." Professor Phoebe called out to us as we filed out of the theatre.

"Elephants?" I said.

"Or maybe a wooly mammoth." Professor Phoebe flashed a wicked grin.

"Meal time!" Don strode past me. My stomach grumbled as soon as he said it.

Hera sauntered up beside me. "Hey, you wanna catch a meal down in the Agora?"

To say my curiosity had been piqued by Hera's offer to go to the Agora would have been a gross understatement. I paused for a moment, watching everyone else walk past me. I thought of the earlier conversation in the Andron about Hera never eating with everyone else.

"Sure. Why not?" I replied. "They have food down there?"

"The best." She nodded. "Besides, you'll need some writing supplies for Rhetoric and Philosophy tomorrow."

"You coming with us?" Meter called casually over her shoulder as she walked toward the Megaron. Her smile was easy and innocent.

"Zeus and I were just heading to the Agora." Hera looped her arm through mine. The lion's heads from her armlet bit into my bicep. Her lips curled as she led me away.

"Wait, I can come with—" Meter said.

Hera's head whipped around. "We're not riding a three-wheeled chariot."

Meter stopped, looked Hera over, and then marched off.

A sudden burst of wind stole up the path and rustled Hera's red tunic. I wondered if I was the only one following dress code. Actually, Meter always wore the standard issue tunics. I cast a sidelong glance toward Hera as we walked in silence. I wasn't sure what to say. The crunch of shale underfoot sounded like steady percussion to the wind-chime tones of the bangles on her wrists.

They reminded me of the ones Amalthea had worn back home. "Do you make those?" I asked.

"These what? The bangles?"

"Yeah *those*." I looked up and smiled. Her cat eyes warmed, a nice change from their standard intensity.

"No. I could never make anything as beautiful as these. This is all Tia. The trinkets she creates are amazing." Hera stopped and turned toward me. She extended her wrist and wiggled it. The brightly colored bangles danced around her wrist, some wooden and some metal.

I gazed at the bow of lips. I could have listened to her raspy voice talk about anything all day. I loved the sound.

"What about the armlet?"

"Also Tia's." She flexed her athletic arm. Her bicep pressed against the metal.

"So Tia makes jewelry? A girl of many talents."

"Back before the schools split, the Cyclopes taught Metalworking, Weaponry, and Geology. You should've seen them. One-eyed behemoths. Still, they were great teachers. And Tia would always go to the Forge and try out different jewelry designs."

"Where's this Forge?"

"Under the gym. Somebody'll show you one day. Now it's just a concessions area for sports contests in the gym. Ever since the Cyclopes went over to Othrys, we haven't had anyone to teach what they taught. That's probably how they beat us in War Games last year. Better weapons."

"So you use real weapons in War Games?"

"Yes, but they can't cause killing blows. They do hurt, though."

"And, the girls fight alongside the guys in the War Games competitions?"

She looked me squarely in the eyes. "Absolutely. Wouldn't miss it."

"Funny, I can't picture Tia fighting." I stared into her eyes.

"Don't underestimate Tia, or Meter for that matter. They're fierce." She picked up the charm that hung on the end of her leather necklace. The small, roundish, hammered piece of metal sparkled in the sun's gaze before she placed it between her teeth and pressed her lips against it.

"Tia make that too?"

"Nah," she chuckled, removing it from her mouth. "This one's mine. Can't you tell the difference?" She lifted her bangled wrist to be close to the necklace's charm for comparison. "I basically found a piece of scrap metal in class, flattened it out, and then hammered this 'H' in the middle. Can you see it?" She bent her neck toward me, holding the charm out. The soft, floral fragrance from her hair rushed my senses. I barely saw the charm.

This close, her eyes looked less green and more like the aquamarine of the ocean. She held my gaze for a moment. Warmth pulsed off her skin in subtle waves. Or was that from my own cheeks?

"The charm." She raised her eyebrows, tilting her head slightly. "Do you see the 'H'?"

"Oh yeah. That." I laughed as my gaze dropped to her necklace.

She straightened back up. "We all have one. A charm necklace, I mean. We made them in Metalworking class. Somehow we need to get you one."

"Maybe you and Tia should work together. Make a little collection of jewelry."

"We've talked about it. But her designs and abilities are out of my league. We each have to stick to our strengths." We turned down the path toward the Cloudwell. "She *makes* jewelry. I make jewelry *look good*." She flashed a sidelong smile.

Yes, she did. Remembering Tia's warning, I asked, "What are your thoughts on romance?"

She smiled. "There's a place for it, I suppose."

"Explain?"

"I mean, we can't engage anyone here at school now. But, maybe once I figure out what I want to do, what my life is going to become, perhaps then I could find someone meaningful. A strong, honest relationship would be important, you know? I can't tolerate liars."

My mind wandered to Amalthea, *my mother*. She'd never found a true love, I don't think. At least not that I'd seen. I wondered whether she'd even wanted one. Wouldn't anyone? She'd never spoken of it. At one point, I suspected a love connection between her and Aristeaus. There still could be. I hoped she had recovered from the wound. Somehow, I'd have to get back to see or check in on her.

"Hope you didn't mind what I did back there with Meter," Hera said.

I shrugged.

"Don't get me wrong. I like the tree-hugger. But sometimes she's a bit naïve. I'm a take-charge kind of girl. She meanders a bit."

We reached the Cloudwell. I tensed, knowing what waited at the bottom.

"You all right?" She half-laughed.

"Sure." I stared down the descending clouds.

"You've been here before, right? You and the boys went to Othrys Hall last night. Oh … that's right, you got sick or something, didn't you?"

My cheeks flooded with heat. "I wasn't *sick*. Someone threw a dagger at me and it—" And then I remembered. I did get sick on my maiden Hurler voyage.

"A dagger? Really?"

I wasn't sure I should say, but I had the urge to tell Hera everything. I nodded.

"You're serious?"

"Something sharp, at any rate. And it lodged into my back, just as I put my hand on the Hurler."

She inhaled sharply through clenched teeth. "Oh man. You know what that means? That dagger and its metallic composition are part of you now. The Hurler incorporated its properties into your body when you transported. It's in your blood."

I tried to wrap my mind around this new information. My arms and legs looked normal enough. My skin prickled with the anxiety of having this foreign substance inside of me.

"If you're scared we can always—"

"I'm *not* scared." I needed to face this Hurler again. At least there was no dagger sticking out of my back this time. I took a deep breath as we approached the post.

"It's all right to be afraid." She gazed at me intensely. "Admitting a fear doesn't make you less than … It makes you self-aware. Acknowledge the fear, and do it anyway."

Apprehension knotted my stomach. I dabbed my finger on the sweat on my upper lip. I couldn't be shown up by both the girls *and* the guys here.

I looked into Hera's eyes and knew I could trust her. I slammed my hand on top of the Hurler even as fear curled through me.

Hera smiled. "See, this is why Meter had to stay behind. She'd never be able to push you like I can. I have to know what you're about. That you're not just another handsome face. That you won't mind mussing that hair of yours. You're still a bit scrawny, though. Don't worry, Calisthenics class will fix that."

I smiled, unsure if I was mad at her or intrigued. "I'm my own man. I do what I want."

"Whatever."

"I'm serious."

"Then why didn't you stay back there with Meter and go to midday meal in the Andron? I know you wanted to. You looked so cute together during class."

I paused.

"That's what I thought." She placed her hand on top of mine and we evaporated into the humid air.

Moments later we reconfigured in the middle of a semi-circular, tree-lined clearing. I wobbled for a moment, and then stood straight. Once I got my bearings again, I checked myself over. Nothing strange or out of place.

I shook off the ride and turned to Hera. "Is there anything you're afraid of?"

"Failure," she replied without missing a beat.

After several steps, I asked, "What do you fail at?"

"Nothing, if I can help it. And don't confuse failing with losing. Losing is all right in the short run, as long as you win in the end. Failing means you've given up trying. I never want to be in a situation that's so bleak that giving up is favorable to trying again."

"Your parents teach you that?" I asked.

"What parents?" she scoffed. "I grew up on Samos until I started lower academy. That's when I was shipped off to Euboea. No idea who my parents are. If I ever found them, they'd get an earful."

"Wait." I stopped walking. My brain connected two important dots. "That's where Don went to lower school."

"Seahorse pride. Yes, indeed. Are you writing our life story on a scroll? Let's keep moving."

"But back to your parents … or not," I said. "You don't know yours? I don't know mine either."

She paused and turned. She chewed on the inside of her cheek for a moment. She turned glances over her shoulders as if she thought someone was listening to our conversation. "Let's get one thing straight. I do not talk about my parents. Whoever they are, they abandoned me and I have gotten where I am largely on my own power. End of discussion."

I clamped my lips shut for the remainder of the walk down the colonnaded corridor. But like it or not, we had a definite connection. Not romantic, obviously. But something.

We turned left from the corridor and stepped through a tall arch into a huge courtyard. It was completely enclosed on all sides by buildings of various heights and widths. My mouth fell open. The structures were amazing. I'd never seen anything like it. It was its own miniature community. This entire concept was so impressive.

"First we need to get you a few blank scrolls, a wax tablet, and some styli for Rhetoric and Philosophy." She led me to a two-story, faded yellowish-brown building. The carved wooden sign above the door hung on rusted hooks. It read, *Stone, Scroll, and Sword.*

"Is that what they sell here, stones, scrolls, and swords? Interesting combination." I chuckled after I said it.

"Not exactly. Kreios sells all sorts of odds and ends. But it does house a collection of rare scrolls on many subjects," Hera answered. "The store's actually named after the game. You've never played?"

"What?"

She held her right hand out, palm up and raised her left fist in the air. "Do what I do."

I matched her, my left fist raised to eye level.

"All right, here are the rules," she said. "Stone crushes sword. Sword cuts scroll. Scroll covers stone. Got it?"

I nodded.

"So now you pound your left fist on your palm twice and then pick one. Stone, make a tight fist, scroll, hold your hand flat, or sword, thrust your hand and arm forward. It's always the best out of three. You ready?"

I nodded. We pounded our fists to palm twice. I chose sword. She chose scroll.

"Ha! Beginner's luck. Round two ... " she said.

I beamed. We raised our fists and then pounded them twice again. I chose stone. She chose stone.

"We tied, rascal." She smiled. "All right, get ready."

We played again. I chose scroll. She chose stone. I laughed. "I like this game."

She bumped me with her hip. "Psssht. I let you win. Don't get too confident. Let's go inside the shop."

CHAPTER FOURTEEN

I sneezed as soon as I stepped inside the semi-dark room. Dust particles drifted toward me through the shaft of light that streamed into the front window. My eyes widened as I took in the sights. Paintings of wild beasts hung on the walls. Wooden checker sets piled on a table against a far wall. An iron bucket sitting in the corner with twenty or so blank scrolls sticking out of it.

"Bucket-o-scrollsss is what that is!" a loud booming voice came from behind a stack of wooden tablets. A bearded mass of a man stepped from around the tablets, emerging into the orange haze of candlelight. "'Ello there, Hera. Pleasant to see ya this Gaimera. Who've ya brought with ya?"

She strode over. "Kreios, this is Zeus, new student at MO Prep. Zeus, Kreios."

"New student, ya say? Sssplendid. Splendid indeed. Well, you'll be needin' supplies 'ere wontcha, boy?" He lumbered his large frame over to the scrolls. "Now, lemme tell ya about these 'ere scrolls. We've got papyrus ones from the Egypt and the Sumeria. This Blue Nile brand is good. It's the original, ya know? Not that fake stuff ya might see elsewhere. Like this Lion's Gate brand from Sumeria is just a knock off. It's all right, but ya gotta watch what ink ya use on it."

Kreios pointed to a shelf under the window that over looked the courtyard. "Now 'ere is your inks and styluses."

Hera whispered in my ear as she passed, "*Styli.*"

I picked up a stylus and ran my finger along the metal instrument from the pointed tip on one end to the flat edge on the other. Laid out in my hand, it covered the distance from the tip of my middle finger to the heel of my palm. It appeared similar to the ones we used on Crete.

A box hung on the wall next to the window. I approached cautiously and opened the box slowly. "What's in this? Another stylus?"

"That, boy, isss the Dragon's Claw Stylusss. We used to award it to the best student at MO Prep. Until the split, that is. Now we award two at the end of the summer term."

I reached for the stylus. "May I?"

He nodded.

I turned it over in my palm and felt the substantial weight of it. This was definitely *not* like anything I'd encountered back home. It emitted a dull rumbling vibration. Slightly shorter than my forearm, it was solidly constructed. "Is this a ... *real* dragon's claw?"

"Yesss, boy. An' it's a devil of a time gettin' 'em too."

"A dragon hunter got this for you, didn't he?"

"Quite right, my boy." He turned to light a torch on a wall near the door. "Though, we're in desperate need of the huntersss nowadays. Population control, dontchaknow."

My arm continued to vibrate slightly as I held the dragon's claw stylus. Not enough to alarm. I pressed it into my other palm. Same thing. "Is it supposed to do this?" I asked.

"Do what, boy?" Kreios cocked an eyebrow. "You're not doin' anything. You want somethin' to write on?"

"Umm, yeah." I questioned the vibration I felt. It could've been residual weirdness from shapeshifting, or from the Hurler, maybe. That was a lot for one day.

He brought me a roughly torn parchment scroll others had written on before. He anchored the curled edges of it with a small well of ink whose label read, Erebus. "All right, 'ere we go now."

I dipped the stylus into the ink, dark as the night sky.

"Only takes a little." Kreios looked over my shoulder.

A jolt shocked me as I touched the point down. My arm muscles tensed.

"Never seen that before," he said.

Each stroke I made against the paper drew a bright goldenrod streak before the ink turned black and seeped into the scroll. I blinked rapidly.

"Hmmm," uttered Kreios. "Lemme see that thing."

Hera joined us. "What's going on?"

Kreios kept writing my name over and over. The yellow streak never happened for him. He handed the stylus back to me. "Do it. Make it do what ya did."

I took the stylus back, dipped it, and wrote my name. Sure enough, the vibration returned. The golden streaks returned. Lingered, but never stayed.

I set the stylus down with a thud and stepped backward. Tiny pricks and tingles radiated through my quivering hands. "I'm all done. Thanks."

"Well, boy, you're a special one, aren'tcha?"

Hera smiled. "You should've seen him today in Shapeshifting class. A real natural."

She'd noticed.

"Well, Zeusss, if you're the best student at MO Prep, so chosen by your Headmaster, you can 'ave it. Or one like it."

I wasn't sure I wanted that thing. "So who's won it in the past?"

"You're lookin' at her," Kreios smiled, pointing to Hera who beamed as if he'd patted her on the back.

What if I could become the best student and dethrone her? What an achievement that would be. School used to be a nuisance. But MO Prep was amazing at every turn. No more boring classes. I wanted to prove I could be the best. Though, I knew it would be a tall order.

"All right," Hera said. "Let's grab you some blank scrolls, a pad, and a few styli and get going."

Kreois handed me a small woven bag. "Oh, Hera, d'ya hear about the big wrestling showdown? Looks like it's gonna be Dagda against Poseidon again. Such a classic matchup. Though, I'm a bit miffed that it wasn't Menoetius."

My ears perked. "Dagda?"

"Yesss, boy. Dagda from the Celtic Academy of the Emerald Isle. My sonsss told me this morning. He beat Menoetius pretty bad to win the match."

I froze. Sons? No way. I thought about the knotheads at the wrestling match. Atlas was the only name I remembered.

"Do your sons wrestle?" I asked.

"No, boy. But they love War Games."

"Pallas, Astraios, and Perses are his sons," Hera said. "But they're harmless. It's Atlas and his brothers you have to worry about."

"Ya got that right. They're bad eggsss. My brother Iapetus put those boys on a crooked path, I tell ya. They're little hellions now. Used to be nice boysss."

I scribbled on my new wax pad:

Kreios: Pallas, Astraios, Perses

Iapetus: Atlas, Menoetius …

"Whatcha writin' 'ere, boy?"

"Just trying to keep all these names straight. Does Atlas have two or three brothers?"

"Three. Who do you have so far?" Hera said. She looked over my shoulder. "Oh, you're missing Epimethius and Prometheus"

Their images flashed before my eyes. I remembered because they were walking *behind* Atlas. "That's right. Epic and Promo. Hard to keep them all straight. But you never know when you need info like this." I wrote the other two names.

"Hmmm," Kreios mumbled.

"Thank you," I said as I turned to leave. "Oh wait, is that it? Do I owe you anything?"

Hera spoke up. "Headmistress has an account set up with all the vendors in the Agora. That's one of the advantages of being an Olympian."

We exited into the sun-drenched courtyard, where more people milled. I loved the energy of the place. It was such a contrast from boring Crete. Guys played lyres while girls danced in a line around the fountain in the center of the yard. My gaze traced the top edges of the Agora buildings, which were framed by steep mountains on two sides.

At the far end of the rectangular yard, a bold set of columns flanked the entrance to a theatre. As we drew nearer, I recognized it as similar to the sunken, half-moon structure on campus where Shapeshifting class was held. The word 'Odeon' had been chiseled above the entrance. The skene behind the stage was twice as large as the one back on campus. Three doorways stood as immense, rectangular black holes against the ornately carved skene. Rolling Thessalian landscape framed the theatre on both sides.

Two of the white and silver-haired Muses from MO Prep looked to be arguing down on the floor of the theatre. I watched the intensely exaggerated gestures.

"They're practicing for the end of term performance. They're so good."

"A play? I remember reading those in language arts."

"Yeah, you'll learn about that in Drama class." She turned to me. "In lower school we read plays, but here we get to act them out."

As we strode away from the theatre back toward the center of the Agora, Atlas, Money, Epic, and Promo came from the other side, approaching like a pack of wolves, encircling us. They must've just recently arrived.

"Look who we have here, boys—" Atlas asked with his hands spread wide. "A mouse and a rat?"

Money turned to Atlas and thumbed to me. "*This* is the guy? I can't see it." Money ran his palm over the dark olive toned skin on his bald head. His muscular frame was even larger in close confines than when I'd seen him at the wrestling match. He turned back to me with a smirk that was higher on one side than the other. "Don't have your boys here to protect you now, do you?"

"Then again, why do I need them?" I fired back. "You can't even beat Dagda."

Money got in my face. His cheeks turned red as the setting sun. "I have standing orders not to maim you, but rules are made to be broken, huh?"

I moved my nose to within an inch of his. My heart froze still for a split moment, and then thudded with renewed intensity. The pulse in my ears nearly deafened me. I clenched and unclenched my fists.

Hera pulled my arm, "Let's go."

Atlas pointed to me. "First you get saved by Poseidon and Hades ... now Hera." He threw his head back and laughed. "I take back what I said earlier." He looked straight at me. "You're a mouse too." Epic and Promo echoed laughs behind him.

Hera stepped toward Atlas. "Tough words coming from someone who can't even beat Money in wrestling," she said, thumbing to Menoetius. "Oh yeah, and he can't even beat Dagda. So that makes you both losers."

Money scowled. "I could snap you in three pieces over my knees—"

I dropped my sack to the ground. Hot blood coursed through my veins like a torrent. "I've no issue with you, *Malicious*—"

"It's Menoetius," he said through clenched teeth.

"Whatever." I glared at him. "But if you don't move, your school is gonna be missing a student."

"Is that a threat?" Money stepped toward me just as Kreios pushed through the group of us.

"Boysss! Run along now, ya hear? Iapetus won't be too 'appy 'bout ya hasslin' MO Prep students in the Agora," Kreios said.

Atlas stepped forward. "We weren't doing anything Kreios. Just settin' a couple of mouse traps." He sneered at me. "This isn't over. It's just the beginning. Titans never back down."

I bent over to pick up the woven sack Kreios had given me in his shop, but my fingers shook too much.

Hera grabbed it for me. "C'mon."

I glared at Money and Atlas as we walked away. Once we were out of earshot, I turned to Hera. "I ran into Atlas at the wrestling match. It's like we're on a collision course or something."

"That was invigorating back there. I love getting the old ichor blood pumping, don't you?" She smiled up at me. "But, we gotta get you some more nectar and calisthenics. Atlas and Money could've crushed you."

"Thanks for the vote of confidence." I thought back to Atlas' hand nearly collapsing my chest the previous night.

"What? You don't like honesty?"

Savory scents wafted past my nose. I looked until I saw a crowd of people standing around a place whose sign read, *Lambda, Lambda.* "Let's go there," I suggested.

She smiled. "I knew we'd end up over here. They make the best gyros. Lamb, flat bread, yummm."

We serpentined through the crowd to the window to order. Two thick cypress tree trunks formed the sides of the window. The aroma of spit-roasted lamb was maddening in a good way, making my stomach growl. We ordered two gyros and two goblets of water. Hera also ordered something called ambrosia. She said it was a food and an exfoliant.

"An ex-foli-what?"

She laughed. "It scrubs the face. Leaves my skin all aglow. See?" She turned her cheeks to one side then the other. I had to agree, though my mind couldn't quite wrap around rubbing food on your face. She continued, "It's nectar mixed with honey. Meter makes her own ambrosia that I use. But I didn't feel like waiting."

The lady at the window handed us our tray and we stood there, eating, wrapped in our own silence. Two souls connected by gyros. The charred lamb and fresh vegetables on flat bread were savory goodness. I opened my mouth to speak several times, but nothing more profound than perfect silence sprung forth. So, I remained cocooned in the moment.

We finished our gyros and headed back to the Hurler. I eyed it warily given that I had just eaten. I rolled my sack tightly, careful not to crush the scrolls, and then bravely placed my other hand on top of the Hurler. "What happens to my bag and scrolls and stuff?"

"The Hurler doesn't discriminate. It'll vaporize anything on you, that you're holding, or in you. Like I said before, that's why that dagger got sucked up inside of you. Anything in you or sticking out of your body will become a part of you. Just remember that."

As I put my hand on the Hurler, Atlas' words echoed again in my ears. *This isn't over. It's just the beginning.*

CHAPTER FIFTEEN

Three busy days later as dusk slid into night, I sat wide-eyed in my first Astronomy Class. I'd gazed at the night sky back on Crete. I thought I knew the stars, but Headmaster Ouranos *owned* the Heavens. He knew every star. Every planet. Every speck of dust. They all had names. Yet, my muscles still tensed whenever he passed me in class. My nerves still sat on edge, waiting for him to deliver another unfriendly comment toward me.

Ouranos sauntered around the lab tables in the Observatory offering assistance in seeing the different star groupings. We studied the rising moon chariot on its nightly journey. The sliver of moon we saw that night looked like an ivory longbow pulled taut. Or, a winking eye. His silvery hair was as animated as I'd seen it. My mind drifted to the times Tos and I had raced, climbing trees at night to see who could get closest to the stars.

"Remember pupils," Ouranos said, snapping my attention back to the lesson. His sky blue-eyed gaze trained on me. "No matter what we see with our naked eyes, the moon always has two faces—"

Before he'd finished his sentence, a brilliant white light flashed in the sky and exploded into a kaleidoscope of fractured colors. I ducked under the table as a flashback to Crete assaulted me. Gasps circled the room amid murmurs.

"What was that, Headmaster?" Meter asked.

He massaged his beard and smiled. "That, pupils, is a stellar burst. When an aging star reaches the end of its life, the core of it collapses, releasing enough energy to cause the explosion you just saw."

Everyone stared slack-jawed at the wondrous heavens.

"Bursts like that one spray cosmic dust across the sky dome, as Hestia can attest from her studies, and help create new stars," Ouranos continued. "And in that way, cosmic dust not only drives the mass loss when a star is nearing the end of its life, but it also plays a part in the early stages of star formation."

"Wicked," I muttered.

"Make sure you have your projects turned in by next week," Ouranos said.

"Professor—" I raised my hand. "There's no way I can put together a research project in one week."

"And yet I've heard tales of your first-timer, legendary prowess in some of our most difficult courses," Ouranos said. "I'm sure you'll figure something out."

I knew a confrontation was coming. "You've not quite warmed to me, have you Professor?"

He took a breath. "I am cold and calculating by nature." His face softened despite his harder tone. "And there's been such *turmoil* and upheaval lately that I've likely turned more so." He leaned closer to me. "That prophecy you mentioned before has huge implications, ones I fear I may not see through to the end." He drew his lips to a tight line. "I had unfair misgivings about you when you graced our doorstep and for that, I apologize. But don't make me regret my reversal."

"I'd never dream of it."

"What if he helped me with my project, Headmaster?" Tia asked, crossing the lab. "This class is different from the others. How could he possibly research a term's worth of material in one week after missing all the lectures and labs?"

Ouranos drew a deep breath and sighed. His eyes narrowed. "Let's be clear. I want a detailed summary of your contribution to the project from this point onward."

I sighed. The knot in my stomach uncoiled. Out of the professor's eyesight, I mouthed, "Thank you," to Tia.

As we left the Observatory Tia asked, "So, how'd you like your first Astro class? Professor O knows his stuff, huh?"

I laughed. "I felt like a planet out of orbit in there. Definitely a lot of ground to make up in that class. I enjoyed the bit about the cosmic dust, though. And I've always enjoyed my science classes, especially the interplay of energy in our vast cosmos."

"Oh, yeah. That's where real power is. The alpha and the omega. The cornerstone of all that we are. Wait until he takes you into the sky to see the dust particles up close. Teeny tiny iridescent flakes, barely visible, just floating through the air. You put your hand up and they just pass right over you. Of course, the flecks actually land on Professor O. He soaks them all up. Weird, huh? He's like a conductor or something. Oh, and you know that the Hurlers are powered by the cosmic dust. Did you see the post in the corner?"

"Maybe that's why I had such a bad experience the other night."

"Hurlers can be downright traumatic on your body, especially for first-timers who don't have enough nectar in their systems. But we all get used to it. And so will you. It's part of what I'm researching for my project; the power of cosmic dust." She took a breath and tapped her fingers together. "So what'd you think of the Agora? Sometimes we just go down there to sit in the Odeon and read. Meter has her own little corner that she keeps to. The view into the valley is stunning."

"It was nice, except for a run-in with Atlas and Money."

She laughed. "Those two cock-a-doodles belong under a rock

somewhere. It's a shame … Atlas and Money are seriously lava-licious." She fanned her face. "They're just crazy as all Tartarus."

"And we also went to the Stone, Scroll, and Sword. Kreios is a hair on the odd side."

"He's such a nice man, though. And his sons are all decent. Pallas was interested in me at one time. We walked and talked together for a while. But, now he's over there, and I'm over here. Long distance relationships are hard, you know? I also had one with a guy from Matterhorn Scuola Roman Academia. They just never work."

"I can see how that'd be challenging." I thought back to Telesto.

"Or maybe I'm just difficult." She brought her hand to her mouth and stifled a laugh. "Just paint 'does not play well with others' across my forehead. I'll probably be alone until forever shadows my doorstep. What about you? Did you leave anyone special back home on Crete?"

I felt pressure build in my nostrils. My eyes stung around the edges. "Yes and no."

Her face wrinkled.

"I met a nice girl right before I came here. But I wouldn't call her special. I mean, she is special in her own right. Just not *special* as in a relationship. We only hung out one time." I sighed. "We kissed. It was magnificent."

"What's her name?"

"Telesto. Daughter of Okeanos."

"I've heard the name before, oddly. Rings a bell somewhere."

"But I also left someone else. Not a *girl*. It's my mother, or rather the lady who raised me." My voice cracked. "I left *her*. She was hurt badly when my village was attacked. And my friend Anytos was killed."

"Oh my." She gasped and covered her mouth with her hand. Her green eyes softened. "I had no idea. I'm so sorry to hear that. Must've been awful."

I inhaled deeply. "Yeah. It was bad—" I paused and wondered

how much to divulge … and who else was listening. I ultimately stopped talking altogether and pressed my lips tightly.

She pulled me close to her shoulder. "You're going to be all right. You hear me? I want you to know that. Lean on any of us for anything."

"Thanks."

Tia looked into the distance. "I was raised on the island of Kerkyra. Ever heard of it?"

I shake my head. "Was there a lower school there?"

"Yes, actually. I sort of stuck to myself amidst the Oceanids and Potamoi—"

"Me too! Eastern Crete was overrun with them. Telesto was an Oceanid."

"I am not quite sure who my parents are, really. None of us here are. We're all misfits and orphans." She smiled with a faraway twinkle in her eyes. "I remember when Headmistress came to Kerkyra Lower Academy. After talking to the guidance counselor, she pulled me out of class and asked me if I thought I could handle the rigors of MO Prep."

My eyes widened. "Wow."

"I asked her 'when do we leave?' I couldn't wait to get off that island." She turned to me. "I gotta get some sleep. Take it easy, all right? I'm serious. Everything is going to be all right."

She strode into the dark woods toward her cabin while I made my way home. I still had a hard time calling it that. *Home.* I'd gotten used to sixteen years of a damp, musty cave.

I stepped through the doorway to the bungalow. The candle cast a cheery orange glow around the space. Shadows danced against the walls from the fire's flicker. Of all the things that could make a place home, though, Amalthea topped my list. Her gentle voice. The reassuring comfort of her presence. The strength of her embrace.

I picked up and changed into the tunic I'd worn when I arrived from Crete. It was tattered, dirty, and bloody … but still comfy. As soon as I slipped it on, I felt the gentle breezes of Crete's shore, the warmth of the dry days, and the crisp coolness of the nights. The next day, I had to find out how to wash my clothes. The blood would likely never wash out, though. That would be all right. I couldn't completely erase Tos.

Tos haunted me. Not in a creepy or scary way. His soul begged me for retribution; to never stop searching for the ones responsible. All the classes were nice, but they wouldn't help me find Kronos, Hyperion, or the guys who assaulted us.

I wondered how I'd ever find them. If I could shapeshift into a bird, I could at least fly high above and find them that way—Wait! Every nerve in my body sparked to life. At some point, I needed to find a bird.

CHAPTER SIXTEEN

I pushed open the wooden gymnasium doors the next morning with nectar coursing through my veins and determination in my soul. If I couldn't find Tos' killers just yet, I could at least be ready for them once I did.

It was time for Calisthenics class. Finally.

Coach Pontus stood at the center of the grass and sand gym floor. Wind rustled his royal purple tunic around his burly, athletic frame. Don walked ahead of me with a particular swagger in his steps.

"Game day!" Pontus growled. "You ready, Poseidon?"

"Never ready! Always striving! Mu Omega Pi!" Don yelled.

Every hair on my body stood at attention. Mu Omega Pi. Mount Olympus Prep. That's where the Omega thing came from. A warmth of pride filled my chest as I began to stretch from side to side. I finally belonged to something larger than myself.

"That's my boy." Pontus smiled. "All right, my little kids and bucks. I have the usual stations set up. Don't take it easy on Zeus. We have to destroy him in order to rebuild him."

I stopped mid-stretch. My eyes bulged.

Don and Hera chuckled while my stomach knotted. I forced it to unwind. If I wanted to be one of the most powerful students to ever walk the paths at MO Prep, including Poseidon and Atlas, this is where I needed to make it happen.

We began with a light jog around the track, nothing too strenuous. My breathing flowed well. My calves felt loose. At that pace, I could have run forever. Running was one of the only things I'd done consistently back on Crete.

As I ran, Hyperion and his monkeys pushed to the forefront of my mental focus, causing my pace to increase even more. At certain intervals, Pontus tamped his staff into the soil and the collective pace of our running sped up. Meter darted far ahead of our pack like a gazelle, moving with fluid grace as her dark mahogany braided ponytail bounced from side to side.

By the end of our run, we were flat out sprinting, our feet barely touching the earth except to change direction. A burning sensation spider-webbed through my lungs. Meter still held the lead, followed closely by Hera and Shade. When Pontus finally stopped us, I'd moved into third place, just ahead of Shade. But as I looked around, my lungs floundering as if I had been held underwater, no one else was even breathing hard.

Don clapped me on the back. "That's just the warm up. Now the real fun begins."

No one chuckled or joked like in other classes. Everyone wore a stone face, even jovial Tia. Well, not quite so jovial at that moment. She smoothed back her auburn ponytail. Her demeanor was all business.

Don led us through lunges across the gym floor with thick logs atop our necks. My legs melted into something akin to the jellyfish that used to wash up on the south shore of Crete.

After several rounds of push-ups, pull-ups, and sit-ups without rest, my arms shook. My chest felt like an iron breastplate had been hammered into it and my stomach was hot to the touch, as if six burning embers were pushing through my lower torso.

"All right, Olympians," Pontus yelled. "Time for the Grinder!"

I bent over with my hands atop my knees. Physical fitness class at Eastern Crete had nothing on this. I didn't think I had more energy to pull from, but I refused to quit. Pontus ordered us to an obstacle course. We hurdled logs, crawled through the mud under a wide, flat stone, and scaled a series of walls slightly taller than ourselves. The course concluded with climbing a knotted rope to the top of a sky-scraping column.

Don climbed up first. Once he reached the top, he leapt impossibly far to the next column, landing directly on the top. Five columns stood in a row. While Tia climbed next, Don leapt from one column to the other until he reached the final one and eventually repelled to the ground.

Meter went next. Then Shade. Lastly, Hera climbed with the fluid movement of a cat.

I stared up the curved face of the column. A cloud passed overhead, obscuring the column's summit. Hera disappeared into the cloud when I grasped the rope. Hand over hand, I climbed. One knot at a time. Hera leapt to the next column just as I reached the top. I scrambled atop the platform. And then I looked down.

Huge mistake.

Looking past the platform of the column, the cloud dissipated and the ground melted away from my vision. Certain details became blurry while others sharpened. My stomach cramped and then flipped. I tried looking away from the ground, but it held my gaze. My head refused to turn, eyes refused to close.

"Jump, Zeus. You can do it!" A muffled voice rose from the ground.

The column shook. My entire body tensed and I grasped at the air reflexively. I stumbled, waving my arms wildly.

"Zeus!"

I finally caught my balance.

"Zeus. Kneel down and close your eyes!" someone said.

Yeah, like closing my eyes would've helped me at all. I figured out who was talking. Hera. I forced my gaze upward. She leapt back from the third column to the second.

"Close your eyes, Zeus. Do it now!" Hera demanded.

I crouched in my stance and found enough inner strength to close my eyes. My fingers, however, still gripped the edges of the platform like a vise.

"All right," Hera said, sounding closer than before. Even at that distance, her voice whispered in my ear, to my soul. "Don't open your eyes yet. Picture something important to you, something that makes you feel good."

I paused for a few moments. Deep inhales. Slow exhales.

"Do you have your warm and fuzzy picture yet?"

I pried my fingers away from the edge of the platform and rested my hands on my knees as an image of Amalthea appeared in my mind. She stood amidst our beloved herd of goats. A gentle breeze rustled her wild, dark curls. Her broad smile warmed me.

"Ahh, your body language says you've found your picture. Better not be some girl from back home." She chuckled as she said it.

I had to smile at that. Perhaps that's what she wanted. To relax me. It worked.

"Now," she said in a commanding tone. "Stand up, open your eyes, and project your picture onto the next platform."

I tried to stand, but my limbs locked up.

"Easy does it." Hera's encouragement floated to me in soft whispers across the expanse. "Stand. Slowly."

I rose to my feet. My final posture felt crooked. I opened my eyes one eyelash at a time. The yellowish, sparkly stars in my vision dissolved and I saw Amalthea standing on the other platform.

"When you're ready," Amalthea said. "Jump to the picture you've projected. Do not look down. Jump to me. You have no greater desire than to jump to me."

Amalthea held her arms outstretched on the next platform. With my chin up, I edged to the back of the platform. An odd combination of fear and exhilaration surged through me. I rocked backward, took two steps, and launched myself over to her. Arms flailing, running on air, I sailed across the space and landed in her arms. Safe.

"Good boy," she whispered. Her grip tightened. "Who knew you'd be afraid of heights?"

My ears registered the voice as raspy. Amalthea's had not been. "I've got you." Hera held me, her warmth transferring to me, threading through me. "Now we need to get through the rest of the jumps. Just don't look down."

She turned and leapt to the next column like it was nothing. Every nerve ending in my body craved Hera's support. Following her advice, I projected Amalthea to the next column, and jumped, successful again.

I no longer needed to project Amalthea. I leapt to the next column. And then the next. Until I found myself repelling down the final column. My legs failed to hold my weight once I reached the ground. I crumpled in a heap.

Applause greeted my descent, including Ouranos. I hadn't even noticed him arrive.

Ouranos strode up to me. "You have more power and ability inside of you than you know. It's our job to bring it to the surface and then to push you to the edge. And past it. Good job up there."

"Thank you, Headmaster."

He placed his hand on my shoulder. "Fear is an illusion, an empty emotion. It's simply a reflection of an event that has not come to pass, and may never do so. Just focus on the task at hand, what is directly in front of you. And sometimes, the thing you fear the most, is the very thing you *must* do. Do you understand?"

I nodded, and then drew in a deep breath.

"All right, class dismissed," Pontus said. "Rest up for tonight's festivities. Poseidon, come back later for pre-game."

"Yes, Coach," Don said. He turned to me. "I don't know what Hera said to you up there, but that was the gutsiest thing I've seen in a while between the two of you. We've never seen someone who's afraid of heights before. I like that you pushed through it, though. It tells me a lot about you. And I'm glad Hera helped you."

Hera rifled her hands through my hair. "You can thank me later." She winked as she turned to leave the gymnasium.

New admiration for her welled up within me. An unfortunate whiff of my own body odor wafted past my nose. I wrinkled my face, smelling worse than a wet goat. I strode out of the gym and around back to the boy's bathhouse. Funky aroma is no way to win friends and influence people.

After entering the large, rectangular vestibule, I removed my sandals. Two sets of sandals lined the wall already. Then I pulled aside the curtain and entered the inner sanctum between two columns into the hexagonal hygiene area. A circular cold water pool rippled in the center of the room. I peeled out of my tunic, and then spread pumice and ashes over my body. I doused myself with olive oil and began to brush off my body with the strigil, a curved metal scraper. Once clean of all the muck, I walked to the back of the bathhouse where there were a collection of twenty individual heated baths, and then lowered myself into the warm water.

I looked my body over, holding my still trembling arms outstretched. Peaks and valleys existed where flat plains had once stood. My veins stretched out like rivers through rolling hills, dark like the Erebus ink from the Agora. Tremors quaked through my limbs as I submerged more into the water up to my neck.

Don and Shade both relaxed in their own baths already. Neither talked, which was fine by me. I still hadn't the energy for conversation.

The warm water triggered thoughts of Hera's embrace. Up on the columns, she'd melted away my every apprehension. The fierce look in her eyes filled my mind. Even sweaty and muddy, she still surpassed Tia and Meter in beauty. But she was also still very off limits.

Maybe Hera was just being nice. Every girl here had been incredibly helpful. Tia showed me around campus and assisted with Astro class. Meter guided me through Shapeshifting. Hera took me to the Agora and helped me conquer my fears.

But something else about Hera stirred me. It wasn't her simple beauty, although she had more than her fair share. It was her substance, her depth. Her dizzying intellect. I loved the way she pushed me to be more than I thought I was. I relaxed and allowed the memories of the Agora and Calisthenics class to embrace me as the water did.

After bathing, I put on a fresh tunic. Shade and Don waited for me in the vestibule. The sun shone bright overhead when we finally stepped out, so it took several moments for my eyes to adjust. But what I saw when my eyes cleared caused my muscles to tense. I inhaled sharply.

"Here comes trouble," Don said.

CHAPTER SEVENTEEN

Headmistress approached and cast a solemn gaze toward us. Her blue eyes were colder than usual. Metis walked at her side. Her tight, blonde ringlets bounced with each step. But something was off about her. Her downcast eyes spoke volumes.

Her hair parted over her right eye and flopped over to the other side of her head, falling over her face the way it had at the wrestling match. Her hand caressed dark marks on her left arm and when she looked up, one of her eyes had significant bruising around it. She turned away and her hair hid it again.

A spark of anger shot through me as I remembered Atlas' grip on her arm at the wrestling match. I took half a step toward her, but was arrested by her glassy-eyed gaze.

"Boys, I assume you remember Metis," Headmistress said.

Don and Shade nodded. I managed to not react. At least not visibly. Internally, I ached. Chills crawled up my arms.

Headmistress looked directly at me and continued. "Metis is rejoining our school, and will begin classes anew next term. She remembers where everything is, so an exhaustive tour isn't necessary, but I at least wanted her to meet Zeus, given that he is new here."

Shade and Don both turned toward me. I drew a deep breath. Headmistress gazed upon me with a piercing, icy stare.

"But it seems you two are already familiar." Headmistress looked from me to Metis.

I inwardly cringed. I'd totally forgotten she could read minds.

Metis extended her hand. "Nice to meet you again. Zeus, right?"

"Yes." I managed a weak smile.

"Let's welcome her back into the fold, shall we?" Headmistress glared at both Shade and Don. She turned back to Metis. "I'll show you to your new cabin and then you're on your own. Oh, and you know we have the wrestling finals tonight, right?"

Metis nodded. The corners of her mouth threatened to turn upward, but never did.

I studied her movements. My heart squeezed and my stomach knotted in frustration as I considered what could have happened to her. I had a hunch, though.

Headmistress glowered at me, and then turned to lead Metis toward the girls' cabins. Don, Shade, and I walked around the corner of the gym. Once we were out of earshot and mind reading-range, Don turned to me.

"Look, I'm not telling you what to do," he said. "But if I were you, I'd stay twenty-four-and-a-half paces away from her and whatever her problems are. She is a total drama magnet. Incredibly smart girl, but she likes trouble. And you remember who her boyfriend is?"

Shade laughed. "Yeah. It's all fun and games till someone gets a dagger stuck in their back, eh, Zeus?"

I cut my eyes at Shade, and then spoke to Don, "Why twenty-four-and-a-half?"

"That just seems like a nice safe distance."

"Although, if she's over here," Shade said, "maybe she's finally moved on."

"Let's hope so. If you talk to her even while she's over here, he'll find out and go volcanic. Are you looking for trouble or what?" Don chuckled.

"So the fact that she's clearly bruised up means nothing to you guys?" I asked.

"Sure, it means she needs to leave Atlas, like yesterday." Shade said. "But she *is* kinda cute. I'll give you that."

Don clapped Shade on the back. "My boy here doesn't have to worry, because none of the girls like him anyway."

"No. That's where you're wrong." Shade rubbed his hands together. "Meter is warming up to me. You'll see."

My eyes widened and I laughed internally. From what I'd seen between them, Meter was far from warming.

"In any case," Don said. "I need some extra helpings of stag meat and nectar today, boys. Got the fight of my life tonight."

$$\Sigma$$

That evening after dinner, I returned to my bungalow to consider tunics for the night's festivities. I settled on black for no other reason than it looked badass and made my arms look even bigger. I liked my new physique. That nectar must be some wicked drink.

I walked down to the gym as dusk settled. Large urns above the gym sent gaudy flames skyward. Orange and yellow light licked the gathering indigo of nightfall.

A crowd milled outside the gym doors. Some had painted their faces with school colors. Others feigned some of the wrestling moves that were sure to be on display later. I recognized the Muses, but no one else. More people arrived from the Cloudwell area, including visitors from other Pantheon League schools wearing strange clothing. I ambled down to the Cloudwell to watch them all arrive by Hurler or other means.

A massive cloud slowly approached from the west, gliding over the Thessalian valley. It docked right next to the Cloudwell. Diffused green light emanated from the core of the mist. Seven fairly odd looking people disembarked from it, four guys and three girls. Two hulking guys with strange markings and piercings effortlessly hauled a cauldron that was larger than the two of them put together. One of the girls carried a large harp.

They all ascended the Cloudwell. The guy who walked in front almost doubled Poseidon in size. Anger flashed in his eyes as he neared. He rolled his neck and head at random intervals and face-palmed himself repeatedly. I guessed by his swollen appearance and chaotic disposition that he was Don's opponent, Dagda, from the Celtic Academy on the Emerald Isle.

I followed the odd entourage to the doors of the gym. The crowd parted easily for the mountain of a young man and his fellow travelers. They slipped into the gym and disappeared. Pontus closed the doors behind them. No spectators were allowed in yet.

I stood in the middle of the quad as the throng of spectators grew. A tall man and two young guys I didn't recognize walked down the path from the Observatory. At that distance I couldn't make out any details in the dusky light.

Then, Metis rounded another corner. Alone. Ambling. Aimless.

The conversation with Don and Shade replayed in my head, so I remained rooted to my spot. She walked in measured, uneasy steps, rubbing her hands over her arms. The firelight from the flaming urns danced on her golden hair and semi-bare shoulders. Her white chiton looked similar to the one she'd worn when I'd seen her at Othrys Hall. Absolutely alluring, and not even close to dress code.

Wearing a bright yellow tunic, Tia strode up with Meter from the right side of the gymnasium. "Hey, you," Tia said in her normal chipper manner. She handed me a reed flute.

"Hey, yourself. I've seen flutes before, but what's this one for?"

"To cheer, silly. While they're wrestling you just blow into it and make noise to support Don. You know, like this." She wrapped her bejeweled fingers around the flute and blew into the instrument. My ears cried mercy.

"Phew. I swore these things were made specifically to make music," I said.

"Uhh, yeah." Tia wiggled her head side to side. "If you pay attention in music class. Music is my hardest subject. So I just play it during wrestling matches. It works."

"I bet it does."

"What's wrong with you?" Meter asked. The gold flecks in her irises twinkled. "You don't exactly sound like you're ready to watch Don whoop some rear flank!"

Tia looked around. "Where's Shade?"

I shrugged.

"What's the matter?" Tia shook my shoulders and jumped around in front of me. I let out a half laugh.

"Ohhh, I think I know." Meter extended her leather-clad arm and pointed across the quad. Metis stood at the far end of the thin, imaginary rope her finger cast. "I wonder what she's doing here. She never struck me as the sports loving type."

I tried to act like I wasn't looking at Metis. But, I was truly concerned, and I'm certain my eyes betrayed me.

"Oh wait," Tia added. "Is she over here now? I hope she's finally left Atlas."

"She is going to MO Prep again," I said. "I saw her earlier with Headmistress."

Tia raised their brows.

"That's straight up poisonous," Meter said. "And possibly dangerous. Though, maybe she's turned over a new leaf."

"I have a really good imagination," Tia said. "But I can't imagine that."

"I also saw some bruising on her that I want to ask her about—"

Meter gasped. "Bruising?"

Tia spoke with a sharp tone. "Atlas is such a mule's ass. Maybe you can get her to finally break ties with that boar. Let's hope."

"Tough language, girl." Meter laughed.

"I never liked Atlas." Tia folded her arms. "Metis can do much better." Tia winked at me.

The doors to the gym opened with a clang and Professor Phoebe waved everyone in.

"Come on, Tia," Meter said. "Let's leave Zeus to his mission."

As Tia and Meter walked away, a crisp gust swept across the quad, causing Metis to hold down the sides of her chiton against the wind. *Great Gaia.* I loved the way it clung to her curves.

Metis walked toward the entrance to the arena. I imagined she was lonely and thought about walking up to her. This was my chance to find out the specifics of what had happened. But, then a dark-haired girl approached. They kissed one another's cheeks and entered the gym together. The other girl looked familiar, but I couldn't remember where I'd seen her. Othrys was my best bet.

I tried not to be Admiral Obvious, following them in and clearly trying to get a closer look. But as I took a step toward their departing figures, noises to my left distracted me. Students from Othrys Hall. In what felt like a blink of an eye, the quad was overrun in blood-red tunics. As boisterous voices howled, I steeled myself for showdown number two with Atlas. There was no doubt he was here amongst the crowd.

CHAPTER EIGHTEEN

The crowd inside the gym pulsed with energy. I snaked my way to the back corner, where Shade and I had arranged to meet, and caught up with him. We ducked inside a stone-framed doorway and descended two flights of torch-lit stairs. At the bottom, we stepped through a huge doorway, over which was carved, The Forge.

Tables of food stretched beneath an array of weapons that hung from the walls. Axes. Swords. Two crossed spears. A few people in red tunics strolled by. For the first time, I noticed that on the chests of their red tunics were two crossed sickles. My pulse quickened for a moment, and then subsided. The red tunics up close made me think of Atlas and his crew. I saw no one we knew, or at least no one I recognized like Money, Epic, and Promo.

"If you're looking for nectar, you won't find it," Shade drawled.

"Huh? Why?" I tore my eyes away from the table and back to Shade.

"Since this is a Pantheon League-wide event," Shade said. "We don't serve nectar. Nectar is only for *us*. Not them." Shade pointed to some people who were neither MO Prep nor Othrys students.

I swelled with pride. Omega pride.

"Let's grab some food and find a prime spot so we can see the opening ceremony," Shade continued. "Sometimes the Muses recite poetry or act out battle scenes. Ouranos has been known to rain meteor showers across the sky."

We took our food from The Forge back to the gym floor. The crowd had thickened in our absence. It was difficult to imagine that just a few hours before, I'd been through the Grinder in this gym. As we leaned against a rock at the far edge of the gym floor, I smiled to myself, giving it a playful push. It was the same odd-shaped rock I had seen Don and Shade tossing back and forth when I first arrived.

It moved, if only a few inches. But it moved. I shoved it again just to make sure my eyes hadn't deceived me. They had not.

"Hey, genius, would you stop shoving the rock so I can lean back on it?" Shade joked.

I was impressed anew with my physical transformation. Confidence swirled through me as I leaned back and anticipated the opening ceremony.

"Interesting trivia about this rock," Shade began. "The story goes that way long ago, Headmistress presented this stone to Kronos as a symbol of strength for being our intermural athletic director. In classic Kronos form, he rejected it as dispassionate and thoughtless. So now we use it to train with."

Pontus stepped to the center of the gym floor and threw a torch into the middle of an enormous woodpile. A roaring fire erupted. The crowd's applause competed with the loud crackling of the flames.

"Where are they supposed to wrestle if that huge fire is out there?" I asked.

"Pontus calls that seasoning the grounds," Shade explained. "We've done it for every championship match. It gets the ground good and charred—ready for battle."

The Muses serenaded the crowd on flutes and lyres. A girl from the Celtic Academy joined with her harp. Then three hooded women I didn't recognize strolled up to the crackling fire with goblets in their hands.

"Fire-spitters," Shade said before I could ask him. "Also known as Oracles. You'll like this."

The first woman turned her goblet up to her mouth and then spat into the fire. Blue flames rose majestically, retreated, and then streamed upward from the center of the woodpile. An image appeared of a stately man holding a long, slender, crackling shaft of yellow fire above his shoulder. He hurled it high into the air.

I held my breath as the shaft pierced the heavens and then took a severe nosedive. Wide-eyed, I watched it descend toward me. I stumbled several paces away with uneasy steps and jumped backward just in time before it struck the ground near where I stood.

The shaft burned and crackled for a short while, sparks falling to the ground all around it. Then it dissipated into the air like it had never even been there, leaving a charred circle of soil in its wake.

The crowd fell silent. Everyone turned toward me. Goosebumps rose on my shaking arms. Applause circled the gym floor. Shade just laughed.

"A-a-amazing!" I stammered as I tried to calm my racing heart.

"Told you."

The first woman stepped back as the second lady stepped forward. She poured the contents of her goblet into her mouth, and then spat powerfully into the fire. Red flames spiked into the air, but the image fizzled before it could form fully. She stared into her cup as she stepped backward.

"Awwwh," the crowd groaned collectively.

The third woman walked forward and spat her liquid into the inferno. A pillar of orange flames streaked high into the air, divided, popping and hissing, and eventually morphed into a picture of a beautiful woman. She looked oddly familiar. Almost like she was someone I knew, but a little older. The heat from the image caused me to shield my face. Then, it evaporated, surrendering to the dark night sky.

The second woman approached the blaze again and spat her elixir into the flames. A column of red flames stretched toward the heavens. It fanned out to form the vision of a man sitting upon a throne. After a moment, the man disappeared, leaving an empty throne. The flames turned colors from reddish-orange to golden. Then, the entire picture dissolved. Sparks fell like shooting stars.

Raucous applause erupted throughout the crowd. I clapped so hard my palms stung.

"Absolutely wicked," I said.

"Sometimes the Oracles have straightforward messages when they perform their spitting image ceremonies," Shade said. "Other times, like tonight, you just never know."

I remembered Ouranos' earlier comment about the Oracles; *"They speak with three tongues."*

Pontus threw a humongous pail of water on the fire to quench it. Steam and smoke billowed. Then as if by deity magic, a gust of wind cleared the smoke from the gymnasium. Pontus then used a giant rake to pull apart the fire's smoldering logs and arrange them as a square boundary for the wrestling circle in the middle of the gym floor. When he finished, Pontus leapt into the middle of the ring saying, "Thank you one and all from pantheons far and wide. It is our greatest pleasure to once again host the Pantheon League wrestling championships. Tonight's combatants are as follows: From the Celtic Academy on the famed Emerald Isle, Dagda, the challenger to the crown of laurels."

The boy with swollen muscles that I'd seen earlier pushed through the crowd and bounded into the center of the ring. He had a prominent mark on his chest; three joined spirals. It jumped each time he flexed his muscles. Everyone applauded.

Pontus continued, "And from our very own Mount Olympus Preparatory Academy, Po-Sei-Don!"

"Don!" The crowd cheered over and over as he strode out. I was stunned that he had such a following from other schools.

My gaze stopped on Metis as he strode past her. She looked like a flower being tossed in the wind as she glanced around the room, clearly looking for a place to stand and watch the match. When she found a wall near the edge of the gym floor, she walked over and leaned back against it, looking around like she expected someone. Atlas, perhaps?

"Hey, Shade, hold my spot here," I said.

"Wha—" he responded. "Where you goin'? The match is starting."

I pushed my way through countless spectators. Soon, I stood within mere paces of Metis. I felt a tug at my body, pulling me closer to her. Gravitating gently. Nothing strong or overly noticeable. Just a feeling of being in her orbit.

I hadn't the foggiest idea what to say to her after the Othrys Hall encounter. Particularly after my recent conversations with my classmates. But as I drew closer, she looked up at me from under long eyelashes, her big, sad hazel eyes casting a pained gaze.

I looked for the bruising I thought I'd seen earlier. "Metis?"

She nodded, looking around warily. Her voice quivered, approaching a whisper. "Why are *you* here?"

I was unsure how to answer. Was she asking about here at the school? Or here at the match? In the silence, I bounced back and forth as to what to say.

"Well, I'm from Crete," I began telling my life story. "And—"

"I mean why are you here talking to me? I'm a mess."

I didn't dare tell her it was because of how attractive she was. It didn't quite fit the situation. But the dam broke. The words raced out of my mouth before I could contain them. "Because your beauty shines despite your tears. Despite your pain."

She looked at me all glassy-eyed. "Shut up." She smiled. "You just wanted to play hero and save me from Atlas. Some things can't be fixed. Some people can't be saved."

As I glanced back toward the match, I saw Dagda and Don circling one another like a rhino pacing around a lion. Thickly-muscled Dagda towered over Don even as they both crept in hunched, coiled postures. Swift charges resembled snake strikes. The combatants lunged for one another and locked arms. Strong stances punctuated the melee.

"You like wrestling?" I asked in an attempt to lighten her mood. I glanced sidelong at her face, searching again for any bruises.

She shrugged, hugging herself a bit tighter, rubbing her arms. Her hair shielded her eyes again. "It's alright, I guess."

"Are you waiting for someone?" I switched tactics. "Don't tell me you brought along your old ship's anchor?"

Her face wrinkled. "You mean Atlas?" She looked downward again. "I don't think he cares about this match. Once Money got knocked out of the championships, Atlas lost interest. He's all about War Games. He probably won't even be here tonight." Every word she spoke, she pronounced crisply.

"So if you don't fancy wrestling, why'd you come to the match tonight? You waiting for anyone else? Epic? Promo?"

She cut her eyes at me. "My friend, Amphitrite. She moved closer to the ring to get a better look at the match. Funny thing, before she left she told me to stay out of trouble. And yet, here *you* are."

"I can't even spell trouble."

That's where I'd seen the dark-haired friend. Amphitrite was Don's girl over at Othrys. Scanning the crowd, I leaned back on the wall beside Metis. Our skin almost touched. We watched the wrestling match. Together. In silence.

Suddenly, Don and Dagda lunged forward, grasping one another behind the necks. After several circles around the ring, Don sank and threw Dagda over his shoulder. Dagda dexterously avoided hitting the ground hard and the crowd roared its approval.

I closed my eyes momentarily, enjoying the floral scents emanating from Metis' hair. I turned toward her again. She was actually engaged in the match. Or at least seemed to be. I slid closer to her on the wall. My arm grazed hers, sending a slight shiver down my spine. She didn't move away. I turned back to the wrestling action. Dagda and Don had tangled arms and hands behind one another's necks again.

My hand fell to my hip. It was close enough to feel her warmth. I uncurled and extended my fingers. Stretching. Seeking. The first two knuckles of my right hand caressed her chiton-clad hip like a whisper. She inhaled sharply. Then I realized that my hand hadn't actually moved. Had I imagined that whole sequence?

"Oh great," she uttered, snapping my moment in half.

A large, imposing dark-haired older man and two slightly shorter blond guys parted the crowd. The rugged and chiseled dark-haired one walked with an uncommon swagger, as did his cohorts, all filling their red tunics to near bursting. You'd have thought they could at least have found clothes that fit.

A trio of images sliced through my mind. Amalthea. Anytos. Two muscle-bound guys leaping off the back of a chariot. A sharp pain streaked through my head.

I whipped my head back around. My eyes stung with anger. I clenched my teeth. There they stood. Laughing. It was *them*. I was certain. Although the tall man wasn't Hyperion, the younger ones were definitely the attackers from Crete. My eyes darted between them as I tried to figure out what to do. Walk away. Fight them. Run away. Stand my ground. *Kill them where they stood.*

"What's wrong? Are you all right?" Metis asked, her arms still crossed. "It's only Kronos."

CHAPTER NINETEEN

Kronos.
I'd stepped forward several steps before I even knew my feet were moving. My vision tunneled as I focused on the two guys beside Kronos. The people. The noise. The match. Everything faded away. I heard nothing except my thudding pulse. Rising. Racing. Rushing.

"Hey, you never came back to the rock." Shade appeared from out of the shadows.

"What?" I jumped, looking at him blankly. "Huh?" I flashed a glance at the blond guys. Still there. I turned to Shade. "Where'd you come from?"

"I saw you walking so I—hey, were you talking to Metis? Is that why you told me to—"

"Hold on, Shade. My world just exploded. Again."

"Again? What are you talking about?"

I turned toward Kronos and company. Their smirks and laughs churned my stomach. They stood with their arms folded across their massive chests, occasionally chuckling. They hadn't see me. Not yet.

"Where is the boy ... " Hyperion had asked.

"You're pale as a cloud. What's wrong?" Shade asked. He then noticed where my gaze had been fixed.

There was no mistaking who the guys were. My blood temperature rose. Coursing. Darkening. Inky veins webbed across my arms and clenched fists. I had no weapon except my hands.

"Watch my back," I said.

"Wha—"

I took off at a light trot, weaving through random spectators. All my senses went flat. I had no peripheral vision. I heard nothing. Felt nothing. Smelled nothing.

My trot turned into a full sprint after several strides. I neared the blonde guy on Kronos' right. Remembered him well. I cocked my arm back. My final steps shortened. Three. Two. I elongated my final step and snapped my arm forward, punching the closest guy's ear. I threw every ounce of my weight through my shoulder and arm.

My fist sounded like a hammer striking an anvil. His head flopped over. "That was for Tos, you bastard!" I yelled.

He crumpled to the ground in a heap.

Kronos whipped his head around. "You're going straight to Tartarus, young man!" His thick eyebrows seemed to be a step ahead of the rest of his body as he neared me. Close up, he stood taller than Hyperion and Ouranos. Then he stopped abruptly. He narrowed his eyes and peered at me. Through me. Searching me. Studying me.

I glared back at him, fists curled into balls of fury.

The other muscle head scrambled toward me. He looked downward. "Pallas?" he called to his unconscious friend. Pushing his hair off his forehead, he glanced up at me and took another step forward. "You! I should've taken you—"

I lunged for him, connecting on a punch to the jaw. He swung and missed. I ducked and launched into his midsection. His back hit the ground with a thud. He wheezed. Sitting on his chest, I hit him with a flurry of strikes to the jaw, nose, and temple.

I was abruptly lifted into the air. When I touched ground again, some invisible energy field held me in place. The blond guy stood up and charged again.

Kronos halted his progress. "Easy there, Perses," he said without removing his gaze from me.

Perses stood there, breathing hard through his bloodied nose like a seething bull. Pallas still lay on the ground, motionless. *Perses and Pallas. Kreios' sons.* The ones Tia said were such nice guys. My breathing huffed in short bursts as I returned their glares.

Shade caught up to me. "Great Gaia, boy! What's gotten into you?" He asked over my shoulder. He grabbed my arms and pulled me back a few steps. I bristled at his grasp and pulled away.

My gaze remained riveted to Kronos and Perses, but I couldn't move any closer. Something held me in place. Another vision of Anytos flashed through my mind, his body flying backward from the force of the spear's impact. I tried again to lunge for the other guy's throat, but couldn't move. Kronos stepped between us.

"You have a lot of fire in you, boy," Kronos said in a measured tone. "Reminds me of myself when I was your age. In fact, you look like me at that age, so raw with emotion." He extended his massive hand to me. "In case you hadn't figured it out yet, I'm Kronos."

"I know who you are. Did you send these guys after my mother?" I pointed at Pallas and Perses, leaving his outstretched hand hanging.

Kronos' eyes morphed from smug to concerned. Shock played across his face and his features softened. He narrowed his gaze a bit more, but still didn't speak.

"What are you talking about *now*?" Shade asked.

I waved him off.

"What do you want from me?" I demanded with more force.

He chuckled, "So you're the one, eh? *The Boy.* Never quite knew what I'd do if I found you."

A throng encircled us. I swelled with confidence. Kronos looked back and forth, running his tongue over his bottom lip rapidly.

"I'm the one what?" I growled.

"Yeah," Shade chimed. "The one what?"

I turned to hush Shade again. I briefly caught sight of Metis' concerned eyes gazing past Shade's shoulders.

"Clearly these boys here made a mistake." Kronos chuckled again with a hint of nervousness. His gaze darted through the crowd. "I told them to find a boy I thought had stolen a goat of mine. I have no idea why they attacked your mother."

"Well they did!" I struggled toward him again. "And killed my best friend!"

Perses chimed from behind Kronos, "We were just doing what yo—"

Kronos whipped around and grabbed Perses by the throat. "Not. One. More. Sound." He wheeled back to me. "So now, where were we? Oh yes." He looked deeply into my eyes. "What's your name, boy?"

"Zeus," I hissed.

"Well, Zeus, we should talk." He stepped toward me.

I backed away. "I have nothing to say to you. Not until you answer my questions."

"I told you," Kronos spoke through clenched teeth. "These imbeciles made a mistake. They will be dealt with. I assure you. Now come. Let bygones, be bygones."

"Look, my friend is dead. And my mother was close to death when I left. I will not stop until I find whoever ordered that attack. Was it you?" I tried to step forward and was still held in place.

"Strong words, boy." Kronos' demeanor swung back to smug. "I'd mind my tongue if I were you."

My gaze never wavered.

"Besides," Kronos continued. "You need look no further than the owner of the sun chariot to find the orchestrator of that attack."

I paused. "Ohhh … I never said anything about Hyperion." My eyes narrowed. "So why would you even mention a sun chariot?"

"Just because I know about the attack, doesn't mean I ordered it," he growled. "Now if you want to go sniffing around Hyperion, be my guest. But he's not exactly the social type. And he has anger management issues."

"So Hyperion decided to attack my family on his own?"

"Well now, I can hardly speculate as to the mental goings on of a man who spends his day hauling a fire hazard across the sky. But if you think you're man enough to toss around with him, then by all means … "

I thought back to how effortlessly Hyperion had dismissed our spears. And how he summoned the one spear back to his hand.

"Now," Kronos said sternly. "Looks to me like you have two choices. You can come to Othrys and I can make you the most powerful young man in the world. We can defy even the Oracles and their gibberish." He paused for effect. "Or, you'll go straight to Tartarus. Fighting at Inter-Pantheon events is strictly prohibited."

Ouranos and Headmistress pushed through the crowd. "Our students don't respond to ultimatums, Kronos," Ouranos bellowed.

"If Zeus goes to Tartarus," Headmistress said with an icy stare. "It'll be by our hands, not yours."

"Well, if it isn't daddy rabbit and the little pussy cat," Kronos jeered.

"That'd be lioness to you, Kronos."

"Rhea, must we engage in such petty banter?"

Headmistress *did* have a name. Wait, *Rhea*? The one who issued some warning to Amalthea about me?

All this time she was right under my nose. And could've answered all my questions.

For now, simply address me as Headmistress.

You will find all the answers you seek … all in due time.

I clenched my teeth. The ground beneath me shifted in odd ways. I grabbed at the air to steady myself, but the world around me twirled in the opposite direction. Someone grabbed my left arm.

I looked over. It was Shade. I sighed. A stronger hand gripped my other arm.

"Listen to me," Kronos said. "This is a complex world we live in, one where things are never as they seem. And the more layers you peel away, the more things move from black and white to gray."

Ouranos stepped in front of me, panting like he'd been running from the other side of the world. "That's enough, Kronos. Whatever punishment he deserves shall be issued by us. You may take leave of this campus."

"May I, now?" Kronos sneered.

After a mini staring contest, Kronos helped Pallas from the ground. I felt emotionally turned inside out. Exposed. My feet paced backwards without telling me they were doing so. I bumped into people, stepped on toes, and almost tripped.

"Zeus," Shade called out. "Wait."

Tiny pinpricks stung my eyes. Pressure built rapidly in my nostrils.

Metis stepped in front of me. "Hey, you all right? What was that all about—" I pushed past her. The residual coolness of her caress lingered on my arm. Her concern transferred through my skin.

Shade was hot on my heels. "Wait up!"

The crowd behind me roared. Something must've happened in the wrestling match. I kept walking out of the gym toward the housing area. Through blurred vision, I eventually found my bungalow. Rage-filled blood coursed through me.

My vision darkened. The room spun and before I knew it, I'd crashed onto my bed. The confusion and anxiety all rivered down my cheeks.

Abandonment. Amalthea. Anytos.

Death. Hiding. Hyperion.

Rhea. Kronos.

No mother.

No father.

Who was I?

CHAPTER TWENTY

I awoke some time later to the painful throb of my bruised knuckles. As I pulled my hand up to my face to examine it more closely, a hand touched my shoulder. I wiped my eyes and looked up to see a cloth dangling in front of my face.

I rolled over. Tia's smile lit up the room more than my candles.

"Tia—" I grasped the cloth to wipe my eyes and cheeks.

"Hey," she soothed. "I heard about what happened. So, you laid out my ex, huh?"

"Who? Pallas?" I responded. "He had it coming."

I sighed and sat upright. Shade, Meter, and Hera stood behind Tia. Hera covered her mouth with her hand. But her eyes spoke to me, even from that distance.

"What did Pallas do to earn such a headache? I didn't even know you knew each other." Tia said.

"We still don't," I said. "He knows my fist, though."

"Doesn't make sense. Pallas can be a hothead sometimes, but how'd you get crossed up if you don't even know him?" Tia massaged my shoulder in a motherly way. "And what would Kronos want with you?"

Before I could manage my mouth, all the words tumbled out. I summarized and explained everything from Hyperion to Kronos and from Amalthea to Anytos, ending with my journey from Crete to MO Prep. I found the story itself rather exhausting.

"Wow! I'm so sorry." Tia hugged me. "I'm no math scholar, but something still doesn't add up. What business would the Elder Sun Deity have with a goat herder on Crete?"

"Hyperion was searching for a boy mentioned by the Oracles."

"But why?" Meter asked.

I shrugged. "All I know is that I need to find Hyperion. Or find whoever ordered the attack. Either way, if Hyperion acted alone, he is in for the fight of his life."

"Yeah?" Shade scoffed. "And how exactly do you propose to fight him with all of his Elder Deity magic?"

"I haven't figured that part out yet. But I think Kronos knows more than he's letting on."

"Be careful." Meter crossed the room and sat down beside me. "Kronos is more powerful than you realize. And Hyperion too."

I thought back to Hyperion's powerful display on Crete and Kronos' ability to pin me in place at the wrestling match without touching me.

"While you're thinking that over, let's go down to the Agora. There's a big celebration for Don tonight. He won the match." Shade rubbed his hands together.

My eyebrows rose.

"Yes. He won. Again," Tia said in mock exasperation before laughing at herself. "I told you, Zeus, we don't lose."

"Give me a moment to collect myself," I said. "And rinse off my knuckles."

"You sure?" Shade said. "I need to catch up with Don. He's in the baths now. Just meet us down at Dragon's Breath Taverna."

"It's at the end of the Agora near the Odeon," Hera said. "But count me out. Wine turns boys to animals, even if it is diluted. I'd hate to have to hurt someone's feelings tonight."

"You boys have fun," Tia squeezed my shoulder one last time. "I have to put the finishing touches on my Astro project. Just a bit more research."

"Tonight?" Meter joked. "Girl, just finish that thing tomorrow. Or the next da—"

"You know me." Tia stood up and walked to the door. "Be well, Zeus. You're in my thoughts."

"Oh that's right. The Astro project!" I palmed my face. "Can I do anything? I am supposed to be helpi—"

"You have *more* than enough on your plate," she said. "But, if Professor O asks me anything, I'll swear north and south you helped me." She winked and left.

Hera, Shade, and Meter followed. I was alone again. I rubbed my arms, massaging the goose bumps that rose in Tia's absence. I leaned back and closed my eyes. Kronos was a hairy goat's scrotum. I didn't trust him—or Hyperion—at all.

I still didn't know why they were looking for me or why they had tried to kill Amalthea and succeeded in killing Tos. Had Amalthea abducted me?

I had too many questions and not enough answers. I doubted that I'd ever find my real mother at this rate. And, worse, Rhea had known the entire time. If she warned Amalthea and the Kouretes, she knew I was there! *Call me Headmistress, my ass.* I pounded my fist on the bed.

I couldn't decide if I wanted to go to the party in the Agora or not. I kind of just wanted some time to myself, to process everything that had happened this evening. Also, what if Atlas and Money were down there? That would be just asking for more trouble than I needed right now.

I clenched my teeth and tried to untangle my mind. After several deep breaths, I'd calmed myself and closed my eyes again, leaning my head back against the wall.

CHRIS LEDBETTER

My eyes were lured open by light rapping on my doorframe.

"Metis?" I rubbed my sore eyes at the sight of her.

"Hey," she whispered. Wavy golden tendrils fell across her face as she tilted her head. "I wanted to check on you. How are you doing?" She leaned against the wall just inside the door, her soft, floral scent floating toward me. Her chiton clung so tightly to her hips and breasts that I momentarily forgot my plight.

"I meant to tell you earlier … " I grinned. "You're not even remotely in dress code."

She cast me a searing glance. "Should I take it off, then?"

I had half a mind to help her out of it. I stood and walked toward her, forgetting all my anger and frustration.

"That was quite a show you put on out there." She tugged the bottom of her chiton up slightly. "I don't know—such power—it did something to me."

I felt her draw me in. The pull to be near her, to touch her, was overwhelming. I ran my hands over her waist and hips, looking directly into her eyes. Her lips parted slightly, before she smacked my hands away and smiled.

"I have a boyfriend, remember?" she purred, slipping from my embrace and moving across the room. She sat on my bed and propped her leg up.

I crossed the room, moving as smoothly as a panther. "Yeah, about that—"

Her coy smile drove me insane. I'd almost reached her when I was startled by a noise behind me. Metis' eyes bulged.

When I turned around, Headmaster Ouranos stood in the doorway. "Metis, you may return to your cabin. Now."

"Yes, Headmaster." She scurried out, leaving me in a puddle of utter need.

Headmaster watched her leave, and then turned back to me. His blue eyes cast a frigid stare. "Zeus, come to my office tomorrow after morning meal."

CHAPTER TWENTY-ONE

My vision hazed as I walked to the Megaron the next morning. I scratched the back of my neck and fingered the collar of my tunic. I still stung from my encounter with Kronos and I desperately wanted to ask the Othrys Headmaster more questions. I also had some for Rhea, but I wasn't entirely sure I wanted to know the answers. I wasn't sure how much more bad news I could take. After Ouranos left my bungalow last night, the events of last night caught up with me and I ended up not heading down to the celebration. I was certain Tartarus was in my future for the fight last night. Whatever Tartarus was. And then, there was the "incident" with Metis in my bungalow. Though I might be able to talk my way out of that one.

When I entered the Andron, the delicious aromas from the array of food stirred my appetite. Professor Mnemosyne, teacher of Rhetoric and Epic Poetry sat at a nearby table. Nemo, as all the students called her, smiled warmly when I passed.

I grabbed a plate of food and joined Don and Meter at a far table near a window. "Congrats, Don! I heard the great news."

"Thanks. Float like a manta ray, sting like a jellyfish," he said, standing to clasp my arm. "Say, what happened to you last night? I heard you got in a seismic scuffle. Laid Pallas out, did you? Good man."

I laughed, massaging my bruised knuckles.

"Yeah," Meter added. "Shade said he'd never seen a punch like that before."

Shade strode into the Andron. "Spruce, what happened to you last night?"

"What do you mean?" I looked at him incredulously. "You were there. You saw the whole thing."

"No. I mean the after party at Dragon's Breath. Why didn't you come down?"

I thought back to Metis in my room the previous evening. "I was spent. I'd have been horrible company."

"Gah, you missed a great party, brother," Don said. "We played spin the amphora. Girls were belly dancing. It was great."

My posture sank. I hated that I had missed the festivities. It sounded epically more fun than anything I'd done on Crete, even the bonfire. Of course, if Ouranos hadn't cut me off at the kneecaps last night, I would have had plenty of fun on my own.

Headmistress Rhea rushed into the Andron. Her normally well-maintained hair looked like wild brush.

"The Observatory is a wreck!" she said. Her hand gripped the fabric of her tunic over her heart. "Stop what you're doing and come to the lab. I want to make sure everyone is accounted for. Go find Tia and Hera. Who else are we missing? Metis? Find her too. Now."

"You all know where to find them?" I said to Meter, Don, and Shade, my heart racing. "I'll go with Headmistress."

I rose from my half-eaten food and walked quickly to catch up with Rhea, my gaze shifting everywhere except for her eyes.

"Mnemosyne, you and the rest of the instructors should split up and stalk the main entrance and the Cloudwell," Rhea said. "Report anything suspicious to me. And if you see Ouranos, tell him to come to his lab, immediately."

"Done," said Professor Nemo.

As I followed Rhea, I thought of the confrontation with Hyperion on Crete. This situation had the same immediacy. The same tension.

"Did you go to the Observatory last night for any reason?" Rhea asked me.

I shook my head. Tia popped into my head. "I think Tia might have, though. She was working on her—"

"Oh dear Gaia!"

We jogged up the path, winding through woodsy and pungent cypress trees on the hillside. We climbed the steep flight of stone stairs leading to the Observatory, which perched on the edge of a cliff. At the top of the steps, Rhea stopped and turned to me.

"Zeus, I don't want you to fret. The scene's messy up here. Pontus is already in there. The only reason we're showing this to the students is because we all need to be aware of what's going on. We don't shelter anyone here. Full disclosure. Also, the more eyes we have searching, the less likely we'll miss something."

"I'll do whatever I can to help."

Rhea studied me for a moment, and then tightened her lips into a half-smile. "I know you've been through a lot and have a plethora of questions. But don't concern yourself with Kronos. He can't harm you here."

I tried to turn off my brain. No more thoughts. I didn't want Rhea invading my brain.

She pushed the blue door to the Observatory. It groaned open, revealing a chaotic mess. As we entered the lab, I found myself blinking several times. A faint sulphuric scent filled the space. Lab tables lay on their sides. Clay tablets had been strewn widely across tables and the floor, some broken. Unfurled scrolls curled up from the floor like eyelashes. The images overwhelmed me, searing into my mind. The implications were staggering.

Pontus looked up from gathering scrolls. "Where's everyone else?"

"They're all coming, Pontus." She turned to me. "Look around for clues as to what might have happened here, or whom might have done this. Call me over if you find anything."

I approached a stack of uncharged Hurler posts, struggling with the weight of one when I picked it up. The post was solid.

A pink flower bloom rested innocently on the floor and beside it, a necklace lay coiled. On the end of it hung a decorative charm similar to Hera's, except it had the letter 'T' on it.

"Headmistress," I said as my throat constricted. "I think this is—"

She took the necklace from my hand. "Hestia—" she breathed with her hand covering her mouth. "All right, we need a clearer picture of what happened here. Keep looking." Her voice was like the dense forest at night, calm with a hint of danger around the next bend.

My shoulders tensed. A shaft of Hyperion's sunlight shot through the open ceiling of the Observatory, illuminating the madness on the floor, a stark contrast to the sterile, white walls. In a corner of shadows, an active Hurler post stood, casting a blue halo.

A trail of dried ichor blood led into the alcove, right to the post. The blood had a muddy goldenrod tone. My stomach turned as image after image of Tos flashed before my eyes. "You might want to see this," I called to Rhea on the other side of the room. She strode over next to me, gasping and then collecting herself with a sigh upon noticing the blood trail.

Pontus said, "And what's this?"

A spear leaned against the wall. The metal tip and onyx shaft were also streaked with ichor. And, on the wall, a message stained the wall in swirls of darkest gray and bright golden-yellow blood.

Prophecies Are Meaningless
Stars Come and Go
Time Marches On
Residual blood had dripped down the wall like tears. My heart

pounded an irregular cadence.

Rhea's eyes looked glassy and liquid. Tears threatened to burst from the corners as her brow furrowed. "How could this happen on our campus? How could I not have sensed it … read the person's mind who planned it?"

"Rhea." Pontus looked at her. "This is not your fault. You can't blame yourself—"

"How can I not? There are few in this cosmos whose minds I can't read. So how didn't I feel this?"

"Let's focus on the message," Pontus said. "Zeus, write this down so we can analyze it."

Pontus grasped the spear. Careful not to touch the blood, he pulled it into the sun.

"Look at that," Rhea said, pointing to the shaft. "The shaft doesn't reflect anything. Even in broad sunlight."

I finished copying the message onto a piece of parchment and handed it to Pontus. When I got a closer look at the shaft, my mind snapped to the demonic spears Hyperion's henchmen had used. Aristaeus' words echoed in my ears.

Deity magic is unparalleled.

My voice quivered. "This looks exactly like one of the spears we were assaulted with on Crete."

Rhea's head whipped toward me. "Hyperion had a spear like this one?"

I nodded. She and Pontus looked at one another.

"I've never seen anything like this," Pontus said. "It's certainly not one of ours. Furthermore, why would the assailant leave his weapon behind?"

"Perhaps he was in a hurry?" I asked.

Pontus twirled the spear in his hand. "What's ironic is I would've normally gotten Ouranos to examine a weapon like this." He stroked his shrub of a goatee. "But he's nowhere to be found at the moment … which is a low concern. Elders can't die. Killing weapons don't exist—"

"Don't they?" Rhea snatched the spear from Pontus. "We have no idea what this is capable of." She held it up to the light again. "Wait. What are those markings?"

Three rows of runes glowed near the butt-end of the spear. Their visibility seemed to be activated by the sunlight.

"What pantheon uses these marks?" Pontus asked.

"I don't know." Rhea's eyes turned cold. "But I intend to find out."

"Let's hope that the other students find Hestia, Hera, and Metis. Then we'll only have to worry about Ouranos," Pontus said. "Keep looking for anything else."

I stepped over debris toward an archway in the back of the lab. Curiosity got the best of me as I peeked at the stairwell that led upstairs.

"Come back over here," Pontus commanded.

"I wasn't doing anything."

"The Sky Throne is up there. It's forbidden to all except Ouranos."

"I just wanted to look at it. Tia already warned me not to try to sit on—"

"That's right! Do *not* sit on it. Don't even approach it. I can't undo whatever it would do to you."

"Got it." I climbed the marble stairs, which stopped at the top of a covered tunnel. Above me, the sky opened in every direction, cloudless and vast. I inhaled deeply, crisp, clean air filling my lungs. I'd almost forgotten my mission.

"Zeus," Pontus called from below.

Looking upward and down the tunnel, I didn't see a throne, let alone a *Sky Throne*. I didn't even see a chair of any sort. "Just looking around for more clues," I lied, holding on to the sides of the angled, vertical tunnel to hoist myself higher. Smoothing my clammy hands on my tunic, I inched upward as if I were being pulled.

I reached the top of the tunnel. A panoramic view of the Aegean spread out before me.

"Just don't look down," I whispered.

But—of course—I did, my gaze fixing on the dizzying drop toward the earth. My limbs stiffened and my stomach lurched into my throat like I was already falling. I could barely breathe.

I lost my balance, collapsing onto the top stair inside the tunnel. I fell backward the opposite way and hit something hard behind me. Turning around, there was nothing but air. The area behind me felt solid, smooth to the touch like the marble.

The wide view from Mount Olympus stole my breath. Ocean waves crashed far down to my right. Lush, green hills of Thessaly rolled to my left. The highest point on the earth, eh?

"Zeus! Get down here this instant!" Rhea called from below.

If I was ever going to sit on the Throne, this was my chance. They'd never let me this close again. If I could access the power inherent in the Throne, I could stand up to anyone. Hyperion. Kronos. Anyone. I edged higher, but my fear of falling constricted my throat. I wiped my damp brow.

"Zeus!" Pontus climbed halfway up the stairs. "Down here. Now."

I finally relented and inched my way back down the steps, scooting on my rear end. Pontus gripped my arm like it was his last meal. His muscles flexed as his fingers dug into my bicep. "*Do not* mount that Throne. Do you hear me?"

"Yes. But—"

"No buts!" Pontus said. His hair pulsed as he talked. Rhea glared at me over his shoulder. Don, Meter, Shade, and Hera stood behind her, wide-eyed.

"All I was going to say was—"

"Do you want detention? You've not mapped the Underworld yet. It's Tartarus for you if you don't scrap this idea of going near the Throne." His voice rumbled with barely impatience.

Rhea stared at me with an icy gaze. "Frankly, it doesn't matter what you were going to say. We're not about to lose a student to insubordination. The rules of this school exist to ensure your safety. And they are non-negotiable."

CHAPTER TWENTY-TWO

"Ouranos is nowhere to be found. His lab is a mess. We've got students missing and one trying to climb the Throne. What else could go wrong today?" Pontus glared at me.

I avoided his eyes and stepped around the scattered evidence, a ball of anxiety knotting in my core. Don's disapproving stare hollowed me. Meter tightened her lips. My heart broke to think I'd disappointed them. Just behind Shade, Hera stood with her arms folded, her weight on her right leg.

"Where is Metis?" Rhea voice creased the silence. "Two students missing now?"

Everyone shrugged.

"I'll go look for Metis," I said. Anything to get out of there. I inadvertently brushed against Hera's shoulder as I exited the Observatory.

"Report to me immediately if you find either of them," Rhea said.

Hera caught up to me when I reached the bottom of the stairs.

I shot a sidelong glance toward her. "Hey," I whispered.

She nudged me with her shoulder. "What's with the sad eyes? They do absolutely nothing for those nice thick eyebrows you have."

I whistled an exhale, thinking about how much trouble I got into at Eastern Crete and how my behavior over the past day had been just as contentious. "Rhea's probably going to kick me out of school."

"If that were the case, she'd have done it. Your place at this school is safe. So far, at least." She smiled. "But, more goat-foolery like fighting at an Inter-Pantheon event and that mess you just tried to pull up near the Sky Throne *will* get you sent to Tartarus. Trust me. You do *not* want to go down there."

I sighed.

"Chin up. You still have all your fingers and toes."

I instinctively looked at my fingers. And toes. "Aren't you concerned about that mess back there?"

"The blood is unnerving. And the mess. But we don't know enough yet to be concerned. Ouranos is frequently gone. And the couple of students who happen to not be around ... yeah, not a huge deal either. Not yet anyway. It's Hemera Kaos ... rest day. Now, if they're not back by Hemera Gaia, two days from now ... we can worry."

I acknowledged her confidence.

"Oh, and just to let you know, I adore what you did back there in the Observatory."

"Which?" The corners of my lips turned down. "Almost killing myself trying to find the Throne? Or almost getting myself thrown in Tartarus?"

She laughed. "Both. Equally. Takes real courage to go after what you want, critics and consequences be damned."

"Who wouldn't want the power of the Sky Throne? The power to rule all the heavens? Sign me up." I smiled. "Besides, I have a debt to settle with Hyperion."

"Good luck with that." She snorted. "You'll need to get bigger *and* stronger before you start picking on Elder Deities."

"I *have* gotten bigger. And stronger." I flexed my biceps.

"Mmmm, yes you have." She slipped her fingers around my bicep and squeezed. Her fingers and palm felt hot on my skin. "But you're still a mere babe compared to their power. We all are. The only thing that could help you gain their strength *is* the Throne."

I paused for a moment. "I know the Throne *could* kill me ... but what if it didn't? What if the threat of death is just a story created to keep students off the Throne? You can't have everyone up there controlling the Heavens, right?"

"When I rule the heavens one day, I'll let you know. I was the best student at Samos Lower Academy before getting shipped to Euboea. After conquering that school too, I came here. I was the best student here at MO Prep before the schools split. And I'm still the best. Nothing's going to stop me from getting what I want."

"Which is?"

"To be the most powerful being on earth," she deadpanned. "Elders included."

I countered with a half laugh. "Why stop there?"

"I won't." She tossed her dark wavy hair over her shoulder. "I *will* rule the heavens and the earth one day. Watch me."

"That would mean that you'd have to rule the Sky Thr—"

"Exactly. Which is why I found it so endearing that you crawled up there. In front of everyone. Brave. Possibly stupid."

"If you want to rule the heavens so bad, why haven't you mounted the Throne yet?" I goaded her.

"Just waiting for the right moment."

"You're not afraid the Throne might kill you?"

"To be the greatest, you have to overcome the greatest obstacles."

Her ambition struck me. Deeply. The nymphs had been fun back home, but I'd never gotten a sense they had aspirations. Telesto wanted to be a teacher. But here was Hera. She wanted to command the cosmos. There was something alluring about a girl going after what she wanted.

"Let's check out Tia's cabin. See if she's back yet." Hera said. "We checked earlier, but—"

"What about Metis—"

"What about her? She's probably visiting Atlas or something. I didn't even know she was going to MO Prep again."

My mind scrambled. I had to find a way to permanently get her away from that goat's scrotum, especially if he was responsible for those bruises. I wanted to give him a taste of what I'd given Pallas.

Ahead of us, the path divided and wrapped around a clump of trees. Nearing them, Hera stepped to the right. I veered to the left. She grabbed my arm and yanked me. "Don't split the trees."

I laughed. "I'm sorry. That rule wasn't in the code of conduct."

"Shut up. Like you even read that fire starter."

We kept walking past the clump of trees. Violet, yellow, and bright pink flowers lined the path, vibrant and fragrant.

Hera noticed me looking at the flowers. "Meter planted those. She's masterful with plants. You should see her cab—" She stopped abruptly, slicing off the end of her last word. "Then again, maybe not. I mean it's all right. If you're into that sort of thing. I ate a pomegranate once down in the Agora and it was so delicious that I asked Meter if she could help me grow a pomegranate tree in Horticulture class. She said she was going to do it this year, but never did. I still want my tree."

We finally reached Tia's cabin. I stepped in front of Hera. "Wait here." I placed my arm across her torso to block her advance. "There might be danger in there."

She chuckled. "And what are you gonna do? I'd do better if I went in there by myself."

"Did you not hear about the punch I leveled on Pallas?"

She didn't answer, brushing my arm aside and walking past me through the door as she called Tia's name. The doorway had a wispy opaque curtain hanging over it from the inside. It smelled like honeysuckle.

"Where's Tia?" Hera wondered out loud. "It's not like her to miss meals *and* be unaccounted for. If anyone's a goody-two-sandals, it's her."

A series of dark, square cubbyholes hung above her desk, each stuffed with one or two scrolls. While Hera inspected the bed and closet for clues, I examined the spotless wooden desk. Each cubby was labeled with marks chiseled into the wood. The cubby for Astronomy was empty.

A potted flower anchored the back corner of the desk. The dark cubbies framed the flower's splash of green. Five little heart shaped rocks sat in a row on the windowsill. Each was different in shape and size. I smiled because I could totally see her collecting something like that.

"Oh well, I don't see any notes or indications that something malodorous happened here. Her theatre script is over there. She's still gotta turn that in. Other than that, per usual, nothing's out of place here. I hate how organized she is. Maybe she went down to the Agora." Hera turned to leave.

"What would she be doing down there?" I asked. Then I remembered her saying she liked to go there to read. But still, between Tia missing, her empty Astro cubby, and the mess in the Observatory where she supposedly worked on her project last night, something didn't quite add up.

"Oh who knows with that one? She could be grabbing a gyro. Could've gone home with some cute boy from another school. Not the first time." Hera walked toward the door.

"But wait … " I put my finger in the air. "What about Tia's necklace, the one like yours? I found it in the Observatory. Why would that be on the floor in the corner?"

"Now, that does concern me." Hera pulled on her bottom lip. She sighed and fingered her own necklace, bringing the charm to her mouth. "That's easily the most damning clue we have."

"And what about the blood smatters?" I asked.

Hera paused for a moment and massaged her temples. "Once you drink the nectar, the cosmic dust within the nectar binds to your cells and allows you to heal at such a fast rate that weapons can't kill you. They do hurt, though." She shook her head. "The blood is bad but not as bad as the necklace." Hera pinned me with a stern glare. "She'd never take that off. We need to keep searching. Come on."

I joined her just as Meter poked her head through the gauzy curtain. "Oh there you are, Ti—" Then her face wrinkled when she saw Hera. "You're not Tia."

"That's how you greet the queen of the world?"

"In your damn dreams." Meter cut her eyes. "I guess we still haven't found her?"

CHAPTER TWENTY-THREE

"Zeus and I were just getting ready go look for Tia at the Agora."
Hera eased her arm over my shoulders and began to pull me toward the door.

"I see—"

"Hey, by the way," I said to Meter over Hera's shoulder, as we walked past her. "I like your flowers outside along the path."

We walked to the Cloudwell and hurled to the Agora. I tried to shake off the rough ride. "I wonder if I'll ever get used to that thing?" I muttered.

"And you thought you could mount the Throne? Give me a break. I'll rule the heavens before you will." Hera laughed.

I gazed into her eyes. "Is that a challenge?"

She returned a wry smile.

We inspected the busy Agora, my eyes keenly searching for anyone resembling our bright and vibrant Tia. As we passed Dragon's Breath Taverna, I peeked through the doors to see a bit of what I'd missed the previous evening. The sprawling, pavilion-style room smelled like death. Well-used target games lined one wall opposite a serving counter on the other. Plates of half-eaten food and overturned goblets littered the tables and floor.

"Seen enough?" Hera joked. "I don't think she's in there."

We searched through the Odeon theatre, asking several people if they'd seen Tia, and eventually made our way back down the opposite side of the Agora. A shop sign hung over an entrance I hadn't seen the last time, *The Golden Himation.*

"I'm guessing they sell cloaks here?" I asked.

"And other things," Hera said. "Sandals, cloaks, tunics, chitons, brooches, girdles. You name it. They even sell some of Meter's Kosmetikos. Masks. Bath soaks. Eyeliners. Lip stains. I told Tia she should make jewelry for this place."

"Let's stop here and ask if they've seen Tia." I pushed through the doorway. Tunics in all the exotic colors Tia wore were folded neatly on wooden displays. I smiled for a moment, remembering the first day I met her.

I approached an elderly woman who sat near the back of the establishment. "Do you know Tia, er Hestia, from Mount Olympus Prep?"

"Why, yes I do." The woman's voice sounded fragile. She reminded me of our guidance counselor. "She's one of my best customers."

"Have you seen her?" I asked.

"Why, no I haven't. Not in a week or so now. Maybe Rhea got tired of paying that girl's tab."

Several random people I didn't know entered the shop. My head snapped toward them, but none of them were our Tia.

We made our way to Stone, Scroll, and Sword.

"Kreios?" I called out as I popped my head through a half-open door. Then I remembered my knuckles and whom they'd hit. *Yikes.*

No response. I looked at Hera. She shrugged and nudged me forward. I almost jumped from my skin when the door squeaked on its hinges as I opened it wider. Hera held fast to my waist.

"I got you," she whispered.

Kreios rumbled out of the back, wringing his hands. His dark hair was wild. "Ohh, Hera and Zeusss. I didn't hear you come in."

"We haven't been here long," I said. "We're actually looking for Hestia. Have you seen her?"

"Goodnesss no, boy. I've not seen her in agesss. How is she?"

"We can't find her. In fact," Hera added. "Professor Ouranos is also unaccounted for—"

"That ol' kook." He spit a little and massaged his beard. "That man keeps his head in the clouds, he doesss." He elbowed me in the shoulder. "If ya know what I mean." He let out a raucous belly laugh.

Hera and I looked at one another.

I took a more serious approach. "Kreios, what do you know about cosmic dust?" I wanted to wrap my mind around this substance and how it made Hurlers work and such. Hera gave me a quizzical look.

His face morphed, matching my tone. "Whaddya be needin' that information fer, boy?"

"After searching around Ouranos' Observatory, I got an itch to learn all I could about it."

He glared at me. "Why dontcha just climb up to the Sky Throne and find out fer yourself?"

I took a half a step backward. Hera held my back.

"I know you have rare scrolls. Do you have any on cosmic dust or not?" Hera said, a little more directly.

"I have one scroll on cosmic dust. But you'll hafta play me fer it."

"I'm sorry … play you?" I could've sworn he'd been nicer the last time. Then again, I had just punched my fist through his son's brain last night. I folded my hands into my armpits to hide my bruised knuckles.

"Yesss, boy. You do know the game, dontcha?"

Stone, scroll, and sword. I narrowed my eyes. I was getting really tired of his hissing lisp. "Don't you think this is a tad childish?"

His face drew close enough for me to smell his lunch. "If it's so childish, ya ought to win, ought'nt ya?"

"You got this," Hera whispered in my ear.

Kreios stepped backward. "I'm the best there is, boy. I invented the game. If you win, you get my scroll. But, if you lose, all three of m' boysss beat the nectar outta ya. Deal?" His neck bones cracked as he twisted his head back and forth.

So he *did* know about the punch. I wiped my moist palms on my tunic and stared into Kreios' aged, cloudy eyes. "I'm ready when you are."

We both stuck our left palms out. I raised my right fist. My bruised-knuckled right fist. He stared at my knuckles, then back at me before raising his own calloused hand.

Pound. Pound. Pound. I chose sword. He chose stone.

"That'sss one, boy." His cheeks plumped into a fiendish smile. "Best outta three."

Damn. I should've known he'd choose stone first. *Lumbering oaf.* My heart thudded as we prepared for round two.

Pound. Pound. Pound. I chose sword again. He chose scroll. I won. Yes.

A growl rumbled through his clenched teeth. "Last one, boy. Don't get nervousss."

Based on his going stone first, and scroll next, I was sure he thought I would go with stone next to try and block his sword. But, since I did sword twice, he probably thought I'd either do sword again, in which case he'd go with stone again. *How can I win this match?*

"Raise yer hand, boy. No thinking game. All instinct."

I raised my hand. My pulse vibrated against my wrist.

He flinched his hand downward and then laughed. "You ready? Don't think too long. Always go with your first choice."

Pound. Pound. Pound. I chose scroll. He chose stone.

I pumped my fist and looked straight into his eyes. "Now, give me the scroll."

Kreios huffed and disappeared into the back of the shop. He returned a moment later and shoved the scroll in my face with his gnarled hand.

I slowly unrolled it. "Wha—"

"You were smart enough to win it from me," Kreios said. "Now be smart enough to read it. Good day, boy."

"But it's blank."

"Is it?" Kreios snarled through clenched teeth, beginning to stalk toward me.

I backed toward the door, with my gaze trained on Kreios. Hera and I exited the shop and made another sweep around the Agora. No sign of Tia. The people at *Lambda, Lambda* hadn't seen her either. I closed my eyes and massaged the bridge of my nose.

"Let's get back to campus," I said. "Maybe she's turned up by now."

CHAPTER TWENTY-FOUR

As we climbed the Cloudwell, Shade shot past us from the housing area. "Assembly in the Andron. Better get moving. Pontus is fired up!" he called over his shoulder.

Hera sighed. Her voice approached a whisper. "I hope it's not bad news about Tia. I always liked her."

"*Liked?* As in past tense?" I fidgeted, picking my fingernails. "Don't think that way."

"She was always more headstrong than Meter. I'll give her that. But not more than me."

I chuckled. "Is anyone as headstrong as you?"

"Not likely."

"Hurry up!" Shade called from across the quad.

She turned to me. "We probably should double time it. Pontus is such a bear when he's angry."

"Nice of you to join us," Pontus hurled the words toward us like a javelin when we entered the Andron. "Where've you two been?"

Rhea stood to Pontus's right shoulder and glared.

"I told Hera to come on," Shade said, stirring the tension.

Hera marched toward him.

I grabbed her arm out of concern. "We don't need any fighting right now."

Hera's head whipped around. "Don't you ever touch me like that again." She yanked her arm from my grasp.

A hush swept through the room.

"And as for you, Shade—" Hera started toward him again. A scowl darkened her face. "You better keep my name out of your mouth. You hear me?"

Mental note: Do *not* get on Hera's bad side.

I caught a glimpse of Metis out of the corner of my eye. At least she still wasn't unaccounted for. I smiled as I remembered her on my bed after the wrestling match. I strained to see if she had on a chiton like the one she was wearing last night. But she wore our standard issue, white MO Prep tunic with gold trim. *Drat.*

Suddenly, I felt a heated gaze on the back of my neck. I turned to witness Hera glowering at me as she returned from confronting Shade.

"Settle down. Everyone have a seat." Rhea clapped loudly. "We have a serious issue at hand. Obviously Ouranos is missing and someone's blood is smeared across the Observatory. I'm not worried that he's missing. He takes off from time to time, especially near end of term. But the ichor *is* cause for concern. If he doesn't return by Hemera Gaia, two days from now, we'll have to report the Sky Throne vacant to the Khaos Council who oversees our school system."

Nervous shifting and uneasy throat clearing filled the room.

"More pressing and slightly more troubling is Tia's absence. Has anyone seen her?" Pontus stepped forward. "I can't make sense of it. There's no note. Nothing out of place in her cabin."

"Boys and girls, this smells immortally foul to me. We have ichor trails, Hestia's necklace, and a mysterious spear. Aside from that, we don't know where to begin." The lines around Rhea's eyes deepened with her concern. "If any of you find information, you are to report to me immediately. And I'll know if you know anything because I will be pushing my mental faculties further than normal. I am the leader of this program now."

We could have heard a feather hit the floor.

"Additionally, I will make rounds to other Pantheons, especially Kerkyra Lower Academy and Matterhorn Scuola Roman Academy. Tia used to be close to a boy from The Horn. Pontus will check over at Othrys. No student comes or leaves until we return. You are hereby ordered to remain in student housing except for meals and to turn in assignments. All projects are still due. Turn them in to my office. You all must use the buddy system. Anyone caught by themselves will be reprimanded. That is all."

We filed out of the Andron. A hand caressed my shoulder blade. I turned. My face softened when I saw Metis.

"What do you have there?" She nudged my arm.

"Just a scroll from Kreios," I said. "In fact, we had the weirdest run-in with him. Do you know Kreios down in the Agora?"

"Everyone knowsss Kreiosss," she said, imitating the man's lisp. "You forget, you're the newbie around here."

I smiled and nodded.

"So what's on the scroll?" She reached for it.

"Nothing you'd be interested in," Hera interjected. "Why are you back anyway? Shouldn't you be sniffing up Atlas?"

"If you must know, we broke up."

"What is this, the eleventieth time?"

Metis stared Hera down. I actually admired that she didn't back down. "Is there something you wish to say, Hera?"

"Pretty sure I'm saying it."

Metis squared her shoulders. "If so, then you need to go back to remedial Rhetoric because your argument lacks vigor." She turned and left.

Hera's cheeks were as red as a radish. I glanced down at her shaking hands. "You all righ—"

"I'm. Fine."

I drew in a deep breath. "Well, we need to figure out a way to read this scroll. We should try to retrace Tia's steps. She was my Astronomy partner, after all. I feel responsible." I turned away from Hera, shaking my head slowly. "When she said she was putting the final touches on our project last night, I should've gone with her. Pretty sure it had something to do with cosmic dust."

After several calming breaths, Hera shook her hands out. "Then, we need to find her research and/or project."

"We need to find *her*."

CHAPTER TWENTY-FIVE

Two days later, tension was as thick as nectar in the Andron when I entered with Shade. It was Gaiamera morning. If Ouranos didn't turn up by the end of the day, the school would probably go into emergency lock down. Even more than it had been. Meter ambled across the floor with her veggie plate. Don stared out the window, his eyes vacant. He hadn't even touched his food. I grabbed a plate and piled some goat meat and figs on it. After I sat down, I couldn't help but notice Hera picking at her food. It was already odd that she was actually eating in the Andron along with everyone.

Shade stood near the windows. "Something is brewing outside."

"A storm?" Meter asked.

"The worst kind, I'm sure," Shade said. "Kronos just walked up from the Cloudwell."

"No way." Don bolted from his seat and rushed to the window.

"Does that mean they found—" Meter's words fell off.

Loud voices rose from the grassy quad outside the Megaron. We all hurried to the windows.

Pontus stepped across the pebbled path toward Kronos. "Your father always liked you best, didn't he? That is, until you turned psychotic."

"I'd be careful how I talked to your next Headmaster—"

Upon hearing that, Don swung out of the second floor and sailed toward the ground. My eyes widened, knowing I'd never be able to pull off that move. Scampering to her feet, Meter just barely beat Hera and myself to the doorway. I clenched and unclenched my fists in an effort to calm myself. My blood ran hot at the thought of coming face-to-face with Kronos again. We scrambled down the stairs, through the halls, and burst through the doors onto the quad.

Don and Shade stood beside Pontus. Shade must've jumped through the window at some point too. Rhea jogged down the path from the Observatory and reached the eye of the storm as we did.

"Kronos, what are you doing here?" Rhea asked. Her regal golden robes swished around her as she walked. "We have enough to contend with at the moment—"

"You do indeed, Pussy Cat. But, you haven't found our father yet, so I've come to spearhead this investigation."

"We have enough hands on deck." Don stepped forward.

Pontus held his arm in front of Don. "Stand down. We will handle this."

"Exactly," Kronos sneered. "This sand box is a little large for you, Poseidon."

"Kronos, I know you wish to find out what happened to our father, but you may take leave of us now. We need to continue our searches." Rhea folded her arms. Her eyes shot ice daggers at Kronos.

Kronos took two deep breaths. His eyes glassed over. "Not until I see the scene for myself." Kronos walked toward the Observatory. "And you'll also present me with any evidence you've already found. Catching whoever did this is my first priority."

Rhea followed him at a brisk pace. "I am the leader of this program now and commander of these grounds. We are under a full examination and I order you to stop at once."

Kronos wheeled around. "As soon as I've had a look around you can resume your searches ... under my supervision."

Pontus led the rest of us just behind the gathering storm front as it surged up the path. He turned to us. "Students, if this turns ugly, go immediately to the armory and suit up."

"Ooooh," Hera uttered.

"The armory?" I asked.

"I'll fill you in later," Don said.

"Dammit, Kronos," Rhea's voice rose considerably. "I want to find out what's going on as much as you do. But running through *my* campus like a bull is not helping matters. You already splintered our school once. I won't let you do it again."

Suddenly, as if from the ether, three shafts of sparkling energy descended from the heavens to the ground. The one on the left gleamed shining gold with sparks of white crackling and revolving around the edges. The middle pillar shone brilliant white and stung my eyes. And the third column was solid black with tendrils of dark smoke wisping from it.

My heart rate increased as three men the same color as their energy appeared where the shafts had touched down. It's almost as if they'd hurled here without using Hurlers. Kronos took a step backward when they walked toward us.

The one with pale white skin spoke first. "Good. You're all here in one place awaiting our arrival," he said in a booming tone betraying his clean-shaven, boyish face. "That means we shan't have to search for you all as well. The gravity of an empty Sky Throne must not be underestimated ... which is why the Khaos Council is here. We are henceforth in charge of this investigation. I am Eros, for the uninitiated."

"But, I can handle thi—" Kronos said.

"You ... are ill equipped to handle an investigation of this magnitude." Eros' piercing blue eyes cast a sharp glare at Kronos.

"This is a matter to be reconciled by Primordials. Period," said the black-skinned man, his visual presence a stark contrast to Eros's.

"But Eros," Rhea pleaded. "If you can give us a bit more time, we can resolve this."

"Time is not on our side," Eros said crisply. "We've seen these types of Sky Throne vacancies in other pantheons before and they never end well … for the incumbent that is. You agree, Erebus?"

Black-skinned Erebus nodded. "We have entered the Time of the Empty Throne. We will suspend school operations in seven days if we can't find Ouranos or discover what happened to him. Students' safety is paramount. If we are under attack from an external force, we need to protect our own first."

"But—" Kronos stammered.

"In fact, first we need to secure the Observatory." Erebus pointed to the third man in his group, whose golden skin glinted in the sun's gaze. "Phanes, stand guard at the lab until we can assess its contents. No one in or out."

"Done, Erebus." Phanes nodded and walked back up the hill to the Observatory. He gripped his staff tighter. The orb at the top of it emitted a light so intense that we all shaded our eyes.

"Rhea." White-skinned Eros brushed past Kronos as if he wasn't even there. "We will set up a command center in the Megaron. I expect to see everyone present and accounted for just after midday meal so that we can ask a few questions. This will give us time to perform our diligence."

"This is my father we're talking about here!" Kronos threw his hands in the air. His bottom lip quivered. "I demand to be a part of this investigation."

"And so you shall," Eros said. "Do what we ask of you and there won't be any trouble." He paused, staring into Kronos' eyes. "Or will there?"

CHAPTER TWENTY-SIX

After waiting around in student housing for the remainder of the morning and reconvening for midday meal, all of us waited against a wall outside a room in the Megaron. Shade stood at the front of the line, waiting his turn to enter and be questioned. I was fourth in line, barely able to see around Don's thick-muscled frame into the darkened room. Hera tapped her foot just ahead of me and Meter's hand rested right on the small of my back.

Finally, we saw Professor Nemo exit the room with an exhausted expression and downcast eyes. She'd been the last of the faculty to be questioned. She cast a tight-lipped glance toward Rhea, who leaned on the wall opposite the interrogation room. Rhea tapped her fingernails against her teeth. Her leg bounced like it had a mind of its own.

The line inched forward as Shade stepped out. He cast a sidelong glance back toward Don as he entered the room. I turned toward Meter, noticing a tear sitting at the corner of her eye. Metis stood behind her with arms crossed. This felt like Crete all over again, except I did nothing wrong this time.

This waiting caused my heart to beat erratically, filling my chest with an unpredictable cadence. I closed my eyes and tried to steady my breathing, but questions flashed through my mind. Where was Ouranos? What happened in the lab? What kind of questions are they going to ask us?

Before I realized it, I was next. Phanes greeted me before entering the room by stretching his arm across my torso, halting my progress. His golden skin still gleamed as if we were outside.

"What is your name?" he asked.

"Zeus," I answered.

He waved his staff over my entire body from head to toe. "This process is to ensure you are who you say you are. False identities are forbidden in these proceedings." I felt scraped raw by the end of the search as if he were taking tiny rakes and scrubbing my body from top to bottom from the inside. "You may proceed." He motioned me in and closed the door behind me.

In the middle of the dark room stood a single wooden throne. Nothing overly elaborate. Eros paced back and forth while talking to Erebus whose features and robes melted into the shadows.

Eros looked at me with severity. "We have before us the dilemma of a missing Headmaster and Sky Throne master. The fact that he is Headmaster concerns us not. But the Sky Throne vacancy is of utmost import."

Phanes approached. "It is our intention here to bring the truth to light. If you are found guilty of a stained hand in the disappearance of Ouranos, heinous disciplinary measures await. Do you understand?"

I nodded, running my palm across my torso. My eyes had finally adjusted to the lack of light in the room when a bright light pierced the darkness. The sphere atop Phanes' scepter lit up, blinding me while shadows moved behind it.

"Now then," Eros said. "Let us begin. Erebus, you're up first."

I squinted to see Erebus behind the brightness of the scepter's orb. "Zeus," he said in a commanding baritone. "How long have you attended this program?"

"I haven't been here long, actually," I said. "I arrived from Crete a few weeks ago. I've been to a few class—"

"You're new, then? As in you have never attended classes here before?"

I nodded. "What does being new have to do with anything? Metis is new here also." The words flew from my mouth recklessly. I gasped as a pang of guilt slammed into my chest. I shouldn't have mentioned her name.

Eros whispered something to Erebus in the shadows.

"Thank you for your candor," Erebus said. "We'll be sure to inquire about that when she enters the chamber."

Dragon Balls! I couldn't believe I'd just done that. My dry mouth hung open as my gaze shifted toward the darker recesses of the room, simply to find brief respite from the blinding light of the scepter. I clasped my shaking knees together.

"What is your lineage? Who is your father?" Erebus asked.

I shook my head and shrugged.

"What about your mother?"

My lips tightened as I shook my head again. "I don't actually know. Not for certain, at least."

"You don't know *that* either?" Erebus asked. He paused and cleared his throat. "All right. Tell us everything you did on the night in question. Begin with the wrestling match."

I inhaled deeply and combed through my mind. I'd almost forgotten what happened that night. "Uhmm ... " I stammered. "I went to the match. Then I left and went back to my bungalow."

"Can anyone vouch for your being in your bungalow after the match?"

"Sure. Tia. Shade. Hera. Meter." I paused for a moment, unsure of whether or not to say the next name. "Metis."

"And by Tia, Shade and Meter, you mean?"

"Sorry ... Hestia, Hades, and Demeter."

"So all students, yes?" Erebus asked. "Any faculty?"

"Yes, actually—" I said, before realizing that I could've been the last person to see the Headmaster. I would've given anything to take back those last two words. Sometimes silence is golden.

"Out with it," Phanes demanded, "You said yes ... who is it? Give us a name."

My voice thinned. "I was going to say that Ouranos, were he here, would vouch for me."

"Were he here—" Phanes said in a grim tone. "I'm sure that he would."

"So let's recap," Eros said. "You ... saw Hestia *and* Ouranos *in your bungalow* ... on the night *both* went missing."

"Yes, but—"

"It wasn't a question." Eros' face appeared just above the bright orb. Light shined upward, casting haunting shadows across his face.

I gnawed on my lip and rocked back and forth in the throne. My mind raced. Thoughts blurred. I blinked rapidly under the assault of the brilliant light, wanting to shrink into the recesses of darkness in the room.

"*Zeus*. Answer the question, please. Were you in your bungalow all night?"

"Wha—" How had I missed his question? I shook my head to clear it.

"So you were *not* in your bungalow the entire night?" Erebus asked with emphasis. "Where were you then—"

"Yes, I was there." My voice was laced with frustration. "I was there all night."

"But you shook your head," Erebus said. "Which is it?"

"Great Gaia!"

"I will instruct you not to raise your voice in these proceedings." Phanes stepped into the orb light. "Now, were you or were you not in your bungalow all evening?"

I growled out a deep sigh. "Yes! I was in my bungalow all night."

I shifted my gaze away from the light.

Eros stepped forward. "Can anyone vouch for you being in your bungalow all night?"

I exhaled sharply through my nose. "No. I suppose not."

"Very well then, let's continue," Erebus said. "I gather from others that you and Hestia were working on a project together?"

They gathered this from others? Was someone trying to set me up? "Yes, we were."

"And it is our understanding from previous conversations with Ouranos that Hestia had some impressive research. That is, research many might kill for. Do you understand that to be true?"

"I knew it was something big, but who would kill for it?"

"We ask the questions!" Erebus growled. "Now, you were, in fact, helping Hestia with her project that night, were you not?"

"No, actually."

"No? And why not? Can't pull your own weight?" Erebus asked.

The heat of my blood warmed my skin's surface. I swiped the beaded sweat that had gathered from my brow. Memories of that day and night swirled. Metis' bruises. The fire-spitting opening ceremony. Kronos. Pallas. Rhea.

I spoke with a measured pace. "I had a lot on my mind that night."

"So it seemed. Isn't it correct that you knocked an Othrys student unconscious with a single punch?" Eros asked.

"Wait. How did you know abo—"

"A move that was unprovoked as far as all could see," Eros continued. "Isn't that correct?"

My mind spun on hyperdrive. I gazed at the floor and dragged my sweaty palms down my tunic. I couldn't believe they threw that in my face. "But I was attacked before that!"

"That's not what the witnesses say," Phanes said. "And it was not your first violent encounter since you showed up here, was it?"

"What? Wait a minute … you don't think that I had—"

Eros crossed his pale arms in the shadows. "We are simply collecting as much information as we can. Answer the question."

"But it sounds like you've already made a decision." My blood ran even hotter beneath my skin, so much so that I wished I could go jump in the ocean.

"Yes," Erebus said. "I am not going to lie. It doesn't look good for you. Best you can do is answer our queries honestly."

"Are we done?" I asked.

"I must confer with the council," Eros said. They walked to the corner of the room, talked for a few moments, and then returned.

"One more question," Phanes said, bringing forward the spear we'd discovered in the lab. Erebus grabbed it and his skin was the same color black as the spear's shaft. "Have you seen this spear before?"

My mind ran rampant with theories as to what might happen if I said 'no' given that I'd already told Rhea and Pontus that I had seen a spear like it. That wouldn't have been a lie, though. I hadn't seen that particular one. Or had I? What if it were the same spear Hyperion had used?

"You will answer the query posed to you," Erebus barked. "Have you seen this spear before?"

And then my mind snapped to lucidity. "Yes. It is Hyperion's." I wanted to throw that bastard under the chariot. If I couldn't find him, maybe they could.

Eros took a step backward. "Hyperion's?"

I nodded. "He's the one you should be investigating, not me."

They looked at one another. Then I disclosed to them how I had first seen the spear during the attack on my family. I explained about my mother's health and of my friend's death.

The three of them retreated into the corner of the room after my explanation of how Hyperion was involved. They returned with solemn gazes.

"Zeus, you have provided us with a great deal of information," Eros said finally. "But at the end of the day, we know this: you are new here, you have a history of violent tendencies, you saw both missing parties late on the night in question—at your bungalow no less—you have no alibi for your whereabouts for most of the night, you were involved with the research of one of the missing parties, and you admitted to having intimate knowledge of what could be the weapon used to kill one or both of them."

My mouth went dry.

"In other words," Erebus said. "You are our number one suspect."

CHAPTER TWENTY-SEVEN

I couldn't breathe; the weight of that last statement sat on my chest like a rhinoceros. I rose to my feet. "I didn't do anything!"

"There's that temper." Phanes studied me.

"I'm serious. I had nothing to do wi—"

"You would do well to sit back down in your seat." Phanes pointed his staff toward me. "Don't force me to use this."

"Erebus," Eros said. "Fetch Rhea."

He swept across the room through the darkness. Light pierced the room as he opened the door and called Rhea's name. As she entered, her footsteps as light as feathers brushing across tiles, I couldn't bear to raise my gaze from the floor.

"Rhea, I must apprise you of the severity of our preliminary findings," Eros said. "For reasons I'll divulge in due time, Zeus is our primary suspect."

Rhea covered her mouth with her hand.

I dropped my head.

"Somewhere between the darkness and light lies the truth," Eros said. "And we will uncover it."

"Rhea, as acting headmistress we must ask you if you are impartial enough to restrict Zeus' travels until we can further investigate the other leads we have."

"So, you do have other leads, then?" Rhea asked.

Phanes nodded slowly.

Rhea cradled her forehead in her palm and shook her head. I felt like I was imploding on myself. I forced every stray thought from my mind to the point of even holding my breath. If I could've stopped my heart for that moment and a half, I would have. Her eyes raked over me. Searched through me.

She turned back to Eros and sighed. "I can guarantee that he will remain on campus until you need him further."

"Very well," Erebus said. "He is remanded into your care. If so much as a hair from his head leaves campus, you will be held as guilty as he."

She nodded, putting her arm around my shoulder and leading me from the room. Metis gripped my arm as I passed her. Her gaze reflected all of my agony and confusion, like she somehow knew everything that happened in the room without needing me to speak a word. Rhea tugged me forward and Metis' fingers slid to my hand. Our pinkies locked for a moment and then released.

When Rhea and I reached the end of the hallway, she turned to me. "I want to believe in your innocence. So far you've not acted in a manner inconsistent with your thoughts."

"You can read minds," I said. "Search me. I'm clean. I swear."

"I know you are."

"Thank you," I murmured.

"When you find yourself in a storm-bent, roiling sea, you have nothing but your internal strength on which to rely. And you only discover its true power when the storm winds are highest. The side effect? Once you recover, *if* you recover, you won't be the same person who entered the storm. Go get some rest. I'll check on you later."

Σ

At daybreak the following morning, I walked near the Cloudwell. I wasn't sure how I'd ended up there. I'd simply followed my feet.

Gaia's beautiful Earth stretched out before me like a humongous, sage green woven rug over the peaks and valleys. Earthen pillars and jagged rocks rose as if trying to offer themselves to the sky.

A bird called in the distance. Then a dark brown eagle leapt from its perch near the top of a tree. I stared in awe at its strength and grace as it circled above. I clapped my hands loudly. There was the bird I needed, my escape.

I waved my arms, but as it turned toward me, I retreated several steps. I hadn't actually expected the bird to acknowledge me. It stormed toward me and buzzed me a few times. The eagle would've taken my head off if I hadn't ducked. It climbed effortlessly back into the sky. Flap. Flap. Soar. Coast. Turn.

With a sudden swoop, it dove straight toward me again. I turned and cringed.

Just before it plowed into me, the eagle spread his wings and hovered right above my head. Its dark brown wings whipped the air as I looked into its eyes and soul. He returned my gaze like he knew me.

He landed near my feet and folded his wings in. He paced around me in a circle, studying me. It creeped me out, if I'm being honest. But something drew me out of myself. I extended my hand and smoothed over the golden brown feathers on its head. It nuzzled into my palm, then leaned back and emitted an ear splitting call, "Weee-awwwww!"

I snapped my hands to my ears and turned away. The bird stared at me and stepped forward. "There we are. Nice birdie." I stroked its feathers and he opened his mouth as if to speak. I glared at him. "Don't you dare call out like that again."

I closed my eyes and tried to focus on the bird's energy. Nothing happened ... and then I gasped, inhaling sharply as the strong jolt of the eagle's essence surged into my hand. The bird's energy filled me, and suddenly my eyes were not my own. My gaze sharpened. I could see deep into the valley with such detail that I never had before. I nearly shed my feathers when I saw my feet. Or rather, my talons.

The eagle beside me rustled his feathers, spread his wings, and took flight. I desperately wanted to do what he'd done. To fly.

My talons dug in the soil, refusing release. Shapeshifting into the bird had been easy. Ignoring my fear of heights was not. Yet the soul of the beast roared within my chest. Pushing me. Daring me to fly.

I extended my wings and launched into the air. I climbed higher and higher, relishing the wind swooshing past my face. The freedom was incredible, as I was neither shackled by gravity, nor hindered by space. Each flap of my wings brought me closer to peace.

I tilted my head downward and toward Gaia's earth. To my surprise, I didn't feel an ounce of fear. Over the expanse below, I could clearly see small animals scurrying on the valley floor. The other eagle soared below me. I pinned my wings to my sides and dove.

My hooked yellow bill leading the way, I tore through the air at an unnatural speed. The ground drew closer. The wind swept past me until I spread my wings and the nosedive ended abruptly. Air caught beneath my wingspan and I rose again.

"This is amazing!" I yelled to no one in particular.

The other eagle glided up beside me. "You find any food yet?"

"You're joking right? Yeah, just as soon as I get my stomach out of my throat."

"What?"

He obviously didn't understand. And then it dawned on me ... I just communicated with an eagle!

I regained my focus and wondered if I might be able to hunt

down Hyperion in this form. The sun inched across the heavens high above. If I couldn't find him elsewhere, I could definitely find him in his chariot.

I swooped down and then sharply upward, flying higher and higher. The air grew thinner and bluer and colder the higher I climbed. But no matter how fast I flew, Hyperion's chariot never felt any closer. With mounting frustration, I turned back toward the ground.

Once I returned to a reasonable altitude, I focused on looking for Tia and Ouranos. I skimmed treetops all the way to the Agora, turning my keen eyes to the valley floor. Even with my amazing vision, I still needed a closer vantage, so I scoured the countryside. I swerved in and out of tree clumps, banked left and right through crevices, gorges, and rock formations all over Thessaly.

Seeing no one who looked like Tia or the Headmaster, I was ready to find solid ground again. I sailed toward campus, caught a gust of wind, and pushed past the Cloudwell to my bungalow. Through the trees, I nimbly landed on a branch outside my window.

After jumping to the ground, I shifted back into myself. I blinked several times as my eyesight changed back to normal. I already missed my eagle-eyed vision. After several moments, I checked myself over to ensure the rest of my normal body had returned. My legs wobbled slightly as I walked around my bungalow toward its entry. But, I smiled like a fool after having experienced the wildest ride of my life.

Metis startled me when she seemingly appeared out of nowhere, walking around the corner of my bungalow. Goose bumps prickled my skin. She pulled down the hood of her cloak, smiled, and spoke evenly, "Do I make you nervous?" Her golden hair fell to frame her face.

I narrowed my eyes, thinking of something clever. "Hardly. I often find beautiful girls hanging out at my bungal—"

"Bull patties. I was the first. I could tell by how your eyes lit up that night after the wrestling match."

I laughed as I recalled the incident.

"Look at you. Your soul is smiling."

I tried to hide my smile, but I couldn't. "I guess it is," I said, clearly under the influence of both the eagle's flight and Metis' charms.

"That was a neat trick you just pulled there." She looked at me like she knew all my secrets. She teased her fingers through her wavy, blonde hair, folding a mass of it over to the other side of her head. "Just hope you don't get in trouble for shifting off campus. Or for leaving campus at all."

"But I didn't. I shifted at the Clou—"

"Yeah." Her lips twitched with a half-laugh. "And proceeded to fly ... off ... campus."

"You saw me shift? How?"

She arched an eyebrow and flashed an absolutely wicked smile. "You liked it, didn't you? Admit it."

"What?" I attempted to be coy, but she saw through me.

Her gaze intensified. "You *liked* it. The ride. The exhilaration. The freedom. The escape."

I took longer to confirm than I probably should have. Eventually I nodded, almost against my conscious will. I didn't *want* to agree with her and wasn't sure I wanted someone else knowing my inner workings that well. But I had enjoyed the heady rush of adrenaline. Or maybe it was just Metis.

"You're an outsider at this school, aren't you?" she asked. "Not sure you belong. Not sure whom to trust. Alone in a crowd. A leaf caught on the wind's whim."

I'd certainly felt that way. My life wasn't my own anymore. The leaf analogy was a direct hit.

I stared at her, wanting to speak, but my mouth wouldn't form words. She moved closer. My body was light as papyrus, weightless under her gaze.

"I totally get it," she said. "I've been there. I *am* there. Something inside you just wants to escape sometimes. And becoming that bird allowed you to do that, if only for a moment." She caressed my shoulder, but it felt like she was reaching inside of me, opening me up. I tensed as the hair rose on my arms. An odd tingle crawled down my spine, and I stepped back even though I wanted nothing more than to step into her embrace.

"I've struggled to find my place in this cruel world," she breathed just above a whisper. "I have more siblings than you could count in a lifetime. There are thousands of us Oceanids. I grew up on Kithira Island, away from mommy, Tethys, and daddy, Okeanos. To get my parents' attention, I'd always felt I needed to become something or someone extraordinary. But many times, I simply wanted to run away. Find somewhere to exist. They'd never miss me."

I remembered Aristaeus telling me once I had siblings. *If there are any left, he said.* I still didn't know who they were. Perhaps I'd never know. "At least you know your parents and some of your siblings. My entire life, I thought one woman was my mother, only to find out that she wasn't. I guess my *real* mother abandoned me."

Her mouth gaped and she covered it with her hand.

I studied her eyes. The high arc of her eyelid. The black line around her hazel pools. The way her pupils dilated whenever we were close, like she was taking in more of me.

"And I don't even know who my father is—" My voice quivered, off balance by how easily she'd opened me up. "You do *know* your parents, right?"

"I know who they are … but I don't really *know them*. When you have as many siblings as I do, you become a number, you know? I think my mother had like eight or ten children at a time, overly fertile freaks of nature." She paused to reflect. "You're from Crete. Tell me about dear old mom and dad."

I recalled my tenure at Eastern Crete … various run-ins with the headmasters … my final act mischief. I figured I'd leave that out. "Tethys and Okeanos were larger than life on campus. Overall, they were nice. I had no problems with them. The Potamoi, on the other hand …"

"Ahh, those knuckleheads," Metis said. "My brothers are always trying to be big fish in small ponds."

Then I thought back to Telesto. I suppose she and Metis would be sisters. After weighing whether or not to ask Metis if she knew her, I passed on that idea too.

"At Kithira lower school, I pretty much kept to myself when I wasn't hanging with Amphitrite," Metis said. "I closed up inside my loneliness. Not letting anyone in. Until Atlas came along once I graduated to MO Prep. He's a great guy. Or at least he is, until he turns."

"Turns?"

She looked away. I touched her shoulder and after a few moments she turned back to me with glossy eyes. "He showers me with attention. Takes care of me. Makes me feel like I matter. But he has rage issues. It's why he can never win wrestling tourneys. He blacks out when he gets angry. Sometimes it's good, but a thinking person can outwit blind rage any day."

"Are these issues recent?" I remembered the bruises she'd had. "Does he ever ... turn his anger on you?" I didn't want to come straight out and ask her if he'd caused the marks I saw when she'd shown up at MO Prep. But, I remembered his disposition in past meetings. I wouldn't have put it past him. I finally blurted, "Did he hit you?"

"He's always had anger management issues. We've broken up many times because of them. I've tried looking past them. He kept promising to change."

My voice rose. "Did he hit you?"

"The concern in your voice is cute." She looked away again. "He's the first guy who ever showed any real interest in me. And once he claimed me as his, no one else would even look at me. I've always felt like a shadow, hidden in plain sight." Her words caught in her throat.

I wrapped my arms around her. "You don't have to put up with that, though," I whispered into her golden hair. Her body shuddered against mine. I held her at arm's length and watched tears stream from the corners of her eyes. "The attention he shows does not grant him the freedom to act like a goat's rectum."

"It's said that we all have five senses, right? Love is the sixth sense," she said. "But it's fallible like the rest."

I narrowed my eyes into a sidelong glance.

"Every sense has a false read. Haven't you ever seen something that wasn't quite what you thought it was … or heard something one way and it turned out to be something else?"

My mind churned.

"All of our senses are flawed. Love is no different."

"But love's not a sense," I scoffed.

"All of our senses are tied to body parts, right? Love is tied to the heart. I fell for Atlas, the softer side of him, the side I *wanted* to see."

"So when he showed you his true nature, why didn't you believe him?"

Tears streamed from her eyes. She shook her head. "Sometimes, the heart provides the falsest read." She sighed hard. "I don't know—"

Her beauty really was quite astounding. Even crying, I was drawn to her, to the vulnerability that belied her outward strength. Perhaps it was because her truest beauty, I found, lay beneath the surface. Her open soul and refreshing spirit.

"Hey, that night at the Othrys wrestling match, what was all of that stuff with Atlas about?"

She shook her head. "He's such a jerk."

"Yeah, but you were crying. Why?"

"He accused me of cheating on him with Pallas. You know, the guy you laid low at the wrestling championships?"

My teeth clenched. Pallas. "Yes. I remember him."

"But, I didn't. I'm not like that. I wouldn't do that." She stepped a little closer to me, looking up into my eyes. "Please believe me."

As my head spun, I realized I didn't know what I believed anymore. A knot twisted in my core and my breathing shallowed.

I did know one thing ... that I absolutely had to keep Metis away from Atlas.

As she drew closer and placed her palm over my heart like she owned it, I declared something I wasn't sure I wanted to. "I'm so drawn to you."

She looked up with wide eyes. A rogue tear streaked down her cheek. I reached to swipe it and she playfully smacked my hand away. She chuckled, shaking her head. "You don't mean that. I'm a complete mess. I just understand you."

I rested my hand against her cheek. She leaned into my palm and closed her eyes. The space between us evaporated. Her lips were inches away when I heard a voice.

"That's a tad close. Can you see her stomach from that vantage?"

CHAPTER TWENTY-EIGHT

Don and Shade stood ten paces away. *Damn.* Another kiss with her had been ruined. I pivoted my head to see if anyone else was with them.

Don stepped forward. "Sinking your teeth into Zeus, huh? Atlas not enough for you?"

She cut her eyes at him.

"Back off, Don. Seriously," I said.

"Woo-hoo-hoo-hoooo." Shade looked at Don. "If I didn't know better, I'd say there's something serious going on here."

"Just remember what I told you." Don glared at me.

Metis turned to me with raised eyebrows. I didn't have the nerve to tell her what he'd said ... that she was trouble.

I glanced from Metis to Don. But when I looked back into her eyes, and her damp cheeks, I knew Don was wrong. The connection between us was so strong that our spirits threaded into a tight braid, almost like we'd known one another before now. That I found her irresistibly attractive was just a bonus.

There was no explaining or rationalizing our connection, but if nothing else, I knew I had a good friend who identified with me. Not that friendship was all I wanted from Metis.

"Come on, kid. We need to get some food in our bellies," Don said. "Pontus wants us to meet him in the gymnasium after morning meal."

I looked at Metis and sighed. I worried that a moment like the one we'd almost just had might not come again. Even now, as Don and Shade walked toward the Megaron, my feet refused to move.

"I need to stop by my cabin," Metis said. "I'll catch up."

It's almost as if she read my mind. She caressed my arm and sauntered away, releasing my feet from their rooted condition. I jogged to catch up to Don and Shade. The sky above had turned iron gray with clouds. It mirrored the entire mood on campus.

"I hope you know what you're doing, Zeus. Helping you fight over a girl is not my idea of fun," Don said. "And you're setting yourself up for a collision. It's just a matter of time."

I made a beeline for the food table as soon as I entered the Andron. I sat down next to Don and Shade and faced the door. Meter joined us with a plate piled high with vegetables. We ate in relative silence, our long faces reflecting the fog of sadness that hung over our mountain home.

Metis strolled in not long after me. I immediately looked at my food to make sure nothing had fallen over the sides of my plate. In truth, I wasn't sure what my eyes would express if I met Metis' gaze at that moment. She could read me like a scroll.

"Have any of you seen Hera?" Meter asked. Heads shook all around.

"Sheesh, like we need more drama around here," Metis said in between bites.

The bread I bit into dried my mouth considerably. I raised my eyes slightly, and saw Metis. The corners of her lips turned upward. Quite alluring. I looked back down at my food because I was certain that had I gazed directly into her eyes any longer, my vision would've tunneled. Everyone else at the table would've melted away. And they all would've known.

After the meal, there was still no sign of Hera, so I headed back to my bungalow. I wanted to pick up where I'd left off with Metis. My soul craved our connection with an illogical ache. She fed me far beyond anything I could have anticipated when we first met. Metis was the brightest blues of the vast ocean. Cool. Calming. Refreshing like rain on a warm day.

I reclined on my bed. My eyes hadn't been shut for too long when I heard a soft purring voice at my door.

"You look so peaceful when you sleep."

Metis stood in the doorway, twirling her hair.

"Hey," I said. "Been standing there long?"

"Long enough."

"For?"

Her mouth twitched into a grin. "Don't you worry about what for."

"Sassy."

Her smile filled out, reaching her soft, hungry eyes.

"I just thought about something." I propped myself on my elbows. "You're an Oceanid. How do you have blonde hair when the rest all have some hue of bluish-green?"

"That's my rage against the machine. I got so tired of looking like everyone else, so I rinsed my hair with vinegar and sat out in the sun. After that, it became my signature style. What? Don't you like it?" She folded curly strands behind her ear and twirled the ends.

"No. I do. It's hot."

She grinned. "Good answer."

"To what do I owe the pleasure of your company? Shouldn't you be headed to the gymnasium?"

"Shouldn't you?" She ambled to me as I swung my legs over the side of the bed. "Besides, I wanted to finish what we started earlier before Don—" She cleared her throat, "Interrupted us." She bit her lip. "I hate unfinished business."

She moved between my legs at the edge of the bed, gently nudging them apart. I was clay beneath her palms. She could've molded me into whatever she wanted.

I stared into her hazel eyes. She swept her fingertips across the ends of my hair. Before I knew it, I stood and fisted my fingers in her golden tendrils. She let out a soft moan that rumbled from my ears to my core. I pulled her face slowly toward me, but stopped.

I shot a glance over her shoulder, fully expecting someone—anyone—to ruin this moment for me. She took a finger and guided my chin back to square with hers. I pulled her close again and pressed my lips to hers.

She returned my kiss with such passion I almost pulled her down on the bed. Her arms draped over my neck. I kissed her harder while her torso swayed against mine. Our lips danced. Stealing breath. Giving life. I forced her lips apart again and our tongues arched against one another for a moment before she broke contact.

"Mmmm," she moaned in a low reverb. She dragged her fingernails lightly down across my chest.

I would've responded, but I wasn't sure I had any breath left.

She looked up with her big hazel eyes. "We're going to be late."

"Yeah I suppose we ought to get to the gym, huh?"

"Not like I want to."

I was drawn into her eyes and couldn't pull myself out. Finally, she caressed my shoulder and said, "We should go. And thank you, by the way."

My brow wrinkled.

She smiled sweetly. "For coming to my aid over at Othrys Hall. The wrestling match." She walked to the door. "I never forget a favor. That kiss was just the beginning."

I felt suspended in mid-air. I closed my eyes, thinking back to the incident at Othrys. It seemed like ages ago. In that time, I had collected enemies like Tia collected flowers for her hair.

We exited the housing area and walked down the path around to the grassy quad area between the gym and the Megaron. I was hyper-conscious about who we'd run into on our way given my recent conversation with Don. Had anyone seen us leave my bungalow? I glanced around, not noticing anyone or anything out of place. I really wasn't in the mood for another Don lecture about the girl who'd stolen my heart.

"What's on your mind?" Metis asked.

"Just thinking about Tia." I lied. Actually, it wasn't a total fib.

Metis rubbed my back. "Yeah, that's tough. I just hope there is some way that they're both all right, you know? I'm not sure what that scenario could be, though."

Metis and I entered the gymnasium. Don, Shade, Meter, and Hera stood in the center of the floor with Pontus. A ring of urns encircled them. They all glared. My gaze dropped to the sandy floor.

"Close the doors, Zeus." Pontus said. "And drop the bolt in place."

Metis ambled toward the center congregation as I secured the door. I made my way back to the group. Pontus motioned for me to join them within the circle. I stepped between two urns, noticing that they were filled with water.

Pontus put his finger to his mouth to indicate that we should be quiet. He huddled us close together and then stretched his hands out to the side. A teal color seeped into his fingers, spreading slowly to fill his entire hands up to the wrists. Then the water in the urns levitated into the air then joined together to form a shield all around us. Pontus slowly brought his hands over our heads. The water followed suit, creating a watery shell. *Deity magic is unparalleled.*

Pontus held one fist high in the air. I guessed it was to hold the water in place. "The shell is to keep Rhea's faculties out of this huddle. We are not supposed to leave campus, but I can't sit around here doing nothing. I want to send out a search party into The Thick to see if there are any clues down there."

"What's The Thick?" I asked.

"Where we conduct War Games. Second term intermural sports," Don answered.

"You sure about this, Professor?" Metis asked. "Headmistress said—"

"I'm in," Hera said. "Let's go. Time's wasting."

Pontus looked into our eyes. "I'll leave the gym first to make sure no faculty is around. Then I'll wave you out. Guard your thoughts as you run to the Cloudwell. Can't have Rhea shutting down this search mission."

With such a lack of practice in shutting down my thoughts, I tried really hard to think about Mount Ida back home ... and Amalthea ... and Tos. The watery shell returned to the urns with a splash. Pontus jogged to the gym doors, opened and looked around. We all regrouped and stood just behind him, ready to bound. Pontus waved us forward.

Following Don, we turned right out of the gym doors, and rounded the corner to the white-pebbled path toward the edge of campus. I trained my mind to think of nothing but goats. It's what I knew best. As we descended the Cloudwell though, I pushed my hair off my forehead and considered what had just happened back at my bungalow after morning meal. I'd just kissed Metis. Our entire dynamic had changed.

At the bottom of the Cloudwell, we all placed our hands on the Hurler. I closed my eyes to avoid eye contact as my hand nestled between Hera's on the bottom and Metis' on the top. Pontus plopped his hand on the very top. And then we liquefied.

CHAPTER TWENTY-NINE

We hurled to the Caldron, where the War Games field house was located, and rematerialized in the elbow of a deep valley. Craggy cliffs framed either side. A semi-circle of Hurlers curved around us.

Pontus must've seen me looking at the multiple Hurler posts. "They're for other Pantheon League teams when they come here to play us in War Games."

I nodded, but I still didn't quite understand what War Games were all about.

Some nondescript buildings stood beside the edge of the river. The one on the left was labeled, Laconia Bathhouse. Another building was labeled, Armory. Each building had one door for Olympians and a separate door for Titans.

"Shouldn't the door read visitors instead of Titans?" I asked.

"This is their home field too, unfortunately," Don replied. "So since we both share this armory now, it says Titans on there … per Kronos. Visitors simply use the Titans' room when they're here."

"Listen," Pontus said as we gathered around him. His white tunic peeked from under his royal purple robes as he knelt between us again. "I couldn't say everything back at the gym because of time concerns. There's been a development in the investigation. The Khaos Council has apparently found enough evidence to bring Hyperion in for questioning."

I let out an audible sigh and Metis rubbed my back.

"Any moment now, Selene's moon chariot will eclipse Hyperion's chariot in the sky. She's going up to help bring him in."

"Then who'll steer the sun chariot?" Meter asked.

Pontus shrugged.

Shade huffed, "That's not good."

"Nyx will likely shade the heavens until it's sorted out," Pontus said.

"Or perhaps Helios will have to drop out of Othrys and assume his father's duties." Don crossed his arms. "In any case, our first and foremost concern is the safety of everyone right here."

"Everyone?" Hera cut her eyes at Metis.

My mind raced. Even though I'd mentioned Hyperion in that interrogation, part of me thought they'd never actually go after him. Visions of the attack on Crete splashed through my mind and my body flashed unbearably hot, as if I were still in the fireball's presence. I rubbed my arms.

Meter approached. "You all right? Your cheeks, neck, and arms are red as saffron."

I nodded, checking myself over. "Just had a wicked memory."

"The point I need to emphasize," Pontus said, "is that we still haven't found Tia or Ouranos, which leads me to believe that they were taken or otherwise detained." Pontus closed his eyes and shook his head while massaging his fingers through his thick beard. He led us to the last Hurler in the semi-circle. "Look, I found drops of blood here near this Hurler post as well. It must have been someone leaving though, because if they were arriving, the Hurler would've stitched them up."

Meter bent down to inspect. A severe expression hardened her normally soft features. "Does the Khaos Council know about this?"

"I don't think so. Or else they would've secured the area," Pontus responded. "I'll have to divulge it soon. But first, we search. According to a map I found in Hestia's cabin, she could've been researching something out in The Thick."

"What was she looking for?" Don asked.

"Something to do with dragon's blood, maybe?" Pontus replied. "I know that dragons and wolves run amuck in this valley area known as The Thick. And, I'm certain that Hestia would not have explored these wild lands alone. The only problem is, I have no idea where to begin."

"So we'll need to pair and split up." Don stepped to the center of the circle of us. "Let's gear up and go get our friends."

"Why not stay together?" I asked. "Strength in numbers, right?"

"Don's correct," Pontus said. "You'll never be able to cover enough ground in one group. You'll be fine as long as none of you wanders off alone."

Heads nodded around the group.

"Here we go then." Pontus herded us into the armory. "Get some gear and set out. I'll stay here to provide a home base."

I stepped into the narrow hallway that led to the interior, rectangular chamber. Farther to the left, a darkened corridor stood. A sign above the arch labeled it as the baths. I dragged my palm along the stones as I approached a line of bronze and leather breastplates that hung along one wall to the left. They reminded me of what the Kouretes wore back home. I ran my fingers over the musculature, the Omega symbol prominent across the chest.

I slipped it on and my skin tingled. When I inhaled deeply, my chest pressed against the inside of the breastplate, conforming to it. Filling it. I took another deep breath, staring into the domed ceiling above.

"Fits you well." Pontus' voiced boomed through the space. "Like it's your own skin. First though, grab a team battle tunic."

Five long benches stood in a line in the middle of the floor. Pontus pointed to the one that displayed mesh tunics. I reached for the first one I saw. It had a 'ψ' symbol across the back of it.

Don grabbed it before I could. "That's mine."

The other tunics displayed different symbols, except for a few that were blank. H, Σ, and Δ. Hera grabbed one with 'A' on it. She looked at me and deadpanned. "Alpha."

All of the rest of the tunics were snatched up except the one with 'H' on it. I assumed it was Tia's. I picked up a blank one, as did Metis.

"Now get yourselves a helmet, greaves, gauntlets, a battle skirt, and some weapons," Pontus ordered.

Helmets hung on another wall to the rear of the room. I admired the Omega symbol painted on both sides. Hera brushed against my shoulder as she grabbed a helmet from its hook. "Don't just stand there, pretty boy. Put it on."

Don, Shade, and Meter swarmed through the room, grasping various pieces of armor and weapons. Don strapped on his breastplate. The Omega symbol seemed to flash white when he put it on. Or maybe my eyes were playing tricks on me.

A gate stood to my right. Grabbing the iron bars, I looked through to the other room.

"That's the Othrys Armory," Don said in passing. "There didn't used to be a gate here. But the contests got so heated over the past two years that Ouranos and Kronos thought it best to separate us."

Metis approached the armor tentatively, running her fingers over the leather and metal. I walked over to her.

"Have you ever worn armor before?" I asked.

Her voice shook. "Certainly not. We never had War Games at Kithira. And it's never been a required sport here or at Othrys."

I wanted to put my arms around her, but didn't dare with the others there.

"This mission is for the self-assured." Hera walked over. "Pull on your big girl tunic and let's go."

I clenched my teeth and looked at Metis, instinctively wanting to say something to comfort her. As our eyes locked, Metis' fearful gaze softened and she began to slowly strap on her breastplate. I offered to help her.

"Hey now," Shade called from across the room. "No special treatment. Everyone puts on their own gear."

I stepped away, my eyes trained on Metis. When I turned, Hera's gaze had locked onto mine. I looked away, gathering the rest of my armor, a sword, a bow, and a quiver of arrows. It was a good thing the Kouretes had taught me how to use these weapons. I then headed back outside. The air was clearer there.

In the distance, some guys walked along the river's edge. They approached like a pride of lions, barrel-chested and with swagger for days. As they drew closer, I recognized them.

Atlas, Pallas, Perses, Epimethius, and Prometheus, with Kronos towering above the group from behind. My hands twitched around my sword hilt and I felt like my blood was nearly steaming through my pores.

Pontus stood at my side. "Easy now."

"Do you really think it's that easy?" I looked up at him, gripping and releasing my sword's hilt.

The rest of our team walked up beside me, their collective strength bolstering my courage. I relished the feeling of belonging to something larger than myself.

Kronos' voice rose above the crowd of ten. "Epimethius and Prometheus, what were you two thinking? You nearly got Atlas killed up there!"

Epic looked up at Kronos, then back down. His face was vacant. Expressionless. Promo sulked, straightening his helmet.

"For the love of Gaia, why can't you follow the simplest of instructions? Do you want to be on this team or not?" Kronos barked. "I will replace you tomorrow unless you do what I demand."

Then Kronos' glare landed on me, lingering on my face, before moving to encompass the entire group. "Well, well." Kronos coughed. "If it isn't Pontus' Privates."

They all laughed. We just stared at them dispassionately.

"Practicing a bit early, are you Kronos? The season doesn't begin until next term," Pontus said. "No matter, we have just the combination to take you down this year."

"What? The goat herder and the tramp?" Atlas said.

I stepped forward. "Your parents don't play for us."

"It's a shame we didn't meet under less crowded circumstances." Atlas removed his helmet and flipped his shoulder length hair backward. A scowl darkened his features. "Like in a murky grove of trees somewhere." He turned to Metis and half chuckled. "So, this is where you went, huh? You can take the whore out of the school, but you can't take the whore out of the girl." He looked into the air, feigning pensiveness. "No, that's not right. How does it go?" He looked around at his teammates and laughed. Pallas and Perses sneered.

Almost blinded by rage, I gripped my sword tighter and took another half a step forward. Pontus grabbed my arm.

Atlas continued with a mock thoughtful expression. "No, I got it. You can hold a whore under water, but you can't make her drink—"

He took a step toward Metis. I whipped my sword toward his throat before he could blink. "One more step and I'll feed you to the wolves in bite-sized pieces."

"Is that so?" Atlas took an extra step toward me. My sword point dug into his throat. His glare was chaotic evil. "I'll make you and this sword my bitch."

"Stand down, Atlas," Kronos said. It sounded like he yelled the command from afar, but he stood only a few feet away. Atlas chewed the inside of his mouth, clenching and unclenching his fists. His nostrils flared.

Kronos approached. "You know you're on a losing team, don't you, Zeus?"

"Do I?" My glare never left Atlas.

"Join my school. My War Games team. You and Atlas can fight it out for team captain. To the victor, the spoils." Kronos pushed my sword to the side. "You want to be all powerful don't you?" Kronos looked through my eyes into my soul. "I know. I can give it to you. All it takes is a little time."

"Zeus and Metis are on our team now," Don said. "And Omegas stick together."

"That's right," Shade said as he and Don stepped to my sides.

"You must be afraid of something, Kronos, if you're offering such a plum spot—" Meter said.

"Mind your tongue when you're talking to me, girl," Kronos growled. His eyes flashed anger.

Pontus stepped in front of me. "That's enough, Kronos. I'll not have you stealing or threatening my pupils anymore. Take your team into the armory. We'll have time to settle this on the battlefield next term."

Pallas stepped to the forefront, pointing his spear tip at me. "I owe you one, punk."

"One headache not enough for you?" I stretched my arms to the side. "There's nothing but air between us—"

"Enough!" roared Pontus. "Kronos, remove your team from the field at once or I'll report this to the Khaos Council."

"We don't need to pile anything more onto the Khaos Council. Apparently, they're questioning Hyperion today. It's supposed to be a rather heated affair." Kronos shook his head and waved his team into the armory. Once they'd all filed in there, Kronos turned back to me, his bushy eyebrows wild. "I encourage you to carefully consider my offer, boy. I'll not make it again."

CHAPTER THIRTY

Pontus pulled us to a spot several paces beyond the semi-circle of Hurlers and out of range of any perked Titan ears.

"Pay him no mind," Pontus said. "Do not allow him to discolor our mission."

Don straightened his breastplate. Meter rechecked her greaves. I steadied my breathing, though residual rage still warmed my skin.

"Team up in twos … boy-girl," Pontus said. "I don't want two girls running off by themselves."

"Pardon me, coach," Hera crossed her arms. "I don't need a boy beside me slowing me down."

"No doubt you are as capable as your iron will, Hera, but I'm not bending on this," Pontus said.

Don put his arm around Meter. "Come here you feisty wood nymph. You ready to roll, partner?"

She nodded and slapped palms with Don.

Metis looped her arm in mine when she saw Hera take a step toward me. "Knowing what I know about Zeus," Metis said. "He'll at least keep me out of harm's way."

Hera's eyes bored holes through Metis. Her biting gaze shifted to me, and then back to her. She chuckled and turned to Shade. "C'mon, Shady boy."

"If you find anything, you are to report back immediately," Pontus said. "I'm not leaving home base so you'll be able to find me."

Don and Meter immediately took off on a light trot, shields on their left arms, right hands gripping their spears. I stood still for a moment to collect myself and began to consider potential strategies. The Atlas and Kronos confrontations still had me wound tight.

Shade nodded approvingly. "Stand tall, Zeus. That's all you can do."

Hera brushed by me on her way out, followed closely by Shade. "That wasn't your fight back there with Atlas." She shot an accusatory glance over her shoulder at Metis.

"Wait," I said. "What?"

Hera continued jogging away with Shade.

"What was I supposed to do?" I yelled at her. "Let him punk me?"

"All right you two, better get going," Pontus counseled. "Off you go now."

I glanced at Metis, who was still holding her shield and sword with delicacy and disdain. "Have you ever used a sword?" I asked.

"Once, briefly. It wasn't pretty."

We jogged across the grass and rock area toward the river, and then stopped. Trees surrounded and towered above us. Below, the rushing water hissed. "Sheath that sword. It'll be no good to you or me. Here, carry this spear. It'll help give you distance from an enemy in a fight." I handed mine to her. "Hold the spear overhand and fold your shield across your chest like this." I moved her arm into position. I caught myself looking at her chest, picturing what was under her breastplate. *Wrong place. Wrong time. Focus.*

"I know how to use a spear," she scoffed.

194

"Oh. Well, good then. Whatever you do, don't throw the spear unless I tell you to. Otherwise, just thrust it."

She nodded. A slight smile turned her lips.

We traced the river's edge until we came to a wooden bridge spanning a narrow section. I stopped to consider each direction. Backward was the direction from which we came. Across the bridge is probably where Don went. Thick vegetation blocked any serious view to the other side of the river. There was no sign of any of our schoolmates. I swallowed hard at the thought of the dragon- and wolf-infested wilderness. And to think that I once wanted to be a dragon hunter. I chuckled.

"This area is so vast," Metis said. I loved the way she pronounced every word and syllable with intention. My ears danced to the sound of her voice. "Finding either of them would be like finding a strand of hair in a wheat field. Obviously they're not going to just be out in the open."

"All right then, do you want to dance with dragons or wolves?"

She snorted, holding out her hands like balancing scales, moving them up and down. "Flying, large-taloned and fire-breathing predators versus fast running, snarling, and toothy killing machines? How is a girl ever expected to choose?"

We trudged forward through the dense wood, the treetops arching over our nearly silent footfalls. Not that our stealth would help us much. Any wolves would smell us long before they heard us anyway.

I motioned to Metis to pick up the pace. I didn't want to get caught out here too long after the eclipse. With keen eyes well adjusted to the gathering darkness, I led us farther into the Thick, our route hugging the river's edge in case we had to use it to escape. Neither of us spoke. The quiet was serene. Too much so.

Something rustled in the distance. I turned to Metis, and brought my forefinger to my lips. Wind whipped through the trees, swirling off the river. I tightened the grip on my shield and folded it across my chest. I gestured to Metis to move up next to me so that we could walk shoulder-to-shoulder, shield-to-shield. No way was I going to allow anything else bad to happen to her. Not on my watch.

Metis snapped a twig beneath her feet and jumped. Then a low growl rumbled past my ears. A howl ripped through the air, sending a chill down my spine.

The hair on my neck rose. We were about to step into a clearing when I suddenly sheathed my sword and swung my bow around, halting Metis' progress. I snatched an arrow from the quiver and nocked it. The string groaned as I pulled it halfway back.

"Keep your eyes keen."

A heap lay on the ground by a gigantic cave entrance on the far side of the clearing. I looked at Metis and she returned my silent gaze, both of us wondering if it could be Tia or Ouranos.

Around the edge of the clearing, beady, red eyes popped out in the dim light. Pairs of them. We were surrounded.

My heart rose into my throat and hammered. "Remember," I whispered. "Don't throw the spear unless I say so. Thrust and shift. Jab and move."

She nodded; her gaze intent as she took in the pairs of eyes shifting and coagulating all around us.

Immediately, I shoved her in front of me.

"Run for the mass on the ground over there!"

She hesitated for a moment before shooting off in a dead sprint across the clearing. I followed her with my eyes trained on the tree line. Within a moment, the beasts poured out of the trees. Wolves snarled, their fangs bared.

I shot my first arrow about one quarter of the way across the clearing. It caught a wolf in the shoulder and he fell. I notched another shaft.

Metis gasped and I turned my head. Beasts halted her progress. More wolves surged from the other side of the clearing. I shot another. And another. I heard Metis' spear sink into a beast behind me and then felt her back into me, stopping my progress.

I was almost out of arrows, so it was time to try something other than my bow. I unsheathed my sword, pointing the tip and swinging it in every direction. An ichor-curdling shriek came from the sky. Darkness had fallen in Hyperion's absence, obscuring whatever patrolled above.

As I returned my attention to the wolves, our most immediate threat, I realized they seemed to have stopped their advance. Metis' elbow hit me in the back as she thrust her spear at the bristly beasts.

A lone wolf cocked its head and howled. Not a rallying cry ... A warning! Out of the corner of my eye a dark shadow swept across my vision and, suddenly, two wolves were whisked into the air and sent sailing into the stratosphere. The remainder of the wolves scattered like drops of olive oil in a goblet of water.

CHAPTER THIRTY-ONE

"Great Gaia!" My stomach knotted. An acrid taste rose in my throat as we stumbled into a run.

"What was that thing?" Metis cried out.

"I don't know!"

Twenty paces or so from the woods' edge, two gnarled wolf carcasses fell from the sky with a heart-stopping thud. I shoved an arm in front of Metis. A shrill wail from above threatened to burst my eardrums.

In the next breath, a gigantic, black dragon knocked me to the ground and placed a clawed foot across my chest. Its wings slapped the air as it towered above me. The briny smell of the beast scraped the inside of my nostrils.

"RUN, METIS," I screamed with all of the breath left my lungs.

The dragon's eyes glowed like the setting sun. Silvery smoke wafted from its flared nostrils. It opened its mouth and I could see the furnace within its throat. Wolves' blood dripped from its fangs onto my chest. Fright rose within me like a river swelling over its banks under flooding rains, tremors running through my entire body.

My peripheral vision registered the scramble of feet as Metis ran. I knew I was dead meat. I just hoped she could make it.

The dragon gripped me tighter and looked upward into the sky as if preparing to take flight. Its talons dug through my breastplate and I cried out as the points pierced my skin. Then, suddenly, in the next breath, it stopped.

The dragon's gaze dropped back down to me. The monster tightened its grip again. I felt the low rumble of vibrations through each talon's point, much like the dragon claw stylus had shuddered in my palm. The dragon slowly closed its mouth, gazing at me in confusion.

A wild thought crossed my mind. I grabbed ahold of the dragon's leg and snapped my eyes shut. If I were going to die anyway, what difference would it make for my eyes to stay open?

I focused all of my fortitude into extracting the dragon's essence. First, nothing happened. I tried again. Then, I gasped. My chest heaved. My hands shook as his energy surged into me like lava spewing from a volcano, chaotic and fearless. Every nerve ending I had was fried.

My vision changed. My eyesight grew sharper. Everything got both nearer and farther away as my eyes focused through a red tinted lens. I looked down my torso at my own thick, scaly legs and talons. I rolled to my feet and prepared for an epic fight, but the other dragon abruptly flew away. I almost gave chase, but decided against it. I turned toward Metis.

Too late, I noticed her sprinting full bore at me. It only took her a moment to heave her spear, piercing me in the back. Pain sliced through me, radiating from the point of impact. My scales and outer defenses were not as tough as if I were a real dragon.

Blood oozed from my dragon body, coating the spear's shaft, leaking slowly like my soul was seeping out. I hobbled around the clearing, not wanting to engage Metis, obviously. And she had no idea it was me. I crumpled to the ground near the cave's entrance. Vitality vacated my limbs. The blood loss became severe. Metis saw her opportunity to end me and grabbed my sword from the ground. I let out a wail to try to tell her to stop.

I spit a small stream of fire to let her know I wasn't playing around. She backed up just enough to not be dangerous. *Gaia save me*, I prayed.

My mind fogged over. There were two of Metis. Then three blurred images of her. Back to two again. I tried to remember what Phoebe had said about if you die as the beast you shapeshifted into … but the lesson wouldn't come to me.

I attempted to take flight again, but was too weak. Then, I willed my mind to shift me back to myself, back to normal. My first try didn't work. I fell over on my side. Metis drew closer, her sword outstretched.

If she got within a goat's breath of me, I was gone. I focused again with all the strength I had left. I saw myself back on Crete … running through the twilight on a night raid during a game of Goat-For-A-Sheep. Immediately, I felt able to twitch my toes, a good sign that I had returned to my human form. As I weakly opened my eyes, Metis' mouth gaped wide. She stood directly over my neck, on the downward arc of decapitation.

I held my arms up over my face. Still gaping, Metis took several steps backward, and dropped the sword with a clank, heaving sobs as she knelt to the ground.

"Metis," I coughed out. "I nee—I need your—" Tos and Amalthea flashed into my clouded mind, their fates at the end of a spear.

Metis didn't move. She covered her face with her twitching hands as she wept.

"Metis," I shouted, expending all my remaining energy. "The spear!" It was still lodged in my back.

She uncovered her face and scrambled to my side. "Oh, Gaia! Zeus, I am so sorry. I thought you were—How did you? But the dragon—"

I coughed ichor blood onto the ground.

There was a gentle tug around the wound as she tried to work the spearhead out. My ears barely registered footfalls getting louder. I hoped they were friendly.

"We heard the sounds of a fierce battle near here," Shade said.

"Yeah," Hera added. "What in Gaia's name is going on? And what is the spear doing in your—" She whipped her head toward Metis. "Can you talk? What happened here?"

I opened my eyes. Hera's sword was at Metis' neck.

I tried to sit up. Metis raised her palms to Hera as a means of quieting her. "P-p-put down your sword. I'll tell you what happened. It's too complex to tell here. Let's get Zeus to safety first."

"If I don't like your explanation—" Hera lowered her sword. "I might just remove your tongue."

I groaned.

Hera then cut off the bottom of her cloth tunic and pressed it against my wound. "You're pale as limestone." Then she didn't speak another word.

Between Shade, Hera, and Metis, they took turns shouldering me back to the armory area. The comforting torch lights around the armory came into view. And the hazy blue of the Hurler posts. My consciousness faded toward darkness.

"What happened to him?" Pontus rushed to greet us. "Oh dear … "

I barely opened my eyes when I heard Pontus's voice or when he gently examined my wound. Metis promised to tell everything once we'd gotten back to the school. I hoped she would tell the truth. At this rate, I wouldn't be able to offer much.

"Let's get him back to campus," Pontus said. "This isn't going to end well. I can promise you that."

"I hope he can survive the Hurler to get back," Shade said.

"Anyone seen Don and Meter?" Hera asked.

"Hurry and get Zeus back to his bungalow without the other faculty seeing you," Pontus ordered. "And *please* mind your thoughts.

Your cognitive vibrations will alert Rhea."

My senses dulled. Consciousness waned. I felt as light as a peacock's feather. My classmates' voices became incoherent mumbles as I faded away.

$$\Sigma$$

When next I opened my eyes, it looked like there was a wispy piece of linen over my face, covering it like a veil. I gently reached for my wound, slowly probing the area of my back where I thought it had been. My fingers smoothed over a ridge and then trailed around the circular indentation. My first permanent scar.

It pulsed, an almost imperceptible, dull vibration unless I stilled my mind.

I winced as I raised my body to an upright position. When I spotted the goblet on the desk next to me, I grabbed it and poured it down my parched throat. Nectar. Not exactly the best drink to quench thirst, but it was all I had at the moment.

I thumbed through my memory, trying to make sense of earlier events. They assaulted me, image after image flashing in a foggy gust. Darkness. Red eyes. Snarling. Dragons. Wailing. Shifting. Dying.

Rhea breezed into my bungalow. "Good, you're awake." She pulled me off the bed and her fingers gripped the back of my tunic in an embrace, an uncharacteristic move for her. "I'm so glad you're all right. You gave us quite a scare. Again."

I looked down to the floor, thinking back over the previous months. "Trouble has a way of finding me."

"Trouble will always contest those on the path to greatness."

"Is that the kind of path I'm on?"

"I have to believe so." She sat down next to me. "Opposition is always strongest against those with the most potential. Life is staring you in the face and daring you to grab the reins. Unfortunately, your life will get tougher before it gets easier. Everything seems darkest now, but it's the darkness that allows the stars to shine."

I remained silent for a moment, running my fingers over the wound again. I took another gulp of nectar.

"Do you know why we drink nectar?" Rhea asked.

I shook my head and sipped more.

"It's because nectar is made from cosmic dust; hydrogen, helium, oxygen, carbon, and iron ... the stuff you've been studying with Hestia. Cosmic dust is the alpha particle, the cornerstone to our existence and of deity creation. We're mortal without it."

My brows shot up.

"The easiest mode of absorption is ingestion. But there are other ways as well. In short, the reason you're alive is the cosmic dust in the Hurlers, which reformulated your body's cells when you hurled. We carried you up to your bungalow from the landing site."

It heals wounds ... I thought back to the dagger incident. And then an image of Tos flashed into my head. A Hurler could've saved him.

"The dust particles bind to your cells, strengthen them." She pulled me close. "And yes, it could've helped your friend. But, there's a dark side to cosmic dust that only Ouranos knows."

"I wonder if Tia knew as well?"

"Possibly—"

"Wait, Ouranos *knows*?" I asked. "As in present tense?"

"Yes. Ouranos returned this morning during your search and rescue mission. He'd been out planting Hurlers, as he does from time to time. I'm just so thankful he's all right. Now we can get the Khaos Council off our backs and your name completely cleared. I knew in my heart you did nothing wrong, despite what the Council said."

"That's great. Now we just need to find Tia."

"But wait—" She placed a hand on my shoulder. "Poseidon and Demeter still haven't returned from the mission yet. Pontus is out looking for them now."

"So you know about the search."

She nodded. "That was incredibly foolish of you all. And also stupendously brave. I intend to discuss this at length very soon with the entire staff and student body."

Words rushed out of my mouth. "It was my fault and my idea to go down there and search."

"No it wasn't." She cast a severe glare at me. "Lying is reprehensible. In your weakened state, your thoughts are quite unguarded. I know who engineered this jaunt."

My stomach churned and I dropped my head into my hands.

"I don't know what is going on with those two, but we intend to generate a plan. Clean yourself up and meet us in the Andron. That is all."

I bathed, dressed, and headed to the Megaron. The sky was still dark. So, either nighttime had fallen or the Khaos Council still interrogated Hyperion, which would suit me just fine.

My stomach growled as I entered the room. Headmistress Rhea and Headmaster Ouranos stood within a circle of students and faculty. Long faces met pinched brows and downturned lips. Metis managed a half, tight-lipped acknowledgment when I approached. Professors Phoebe, Nemo, and a few others stood near the rear of the crowd.

"Headmaster, am I glad to see you," I said as I reached the circle.

The smile he offered failed to reach his eyes. "Thank you."

"Have you seen your lab yet?" I asked.

"Yes I have. And I am livid," he said. "But we have more pressing concerns."

CHAPTER THIRTY-TWO

"In fact," Ouranos continued, "one of our most pressing concerns ... is you." Ouranos pointed to me.

"M-me?" I stammered. My posture stiffened. "What did I do—"

"You, and your classmates left campus when you were expressly forbidden!"

"No disrespect, Professo—"

"Headmaster, thank you," he snapped.

"Headmaster, you just returned to campus," I spewed. "How would you even know about the travel restriction?"

"It just so happened that I witnessed part of the proceedings during which Hyperion was questioned. I then traveled to the Caldron to inspect the Hurler post that had blood spatter near it. So yes, I am aware of the transgressions of both faculty and students at this school."

My gaze dropped to the floor.

"Yes," Ouranos continued. "You and Pontus are priority one."

"We're all distressed here, Ouranos." Rhea's voice quaked. Her eyes were red and puffy. "Poseidon and Demeter have yet to return after the mission. They also are priority."

"Indeed." He pointed to himself. "But I will look for them."

Blinding light flashed outside the Megaron window. From the aether, the three primordial beams of energy descended.

"Oh my heavens," I muttered to myself. "That's it. I'm burnt bread ends now."

When my eyes refocused due to the bright light, Eros, Phanes, and Erebus approached the Megaron. Pontus walked ahead of them.

My pulse raced until they stepped through the door to the Andron.

Eros began, "It's definitely nice that you're all together. It makes this job that much easier. Our investigation led us to the Caldron where we found Pontus. Unfortunately for him, he will be reprimanded for endangering students."

"I am returned," Ouranos bellowed. "The Sky Throne is again safe. And occupied. I can spearhead the investigation and handle any staff punishments."

"We still don't know anything about Tia yet," Hera said. "And now we have to find Don and Meter too? It was a good thing Shade and I came along when we did or we'd be out there searching for Zeus too." She cut her eyes at Metis.

Metis swung her hands erratically. "Look, first we were surrounded by wolves, and then a dragon attacked ... and then there were two of them. I didn't know *he* was the second damn dragon, all right?"

"Oh no?" Hera spread her arms as if to goad Metis into a fight.

"Ladies!" Ouranos cleared his throat while Rhea edged between Hera and Metis. "I will not have this. You're arguing like we don't have bigger stags to roast here. There are fierce beasts out in the world. Be glad you're safe at this school."

"Are we?" Hera shot back.

"Watch your tone, young lady." Ouranos gazed sidelong at Hera and continued, "I've been gone for only four days and, in that time, this dire situation arose. And now, we have more students missing." Ouranos folded his massive arms.

Eros stepped forward. "That is why we are here. Ouranos, with your lab in such disarray and your absence, we issue a decree of no confidence in your ability to lead—"

Ouranos slammed his hands on the table he stood behind. His icy blue eyes were more intense than I'd remembered.

"I told you, I can handle this."

Phanes pointed his scepter toward Ouranos. "We are in charge here. And you will obey. Period. Must we restrain you?"

Ouranos stepped backward. His tongue ran over his bottom lip rapidly. "I apologize for my absence. I thought I was only going to be gone two days, but my task took far longer than I had anticipated. But I'm back now, and I plan to give you the support we all need through this trying time."

"You will stand down," Erebus said.

"Since we still have three students missing and Ouranos' questionable travel itinerary, the entire school is officially on lockdown now. By the Khaos Council," Eros said. "I will help the Muses guard the entrances and exits to school grounds. Every Hurler must be manned. No one arrives or leaves. Erebus will restrain Pontus in the gymnasium. And then he will shadow Ouranos."

Phanes spoke, "I will return to the Caldron to continue the search. My scepter will illuminate the truth."

My chest tightened when I thought of Tia and Meter still being out there. Don, I wasn't too concerned about. He could take care of himself. I sighed as I looked at the table in the Andron where Tia and Meter usually sat during meals. I rifled my fingers through my hair, and then pulled my neck downward.

My gaze trailed after Erebus as he led Pontus out of the Andron. Erebus produced a long rope made of black smoke that snaked around Pontus' wrists. I couldn't believe Coach Pontus got in trouble. I mean, it was a ginormous risk we embarked on. And yes, he orchestrated it. But his intentions had been golden. If only Don and Meter had come back. Now, we have to find them too. Damn.

This entire situation had gone from horrible to horrendous!

Rhea and Ouranos exited the Andron as well. Suddenly, I was so hungry, I could feel my stomach touching my backbone. I poured a goblet of nectar and then piled my plate high. While I inhaled my food, Metis, Hera, and Shade looked at me with wide eyes and slacked jaws.

"What? You've never seen a hungry person before?"

Shade shook his head. "Not one *that* hungry."

"I have some major questions," I said between bites. "Like … do we know how widespread these abductions are? Is it only MO Prep? Are other students missing from other pantheon school districts?"

"And what's the connection? Obviously nothing happened to Ouranos because he's here. But why were Tia, Don, and Meter taken?" Shade asked with downcast eyes. His voice cracked. That was the first I'd ever heard emotion like that from Shade. "Especially Meter … what did *she* ever do to anyone?"

I looked up from my food. "I'm tired of being one step behind this mule scrotum … whomever is doing this. We need to figure this thing out."

Hera sighed, knitting her dark brows together. "Let's talk to the Oracles in the Agora. They must be able to shed some light on things despite their usual encrypted messages."

"How in the Underworld are we going to get down there? The Muses will be guarding the Hurlers under the direction of Eros," Shade warned.

"They'll let us go to the Agora, don't you think?" I drummed my knuckles onto my forehead, thinking of options.

"No. I don't think," Hera said. "There has to be another way."

"We have to try," Shade said.

Once we got outside in the quad, I looked around for Rhea, and then whispered to Hera, "I'm going to grab the scroll. Maybe the Oracles can read it or at least tell us how to."

"Good idea. But we still don't have a way down there."

"I'll tag along with you, Zeus," Metis said.

I glanced at Hera, whose level gaze made it difficult to breathe. I looked away and kept walking. Metis trotted at my side.

The sound of our feet crunching the shale underfoot sliced through the thick silence between us. We entered my bungalow and I reached in my closet to grab the scroll I'd won from Kreios.

"Stop," Metis whispered when I turned around. She placed her hand on my chest. "Just stop."

"We have to get back," I said.

"I have to know something ... " Metis stared into my eyes, into my soul. "Are you mad at me?"

I stood with my mouth open for a moment because I knew that my answer would define us, our expectations of one another. I hoped what happened in the Caldron was an accident. But I wasn't sure. So, if I answered yes, that would undercut the trust and understanding we had. Can't be mad at someone for an accident. But if I said no, and it really had been malicious, then she'd think she'd gained my trust enough to harm me.

"Don't answer that," she whispered. A tear crested the ridge of her right eyelid. She sniffled and looked away. "I don't want to know what you believe about me right now. So many have so much to say about me, about us."

"You mean Hera?"

"Whatever lies Hera might've told y—"

"Hera hasn't said anything about you."

"Oh." She folded her hair behind her ear. "Well she always looks at me like I killed her best friend."

Her words hung in the air. I gazed into her teary hazel eyes.

"Zeus, please," she whispered. "I can't take back what happened out there earlier, but I'm so sorry. You have to believe me. I never intended to hurt you."

I nodded.

"I have never actually speared anything before in my life. It all happened so fast. I didn't know what was going on. I freaked out."

Her irresistible magnetism drew me forward. I stepped into her embrace. I failed at any attempt I made to be upset with her anymore. "I know you'd never purposely harm me."

She sniffled again and leaned her head against my chest, right over my heart. "Thank you."

"We should go."

When we returned to the torch-lit path between cabins and bungalows, Shade and Hera were waiting for us. We descended the Cloudwell to find Professors Mnemosyne and Phoebe guarding the Hurler. I swept a sidelong glance at Hera and she took the lead, barely looking at me.

"Hey, Professor Nemo, I know Eros wanted us all to stay on school grounds, but we thought a visit to the Oracles couldn't hurt."

Slightly taller than Phoebe, Nemo folded her slender arms, crinkling her tyrian purple tunic. She spoke with a slow and deliberate cadence. "Absolutely not, Hera. Eros has delivered his decree and I happen to concur. A lockdown is best."

"But," Metis countered. "Isn't it entirely possible that the Oracles could help us solve this mystery?"

"Perhaps they could. Or perhaps not. You never know with those strange fruit," Phoebe said. "I don't know if the risk is worth it." Both professors studied our faces, and then turned to one another.

"I'll tell you what," Phoebe said. Her pale skin contrasted the dark valley of Thessaly that framed her back. "I am just as shaken as everyone here. And in fact, I would love to know what the Oracles have to say about this." She paused and shook her head almost imperceptibly. "To ensure you get to where you're going and don't stray from the path, I shall go with you. There are no beasts in the Agora. Mnemosyne, you stay here on this end."

"No!" Nemo said. Her dark hair swirled about her head like smoke. "I must protest. It's far too dangerous. We have already lost three students."

"Mnemosyne—" Phoebe placed a hand on Nemo's shoulder. "Yes, but we have lost zero faculty. I will ensure their swift return. Just don't tell Ouranos or Eros. If we find something, it'll be worth it. I got this."

Professor Nemo glowered at Phoebe as she huddled us around the Hurler. "We'll be back in no time," Phoebe said, as we all placed our hands upon the Hurler before Nemo could protest more.

Once we arrived at the Agora, in the interest of time, we jogged down the right side of the open-air square gathering and meeting place to the Oracles' Temple. I kept hoping we just wouldn't run into Pallas, Perses, or Atlas down there. At least not with our depleted numbers.

The two-story temple was on the far end of the Agora, directly across from the Dragon's Breath, overlooking the Odeon theatre. A facade of six columns guarded the sole entry. Fake windows had been carved between the columns.

"I'll remain at the entrance," Phoebe said. "Come right back out when you're done."

"You're not going in?" I asked.

"Those crazy witches creep me out," she said.

Cold shadows embraced us as we walked through a sparsely lit corridor, our footsteps sending invisible ripples through the stillness. I brought my fists up in front of me, ready for anything. Several times, I turned back toward the entrance, in case we needed to make a quick escape. A hand stabilized my back. I turned, half expecting it to be Metis. Hera's calm gaze steadied me instead.

My pulse raced as we turned a corner and approached a small interior sanctuary. Wall torches lit the small room. Slits stretched vertically through the ceiling of the room. Three hooded figures sat on miniature columns, still as statues. When we drew closer, they rocked from side to side in unison. In front of them, a cauldron of liquid roiled. Steam rose from its surface and disappeared through the ceiling vents.

I cleared my throat and opened up my mouth to speak. Hera jabbed me in the side with her elbow.

"May we speak to the Oracles?" Hera asked politely.

They stopped rocking abruptly. "Who is it whom deserves an individual account of the wisdom of the universe?"

I stepped forward. "Zeus. And this is Hera, Metis and Shade, er, I mean Hades."

"Ahhh, yes. Hades. Know that name well." The three hoods turned upward to look in his direction. "Do you see sufficiently in the dark, young man? I hope you do."

"What? I guess so. Why?" Shade replied.

"Good. Darkness is your ally."

"I guess that's a good thing since I wear black a lot, huh?"

Hera bumped Shade's shoulder.

"What did I say?" he responded.

Hera brought her forefinger to her lips.

They rocked again, then abruptly stopped and focused on Hera. "What say you, girl wonder? Hera, you are, yes? Ahhh, the sky is the limit for you."

I glanced at Hera. She winked back.

The hoods all whipped in my direction and spoke in unison. "Crackle. Flash. Sizzle."

My face wrinkled. "What in Gaia's name does that mean?"

"No questions, boy," the middle hood spoke.

I raised my hands in an effort to ease the tension. Metis placed her finger to my lips. I nodded.

"But if we ask no questions," I said calmly. "How will you know—"

"But, we *know* why you're here, Olympians plus one," the middle hood said. "Your missing comrades are related to an earlier prophecy we made that you Olympians would defeat the Titans handily in War Games this season. Find out why you'll defeat them and how and you'll find your comrades."

"Well, what in Tartarus does that mean?" Shade blurted.

"NO QUESTIONS!" the Oracles said in unison.

"May we at least hear the original prophecy?" Hera asked.

Silence fell like a swift strike. We looked at one another.

"Very well." The middle hood sighed as the bubbling water gained vigor and steam rose to fill the room. "The Word revealed itself thusly;

> *a school gains a pupil, foretelling a fall*
> *an islander will illuminate the demise and so rise*
> *the great sky will be slain, ichor shall rain*
> *to the victor, permanent altar*
> *only through the stoppage of time can the heavens be restored."*

My mouth dried. I had no words after hearing the exact prophecy that had begun this entire mess. I smoothed my hands down the front of my tunic. My gaze dropped to the floor. My stomach roiled with anger and sadness.

This was the second instance that we'd encountered some variation on the concept of time. On the wall of the Observatory was inscribed: *Time Marches On.* Now, the Oracles had said, *Only through the stoppage of time can the heavens be restored.* The two messages opposed one another.

Hera nudged me and pointed to the scroll.

"One more thing," I said. "I have this scro—"

"Silence!"

"But I can't read this scroll."

All three hoods turned toward us. They spoke simultaneously, "If you can not read it, then you were not meant to. Now leave before we change your prophecies!" the Oracles said.

"You can't do that," said Shade.

Hera yanked Shade's arm and pulled him out of the room. As we exited the temple, confusion clouded my mind more than when we had entered. *Find out why you should beat the Titans and you find your comrades.* And the original prophecy was about as cryptic as anything I'd ever heard. Now I knew what Phoebe had meant about strange fruit … and what Ouranos had meant by they speak in three tongues.

Back at the Hurler, Shade said, "I'm the oldest here now, so I suppose I'll lead us from here on out. When we get back to campus, let's meet at my bungalow."

Hera sucked her teeth. "We've been through this, Shady. You and I both know I can lead circles around you." She turned to me and cast a sidelong glance at Metis. "We should meet in *my* cabin."

Professor Phoebe placed a hand on my shoulder and Hera's. "That's a good idea. You should meet in Hera's cabin. She's a proven leader, whatever task she's leading you on."

"We're trying to go find—" Hera punched Shade square in the arm before he could finish.

"Sorry, there was a fly on your arm, Shade." Hera smiled wickedly. "Yes, we're just still trying to find Tia's Astro project to see if it can offer any clues as to where she might be, aren't we, Shade?"

He nodded sheepishly.

"It's settled," I said. "Hera's cabin after evening meal."

As we hiked back up the Cloudwell, Ouranos roared down the path.

"Where have you been?" he roared.

"I told them not to go, Headmaster," Professor Nemo said.

We looked at one another. Shade spoke up, "We just went to the Agora with Professor Phoebe to—"

"To get something to eat," Hera finished his sentence. "At Lambda, Lamb—"

"Yes, I know the place." Ouranos scowled. "But, Eros decreed that no one leaves campus. Any distortion in that message?"

Phoebe stepped forward. "I told them I'd accompany them to the Agora. I will take the heat on this."

Ouranos glared through her. I thought her skin was going to melt from the intensity of his stormy eyes. "Phoebe, proceed to my office. You will be detained in the gymnasium with Pontus."

Phoebe's head drooped. Her posture slumped. I wrung my hands as she walked slowly away.

"All of you may go," Ouranos said. "Zeus, you stay."

I rolled my eyes and took a deep breath. I waved my friends on and nodded. "We'll catch up later. Where the hare sleeps."

Hera's head whipped around. She smiled out of Ouranos' line of vision and then walked away.

When they'd reached a healthy distance, Ouranos guided me up the path away from Nemo. His demeanor was ragged and disheveled. He fidgeted with his white robe like it itched him.

"Listen," he said. "We have found no clues anywhere regarding where Hestia might be. Or, if she was taken, where she might be kept. Nor Demeter or Poseidon."

My eyes stung.

"It may be time to face the lyre music, I'm afraid. If they don't turn up by next Gaiamera, I'm going to close the school. For your safety of course."

My mouth gaped. "What?"

Ouranos chewed his bottom lip. "What's the point of having a big school like this for just three students? Sorry, four."

"So if you shut school down, then what happens to the rest of us?"

He shrugged. "I suppose I'll have to send you all to Othrys—"

"What? No! Don't force us to go there. Are there any other options?"

"No. I am quite fearful based upon recent events. Three missing students is catastrophic at best. I cannot in good conscience risk endangering you all," the Headmaster said. "But allow me to make one thing clear as aether. If you leave this campus again, the punishment will be swift and severe."

CHAPTER THIRTY-THREE

I ambled to my bungalow after talking to the Headmaster. I'd certainly seen Ouranos volcanic before, but not quite like that. The scowl on his face left an imprint on my brain.

I wasn't about to give up and just let him shut down our school. I'd finally found a place where I belonged, a group of supportive friends, and Metis, a girl with whom my soul threaded. I needed to talk to the others quickly.

I stepped into my bungalow. My crumpled, bloodied tunic from the dragon incident still fermented on the floor near my bed. I picked it up. Some of the blood hadn't yet dried. Small pools of murky goldenrod ichor swirled with bright red blood. The dragon's and mine. After bunching the tunic, I carried it across the room to the window. Blood droplets painted the floor in random splotches. *That* sure was going to be easy to clean up.

I couldn't get to the window fast enough. Blood splattered the desk and a few scrolls. I gasped and panicked when it splashed on the scroll I'd gotten from Kreios. Strike that, *won* from Kreios. That old kook. And to think he was Pallas and Perses' father.

I grabbed the mystical scroll—so sacred no one could even read the blasted thing—and began to try to rub the blood off it. I was pretty sure that my efforts were going to be useless—ichor was terribly difficult to get out of anything—but suddenly, something odd happened. Words appeared.

I narrowed my eyes and tilted my head. Words rose off the page, hovering just above the smears. But not all of it was legible. I needed more blood.

I gently dabbed my hand on the bloody tunic and then again on the unfurled scroll. Rub. Smear. Reveal.

My eyes bulged. It read:

> *Cosmic dust powers all.*
> *A speck is the source.*
> *The alpha and the omega.*
> *From a speck of dust, the universe is known.*
> *An entire cosmos in every granule.*
> *The power to build and the power to collapse.*
> *Absorbed into flesh, deities rise.*
> *Absorbed into metal, the bearer calls the tune.*
> *Absorbed into evil, disaster falls.*
> *Could bring death to deathless ones.*

My mind raced to piece together what I knew and what Rhea had told me with what I'd just read. *Death to deathless ones.* Who were the deathless ones? I needed to talk to the others.

My blood-caked hands shook as I grabbed the scroll and bolted out the door, stopping at the bathhouse to clean my hands. I wasn't about to go to Hera's looking like I just came from a goat slaughter. I shut down all thoughts as I crept around campus except where to place my next step in order to get where I was headed.

Hera's cabin sat way back on the wooded hillside with stone steps leading to it. Shrubbery and growth surrounded it. A vine-covered trellis framed the entrance.

A peacock strutted around the corner of the cabin, barely acknowledging me before it walked away. Shade greeted me as I opened the door. "What's that bloody mess?" He pointed to the scroll.

I swept straight past him, walking to Hera who sat at her desk. "That peacock outside, is it yours?"

"Of course it is. Why?"

"Where'd you get it?"

"I found it walking on campus. Or rather, he found me. Something about him is so regal."

"Wait," I held her gaze for a beat longer than I had to. "The peacock is a he?"

"Of course. Male peacocks are the proud, vibrant ones." Her green eyes sparkled. "I know a strong male when I see one."

Behind Hera, three Dragon's Claw styli hung from nails above her desk. Aside from that, her cabin was spartan and spotless.

I returned to my mission. "Guess what Ouranos just told me?" I continued without allowing them to respond. "He said that if we don't find Tia, Don, and Meter by Gaiamera, he is going to close our school."

"What?" Shade yelled. "He can't do that! He wouldn't."

Hera's face contorted. "No way! I'm not—*we're not* going to let that happen! Did he say why?"

"For our safety." I shook my head and ran my fingers through my hair. "Which makes sense if you think about it. Safety in numbers and all, right? First Tia got taken … then Don and Meter. Someone's hunting down everyone in our school."

"Then we are just going to have to find them. What now?" Shade asked, determinedly.

"I have something that might help." I held up the scroll.

"What in Gaia's name is that?" Hera asked.

"Interesting you should ask," I said.

"Hey, I asked as soon as you hit the door," Shade argued.

I raised my forefinger in the air. "But, Hera knows what this is. You, my shady friend, do not." I spread the scroll on her desk. "This is—" I stopped. "Wait, someone's missing from the party."

"Little Miss Metis," Hera said, wiggling her head. "Can I slap her already for spearing you? Damn, she irritates me. Told you I had a bad feeling about her."

"Hopefully she'll show up soon," I said slowly, still unsure of my certainty about Metis.

"Or maybe she'll get abducted," Hera crowed.

"That was nasty. And unfair," I said before I could stop myself. Hera inched backwards, studying my face.

"Look, I don't hate her. But I definitely don't like her. Tell you what," Hera said, disappointment thickening her voice. She leaned so close to me, I could feel her shallow breaths on my cheek. "When she proves herself to me, I'll let her be. Until then—" She backed up and swept her arms wide.

As Hera and I explained to Shade how we got the scroll, I remembered Don's misgivings, overlaid by Meter and Tia's encouragement. I pictured Atlas' grasp on Metis' arm, and her sunken disposition at the wrestling match. By contrast, Hera had proven herself time and again. If anyone would have my back through thick and thin, it would be Hera.

"But we couldn't read it. It was blank when we opened it." Hera continued the rest of the story. Then she turned to me. "So why, again, did you bring us this bloodied up scroll that we can't read?"

"Ahhh, there's the rub."

"What?" Shade asked.

"Look." I unrolled the scroll again. Hera placed small rocks on the edges to hold them down. It took a few moments, but then the same thing happened. The words appeared; the letters in striking yellow rose against the muddied hue of the blood.

"I'd spilled some blood on here and the words appeared," I said. "But to see the entire message, I had to *rub* more blood on there."

"Oh, *rub*," Shade mumbled.

We read the words over and over. Silently. Aloud. And they sunk in.

"And, Rhea told me something interesting today too about cosmic dust. That it is the essential ingredient in the nectar we drink—"

"Even I knew that," Shade said.

I paused and drove my fingers through my hair. "Let's get to the Sky Throne."

Hera's eyes widened. "Wait, are you thinking what I'm thinking?"

Shade clapped his hands and rubbed them together. "But what if Ouranos is up there?"

"I guess we'll have to stake it out and slip in once he leaves," I said. "He can't stay in there all night, can he?"

"And what about the warnings to stay off the Throne?" Shade continued.

Hera and I looked at one another. Our thoughts threaded.

"Nothing great was ever achieved without risk," Hera said.

I grabbed the scroll and rolled it up. "Let's go. And before we step out of here ... think about the happiest moment you had in lower school so that Rhea doesn't suspect anything." We headed down the earthen path out of student housing. Once the path turned to white pebbles, we stepped to the side so that our footfalls made less noise. As we did, I noticed Meter's flowers along the path were wilting in her absence. I swallowed hard.

The Observatory came into view.

We climbed the steep steps, and then crept close to the door, which stood slightly ajar. It should not have been. I bit my thumbnail and glanced around to see if anything else was out of place. Ultimately, I poked at the door to open it a little.

A slice of air escaped as the door swung wide. I cursed myself for not opening it with more control. My muscles tensed as we tiptoed over the threshold. I braced in case someone was there who shouldn't have been.

"*Absorbed into metal, the bearer calls the tune,*" I muttered as I gazed at the metal Hurler posts stacked in the corner. "What do you suppose that means?"

"It obviously means they'll turn into some sort of musical instrument," Shade said. "A lyre maybe? A bell?"

"I don't know if it's that literal. But, I concede I don't have a better idea."

"Well, I definitely can guess what happens if it absorbs into your flesh," Hera said. "And I'm going to find out. Who's coming with me?" She strode toward the stairwell leading to the Throne.

I loved Hera's drive. Her ambition. Her fire. Shade and I followed her, stepping over the disturbing debris that Ouranos had not bothered to clean up since his return. As I looked around, it occurred to me that, if Tia had indeed been taken, she had put up quite a fight. I beamed with pride even as I clenched my fists at the thought of someone harming her.

Hera climbed the stairs upward through the nearly vertical tunnel. Then she stopped abruptly, causing a chain reaction. I slammed into Hera's back. Not entirely uncomfortable. Shade bumped into the back of me.

Hera yelled up the tunnel. "What in Tartarus are *you* doing up there?"

CHAPTER THIRTY-FOUR

The hair rose on my arms as I tried to guess who was up there threatening the Sky Throne and drawing Hera's ire. Hera climbed until she appeared to be perched in mid-air. My eyes bulged in disbelief. More unbelievable than that though was the sight of Metis standing high above her.

"Get your ass down from there!" Hera dug into Metis verbally. "What do you think you're doing?"

"I could ask you the same," Metis replied with an icy demeanor.

"I knew you were trouble!"

"You know less than nothing." Metis raised her hands above her head. "Your entire world is set to crumble upon your head and you can't even see it."

Hera backed up and her voice dropped an octave. "Now, what do you mean?"

"Yeah, what in the Underworld are you talking about?" Shade called over my shoulder.

"You're right," Metis' voice rose. She tossed her hands in the air. "You're right, Ms. Smarty Pants. I *was* sent here to woo Zeus to transfer to Othrys. To stack up their War Games team."

My mouth gaped. And I could barely breathe. It felt like hands squeezed my heart and throat. And both threatened to collapse under the pressure.

"I *knew* it! You—" Hera climbed the stairs.

"Lock it up, girl. You don't know the half." Metis glared at Hera. "Kronos heard the prophecy that MO Prep was going to beat Othrys handily, so he decided to take out everyone one by one until he forced Zeus to join him."

It was so quiet between heartbeats I could hear the specks of dust drifting through the air. I wanted to yell, but no words formed in my dry throat.

"You sat there ... during the Oracles' prophecy and said ... *nothing*!" Hera growled through clenched teeth. "My friends' lives are in danger and you—"

"Zeus—" Metis cut Hera off in an abrupt change of demeanor. She descended the stairs and approached me, her hands raised in what appeared to be a plea for understanding. *Fat chance.* "I'm so sorry. A few months ago, I overheard Kronos talking to his team and he told them that he needed to find this prophesied boy the Oracles mentioned. That was probably when you got attacked on Crete."

To think, the attack on Crete actually had nothing to do with Tos and me getting back late that morning. Tos' flaming pyre flashed into my mind. The spears. The heartache. At least I now knew that the attack wasn't my fault, even if it didn't do anything to soothe my guilt. Nor my freshly minted anger at Metis.

Hyperion hadn't acted alone after all. Kronos had indeed orchestrated the entire operation. I stared at Metis, memories of Hyperion's assault flashing in front of my stinging eyes. Metis had known everything even back that far. *The entire time.* Through all those talks. The near kisses and near misses. The soul meshing. The spirit threading.

My cheeks and forehead warmed with the unmistakable pricks of humiliation. A gnawing ache that felt a lot like nausea thrummed in my stomach.

"I can't believe you!" I started higher up the stairs. "You said you hoped Tia and Ouranos were all right ... but *you knew*! You knew the plan all along. How could you?"

"Zeus—" she whispered. Her lips parted as tears filled her eyes.

"I even stuck up for you when Don warned Zeus about you," Shade said, shaking his head. The conversation outside the bathhouse with Don roared back into my ears. Warnings unheeded.

"Were the bruises even real?" I asked. "Did Atlas actually hit you?"

"Yes," Metis sighed. "He's as much an animal as you think he is." Her voice trailed off. She looked toward the horizon and inched higher on the stairs toward the Throne.

"You probably lied about your parents and your siblings too, didn't you?" I asked.

Hera started to descend the stairs to console me, but I shrugged her off.

I turned toward Metis. My voice cracked. "How could you?" The words choked out of my quivering throat, if they even made it out of my mouth at all. But Metis clearly had seen the pain on my face. As she stepped down two additional stairs, her face breaking and fathoms of sadness in her gaze, Hera blocked her advance.

Pressure built in my brain as memories of my brief time with Metis flashed by. Of our insane connection. The kiss in my bungalow. And, as if in a windstorm, each memory flattened out, sticking briefly to my face, searing into my skin, branding itself upon me before flying away. I stumbled and collapsed onto the side of the tunnel, almost knocking Shade back down the stairs.

Hera approached me. Metis took a step, but Hera swept a frigid glare in her direction. "Don't. You. Move."

Metis stood still as a statue, crying, shaking her hands. The concern on Hera's face as she moved near me and placed her palm on my cheek warmed and filled me.

"Zeus, I am sorry," Metis called from above. "It's why I'm here right now. It's why I didn't come to the meeting at Hera's cabin. I felt like if I ended it all the voices would stop. The pain would stop."

"You were gonna jump?" Shade asked.

"Atlas caught me cheating on him with Pallas. Pallas liked me and showed me a viable alternative. It was a moment of weakness. Sometimes Atlas can be such a boor."

"You think?" Hera chimed.

"Wait, I thought you didn't cheat?" I whispered because I couldn't speak any louder. "That day ... by my bungalow ... you said—"

"I know what I said," Metis continued in a hushed tone with downcast eyes. Her head shook back and forth as she continued. "It was just a kiss. And so to ruin me for Pallas, Atlas threatened to tell the entire school what a *whore* I was if I didn't—" Her voice choked in her throat and sobs heaved her chest. "If I didn't make out with Money while he forced Pallas to watch ... to prove what a whore I was, to prove to Pallas that I wasn't worth pursuing. I spat in his face and he beat me up pretty badly. He said Money wouldn't want a bruised whore so we'd have to wait till the bruises healed to make good on my end of the bargain."

Silence fell like a hammer. Or perhaps I simply heard nothing save the ringing in my own ears.

"Damn," Hera uttered with downturned lips.

At that moment, I wanted so badly to strangle Atlas that I could feel my fingers tightening around his neck, my thumbs digging into his windpipe.

Metis wiped her eyes. "He said that in the mean time I could perform this little mission Kronos had planned ... to come and get you to switch schools."

I straightened my posture and an arctic shiver of anger raked through me. "Why would Atlas want me there? He's done nothing to insinuate that he wants me at his school, much less within any close vicinity."

"Because, he's Kronos' little puppet. He can't think for himself. He does whatever Kronos wants him to. He's utterly under his thumb. All brawn, no brains. He'll only ever rise as high as Kronos allows him. He would have tolerated you being there to once and for all prove his worth to Kronos. It's sad."

She wiped her eyes and cheeks. "I'm here on this ledge because in my mission to woo you, I got wooed. And I can neither live with what I was supposed to do, nor with what I've done. And I can't go back empty handed. I just can't. They'll crush me. But I can't hurt you either, Zeus. That's why I'm up here tonight. To end all of this."

Hera sat up and turned her head slowly toward Metis. "What?" She looked up into the sky in exasperation. "Gaia have mercy. I don't believe what I'm hearing. See Zeus, that—" She pointed to Metis. "Is the face of a traito—"

I placed a finger to Hera's lips and moved past her on the stairs. I climbed to the highest stair I could actually see.

"Don't come any closer," Metis warned. "I have a splitting headache right now that threatens to cleave me in two. I'm just waiting for my nerve to build and give me the strength to do what I must. You weren't supposed to find me up here."

Our eyes connected across the space. She stepped higher on the invisible stairs, but her eyes looked like they were getting closer to me.

I found my voice. "No, Metis. Stop."

"What? Zeus, let her jump!" Hera said. "She was getting ready to feed you to the wolves anyway. She already stabbed you in the back. She—"

"Hush … " I whispered. The voices in my head were loud enough without adding hers. I glanced down at Hera. In many ways, we were cut from the same tunic. But, I couldn't let Metis go out like that. No matter what her mission *had been*, she'd abandoned it now.

After all she'd done, all her deceit, I should've thrown her off the stairs myself. But I couldn't. I looked at Metis and I just ... couldn't.

"So tell me this, why hasn't Kronos just killed me himself when he had the chance?"

"A couple of reasons." Metis sniffled. "One, you can never truly know what the Oracles intend. They speak in triple meanings. So to kill you outright is foolish. The Khaos Council would punish him severely for that. And two, he probably thought he could outsmart the Oracles. Keep your friends close. Your enemies closer."

Kronos' offer ran through my mind.

"You want to be all powerful don't you? I can give it to you."

"Join my school. My team. You and Atlas can fight it out for team captain. To the victor, the spoils."

"Consider my offer, boy. I'll not make it again."

Bastard.

I reached a hand upward. "Metis come down here."

She didn't move. We stared at one another for a painful moment. She looked wistfully into the distance and inched higher on the stairs.

"Don't make me come after you." My tone had a sliver of bite to it.

"Great." Hera sighed.

"Are you sure you want her with us now?" Shade asked. "There are only three of us left in this mess. We can't afford to have untrustworthy people in our camp."

"Besides, you'll never go up there after her. Heights, remember?" Hera folded her arms, leaning all her weight on one leg. "Zeus, please—"

I turned back to Hera. Hurt and disappointment shaded her eyes. She would never have said it, but I know she felt my desire to save Metis was a betrayal of sorts. One thing was certain, though. I couldn't leave Metis up there.

CHAPTER THIRTY-FIVE

I reached my hand out again. "Metis, I promise no one will take your head off. Come on down."

Hera groaned. "I'm not making that promise—"

"Hera, please ... "

After a few moments, Metis inched her way down the stairs. The closer she drew, I saw how overrun with tears her eyes had become. Her eyes were the color of storm clouds and bottomless sorrow. It broke my heart. She fell into my arms and I embraced her.

The skin-on-skin contact ushered transference of energy that was undeniable. At that moment, I knew I still had to protect her. I also knew that Hera was watching, but it was the right thing to do. Metis needed me. And we apparently needed her for her knowledge of our adversaries.

She trembled as she returned my embrace. A leaf on a tree threatening to fall to the earth. A stiff gust could've ended it all. But inside her, I saw a stronger spirit.

We all climbed back down to the Observatory. The infinite lights of the night sky, the moon, and the stars shone upon us. I sat on the ground while Hera paced like a caged animal. No one spoke.

Shade broke the silence. "Well, that was intense. I need something to drink that's a little stronger than nectar."

Hera inhaled deeply, and then sighed. "I suppose we should go ahead and do what we came up here for, before we got ... sidetracked. I'm going up to see if I can absorb some cosmic dust into my skin. You know, just to see what happens." The grumble in Hera's voice pained me.

"What's this about?" Metis asked.

Hera cut her eyes at Metis, and then continued toward the stairs.

"You'll see," Shade said. "If it works."

We all climbed upward again. I reached out for Hera when she arrived at the top of the stairs, missing her tunic by less than an inch. She kept climbing out over nothing, those peculiar invisible steps. I *hated* them. Who would make invisible steps anyway? Especially ones that jutted over a deep gorge.

She climbed high enough that against the night sky, I could actually see the iridescent specks drifting past her. They glowed against the darkened sky. She stretched her arms wide. The dust washed over her. Several specks stuck to her skin.

"I wonder why it's not working?" Hera waved her arms and hands.

"It *is* working," I called up to her. "Look at your hair and skin. The specks are all over you."

"I want more!" Hera chuckled. "I *always* want more."

Shade stuck his head out of the tunnel. "Are they absorbing?"

"I think so. Maybe." Hera brought the ends of her dark hair around to her face. The dust particles danced on her hair follicles like fireflies.

"Do you feel any different?"

"Not really."

"Well, you don't look dead yet. All right, come down. Let me try." Shade squeezed past me.

"Wait a moment." Hera closed her eyes. Her dark curls pulsed and blew back off her face as if a stiff wind had confronted her. She stood a while longer with her arms outstretched. She turned a half-rotation toward the Throne ... paused and then wheeled back around. "What? These flakes do *not* make me more attractive, Shade. Why would you say that?"

"I didn't," Shade stammered and then covered his mouth. "Hold on. I didn't *say* that ... out loud. But I—" He looked around at me then back at Hera. "I did think it. What? How did you?"

Hera stepped gingerly on her way down. Her eyebrows pinched. She placed the charm of her necklace between her lips and looked each of us in the eyes. Eventually she settled on Shade.

"Shade, you thought I could read your mind before. It's on now, brother. Your innermost secrets are mine." Hera laughed wickedly. "And by the way, I promise not to tell Meter. If we ever find her."

"First Rhea, now you?" Shade placed his palms to his temples. "Get outta my head!"

"*When* we find her," I corrected Hera, thinking back to when I discovered Rhea could read minds. I chewed my thumbnail.

"Sorry, right. *When*." She smiled. "And Zeus, I won't even begin to betray your thoughts." She shot me an intense glare. Her green eyes twinkled with energy and fire. "I'll have a few choice words for you later."

I tried to shut my mind off to keep from divulging anything at that moment.

"Metis." Hera looked deeply into her eyes. They stared at one another for a long, tense moment. It reminded me of the time Metis squared up to Hera in the Andron. Circumstances were a bit different now, though.

"You actually don't have any real malice toward us, do you?" Hera said. "I know that now. Poor thing. Just don't get in our way."

Metis' eyes flooded with tears. Her voice choked. "I won't. I promise. I'll do whatever I can to help."

Hera came all the way down the invisible steps, turning in every direction, looking herself over. Her skin still bore the iridescent marks of absorption.

"I know Don calls you Hare," I imitated Don's voice near perfectly. "But I have a brand new name for you, Freckles."

A slow, engaging smile spread across Hera's face. I glanced sidelong at Metis who revealed a less than enthusiastic, tight-lipped expression. So, I turned my attention to Shade who'd climbed the stairs next.

He held his arms out. Dust particles coated his dark olive skin ... arms, legs, face, and neck. I could've sworn I saw his hair lengthen and his muscles become more defined.

"You feel anythi—" I asked, but stopped short when I saw something peculiar. I closed my eyes for a second and shook my head. "Freckles, did you see that? Shade? You all right?"

Hera gasped as Shade's body disappeared for a half moment then came back. It blinked off again. And then reappeared.

I looked at Hera as Shade climbed back down, flexing his muscles. "I don't feel any different. No fair."

"Maybe you didn't do it right, Shade," Hera joked.

"But something did happen. Either you disappeared or I'm losing it," I said.

Shade's eyebrows pinched.

Hera nodded.

"I don't know. Maybe my eyes played a trick on me. You saw it too, didn't you, Hera? Tell me I'm not crazy." I chewed the inside of my lip. "And your brand is glowing now."

We looked at the 'Ω' shaped brand on Shade's arm. He ran his fingers over it. Sure enough, it pulsed yellow against his olive skin.

"Wicked!" Shade said, rubbing his hands together and staring at his flexed bicep. "Well, it's your turn."

I looked over to Metis and raised my eyebrows.

"I've already been up there," Metis responded with a smile. "I absorbed some dust inadvertently. I'm not sure it made any difference though. Your turn, Zeus. By the way, what's this business you have with heights, anyway?"

"He's just afraid. That's all," Hera said, still admiring her bespeckled limbs. Then she turned to me. "But, if you want to have it all, you're going to have to take the risk. I'm not holding your hand on this one. Go or don't go. But if you don't go, or *can't* go ... guess who won't ever get the Sky Throne."

CHAPTER THIRTY-SIX

I crept up the invisible steps, feeling out and testing each one before putting my entire weight on it. Looking down, there was nothing between the mountainside and myself.

Don't look down, you goat for brains!

I hovered in mid-air with my heart hammering my ribcage. I inched higher atop trembling arms. The solid stairs beneath me felt cold and smooth like marble. I lost count of how many stairs I'd climbed. I snapped my eyes shut to keep from vomiting.

"Sometime today," Shade called from below. If I were able to look down, I'd have heaved a glare at him.

My limbs shook as I stood there, suspended above Mount Olympus. I finally touched something with a different texture. I opened one eye … slowly. Then, *it* appeared. The Throne. The Sky Throne. Its gold trim gleamed in the darkness, if only to me. Shiny. Polished. The inscription on the base read just as Tia had recounted,

'Bestowed Upon The Bearer Of The Throne
Is The Power To
Rule The Heavens Alone'

I pondered that for a moment. Of all the MO Prep professors, Ouranos was the only one who could've sat on it? Not Pontus? Not Rhea? Not Kronos?

I slid upward onto the marble footrest. Tia's voice gripped me. *"Don't try to mount the Throne. It'll kill you."*

I stretched my hand upward and ran my fingers across the smooth black footrest, which, unlike the stairs below, bore no indentation. It was etched with symbols and pictures I couldn't understand. Inching closer, I brushed my fingertips across the rough edges of the markings.

Mount it. Don't mount it. Take a risk. Don't take a risk. What if I never again had the chance to sit on the Throne? But what if it killed me?

"Zeus," Hera sing-songed from the stairs.

I saw Tos' face in the reflection of the polished stone. Sadness strangled me. Then Amalthea's sweet face appeared. Her easy smile warmed my torso against the sudden winds that whipped high above the mountain. And then I thought about Don and Tia and Meter. The unfinished business I had with Hyperion. And Kronos.

Kronos is more powerful than you realize. And Hyperion too.

To defeat a deity, I had to become a deity myself.

Absorbed into flesh, deities rise.

The pulsing energy of the Throne wrapped around my arm like an invisible lasso, tugging me upward. I gasped, unable to break away. The strength of the pull unsettled me. Why would something so dangerous draw me so insistently?

Cosmic dust specks floated past me. Each one hit my skin like a hot rain drop. Searing. Soon, my skin sizzled, covered in tiny iridescent dots. I struggled against the Throne's invisible tentacles, standing with my arms outstretched. Cosmic dust coated my limbs.

Soaking. Absorbing. Entering my soul.

I ripped open my tunic. I needed more. My body warmed as the dust seeped into my blood. Euphoric. Sharp pains stung from the inside of my fingers outward like I'd run my hand through a campfire's flame. A diffused halo of light hovered just above my skin. I felt lightheaded, like when Amalthea gave me wine for the first time. I could've walked on air. Yet, I dared not test that theory.

At that moment, I chose to mount the Throne. I took an extra step upward, felt the cold seat, turned around and sat down. I pressed my bare skin against the back of the seat. Nothing happened at first. Then my body shivered and shook violently, arms were held in place as if they'd been strapped down. My spine suctioned to the backrest.

A blistering torrent surged through my ichor blood vessels. Inky veins stood out prominently against my stinging, yellowish skin. Tiny mountain ranges of goose bumps rose all over.

Frightened, I struggled against the Throne's grasp. They'd all warned me. I hadn't listened. Again. Breathing came in ragged bursts. I felt as if I were being burned alive.

Finally, the convulsions stopped. All vitality vacated my sluggish limbs. A knot of nausea roiled in the pit of my stomach. My head slumped. I glanced down at my friends. Their mouths gaped. Even Hera's. Astonishing her wasn't easy.

My exposed skin was momentarily dark as Erebus ink, illuminated by a night sky's worth of twinkling, yellowish-green stars. My tattered tunic hung limply at my waist. A menacing laugh rumbled up from my core, one I wasn't aware I'd had previously. One I would've pegged on Kronos, and yet I produced it.

I rose to my feet and clapped my hands together. An ominous thunder crack roared in the heavens, vibrating the Throne so much that I nearly lost my balance. I did it again. And again.

I loved the sound of the universe splitting and cracking and then the strong insistent roll and rumble across the cosmos, like giant boulders tumbling down an endless ravine to the bottom of nowhere.

Hera gazed at me with wide eyes. Metis held her hand over her lips. Shade's mouth still hung open.

"What do you think?" I called out to them with arms spread wide.

No one answered.

I brought my hands near one another. Iridescent strings of energy transferred back and forth between my fingers and palms. The tendrils got stronger and bolder the closer my hands drew to one another. I closed my hands all the way and opened them again. Closed. Opened.

"Should I do it again?" I asked.

A resounding chorus of "No!" shot back up.

Hera added, "Um, I think you've had enough fun for today. Get your ass back down here. I'm not asking you."

I was half taken aback by the force of her command and half enticed by it. Hera certainly knew how to push my buttons. And I liked it.

When I looked downward, my fear had vanished. I took a step to walk back down the stairs, but my numb leg wouldn't hold my weight. I tumbled head over heels, going airborne for several steps.

"Zeus!" Metis gasped.

Shade grabbed me to halt my rolling at the bottom of the stairs. "You all right?"

I shook my head back and forth and labored to rise to my feet again. At least I hadn't fallen off the stairs. "Woooo! What a rush."

Shade, Hera, and Metis scrambled backward down the shaft like they were afraid of me. When we re-entered the lab, I lit the inside of it like it was daytime.

"You crazy bastard! You did it. You sat on the Throne," Hera said with a wry smile. "But this ... what's all this?" Her hands made rapid circles around me.

I shook my head and looked down at my glowing skin. "I wish I knew."

"How do you feel?" Shade asked.

"Like I could level whole mountains."

"Wicked."

"Well, you can't stay like that," Metis warned as she walked over. "You'll draw too much attention to yourself. How do you turn it off?" She picked up the torn ends of my tunic and tried to wrap them over my shoulders. She gasped. "You are so hot, Zeus."

"Wow. Thank you. Did you mean to say that out loud?" I looked over at Hera, whose jaw tightened.

"No, really. You are burning hot."

"I feel pretty hot. Nice of you to notice."

Hera huffed. "Give me a damn break."

"I'm not joking around!" Metis cautioned. "Is there some water in here?"

"No."

"Then we need to get him to the bathhouse, like yesterday," Metis commanded. "Hades, give me a hand here."

Hands seared into my skin at various points. Everyone's words ran together. Strings of mumbles and incoherence. My vision blurred like it had the night Metis speared me. Then I saw doubles of everything.

"I hope nobody sees us," Shade said.

"Oh what, this bright sunshiny ball of energy in our arms streaking through the dark of night?" Metis asked.

I felt weightless. Maybe it was because Metis and Shade half carried me down the path from the Observatory. At least I thought it was they who carried me.

"So this is what the inside of your bathhouse looks like?" I asked.

"What," Shade said. "I can't understand you. Speak up."

"The bathhouse. Score. We've finally gotten inside the girls' baths."

"Do you know what he said?" Shade asked Hera. She shook her head. Shade turned back to me. "You're mumbling, brother. Just relax."

They slid me into an empty bath. And then threw buckets of water on me.

"Aggggggggh!" Pain and steam rose from my body. Slowly the iridescent color faded and lucidity returned like the sun burning off the morning fog. They threw a second round of water on me. Shade stood poised with a third.

"All right!" I put my hands up. "I'm good. I promise." I wiped my face clean and looked at my body. My original skin tone had returned, only paler.

I climbed out of the bath and sat like a wet goat. My torn, wet tunic hung from the rope at my waist.

"There's a lesson to be learned tonight, boys and girls," Hera said. "Let's try and stay away from the Sky Throne, all right. We see exactly what can happen."

"Now that we have all that figured out," Shade said. "We still have to figure out where Don, Meter, and Tia are. Do you know anything, Metis? Are they being detained? Have they been harmed? Are they dead?"

"Nooo! And, don't be so morbid, Hades. Have some optimism," Metis said. "Let's begin with how the Oracle said *find out why you Olympians would win at War Games, and you find your comrades.* I think we found out why you might win." They all looked at me. Metis continued, "Perhaps the Oracles knew that you'd ascend the Throne ... and that you'd become ... " she motioned her hands toward me. "This."

"Yeah right." I felt heat rush into my cheeks. "Remember, I nearly got myself killed the other night and tonight."

"Yes, and maybe all of us going up there and receiving certain gifts of deity magic is what ultimately would've led to a win in War Games."

"But how could they've seen all of that? So many things happened along the way. The attack on Crete. Amalthea's injury. Tos' death. Me coming here. Tia, Don, and Meter's disappearance. All those incidences contributed."

Metis touched my shoulder. "You know I'm sorry about that." The emotion in her voice snaked into my core. "Perhaps, that's why they're Oracles, gifted with the deity magic of prophetic vision, foresight, and the ability to sift through the dross."

"Don't you see?" Hera said. "Zeus really is the reason. Aside from your fear of heights, you shapeshifted the best of any first-timer. No one's ever done that well that fast, including me. And besides, I don't know anyone here who has shifted into a dragon, do you, Shade?"

He shook his head.

Hera continued. "And now this incident with the cosmic dust and the Throne and you *survived* it. You're amazing." She said it completely devoid of flattery.

"So what?" I asked. "I'm supposed to help you all win at War Games? And then what?"

"And how does knowing he's the reason help us?" Shade sulked visibly.

"It goes back to what I was saying," Metis said. "Kronos was going to take you out one by one until he forced Zeus to join him. But the other part of what the Oracles said was that once we found the *reason,* we'd then find your comrades," Metis continued. "Let's hope they're still alive."

"Wow, this is deep," Shade said. "I got your back, brother."

"Me too." Hera looked unwaveringly into my eyes. "Whatever it takes."

Metis sat next to me. "Whatever I can do to help out, I'll do. I have a bit of repenting to work on." Her smile still disarmed me in ways I couldn't explain.

Hera rubbed her hands together. "If we're going to fight Kronos and I'm sure other Elders, we're gonna need some weapons. And not those old goat droppings we have down in the armory. I mean some *real* weapons. We need the Cyclopes brothers."

"Oh!" Metis beamed. "Kronos banished the Cyclopes to Tartarus not long ago because they wouldn't make him supreme killing weapons for War Games. I think Kronos had planned to take you all out during a War Games match. Like for real."

"Bastard!" I growled.

"I get it now," Metis began, tapping her temples. "I think the War Games reference was less about the intermural sports aspect. The triple-tongued fruit may have meant something more sinister." Metis paused, possibly for impact. "A real war between the schools."

My heart sank into my stomach.

"You know what I just thought of?" Shade said.

"Yes, but tell us anyway," Hera joked.

"So that scroll said something about *absorbed into metal, bearer calls the tune*, right? Not musical, I get it. But maybe you can make it into—"

"Anything you want?" Hera finished the thought. "Hmmm."

"Maybe that's why we can't find Tia's research, because Kronos stole it from her. Wasn't she on to something?" Shade asked.

"Exactly," I said. "No, wait. It couldn't have been her research. Whatever Tia was studying, the Elders already knew. It had to be something else."

"Clearly Ouranos didn't know about making weapons, or he would've done it," Shade said.

"But he did know how to make a Hurler post," Hera said.

I paced around the hexagonal cold pool room of the girls' bathhouse. "So, Kronos wanted to make these super weapons. Needed the Cyclopes to make them. They refused. He threw them in Tartarus. That much we know."

"Right."

"If we could hold some metal high into the Heavens, like those uncharged Hurler posts, to soak up the cosmic dust, and could somehow craft that metal into a weapon instead of a Hurler," I said, "we would be cooking over a hot flame then."

"We need to extract the Cyclopes brothers from Tartarus," said Shade. "And we can't let Ouranos and Rhea know what we're doing.

Rhea would never believe our story. And Ouranos would never let us go."

"What about Tia, Don, and Meter?" I asked. "School's gonna be shut down if they don't turn up by Hemera Gaia!"

"What?" Metis asked.

"Yeah, that's what Ouranos told me earlier. And that he would send us all to Othrys."

"No! There's no way I can go back to that school," Metis' voice cracked. "I won't go."

"Why don't we just tell Rhea? She'd never let the school close. MO Prep was Rhea's idea anyway."

"She must be beside herself," Hera said.

"If Kronos is behind the disappearances, we'll never be able to defeat him without the Cyclopes," I said. "So first things first. We all agree?"

Heads nodded all around.

"He who controls the Cyclopes, controls the world at this point." Hera said.

CHAPTER THIRTY-SEVEN

Having never been to the Underworld, I asked, "How do we even get to Tartarus?"

Metis' face wrinkled. "By Hurler, of course."

Shade palmed his forehead. "Now, we need to make it to one without anyone seeing us."

"Wait," Hera said. "Have any of us actually been to Tartarus? Otherwise we can't get there by Hurler."

Heads shook.

"There has to be another way in," Hera said.

"In any case, it's not going to be that easy," Metis said. "What's the plan? Go in there, get the Cyclopes brothers, and leave through the front door. Just like that?"

Hera crossed her arms and pulled gently on her bottom lip. "Right. We definitely need a solid extraction plan. Complete with some solid *if this, then that's* built in, got me?"

"Let's meet at my bungalow after we're dressed." I looked down at my soaked, torn tunic. "And be quick. Hyperion will be released soon and we can't afford to get caught in the sun's angry gaze. If we wait too long, we'll never be able to leave campus with the lockdown. Oh, and shut down all thoughts."

On the short walk back to the bungalow, my mind raced, thinking of what we might need to get to the Underworld and back. Food. Water. Weapons. A map would be handy. I remembered that Tia had mapped the Underworld. And then I mind-slapped myself for thinking such thoughts within brain-shot of the watchful powers of Rhea.

I retraced my steps and jogged back to Tia's cabin. At a distance, a light glowed from the inside. My heart jumped. I ran to the cabin and rushed through the gauzy curtains that hung from Tia's doorframe. "Tia?"

"Tia's here?" Hera's head whipped around.

"Oh, it's you."

"Don't sound so excited," Hera snapped.

"I didn't mean it like that. I just thought—"

"No? Well how did you mean it? Were you hoping Little Miss Metis would be in here?"

"That's not fair, and you know it."

Hera grumbled to herself. "Great Gaia, that girl gets under my skin. Fawning over you the way she does. *You're so hot, Zeus.*"

I sighed and massaged my temples.

"Never mind. Let me just get what I came in here for."

"Wait, which was?"

"Tia's maps of the Underworld."

Hera's tone softened. "Her maps are so much better than mine. Like I said, we each have our talents. By the way, from now on, don't think anything you don't want me to know. Just saying."

Hera pulled the maps from under Tia's bed and spread the first parchments out on the desk. Fingers splayed, she pressed the edges flat and set weights down on each curling corner. As I ambled over to see the map, Metis stepped through the door.

Hera's head whipped around. "Speak of the dragon." She sighed and rolled her eyes. "Tell you what … it's suddenly way too crowded in here."

"I'm not here to make trouble," Metis said.

"I know." Hera shot a glance at me. "You guys find a way into that hell-hole. I have to run to my cabin."

Hera left Metis and me alone. I actually appreciated the space Hera provided. And the trust, frankly. Though her ability to read minds probably helped as well.

I motioned Metis over. "Help me make sense of this."

She walked to my side, positioning herself so that we nearly touched. My skin was so sensitive after the Throne incident. Metis' energy pulsed off her body in waves. She nudged into me, her knee pressing the back of my hamstring as she bent across me to point out something on the map. I could barely focus on the map. I closed my eyes to simply feel Metis next to me.

"You need to focus." She looked up at me slowly, seduction clouding her hazel eyes, her blond ringlets falling over half her face and her lips slightly parted. *Damn.* If we weren't in Tia's room and our circumstances were different. It took all the strength in me to not pin Metis back against the wall next to Tia's desk.

"Zeus," Metis breathed, her eyes matching the desire I knew was in my own. "After what I witnessed with you on the Sky Throne, your torn tunic, those abs … " She sighed. "And then subsequently almost losing you, I'm hardly strong enough to resist any advance you made right now … except for the fact that we do have a mission to accomplish." She pointed again to the map with her right forefinger. Her left hand grabbed the back of my head and rotated it so I looked downward. She rubbed my bare back, leaving a trail of heat.

"There's our way in," Metis said. She pointed to what looked like a cave entrance near the mouth of a river, tracing her finger along the river's winding path.

"But that cave is way on the far side of the world," I said. "How would we get there? Also, it looks close to where Hyperion stables his draft horses." I tensed.

"We'll figure that out." She smiled and turned back to the map. "Grab these and take them back with you. I'll be at your bungalow soon."

I returned to my bungalow, while trying to think about nothing but goats. I quickly changed into my black tunic. A knock rattled my door. Startled, I finished dressing, smoothed down my tunic, ran my fingers through my hair, and then opened the door.

Hera stood there in all her fierce glory. Black tunic. Black sandals. No jewelry. All business.

She crossed the threshold. "Can't believe I'm the first one here. Did you and Metis figure out the map?" She nodded. "Of course you did."

Metis tapped lightly on the doorframe next. She cleared her throat. In her hand, she held four medium-sized sacks by her side. As I began to think how attractive she looked in the black tunic she was wearing instead of her usual chiton dress, I immediately willed my mind to not think *anything* about anything. Hera shot me an amused look.

"Anyone seen Shade?" Hera asked.

We shook our heads.

"Hera, we can catch Shade up to speed when he gets here. Here's what we know." I stood in the middle of the floor. "We have Tia's maps and from examining them, we now know where the entrance to Tartarus is. We just need to figure out how to get there."

"And the other maps detail the rivers, and the different levels of the Underworld," Metis said. "Fields of Asphodel, Elysian Fields, and Tartarus are all drawn exquisitely. There's no way we can get lost."

"We just need to get out," Hera said. "Alive."

"Once we free the Cyclopes, they can help us get out." Metis said. "By the way, I made everyone snack sacks with figs, apples, bread, and goatskins of water." She pointed to the bags on the bed.

"That was nice." I looked at Hera. Before I could rein in my thinking, I considered how Hera probably would never have done something like that.

I totally would have. I jumped as Hera's thoughts speared straight into my head.

No you wouldn't have, and you know it. I thought back.

All right maybe not, but don't hold that against me. I'm valuable in other ways.

Yes, you are. I could not believe we were having a conversation mentally. Outrageous.

"Okay," I said aloud, finally. "Let's go get Shade and get down to the armory."

As we headed for the door, a shadowy form appeared as if from thin air. An obsidian ghost. Metis gasped. I instinctively stepped in front of her. My fists clenched and a yellowish ball of energy pulsed around my fist. Then, my eyes registered who it was. "You almost had your life ended."

Shade beamed. "Pretty sweet, huh?"

"Dammit, Shade!" Hera scolded. "Unless you want to go to the Underworld permanently, don't do that again!"

My chest still heaved with heavy breaths as I clasped Shade's forearm. "Yes, that was pretty sweet."

"It's the dust, man. Remember how you said I disappeared up there? Now I can do it anytime I want, I think."

"Just don't come sneaking up on me in the bathhouse." Hera shot him a glare. "I'll know—I can still read your thoughts."

Shade's dark olive cheeks ripened.

My glowing hand cast an eerie light through the cabin. I tried to shake it, but the light remained.

"Your hand all right?" Shade asked.

"I guess." I cleared my throat. "Here's what we need to do. This is just like the game Goat-For-A-Sheep back home. My friend and I were on different teams. One team had a goat. The other a sheep. We hid our mascots in various places through the hillsides. The purpose of the game was to capture the other team's mascot, before they got to yours. Exact same thing. We need to sneak to the armory, gear up to the teeth, and then set out for the river cave."

"How are we going to get to the armory?" asked Shade. "Don't they have all our Hurlers guarded around campus?"

"Maybe." I grinned. "Maybe not."

CHAPTER THIRTY-EIGHT

I raced around my room, gathering up things I might need. An extra tunic. A hooded cloak. Metis' snack sack. "There's an unguarded Hurler in the Observatory."

We stalked back to the Observatory undetected and found the Hurler still radiating a dull blue halo in the corner.

"There's such a high likelihood that someone will be on patrol down at the Caldron," Hera said. "How do we get down there without being seen?"

The group drew in a collective deep breath.

"One of us could hurl down there ... " Metis said, "and then if someone is down there, we could just come back here. They'll only know that we left, but not the actual location."

"That's brilliant," I whisper-yelled.

"I can do one better," Shade announced. "I could render myself invisible and then go take a look around."

"You might just get a hug when all this is over, Shade," Hera said.

Hades puffed his chest out a bit. A satisfied smile played on his lips. "All right team, wish me luck."

Shade closed his eyes and focused. He slowly raised his right hand into the air. After a few moments ... he wrenched his hand into a fist like he'd turned a spigot. And then he vanished.

"Whoa!"

"Here I go," Shade whispered.

"Shade?" I uttered twice. No response came. "I guess he's gone. I sure hope nothing bad happens ... like his deity magic gets interrupted or something."

Hera, Metis, and I waited. I blinked rapidly at the Hurler. Nothing happened. I paced between two lab tables. Hera leaned against the wall with her right foot resting on a stool. Metis rubbed a circle on my back.

Suddenly, Shade reappeared near the Hurler. "All right, this is the situation. It's a good thing we didn't just all go down there. Phanes had just returned from a search of the Caldron and The Thick, I assume. He then hurled somewhere. I watched him. So our window of time here is closing to nearly shut. We have to go. Now."

We scrambled across the Observatory lab, met at the Hurler post, and liquefied. We rematerialized at the circle of Hurlers in front of the armory. The half-light of the sky reminded me of the pre-dawn return from the bonfire. A knot twisted in my stomach. We'd been awake all night planning this act of defiance. Here is where the hot iron would meet the hammer and anvil.

As we dressed for battle—pulling on mesh battle tunics, cuirass breastplates, greaves, bracelets, gauntlets, and lastly helmets—a subtle moan drifted through the building. It was slight enough that I almost mistook it for the building settling itself. Until it happened again.

I held up my fist, signaling to everyone to stop moving. They complied and cast puzzled expressions toward me; I pressed my forefinger to my lips. My gaze darted, searching for the sound.

The haunting moan reverbed through the space again.

"What *is* that?" Metis whispered.

It almost sounded like it had drifted from the other side of the armory. The Titans' side.

As I drew closer to the gate that separated our two sides, I listened again. Nothing.

"Hello?" I called out. "Anyone over there?"

No answer. I was halfway turned back around when I heard the moan again rumble through the silence.

I placed my hands on the iron bars of the gate. As I focused all my strength, a surge of energy flowed from my core, spider-webbed through my chest, and down my arms. My grip tightened, the bars turning yellowish-white and bent beneath my palms. I pulled them apart, stepped back, and admired my handiwork with a stunned expression. "I could get used to this."

"Show off," Hera said behind me.

We stepped out of the torch-lit Olympian side of the armory through the hole I'd made into darkness of the Titan base, our spears extended. Metis held the torch behind us as we walked.

As we moved into the large room of their side of the armory, a crumpled form stirred in the corner. Approaching it cautiously, I wheeled my spear around and poked the heaped mass with the butt end of it. It shifted and groaned louder.

Metis brought the flickering fire forward. I grabbed what looked like a shoulder hidden by a mass of matted silvery hair and rolled the bloodied body toward me. A sickle stuck out of the person's midsection. I carefully removed it and placed it to the side, noting that it was obsidian black like the spear that had impaled Tos on Crete. And the one in the Observatory.

"Wait a moment ... " Hera began, "Headmaster? Professor O? Is that you?"

Hera knelt to prop the body upright. I held his other shoulder.

"Yesss—" Ouranos whispered. His once strong voice weakened.

"Great Gaia!" Shade gasped. "Who did this? Who attacked you?"

Ouranos breathed, "F-f-find K-Kronosss ... "

I gripped the sides of Ouranos' face and turned his head slowly toward me. "Kronos did this?"

Ouranos closed his eyes as if to concentrate solely on his next breath. And then the next. His ageless face showed signs of wear. Wrinkles deepened. Sagging appeared where taut skin once had been.

Shade whipped his head toward Metis. "Did you know about this?"

Metis' eyelids were like dams, struggling to hold back the flood. "No! I swear! This was never part of any plan I was privy to." She sobbed.

I swallowed hard, unable to reconcile the strong Ouranos I had always known with the current vision. At once, my limbs filled with jittery, nervous energy. I gazed into the dark recesses of the Titan armory.

"Air," Ouranos muttered without opening his eyes. "N-n-need air—"

We all grabbed his arms and legs and struggled to haul him outside. His heft weighed considerably more than I'd have thought. The sky had lightened to a bright, rich blue that bordered on lavender. Ouranos took a deep breath and sighed. He moved his head slightly.

"Headmaster," Hera began, "You have been our rock. How are we expected to battle this evil without you?"

"You can and you will. Olympus will fall, if not." He coughed. "Stick together. Remember all we taught you. A leader shall emerge. Follow them through the fire. But ... beware—" he choked out. His head slumped. His pulse slowed beneath my fingers and then finally stopped.

"Beware what?" Shade asked.

But he was gone. My hand trembled against his skin. "If an Elder has fallen, supreme killing weapons exist already."

Ouranos' body became translucent. He levitated off the ground and we all stepped backward several feet. Before our eyes, his body became a million tiny points of light, specks of dust. Slowly, they rose higher in the air until they filled the indigo sky with stars.

My voice cracked. "If Ouranos is murdered what does that mean for—" The names of my schoolmates refused to form in my clogged throat.

Everyone turned slowly toward me. I saw something I never thought I'd see. Tears welled in Hera's eyes, though none fell. Shade's scowl returned. Metis covered her eyes and shook her head.

"Now, I'm really pissed." Hera's soft features hardened. She paced, shaking out her hands frantically. Short huffs of breath escaped her lips. And then she turned her pained gaze toward Metis. "Did you know about this?"

Metis shook her head. "No! I swear. This was *not* part of any plan I ever knew."

Hera glared at Metis. "If I find out your lying, there will be nowhere in this cosmos you can hide from me."

"Trust me," Metis began, glancing into the eyes of Hera, Shade, and myself, "you have every right to hate me. Self-loathing is a dangerous sport. I have a lot to repent for ... and much to prove."

"We should get going." Hera wiped her eyes and glanced around the clearing outside the armory. "Phanes could return. And time is not on our sides here."

We finished arming ourselves in silence and stepped cautiously back into dawn's pre-light. I scanned the landscape for the tiniest of movements, and then suggested our best course of action. "Shade, see if there are some reins and a bridle of some sort in the armory."

"Why, you have a horse up your sleeve?"

"Better."

Shade's face scrunched as he walked off. He trotted out a moment later with ropes and a link chain wrapped in his hands. The chain clinked a little too loudly for my tastes. "Hush that thing up," I whispered.

"Now what?" Hera looked at me quizzically.

"The best part of shifting into the dragon the other night?" I paused dramatically. "I should be able to do it again. So once I shift into the dragon, you all mount my back and I'll fly us to the cave's entrance."

Shade looked around. "Uhhh …"

"I'm driving," Hera blurted. "Actually, I take that back 'cause I don't want you hanging onto me the entire ride, Shade. And I don't want Metis hanging onto me either." She looked at Metis. "Short straw, girl. You're driving. That way Shade can hang onto you."

I closed my eyes and tried to summon the fire in my belly and the iron in my blood that I felt while I was a dragon. I clutched my stomach as an ache grew and then exploded within my core. I gasped and dropped to one knee from the knifing pain. My skin tingled, prickled, and then ignited as it hardened into scales. My heart expanded, pushing a hot torrent through widened veins. My chest and shoulders broadened as my neck stretched and thickened. My eyesight became keener. As I looked down and focused on my friends, I realized they were starting to register on some level as lunch.

Metis reached up, and placing her hands on either side of my broad chin, she gazed into my eyes. She then turned to Hera and Shade. "We need to hurry before the dragon overtakes his being."

Hera gazed at me, and then Metis. "Interesting. I can't read Zeus' thoughts while he's in this form."

Shade approached me with the rope, chain, and bridle.

I lowered myself so they could climb on my back, just above my wings. I shook my head and slapped my tail on the ground to let them know I was ready. Metis pulled the reins, patted my neck, and said, "Let's go."

I stretched out my wings and launched into the air. With powerful strokes, I climbed into the dawn, heading westward. In the east, Hyperion's chariot pushed aggressively against heavy bands of storm clouds, light splitting the darkness in blood reds and sinister oranges.

I reveled in the freedom of the wind slipping past my face and filling my wings. I knew we needed to hurry though, before Hyperion's rays set full-bore over the region.

I spotted the river we sought on the horizon. Without warning, the reins yanked my neck with extraordinary force. I jerked my head around, wondering what had happened. A commotion rose right behind my ears, and then high-pitched shrieks pierced the crisp, early morning air.

I swooped down sharply then climbed aggressively into the air again, turning in every direction to see from where the noises had come. Then I saw *them*.

A murder of heinous winged creatures tracked us. With female heads ringed in manes of serpents, five airborne creatures surrounded us. Their bodies appeared female, but each hand had long talons instead of fingers. Two spears sailed into the air toward them from behind my head. The dexterous beasts dove, swooped, rolled, and otherwise evaded the spears, causing them to fall hopelessly toward earth.

They attacked us from all sides, pure evil glaring from their bleeding eyes. I turned in the air and swatted at them with my wings. Volcanic power roared into my throat. With a strong exhale, I shot a stream of fire straight into the middle of the group. One of the winged beasts exploded in flames as if her blood was made of oil. Another burst into flames as she tried to attack my left side. She disintegrated in midair, smoke and ashes scattering on the wind.

The remaining creatures shrieked, turned, and flew away. They disappeared into the gathering storm clouds. I had no intention of waiting around to see if they would return for more.

Metis yanked the reins and pulled my head back around. I flew faster than before. After gliding just above the treetops, I floated toward the river's surface. I snaked along the river, dragging my taloned feet through the water until I received another insistent tug on the reins.

The cave we sought came into view. Once I'd landed, Metis gave my neck a quick rub and hopped off. Shade and Hera followed. I tried to shift back to normal, but struggled to find my own self within the beast. My skin and hair eventually returned, but it took longer than it should have. My body's reluctance to shift back was worrisome. Professor Phoebe hadn't warned us against that.

I stumbled and collapsed because my legs wouldn't hold my

weight. Metis hurried over to help support me. "The dragon was taking hold, wasn't it?"

"I'm just a little weak," I said. "That shift and that flight took a lot out of me."

"We're going to need you, brother. Don't go getting all woozy on us now." Shade threw my arm over his shoulder. "I got him, Metis." Shade shouldered my weight and helped me walk.

Hera's hair was wild from the ride. She pulled it behind her head and wrapped it into a bun after she found a stick to secure it. "We can't carry you through this." Hera gazed at me warmly. "Once we get inside the cave, you can rest. But only for a little while. It's my job to push you."

I flashed her a knowing smile.

"The sun rises with vengeance," Metis said, her cheeks blushed from the wind.

"Hyperion is free. And probably angry. We need to take cover," I said.

The entrance to the cave towered atop a slight incline. The river split just ahead of us, water strangely flowing up the hill over and around boulders. We walked toward the odd flowing tributary and stepped from rock to rock, traveling up the ravine.

Once inside the cave, we followed the water's edge to where it stopped. The water stopped, but the cave continued. I paused to rest for a moment.

"Now what?" Shade asked.

"How does a river just end?" Metis asked.

Shade scoffed, "How does a river flow uphill? What's really at work here?"

I peered into the darkness that extended beyond the river's ending. It reminded me of looking into my cave back home. The same abysmal darkness, but oddly nostalgic.

"Do the maps say anything about this river just ending like this?" Shade asked.

Hera unrolled one of the maps as if she could actually see in the cave. She quickly rolled it back up and sighed. "Maybe this is the wrong cave. Did you all see any other caves outside?"

Metis pointed into the depths. "Clearly the cave continues even though the water stops here. We could keep walking deeper. A lot deeper. Obviously, Tartarus wouldn't be this close to the surface."

The water's surface rippled with slight evidence of current flowing toward us. "But wait," I said. "So the water flows into the cave, not out of it. The water's going somewhere. Help me find a rock or something to throw in there."

"What are you thinking?" Metis asked.

"That there's no bottom. That the water flows directly to the Underworld," Hera said matter-of-factly.

"But even if it does," Shade said, "What are we going to do? Swim the entire way to Tartarus? I'd rather walk, thank you very much."

"Give me your spear, Shade." I extended my hand.

"Besides, we can't carry all our food and gear if we try to swim," Metis said.

"We might need to make some sacrifices," Hera said.

"And no maps." Metis continued.

I took Shade's spear and tested the stream's bottom. The spear touched solid ground with the water coming halfway up the shaft, drifting past the shaft toward the odd ending place. I walked back down stream, tapping the bottom as I went. Growing increasingly curious, I handed Shade his spear. "I'm going to investigate this thing up close and personal."

"What does that mean—" Before Hera had finished, I plunged into the stream, the frigid water shocking my limbs. I tensed. Every muscle contracted. Then the most insistent force grabbed my legs, pulling me under. I fought my way to the surface just long enough to yelp something incoherent and draw another breath before I was sucked down completely under the water.

CHAPTER THIRTY-NINE

My body was sucked through a small opening in the riverbed. My cuirass breastplate caught on the opening, but only for a moment. My helmet came off and my arms were pinned above my head. I held my breath as I was suctioned down a long, winding chute. Increasing pressure slowly forced the air from my lungs. I could see nothing. I'd no idea how long the chute was, or how long I could hold my breath. My lungs burned as I mashed my lips together. I just had to hold out a few moments more.

As I finally shot from the hole and hurtled through the air, my arms flailing, I gasped in a huge volume of air. My eyes snapped wide and my heart climbed into my throat as I fell for what seemed forever before smacking into a pool of the same water I'd traveled in.

"Great Gaia!" I screamed as I bobbed to the surface. Panting, I looked around. Sheer, black walls enclosed the pool. Treading water, I stripped off my breastplate. Its heft threatened to pull me underwater again.

The hole from where I'd fallen stared down at me like a weeping eye. I was now separated from my team. I had no map and no weapons, no friends and no food.

The water cascaded over another edge in the distance. I wasn't prepared for another steep fall, so I swam with all my unspent might to maintain a safe distance from it. But, an insistent pull drew me nearer to the brink. If only I could have channeled Don's swimming skills.

As I treaded water, Hera's voice entered my mind.

Zeus, are you all right? She asked. *Can you hear me?*

I was so spooked by hearing her voice, I didn't answer straight away. But I'd never been happier to have someone speak to me mentally.

Zeus! She yelled into my mind. *Oh Gaia, why did you do such a boneheaded thi—*

Yeah, I'm fine, I answered mentally. I assessed my surroundings. I was still alone in the water.

Zeus? Is that you?

Yes.

Good! 'Cause when I see you, I'm gonna kill you! What did you do that for? Where are you, underwater?

Underworld. I got sucked through some waterfall. I'm a little shaken up from the fall, but I'm good. Where are you all now?

Praise Gaia! We're still up here where you left us, she said. *Is there any way to come back through to us? Shade was going to jump in after you, but we couldn't risk losing both of you.*

Definitely not. There's no way I can retrace. I looked up toward the hole I'd fallen from again. *In fact I'm about to head over another waterfall.*

Wait! No! We'll never find you!

What? Are you coming through the same way? Be prepared to hold your breath forever.

Do we have a choice? I could leave Shade up here.

My stomach churned with laughter, then tightened. At the

moment, I needed to focus all my energy on survival. Despite my efforts, I drew dangerously close to the other waterfall's edge. With no way to see what perils lay on the other side of that waterfall, I tried to swim away with more vigor.

Hey, Hera said. *You still there?*

Hera's mind reading had limits. At least at this distance. If I thought something to myself, she couldn't hear it. But if I directed a thought to her she could hear it.

Zeus! Hera screamed mentally. *Are you all right?*

Just trying to steer clear of this waterfall.

Answer me when I'm talking to you! She paused for a long while. I was almost afraid to interrupt the silence. *That's it. I can't take this. We're coming to you.*

You mean you're all jumping in the water? No! I nearly died coming through there.

We could walk down, which might take eons. Besides, Shade swears he's memorized the maps. He's discovered he has the ability to create fire in his palms, so he's been reading the maps by firelight ever since.

That could come in handy.

Stay where you are. Don't move a hair. We're coming. All you have to do is jump in, right?

"Oh my—" I gasped. My limbs felt as heavy as logs as I struggled against the current. But there was no place to swim toward. Only a place to swim away from. Darkness on one side. Dim light on the other.

No matter how hard I swam, I couldn't claw myself away from the edge. The current's pull was insistent. I looked over my shoulder and the roar of the falls echoed in my ears. The dimly lit cavern kept me from making out any visual details. I tilted my chin upward to avoid sinking under. Just as I reached the edge, I heard, "Agggh!"

I glanced up to see Shade torpedo from the mouth of the chute, his arms waving wildly. Then Hera flew out next.

"Shaaaaaaade!" I careened over the second waterfall. My soul felt like it was being ripped from my body as I tore through the air for the second time. A translucent shadow of myself lifted out of my body and wisped into the air. I tried to right myself but slammed onto a flat rock below. And then the translucent shadow hammered back into my body.

A thousand hot needles pricked my skin while cool, thick liquid lapped against my lower legs. The impact stole what breath I'd had left. After a pregnant pause, I coughed and gurgled up so much water that I thought my throat lining had risen into my mouth.

I struggled to crawl off the rock, but my body wouldn't move. My limbs refused to obey my commands, as if I were in a dream where I tried to move or scream and nothing happened. I still couldn't take a full, satisfying breath.

My entire world faded into muted grays. I stared into the vast haze above, wanting to close my eyes. Only for a moment, I told myself. With one leg hanging in the murky liquid and pain firing through me, I closed my eyes to summon strength to hold onto consciousness.

Someone yelled. The voice was muffled like it came from the far end of a tunnel. They yelled again, and then a nearby splash sprayed liquid all over me. I couldn't yet open my eyes when someone rolled me over onto my side. My body floated through the air. I opened my eyes just barely enough to recognize that Shade was pulling me onto the riverbank. I'd never been more happy to see him.

"You are one wild and crazy bastard!" Shade yelled. "I can't believe you just did that. And then after talking to you mentally, Hera pushed me in and I was all ... " Shade waved his arms like a maniac. "What a sweet ride that was! My lungs almost gave out, but so damn wicked!"

I shut my eyes again to gather my faculties.

"Come on, Hera! I'll catch you." Shade called out.

He waded to the middle of the dark water where it came up to his waist. I looked upward to see Hera flying over the waterfall. Sure enough, Shade caught her. Clumsily, but he did it. They made a huge splash in the river beside me.

"Dammit, Shade!" Hera scolded. "If you hadn't been in the way I could've shown you some Poseidon-style diving like the ones he performed at the cliff diving championships last summer."

"Pssht, there's only one Don," Shade responded.

"How true."

"Where's Metis?" I coughed out when they climbed onto the riverbank. Hera cut her eyes at me. I meant nothing other than wanting to know whether or not she'd made it.

Shade shrugged.

Hera wiped her face clear and smoothed her hair back. "I asked her if she wanted to go next. She shook like a leaf." Hera paused, perhaps for impact, perhaps not. "So I left her ass standing there. You're too important to me, Zeus. And so is this mission. I don't have time for wishy-washy. To be quite honest, I simply figured she would follow our lead ... as we followed yours."

"I didn't follow, you pushed me!"

"Stop whining," Hera joked. "It really was more of a nudge."

I tried not to wonder about Metis and her motivations. But it was difficult. Metis was up there alone ... or, had she planned to be separated from us all along? I hated doubting her ... again.

CHAPTER FORTY

Shade knelt beside me. "Zeus, are you all right? Can you move? Can you function?"

"Barely," I groaned, rolling to a sitting position.

"What is that putrid smell?" Hera's face wrinkled as she pinched her nose.

Once my faculties returned fully, I caught a nose-full of the Underworld in all its glory. It smelled like hairy goat's flank roasting over a spit mixed with rhino's breath. The stench hit the back of my throat and lingered as if I'd thrown up. The Underworld was definitely a fitting location to punish rule breakers. Incarcerating the Cyclopes for not making Kronos killing weapons was plain crazy, though. I was certain that they would help us bring Kronos down, if we ever found them.

"We need to get moving," Shade said. "The problem is that we now have no armor or weapons. And no maps. But—" Shade tapped his temples. "I've got the maps mem-o-rized."

"Let's hope so," Hera said. "All right, hot shot. Which river is this?"

Shade dug his forefingers into his temples. "This—is—the Styx! That's it."

"You're sure?"

"Ummm, yeah—" He paused and looked in the distance. "Nope. It's the Acheron, because, around the next bend should be a main entry to The Underworld. Then, it's *days* of walking."

"Days?" I gasped. "What about food? I'm already hungry."

"We had to leave the food with *the girl* since you decided to be all impatient and jump into a damn secret whirlpool and get sucked into oblivion," Hera snapped. "We also had to leave the weapons. All we have now is my beautiful mind."

"And my invisibility," Shade said.

"That's comforting." Hera rolled her eyes. "Can you be invisible right now?"

"Fat chance." Shade said. "Let's go."

I gingerly rose to my feet and walked toward the bend in the river. Strength and vitality slowly returned to my limbs. "Shouldn't we wait for Metis?"

"If she were coming," Hera said, "She would've come through by now." Her lips tightened. "Come on. The sooner we get to Tartarus, the sooner we can leave."

Around the corner, the cavern opened. Thick fog rolled across the river. Shadows of the darkest hues of silver and brown draped every surface. Nothing had color. Not even us.

I looked around at Hera and Shade and wondered how we'd cross the river.

"That's a good question," Hera said.

"What?" asked Shade.

"Oh, just wondering how to cross the river," I said.

"You'd almost want some kind of ferry or something, right?" Shade asked. "If I ran this place, I'd for sure have a ferry service, someone to escort everyone across."

"Who'd ever *want* to run this place?" Hera asked.

"It gives me the creeps," I mumbled, looking up toward the ever-receding ceiling of the Underworld. It looked like an inverted mountain range.

"No way!" Shade's voice echoed several times. "A boat." He pointed to a beat up looking dinghy that sat against a far earthen wall.

"Yes!" I pumped my fist as we walked to it.

"Look, it's even got two oars." Shade picked one up and inspected it. I examined the other.

Hera folded her arms. "And if you put both of them together you might get a whole paddle."

The oars were half-eaten by time, moisture, and neglect. They'd likely fill our hands with splinters, but they offered the only option. "If we paddle fast enough, it won't matter that the dinghy has a few holes here and there, right?" I said, trying to muster some optimism in this dreadful place.

"Hey, Mr. Impetuous. Haven't you gotten us in enough trouble?" Hera huffed. "We have no weapons and no food."

"We didn't have a choice." I glared at her. "Go hard or go home."

"Anyone remember the Grinder?" Hera mused. "The column leaping exercise? Anyone?"

I grumbled.

Chin up, Spruce, Hera spoke to me mentally. *Don't get all sensitive on me. Turn your weakness into strength. Then, I won't tease you.* She winked at me.

My blood roiled.

"C'mon, Freckles," Shade said. "It *is* our best option and you know it."

Hera sighed loudly. "When we get back to campus, I'm definitely gonna need a detox from both of you." She paused to look around. "All right, let's hurry before I change my mind."

Shade and I grabbed the rickety boat while Hera carried the half-paddles. We set it in the murky liquid of the Acheron, but then quickly removed it.

"Hera, you get in first. Then we'll thrust it out and jump in."

Hera's face contorted as she climbed in. Shade and I picked up the boat and backed up to get a good running start. We sprinted toward the river, shoved the boat into the water, and clumsily climbed in. Hera handed us the paddles. With racing strokes, Shade and I churned the Acheron to frothy foam. I shut everything out of my mind except the task.

A fair way out onto the water, Hera clapped her hands. "Hurry! The boat's taking on liquid."

As soon as she said it, I felt cold wetness lurking around my toes. I paddled faster, despite my fatigue. Perspiration streamed down my forehead into my eyes.

The liquid rose higher, climbing past my feet up my ankle. Our efforts weren't getting us as far as they had been. Hera cupped the liquid in her hands and threw it out. *Keep pushing. You got this,* she said.

Through the haze, a blueish halo beckoned in the distance.

"It's a Hurler," I said.

"Praise Gaia!" Hera said.

Our dinghy had sunk down so low into the water that the liquid outside looked like it would cascade over the side of the boat and join the rest inside at any moment. The blue halo drew closer and closer. It had to be land. There was no way a Hurler would be in the middle of the water.

Faith is the persistent belief in the unseen, Hera whispered into my mind. At the moment, she was the only thing keeping me going. She reached over to caress my upper back, clearly having heard my thoughts.

Hera shouted, "Almost there—"

The boat slammed into something solid, lurching everyone forward. The boat pitched sideways and flooded the rest of the inside with the dark water. We scrambled, climbing out of the boat and the Acheron, unsuccessfully wiping at the thick liquid that coated our legs, torso, arms, and clothes. I wondered what made it turn so dark and muddy when the river that fed it was clear? Or at least clearer.

The Hurler post shone like a beacon on the shore. "We could use this to escape later," I said.

"Or get some food," Shade said.

"Wait," Hera said. "With all that's been happening at school, we were lucky to get off campus when we did. By now, the campus will be in a complete uproar with our absences. There's no way we can go back now without our friends."

I sighed and hung my head in frustration. My stomach growled at me. "Am I the only one weirded out by not knowing whether it's day or night?"

"I kind of like it," Shade said. "But, I admit to being a bit tired. I bet you could sleep forever down here."

"Let's catch some sleep over there by the Hurler," Hera said. "If anything happens, at least we can get outta here."

The Hurler's brightness against the shaded realm played odd tricks with my eyesight. Shadows passed across my vision. Blue squiggly lines swam before my eyes. I had to turn away from the post to allow my sight to return to normal. Yet, a measure of serenity washed over me.

We agreed to take turns staying awake and standing guard. As I offered to pull the first shift, I couldn't help but hope that nothing bad would happen on my watch.

CHAPTER FORTY-ONE

Hera and Shade settled in as I leaned back against the Hurler post. They'd been asleep for some time when my stomach grumbled so loudly, I thought it would wake them. I could've eaten the north end of a southbound mule. How long could we go without food? And Metis had all our snacks.

I considered Hurling back to campus. Or maybe the Agora. But, I had no idea if it was night or day out there. And I'd look mighty silly walking around the Agora at night. Or ... maybe not.

Perhaps I could blend into the throng, especially if it were nighttime and densely crowded. I was torn, though. At least if I left, I could bring food back. And possibly clothes. Nah, clothing would've been pushing my luck. But would Hera and Shade even be here when I returned? Would they wake to find me gone and then leave themselves?

My eyelids felt like someone was pulling them downward. The window of opportunity was closing. Of course, I could just rouse Hera and tell her my plan. I didn't have the nerve to wake them both.

But Hera would never let me go. At least, not alone. But the three of us together would surely get caught. Dammit, why was this decision so tough?

I cast a sidelong glance at Hera one last time as I placed my hand on the top of the Hurler. No turning back. I pictured the Agora, and off I went.

I rematerialized in the semi-circle of trees where the Hurler was located just off the Agora. Nyx's nightshade draped the heavens, painting the buildings in the darkest blues. I kept to the shadows.

The charred scent of the torches reached my nostrils before I saw a bunch of them dotting the Agora landscape. Girls and guys pranced in a line, arms over one another's shoulders. Melodies danced off kithara and lyre strings as drums paced what appeared to be an end-of-term party. They must not have heard about the drama unfolding at MO Prep. How could they not have heard?

I stopped a tall, thin guy I didn't recognize to inquire about his level of awareness. "What school do you attend?" I asked.

"Othrys Hall," he replied. "I'm new this term. Just came from Limnos Lower Academy."

"The Blacksmiths."

His face brightened. "Oh you know about us?"

I nodded. But I had to move on to my next question. "Hey, have you heard what's going on at MO Prep? Big scandal, huh?"

He frowned and shook his head. "Sad, really. Headmaster Kronos addressed the student body and told us that they had some students run away or something. He didn't go into much detail. Just said to keep our eyes open. And if we saw anything suspicious, to alert him or other faculty members."

"Thanks." I got what I needed to know. I wheeled around.

"So what school do you go to?" He asked in vain because I'd already left his presence.

I walked straight to *Lambda, Lambda* and ordered two large gyros. It took no time for me to inhale them. They looked at me cross-eyed when I ordered four more, but I needed them. I also ordered a goatskin of water to go.

The woman's face wrinkled and she glanced at me sideways after she'd handed me my food on a wooden tray. I requested a sack to carry them. She frowned and scurried to the back. After she returned, I simply took the sack and turned to blend into the crowd.

My attempt at being inconspicuous was working beautifully until I looked back toward *Lambda, Lambda* and saw a burly man emerge through the front door. His head swiveled like he actively searched for something. Or someone. We locked eyes.

I strode in the direction of the Hurler, shooting occasional glances over my shoulder. Rollicking laughter erupted from a gaggle of girls surrounding the Hurler post. The hair on my neck rose. I looked over my shoulder again. The burly man pushed through the crowd, clearly trying to follow me.

I increased my pace, but didn't want to bring more undue attention to myself. The girls still stood around the Hurler, giggling. Just as I reached the edge of the Agora and was about to shoot one more glance over my shoulder to check my follower's progress, a finger dug into my shoulder blade.

"What's your name, boy?" a man asked me. He was totally different from the *Lambda, Lambda* guy who had been pursuing me.

I turned slowly. Not recognizing him, I said what anyone would have. "I'm sorry. Let me just put my food down." I placed my food several feet away and then turned to face the man.

"And why's your tunic so rotten and foul smelling?" he asked.

"You ask a lot of questions." Without warning, I spun around and swept his legs from under him. He toppled backward and met the ground with a thud. I grabbed my food sack and rushed to the Hurler.

Even if he reached his feet to give chase, I'd be long gone. And, he'd have no idea to where I would've hurled. Certainly wouldn't guess the Underworld.

As I reached the Hurler, three shafts of energy descended upon the Agora, the brilliant white and golden shafts easier to see against the darkness of night. The Khaos Council. I couldn't get out of there fast enough.

The man I felled leapt to his feet and gave chase. I probably shouldn't have done it, but I shot him a smug smile just before placing my hand atop the Hurler. "It's time to mistify," I breathed. I pictured the Underworld and immediately became mist.

As I rematerialized, I saw that while Shade still slept, Hera paced along the shore of the Acheron. She glared at me with such fire that, even in the semi-darkness, I could feel the heat of her gaze. And it wasn't the good kind of heat either.

She approached me slowly, stopping about arm's length away, her eyes never wavering from mine. With the speed of a cheetah, she slapped me so hard my neck twisted around.

I stepped toward her and grunted, seething. I'd *never* been slapped like that. By anyone. Then, I turned away in frustration. There was no way I was going to retaliate. After all, I deserved it for leaving them without telling them where I was going.

"That … was for leaving us," she said. "Don't ever make me do that again."

I stared squarely into her eyes. "I know."

"What's in the sack?" She asked after a pause. "It better be some food. Or some clothes."

Her eyes softened when she saw the gyros. She looked at me and her eyes flashed hunger, before landing on Shade. "Guess I ought to save him some, huh?"

I rubbed my cheek as she attacked her gyros without mercy.

Shade stirred and opened his eyes. "What's all the noise? Oh hey, who went for food?"

Hera pointed to me.

"Wait. You left us here?" Shade asked. "By ourselves?" He turned to Hera. "Did you know about this?"

"Shhh," Hera placed a finger to her curvy lips. "Zeus and I have already covered this. I think we understand one another now."

I nodded.

"Where'd you go? Did you see Metis?" Shade asked.

"I figured it was safer to go to the Agora. And no, she wasn't there. How would she get there? There wasn't a Hurler near the cave and we're eons from MO Prep or the Agora."

"I just want this crap to be over," Hera said. "Let's eat and push forward. Or downward, rather."

"Can I finish my meal first? Sheesh." Shade joked.

"I'm just not a fan of being in the Underworld any longer than I have to. Besides, my skin is screaming for some ambrosia." She grabbed her mass of hair "And I can feel my ends splitting."

"Here's my only concern," I said. "We know there is a Hurler right here. But, the deeper we go we may not find any. And might get lost trying to find this one again."

"We can't stay here. Obviously," Hera said. "We also know that there is one when we get all the way to the bottom. So let's just suck it up and push onward. What's the worst that can happen?"

CHAPTER FORTY-TWO

The next few days were painful. I couldn't even be sure they were *actual* days. They could've been long hours. Time meant nothing down here. The nauseating ache of hunger and need for daylight played the oddest tricks on me. Darkness from the tunnels absorbed through my skin and burrowed into my spirit.

No more food. No more water. No more patience. I argued with Shade and Hera about every decision we made. At least we had Shade's memory of the maps, even though it only helped when we were walking straight with no forks in the path. And, thank Gaia for his ability to produce fire. Without it, we wouldn't have any way to light our path forward.

But even that was fading. As was Hera's ability to read my thoughts. Which was probably a good thing.

Our cosmic dust powers, even though I hadn't figured out how to use mine ... whatever mine were, were strongest when we'd recently used a Hurler. I figured that somehow, we fed off the cosmic dust in them. Getting back to that last Hurler would've proven a difficult feat after all the forks in the tunnels we'd passed. There were no signs and no indicators, and our tempers simmered.

I wasn't entirely certain we weren't walking in circles. For as long as it seemed like we walked, we could have encircled the Underworld seven times or more. We came to yet another three-way fork in the tunnel and I'd had it.

"Shade! I thought you knew where we were going! Didn't you say you had the maps memorized?"

"I did. But since we crossed the Acheron, I'm unsure of our bearings. Whose fault is it we all got sucked through a water chute and almost capsized in the Acheron?"

I countered, "Oh what, this is all my fault? My fault that I encountered a deathly whirlpool?"

Hera walked away from us then turned around. "Shut up! Both of you! I'm so frustrated right now I could kill you both with my bare hands. You, Zeus, for jumping into the water up there. *And,* for leaving Shade and me alone when we were asleep. And Shade for not memorizing the maps better. And just for being … Shady."

Shade extinguished the fire he'd produced in his palms. Darkness enveloped us. I saw the same degree of utter blackness whether my eyes were open and closed. My pulse pounded in my ears, drumming through the silence.

"I am sooo done with this place. When we get out of here, I don't ever want to come back," I said.

I waited for a response. The complete void of light reminded me of the cave back home. And then I heard a voice purr out of the darkness. "That's the point."

My eyes shot open, as if the wideness would help me see anything. Shade flickered a weak blue flame and illuminated Metis.

"Where in Gaia's name did you come from?" Hera asked. "And how long have you been standing there?"

"Yeah," Shade echoed. "Is there a Hurler nearby?"

"There is actually. But I didn't use it." Metis stood there with the rolled maps still in her hands.

I rushed to Metis and threw my arms around her. She dropped everything in her hands and returned my embrace. I experienced slight energy transference similar to when Rhea touched my back. Serenity. A sense of calm. Metis buried her head into my shoulder.

"I'm so glad you're all right," I said, knowing fully that my mind had gone to the darker regions of doubt during her absence.

"Trust is earned, right?" she said as she pulled back. "I felt like I still had some work to do on that front." She flashed a tight-lipped smile in the faint illumination Shade provided. "These maps were quite handy. I hoped you'd show up. I've been waiting for you just around the bend there. Had you walked fifty more paces you'd have run right into me."

"But—" Shade scratched his head.

"Yeah, well after you all *left me* up there holding all the supplies, I went back to the sunlight and looked at the maps a little closer. And the initial cave tunnel we were in led me straight here. I did have to cross the Fields of Asphodel, but after that, it was pretty much a straight shot."

"Damn!" Hera said.

"Shhh," Metis whispered. "We are still at a relatively safe distance now, but you don't want to be too loud. If the beast hears you, she'll assume you're escapees from her care and attack you."

"Beast?" Shade asked.

"Campe is the dragon who guards the gates to inner Tartarus. Kronos coaxed her into service to prevent the Cyclopes brothers from escaping. She's the wickedest witch you could ever imagine. She looks like a normal woman as you approach, but before you know it and once you're close enough to her, she'll shapeshift into the fiercest dragon you've ever seen. Or so I've been told."

I inhaled deeply. "This is going to be slightly more difficult than I'd thought. Just getting here was more arduous than I'd expected."

"Tell me about it," Hera added.

"So how do we get past it, I mean her, or whatever?" I asked.

"The only two ways you could get past her are being punished and sent to detention by the Headmaster, or … defeating her," Metis said.

Shade's flame kept flickering on and off. We needed to get to a Hurler and fast if we had any chance of defeating this monster. "What happened to the weapons we brought?" I asked. "Not like I would've expected you to carry them all down here, but—"

"Oh, I left them right by the pool. All except one sword, one shield, and one spear, which was all I could carry. They're propped against the wall around the bend." Metis pointed down the tunnel.

"And where is this Hurler?" I asked.

"This tunnel empties out near a bridge of sorts that spans the River Phlegethon. I've heard the flames of the river can reach as high as the bridge itself. The Hurler is on our side of the bridge."

"Really?" Hera blurted. Her voice carried.

"Shhh," Metis reiterated.

"That makes sense though," said Shade. "That way you'd have to get past Campe and cross the Phlegethon to escape Tartarus. No easy task, I'm sure."

"On the far side of the bridge is where Campe guards the gate that leads to the cells."

"I remember seeing that on the maps," Shade said, still trying to get his blue flames to behave.

"What did you do with our food?" Hera asked.

"I ate it long ago."

I gripped my stomach, which grumbled and ached from not having seen solid food for so long. None of us had. We weren't in any shape to be fighting a dragon. I wasn't even sure I had enough energy to shift into one.

What if Metis was indeed leading us into a trap? What if she'd planned this out with Atlas and Kronos? She kept talking about what was *right around the bend*. I clapped my hands over my temples to quiet the voices.

Nothing about this situation felt right or certain. Metis had been conveniently just close enough to jab me in the back with a spear during the search and rescue mission. What if Hera and Shade hadn't shown up when they did?

It felt just a bit too convenient that three of my schoolmates were already missing and now the last three of us were conveniently *right around the bend* from peril? And Metis was the one that pointed out this cave on the map to begin with. And I was sure even Hera couldn't comb Metis' mind at that moment without first soaking up some cosmic energy from the Hurler. We definitely needed a Hurler to power up.

I hated the doubt. It ate away at all my senses and fed my neurotic, food and nectar deprived psychosis. "All right," I said. "The only way we are going to leave here alive is if we defeat all obstacles in our path. Our first objective is to get to the Hurler. There's no way we can power up and fight without some dust. The second objective is to defeat or otherwise get past this Campe wench. The third objective is to secure the Cyclopes brothers. And our fourth objective is to extract them by Hurler. I am *not* going out the same way we came in."

"All right," Hera said, almost in a whisper. "What's your plan?"

"Metis, please bring the maps over," I said.

She spread the scrolls on the floor of the tunnel, Shade illuminating them as best he could. Hera and Metis crouched close on either side of me, causing my breath to shorten and my head to feel light at their closeness. But I forced my focus to return.

"If the Hurler is here," Metis pointed. "Shade should go first, because once he's powered up he can become invisible and sneak across the bridge."

"Alone?" Shade's eyes widened in the dim light.

"Afraid so." I said. "She'll see the rest of us." I turned to Metis. "That was brilliant. I like the way you think." At that moment, I knew all my doubts were unfounded.

"Before I touch the Hurler, she'll see me anyway." His voice dripped with anxiety.

"Yeah, but then once you disappear, she might think her eyes had deceived her," I explained. "So just go across and stay where it'll be easy to get to the gate."

Shade responded with a shaky voice. "Gotcha. Wait, do I have to hurl somewhere to extract the energy? And then come back? Where would I go?"

"Maybe. That's one way to do it." Although it made me nervous to think we would all have to teleport somewhere and then come back in order to power up, but if that's what we had to do, then so be it.

"Or," Hera said, "what if you just accept the cosmic energy from it the way we accept energy from something in order to shapeshift?"

"What, and shapeshift into a Hurler?" Shade scoffed.

"Seriously, Shade?"

"No, she's correct," I said. "Extract the energy from the Hurler. Now Hera, you need to grab a weapon and go second, because once you're powered you can communicate through your mind and coordinate us all."

Hera looked at me and nodded.

"Then I'll go as quickly as possible because by that point, she *will* attack you, I mean us."

"What about me?" Metis asked. In the dim light, her face showed the same vulnerability I'd fallen for and what seemed like genuine concern.

I took a deep breath. "Metis, the problem is that we don't know what your special powers are yet from getting close to the Throne. I don't even really know what mine are. You and I will have to improvise and help the team as needed."

I steeled my nerves as we crept close to the bend in the tunnel. Diffused light spilled onto the floor just ahead of us, evidence that the opening was as near as Metis said it would be. Moving into the lead, I flattened my back against the rough, dank wall and leaned as far as I could around the bend without falling. I saw the edge of the bridge, but not much else.

Shade poked me in the ribs. I waved him off and edged a little farther out. Finally the Hurler came into view. As did Campe.

Her beauty radiated much in the same way as Rhea's did, except Campe's hair was flame red and wild with curls. She stood on the far side of the stone bridge as expected, appearing quite harmless. It was a shame she might end up turning into a horrific beast and that we would likely have to take down.

I motioned Shade forward. He patted me on the back and then crept around me. I inched ahead as he took two steps and then ran to the Hurler. Metis placed her hands on my waist and peeked around me.

Shade approached the Hurler. Campe rose from her klismos style lounging bench and took several steps forward. She probably wasn't accustomed to seeing people approach from this side of the arched, stone bridge that looked to be as long as the MO Prep gymnasium.

Shade's limbs shook as he accepted the Hurler's energy. His head flopped backward. The brand on his arm glowed bright yellow. Then his body went stiff and he fell to the ground.

CHAPTER FORTY-THREE

I gasped before Hera clamped her hand over my mouth. "Sha—" Hera slid her hand around my waist and held tight. Shade didn't look so good. Had he taken too much?

Campe walked toward the bridge and was about to cross it when Shade disappeared. I breathed a sigh of relief. But Campe's closeness didn't bode well for Hera or me.

"Is everything all right?" Metis asked from behind us. Hera turned. "Shhh."

I nodded. I still couldn't see Shade, which was a good thing, I hoped.

Campe propped her hands on her hips. Her flame-red hair bounced and swung as she looked around. Her chest heaved a sigh beneath the flowing, black chiton dress pinned at her shoulder.

I motioned for Hera to wait for my signal while Campe lingered at the edge of the bridge for a few moments amidst red and orange sparks that began to emanate from and encircle her body. Suddenly, she turned quickly toward the gate as if she expected something. Or heard something.

As Campe sauntered back to her klismos bench, I motioned Hera forward. She glanced toward Metis, then turned and planted a kiss on my forehead. I closed my eyes and savored the feeling of her faint energy. I refused to look at Metis.

Hera crept down the tunnel and prepared herself to run into the opening. With a sudden burst of speed, she sprinted to the Hurler, leaping and grabbing it with both hands. A whimper escaped Hera's lips before she fell to one knee.

Campe's head whipped around and she immediately rushed toward the bridge. I knew Campe had seen Hera and this was my chance to go, no matter what.

I ran to Hera, gazing briefly upward into the void. The half-light that surrounded us was boundless, ascending into a ceiling that was darker than black. The distinct aroma of charred embers stung the rear of my throat. Hera looked punch-drunk on the ground. Her eyelids twitched, half-closed. I held her limp body in my arms, my stomach clenched, as I hoped against hope that she hadn't taken on too much. If any one of us could figure out how to best utilize the power transfer, it was Hera. I even doubted myself.

"No one invades my realm and lives to tell about it!" Campe yelled across the chasm. Her voice sounded as if she were speaking right into my ears. "Identify yourselves or be vanquished."

I wondered if I should try to buy us some time. Hera still struggled to claw her way back to consciousness, and could scarcely contribute. *Is this what happened to Shade?*

Put your hands on the damn Hurler! Hera shouted into my mind. I knew then that she was going to be all right, despite her external appearance. But I had a grand thought. Everyone else should be fully powered before I go. I motioned for Metis to come over. Neither one of us knew what the dust had done to us. But we were about to find out.

Metis ran over.

"Siphon the energy out of the Hurler. Now."

She gazed into my eyes as if to gauge my sincerity. Having satisfactorily seen into my soul, Metis placed her hands onto the post. Her body shook fiercely. Metis let go and stumbled to the wall near the post, barely able to hold herself upright. Luckily, Hera stood just in time.

I tried to reach my hand toward the Hurler, but it refused, almost as if my body knew the agony to come. After a deep breath, I finally edged my hands onto the Hurler. They immediately suctioned to the post. A painful jolt surged through my fingers, up my quivering arms, and radiated throughout my entire torso. My body went rigid as bolts of energy knifed through me. I was unraveling. Pain engulfed me, threatening to rip apart my sanity. My eyes closed and my mouth opened, failing to release the scream that roared up from my core.

But eventually the pain subsided, and when I was able to open my eyes again, Campe stood at the bridge's edge on the far side of the chasm. Her mouth moved, but I couldn't understand anything she said. I realized that my hands still held onto the Hurler post and let it go, falling backward. Hera held me through my convulsions.

"She's changing," Hera whisper-yelled as she laid me on the ground and braced for battle. I cursed myself for having her go second. She had no inherent weapon or defense as a result of the cosmic dust, save her mind.

I struggled to break through my partial paralysis and roll onto my side. As I barely managed to turn over, the beautiful woman across the bridge transformed.

Campe's beastly form filled out into something resembling a half-dragon, half-scorpion. More than ten horns sprouted from her morphing head. Her legs grew as big as tree trunks with sharp silver claws at the end of each foot.

Her entire body scaled over and a long, winding, spiked tail snaked out of her backside and slapped the ground. Her arms extended and formed wings that stretched to either side of the bridge. The alkaline smell stung my nostrils. I wiped the perspiration on my forehead from the sudden spike in temperature in the subterranean realm.

I was still unable to fight yet, but tiny power surges sparked within me. Like the ones I'd felt that night when I'd mounted the Sky Throne. The heat of the sun radiated through my skin, as it turned iridescent and yellowish and inky veins snaked across my muscles.

Suddenly, Campe turned and lashed her barbed tail at a spot right next to her. Moments later I heard something crash next to me and heard, "Umph! Ugggh!"

It was Shade, weak from the fall. He'd been thrown all the way across the river. At least he hadn't reappeared. His invisibility still held strong. "I'm all right. I think. Damn, that hurt."

I whispered to him, "Get back over there. Hera will direct you."

"As soon as I can breathe," he whispered back, crawling closer to me and coughing.

Hera moved in front of me. Her body braced for impact as Campe rose into the air, wings churning powerful gusts toward us.

I struggled to rise to my feet behind Hera, causing her to turn and grip my hand like a vise. Her face paled. "Zeus, I have no weapon," Hera's voice quivered.

I registered a quick flash of movement in my peripheral vision. A spear sailed toward Campe striking the beast squarely in the chest. Metis ran out from behind the corner, beating her shield with the sword and yelling, "Come and get me!"

Hera's head whipped toward Metis. She must've thrown her some message mentally because Metis turned toward Hera and shrugged, and then kept clanging on her shield.

Campe hovered in the air watching us, and then shot a stream of fire toward the river. The Phlegethon erupted in flames that licked up above the bridge. Campe landed on the middle of the bridge and turned her cursed glare toward Metis.

Hera spoke to me mentally, *Campe's going to need to recharge her furnace after that blast. We need to attack her* now.

Pulling on all of my strength, I ran toward the river's edge to draw the dragon's attention away from Metis. Campe turned toward me. Her mouth widened, large enough for me to stand inside. Liquid death dripped from her enormous teeth and I could've sworn I saw her grin.

Metis threw her sword at Campe but it missed. Campe retaliated with a thin stream of fire, engulfing Metis' shield in flames. Metis threw her shield to the ground and tried to retreat back into the cave. But she stumbled and fell backward, striking her head on the Hurler post.

I clapped my hands out of frustration and anger.

Whaboom! Campe startled at the sound of the heavens splitting and the subsequent roll of thunder. I separated my hands. Tiny spikes of pain pushed through my palms. Iridescent strings of energy transferred back and forth between my fingertips. As Campe prepared to attack Hera, the energy mass solidified in my palms. It was then that realized that I could probably heave it toward the she-dragon.

The rotating orb of energy hit Campe in the side of the head. She fell to the ground, her wings smoldering.

"Thank you," Hera mouthed to me as she ran across the bridge and headed into the tunnel.

Campe rose to her feet, fury glinting in her black eyes. Her pupils tightened as she stepped toward me. I hit her with another ball of energy, causing her to stagger backward. I tried to run for the bridge but she anticipated my move, blocking both the bridge and the tunnel with her wings.

I heard Hera mentally ask from behind Campe on the far side of the bridge, *Now what are you going to do?*

I'll hold her attention while you and Shade go find the Cyclopes brothers, I replied.

Campe hissed a stream of fire at me. I dodged and stumbled to the ground. I flung another ball of energy at her, hitting the ridged crown of her head. She staggered again, but I still couldn't get past her on the bridge. Campe's scales pulsed against her body, changing colors from red to yellow to bluish-white.

Metis still lay motionless on the ground thirty paces away. I shook my head when I thought I saw Tos standing there and Campe became Hyperion for a brief moment, until my weary eyesight focused.

"Nooo!" I ran to push Metis farther into the cave. I thought for sure Campe would finish her off to break my will. On the run, I launched another ball of energy at the she-dragon's left flank. But just as I reached Metis, Campe's barbed tail struck me in the side with the scorpion stinger as big as my arm.

The most horrific sound I'd ever heard tore from my throat. I didn't even recognize the voice. My entire being felt like the scream I'd made.

Venom entered my body and staggering pain streaked through me. I looked at the gaping wound. Murky yellowish ichor blood swirled at the wound and dripped down my hip.

Hera! I shot to her mentally. *I'm hit!*

Damn! Hold on, Zeus! She fired back. *We can't find the Cyclopes! There are too many cells down here.*

Tiny explosions of pain erupted all over my body as the cosmic dust fought against the poison. Pressure built in the back of my throat and my chest heaved several times before I threw up. Vitality drained from my limbs as another ball of nausea roiled in the pit of my stomach.

Campe's claws clanked with every step she took closer to me, eyeing me like a meal. I figured I had one last surge of energy left.

I closed my eyes and focused all my strength, feeling power rumble up from my core, across my shoulders, and down through my arms. When I opened my eyes, yellowish-white energy strings swirled around my hands like a violent storm.

I flipped my palms outward. A shaft of energy bolted from my hands toward Campe, lifting her into the air and sending her sailing backward to the edge of the river. She clawed and flapped but couldn't muster enough strength to keep from plunging into the fiery depths of the Phlegethon. Thunder rolled, quaking throughout the realm.

I lay back on the ground, exhausted. Pain wracked me as the venom worked deeper into my body. I felt its slow crawl. My thoughts jumbled together. I could hardly focus on anything outside of my agony. But in a brief moment of lucidity, I thought about Metis, who'd sacrificed herself for all of us. Metis, who had no special powers that I could see, aside from raw courage. Who had stayed the course and continued on the journey into Tartarus *alone* to meet up with us again.

Those thoughts helped me rise to a sitting position. There was no telling what other beasts lurked in this subterranean house of horrors. And I certainly couldn't leave Metis alone. With a heavy heart, I lumbered toward her and slung her arms around my neck to help me pull her up to carry her on my back. I stumbled again on my first few steps but then got a steady rhythm going. I'd almost made it across the bridge when I tripped and fell to one knee, scraping it horribly. Metis rolled off my back and almost over the side of the bridge. My heart stopped for a beat.

I sighed deeply as I pulled her back onto my shoulders and took measured steps across the clearing to the gate leading to inner Tartarus. Once we reached the gateway doors, I had to tilt my neck backward just to see the top of them and the ceiling of the tunnel they guarded. The opening to the corridor was wide enough to drive six chariots through.

Hera, where are you? I'm at the front gate, I said.

You're all right? She asked.

No. But I'm still alive … for now.

Where's Campe?

In the river.

There was a long pause. *And Metis?*

She's here. Not awake yet though. Pretty bad head wound. Hera, I don't feel so good. Campe got me with that wicked tail of hers.

Hold on! We just found the Cyclopes. Stay right there. We're coming up. Whatever you do, don't close your eyes!

I'll try.

I sat down just inside the soaring tunnel and lowered Metis' head across my lap. With pain slicing through me, I stroked her hair, now matted with perspiration and ichor. My thoughts ran through the past few months. A lot had changed. I'd gained friends. And enemies. I'd almost died, several times. I'd been lied to and stabbed by someone I'd cared for deeply. For whom I still cared intensely.

At that moment though, all I could say to Metis was, "Thank you for sticking by us, and for keeping your head when some of us doubted you." Her eyes didn't even blink. I couldn't lose her like I had lost Tos. Now that I'd found someone whose soul threaded so completely with mine, I wasn't ready let her go. I whispered, "I'll never doubt you again. Please come back to *us*. I promise we'll never let Atlas touch you again." I gazed at her, tears gathering in my eyes.

I winced, feeling like my body split in half, as I bent over to lightly kiss her closed eyelids.

My body temperature spiked suddenly. Sweat poured out of me. White spots danced in my vision and the tunnel's darkness collapsed on me. Remembering Hera's last words, I fought against losing consciousness.

Images flashed before my closed eyes. The wind rustling the trees on Crete's hillsides as Tos and I played one day. Tos flashing a bright smile over his shoulder. My hand reaching out to touch my mother's olive-toned, dimpled cheeks. Her soft eyes embracing me.

Something stirred on my lap. *Metis*. Feeling her move helped me find the energy to half open my eyes. Metis' face moved in front of mine like a ghostly shadow.

"Zeus?" she sobbed. "Wake up. Please."

I was trapped within my body, unable to respond.

"Zeus, if you can hear me, please listen," she said between sobs. Her speech was slurred. Or maybe my ears weren't hearing things correctly. "You mean everything to me. I need you to fight whatever is wrong with you." She sniffled while I struggled to open my eyes or speak, and I had the energy for neither.

Metis continued, "I know I wronged you. I own what I did. And, you have every right to be angry. But you can't hate me any more than I hate myself right now. After what I did, you found the compassion to save me from myself. Please don't leave me alone in this cruel world." She sobbed harder. "You make me a better person."

Her words and her energy fueled me. I clawed my way back with new vigor.

Zeus! You're never going to believe what we just found! Hera literally yelled into my head.

Wha– What isss it? My consciousness still waned.

I'll show you when we get back up top. If we ever find our way back out.

CHAPTER FORTY-FOUR

The ground shook with a dull rumble that grew in intensity. I strained to fully open my eyes. I forced them open just wide enough to see Hera bounding around a far corner with a torch in her hand. She smiled broadly as she approached, followed by three gargantuan, one-eyed giants whose heads could scrape the ceiling of the tunnel.

Hera ran up and knelt beside me. "Zeus! Look at you, oh my Gaia! What happened?" She handed her torch to Metis.

My voice was no stronger than a whisper. "Just a little sting."

Hera turned to Metis. "You're awake. How're you feeling?"

"I'll live."

"Good. Nobody is dying on my watch." Hera looked into her eyes for a moment and then smiled. "Wipe your tears. There's no crying in the Underworld." She turned to me. "Look who I found." Hera thumbed back down the tunnel.

"Spruce!" Don stepped from behind one of the Cyclops. He still wore his 'ψ' War Games tunic.

"No way," I breathed. My mouth gaped.

Tia followed behind him. She rifled her fingers through my hair. "Oh my heavens. How are you ... " Her words trailed off as she peeked at my wound. "That's pretty bad. I'm proud of you, lab partner. But we need to get you out of here."

I chuckled at her last statement, but misery flared through me. I clenched my teeth.

Shade walked up, carrying Meter.

"Hold on ... what the—" I stammered.

"She's just a little weak," Don said. "We'll explain later."

"All right. Sappy reunion postponed 'til we get back to campus." Hera clapped her hands. Don helped me up while Tia attended to Metis. "One more thing," Hera said. "Zeus, this is Brontes, Steropes, and Arges, the Cyclopes brothers." She pointed to each one.

I nodded, determined to look each in the eye. Aside from the singular eye that dotted their foreheads, everything else about them seemed normal—except, you know, that they were gigantic. Muscles bulged and rippled all over them beneath their torn and tattered iron gray tunics. Their bodies bore the ashen marks and scrapes of the Underworld across their limbs.

"Nice to meet you," Brontes said in a booming baritone voice.

"So you're the hero we owe our freedom to, yah?" Arges asked.

"I'm no hero," I said. "I just did what needed to be done. We all have."

"Thank you just the same," said Steropes. "We owe you all such a debt."

"Let's just get home, shall we." Hera said. "Zeus, can you walk?"

I struggled to rise to my feet. "I think so."

Don led us through the gateway and across the clearing toward the bridge. The Cyclopes brought up the rear with quaking steps. But just as Don and Tia reached the middle of the bridge, Campe stormed up from the depths of the Phlegethon.

Her entire body burst into flames, bluish near her vibrating scales and yellowish-orange at the fiery tips. She perched on the edge of the bridge and emitted an ear-splitting roar.

Campe twisted her head back and forth, unsure of whom to attack. Don and Tia sprinted to the far side of the bridge.

Brontes yelled, "Somebody distract her!" as he and his brothers ran back toward the Tartarus Gate.

Shade laid Meter on the ground and running to the middle of the bridge, disappeared just before the she-dragon's head snapped forward, and spewed a stream of flames. Suddenly, Shade reappeared near the far side of the bridge, once again disappearing just as Campe attacked. I smiled as an idea sprung to mind.

Weak as I was, I managed to rise to my feet and step forward. "Over here!"

Get back, Zeus! Hera screamed into my head. *What are you doing?*

Ignoring her, I fought to summon my energy. The strings formed weakly in my palms, but never fully materialized. Drained, I bent over, placing my hands on my knees.

"Over here!" Shade yelled as he reappeared on our side of the bridge. Campe's head snapped to focus on him just before he disappeared again.

"No, no, over here!" Hera yelled. Campe reared back and hissed a stream of fire toward Hera. But just before the flames reached her, she was knocked to the side by some invisible force. Campe snarled, swinging her fire toward me. I immediately dropped to the ground, barely avoiding the heat, but it was a close call—I felt it nearly scorch my backside.

Don and Tia waved their hands on the far side of the river. Campe attacked with a fiery burst. Don pushed Tia to one side and dove to the other. The fire missed. So far, all we were doing was dodging ... but we couldn't do that forever.

Campe landed on our side of the bridge. She swung her poisoned barb straight for me, when Brontes came up from behind her and slammed one of the huge, iron gate doors down on top of her tail. She thrashed her tail about so vigorously, I thought it would separate and spew poison everywhere.

Arges heaved the other gate door toward Campe. The impact knocked her backward. However, this time the metal of the iron door melted on impact and slid off her volcanic, scaled back. The halo of flames around her body was *that* hot. The iron door that had trapped Campe's tail also melted.

I labored again to summon energy. My body temperature spiked as my mind focused. Heat flashed through my torso and down my legs. Hot torrential gushes. My skin felt like it would melt at any moment.

Painful pricks pushed through my palms. Sizzling strings of energy flickered and snapped between my hands, filling out into a pulsing, yellowish-white, crackling sphere. I rose slowly to my feet, holding the excruciating energy mass in one hand. It stretched out into a long, jagged, crackling shaft against my palm. The throbbing pain grew so immense that I thought my arm would fall off at the shoulder. Ignoring the agony, I took three steps like the Kouretes had taught me and sailed the bolt toward the she-dragon with as much power as I could muster.

It struck Campe squarely in the chest. A boom of thunder shook the cavernous space so much, I thought the ceiling would collapse on top of us. The bridge rattled as Campe struggled to grip the edge. Chunks of bridge crumbled and fell. Her wings flapped twice and then she plunged back into the Phlegethon once again.

I fell to my knees and closed my eyes. Vision tunneled, hazy on the edges. Voices around me muffled, some closer, some farther away. I felt lighter than goat's fleece when someone picked me up under my armpits. Their pointy fingers seared my skin.

Then, someone placed my hand on top of a Hurler and everything blurred more than it had.

Σ

The next thing I heard sounded like several female voices arguing.

"We have to get him to the bathhouse," one insisted.

I sucked in quick, ragged gasps, each shorter than the last.

"He's hyperventilating. Hurry!"

I closed my eyes. Hot fingertips bit into me as cool air swept over my prickly skin.

Slap. All of a sudden, my cheek stung. As I snapped my eyes open, I saw Don's face, surrounded by steam. Then Hera's face appeared through the mist.

"Is he all right?" Hera asked with a trembling pitch my ears had never registered coming from her lips.

"I think he'll be fine." Don turned to me. "You *are* going to be fine, aren't you?" He held his tightened fist in front of my face. "How many fingers am I holding up?"

"None," I breathed.

"Yeah, he'll be good as new soon." Don palmed my head and rocked it back and forth slowly. "I thought you were a goner, Spruce."

I chuckled. Then I remembered something. "Wait. Where's Metis?"

"She fainted when you did. Poor thing," Don said. "Tia's looking after her."

"And what about Meter?"

"Shade took her out to the quad to soak up some sun," Don said. "Apparently, lack of sunlight depletes her energy stores. I never knew that. Did you, Hera?"

Hera shook her head. "Zeus, can you walk?"

I stood up from the bath, dripping wet. I nodded.

Hera stared at me, her face hung with equal parts admiration and caution. Without a word, I knew the source of each.

I felt reborn. My wound had closed and healed just like after the dagger incident. I guessed Campe's venom would always be a part of me, like the iron from the knife. I could only hope it wouldn't cause major problems in the future.

Don led us all to Metis' cabin. When we arrived, Tia held a goatskin with some water. Meter arranged some flowers she'd picked along the path. Her flowers must've regained their vitality as she did.

I silently reveled in all the attention they showed Metis. She'd had such a black smudge on her since coming back to school, but in the end, everyone rallied around her. As we should have.

Like Don once said, *"We all come together as a team. And keep everyone else out."*

Omegas. Olympians.

"How did Metis even get down there with you all?" Tia asked, dabbing a damp cloth on Metis' forehead.

"Long story," Shade replied, drawing out the word long. He then shot a glance toward Hera and me.

"In many ways, she saved our butts down there," I responded. "Shade was being all invisible and stealthy on the Tartarus side of the bridge. Hera had just energized on the Hurler, but had no real weapon. I powered up on the Hurler, but remained weak. Campe attacked, and Metis threw herself into the fray, taking one for the team."

"Metis *is* pretty mean with a spear." Hera flashed a wry smile.

Don looked at Metis. "Wow, I have a new respect for you, girl."

Tia rose from Metis' bedside and finally gave me a huge hug. She certainly hadn't seemed like herself down in Tartarus. No flamboyant tunic. No flower. But her effervescence had returned. She radiated anew.

"From that first day I showed you around," Tia said. "I knew there was something special about you."

"We're all pretty special," I countered. "Besides, it was your maps of the Underworld that helped us find you all."

Tia's green eyes brightened as she smiled.

"I'd have to agree that you're all special," Brontes boomed, looking through the window from outside. "But, I've never seen such command of energy and matter before."

"Yeah," Meter said as she hugged me. "What was that all about? And what did you do with the Hurlers again?"

"Yeah, seriously," Don added.

"Well—" I began.

"That's a long story too," Hera interjected. "But suffice to say that again, it was something Tia had done, or rather begun, that made all the difference."

I explained how we acquired the sacred scroll from Kreios and how it encouraged us to climb up near the Sky Throne and absorb as much cosmic dust as we could into our bodies.

"You actually sat on the Throne? Are you crazy?" Tia gasped. She looked me up and down. "And it didn't kill you?"

"And then we all got deity magic," Shade beamed. "Look, I can turn invisible." He did so. "And produce fire from my palms." Two little blue flames appeared out of nowhere, and then Shade reappeared. His hands anchored the two flames that had appeared in mid air. His grin showed every tooth in his mouth. "Pretty cool, huh?"

"I'd say." Meter's eyes widened. A warm smile crept across her face as she held Shade's gaze. "I was wondering what in Gaia's name was happening to you in the Underworld. I chalked it up to me being underground too long and losing my vision. What can you do, Hera?"

Hera looked squarely into Meter's eyes and smiled. In typical Hera tone and cadence, she said, "I can read minds."

"She's right," Shade said. "Just like Headmistress."

"Well, that could be useful." Tia was always trying to remain positive. Though, I had to admit that Hera reading minds on a regular basis could be quite interesting, if creepy.

Hera cut a glance toward me and I smiled.

"Students," Steropes said through the window, massaging his full beard. "I would like to thank you again for coming after us. As you likely already know, Kronos wanted us to make killing weapons for the War Games. And when we refused, he threw us into the bowels."

"How in Gaia's name did Kronos get you down to Tartarus in the first place?" Shade asked.

"The Hundred-Handed Ones, the Hecatonchires," Arges answered.

"The Heca who?" I asked.

"Big bullies who are out of control. Ouranos had cast them into Tartarus for being unruly and at odds with the learning process we were building here at MO Prep," Arges said.

"They clamped these shackles to our hands and feet while we slept," Steropes continued. "And we couldn't seem to break free. Something odd about those black cuffs."

"Then Kronos promised to free 'em early if they helped to imprison us, yah," Arges added. "But Kronos tricked 'em after they took us down. And that wench dragon intimidated us all with her horrendous breath. We had no possible way to defeat her until you all came. Did ya see what happened to that iron door?"

We all nodded.

"It was all Zeus," Shade said.

"Yeah, about that," Don said. "So how did you get that particular deity magic?"

I shook my head and shrugged. "I don't have a good answer for that. It just came to me when I mounted the Sky Throne. I can tell you this though. I am still bone tired from all that energy casting. Took a lot out of me. I may sleep for weeks."

Don laughed. "Wild man! I see I'm going to have to watch out for you now, Spruce."

"You're gonna have to watch out for me too," Shade said just before he disappeared. And then flashed back.

"Nice trick, Shade," Don said. "I definitely need to get some of this cosmic dust, huh? Wonder what my deity magic would be?"

"Me too," Meter said. "I can't wait to climb up there to the old Sky Throne now that we know it won't actually kill anyone."

"But, Shade and I didn't actually mount the Throne," Hera cautioned. "Only Zeus was crazy enough to do it."

"True," I said, and then broke the current conversation thread. "So wait, they're still down there?" I asked. "The Hundred Hand monsters?"

Steropes nodded.

"Thank goodness, too, yah? Good bye and good riddance," Arges said in a nasally grumble.

"But," I said. "When we meet Kronos again, we'll have an *epic* fight on our hands. We may need them." I looked at how muscular the Cyclopes were and could only imagine how much bigger and stronger the Hundred Hand guys were.

"And we're definitely going to need those great weapon casting skills of yours," Hera said to the Cyclopes.

"If we're fighting Kronos," Brontes bellowed in a thunderous tone. "I'm all for it! I never liked him."

"Arges. Brontes. Steropes." Rhea's soft but assertive voice sang from outside. "The sight of you all warms my heart. It's been much too long."

"It's good to see you again, Rhea," Brontes responded in his baritone cadence.

Rhea appeared inside the cabin doorway. She brought her hand to her mouth and leaned against the doorframe in one of the only unsteady movements I'd ever seen from her.

CHAPTER FORTY-FIVE

I stood closest to Rhea and noticed her eyes gloss. Her other hand uncharacteristically clutched her heart. Rhea sighed and finally spoke with an initially shaky voice, "I'm so glad that you are all back safely from the mission."

"Back from the mission?" Shade asked. "Did you know?"

"Yes." Rhea straightened up and crossed her arms. "I knew the night you hatched the plan. It's also how I knew you were back." She tapped her temple and smiled. "What I didn't know was what happened to Hestia, Poseidon, and Demeter." A tear streaked defiantly down her cheek. She swiped it.

"Thanks to Metis, Zeus, Shade, and Hera," Don said. "We are alive and well."

Rhea's eyes flooded with tears. She dabbed them with fabric from her loose robe.

"Why are you crying?" Don asked. "Everything all right?"

Rhea smiled. "I'm just so happy to see you all back together again."

"Metis is awake!" Tia's voice sang with a vibrant energy.

Everyone turned their attentions to the bed where Metis stirred. She wiped her sweat-matted hair from her face and took the goatskin of water from Tia.

"Hey, Tia," Metis whispered. Her eyes continued to blink rapidly. "Hey, everybody. Ouch." She grabbed the back of her head. "Great Gaia. I have the worst headache."

Don walked over to Metis and knelt down. "How does it feel to be a hero? Sorry, heroine?"

"Now that she's up," Rhea said. "We need to go and find Ouranos and arrange for Eros to release Pontus and Phoebe."

"And get some food!" Shade's voice was louder than normal. "My stomach has cobwebs in it."

"Cobwebs, that's too funny." Meter cackled with laughter then covered mouth and giggled. "And, get to the bathhou—"

"Wait!" I cut her off. My mind raced. I looked with narrowed eyes into the somber faces of Hera, Shade, and Metis, and then turned to Rhea. "Ummm, Ouranos is dead, Headmistress." In the rush of the extraction, I'd totally forgotten. "We saw him take his last breath and ascend into the Sky."

Rhea gasped. "No, he's not. He's—but—" She gazed into my soul through my eyes. "Dead? How? Are you *absolutely* certain?"

The four of us nodded.

"You can read our minds. You know we tell the truth," I said.

Hera stepped forward. "We were all there."

"But … " Rhea said, "I *just* saw Ouranos in the Megaron not long ago."

Rhea's last words hovered in the air. My jaw dropped as I sifted back through memories I knew I had. Images that had burned into my mind. I held Rhea's gaze as my eyebrows pinched closer together, matching her concern.

"Let's figure this out, shall we." Rhea's glee had vanished. The old austere Rhea returned. She exited the cabin with a brisk turn.

I turned to Metis. "You rest. We'll be back."

"No way. I'm coming with." She bounded from bed, still holding her head.

Rhea led the way with a quick gait, crunching shoal underfoot. All of us students held close to her heels. The Cyclopes brothers followed behind us. Their heavy footfalls shook the ground. I was glad they were on our team.

We rounded the back corner of the gym as Ouranos rounded the front corner. He stopped, his silvery hair wild as snakes.

"Ahhh, well it seems all of our students have returned," Ouranos said, his voice almost unsteady. "Praise Gaia. Very well. Carry on then." He continued walking toward the Cloudwell.

Rhea looked back at us. I shrugged. But something didn't seem right. I know what we saw in the armory. Had he healed somehow? But how? Hera placed a hand on my back almost as if to support my thought.

With everyone right there, including the Cyclopes, I decided to take a risk. I stepped out of the group. "Headmaster," I said. "Were you seriously going to close the school down if we couldn't find Tia, Don, and Meter? Isn't that what you said?"

Whispers and murmurs hissed behind me.

Ouranos stopped and turned. "Son, I run this school. And I can do with it what I please," he snarled. "But since you're all back, let's carry on. I have business to attend to." He turned and strode toward the Cloudwell. "I'll be back before start of new term."

I wasn't satisfied because I knew what we saw in the armory. I walked after him and footfalls followed me. Rhea caught up to me and we walked side-by-side.

Headmaster reached the bottom of the Cloudwell when Rhea spoke again, "Ouranos, just what business must you attend to that overshadows the return of our students? Should you not be planning a feast?"

He stopped about ten paces away from the Hurler and turned, wearing an exasperated expression. "If it's a feast you want, then by all means throw one."

"Headmaster," Hera called over my shoulder as we all continued down the Cloudwell. "How did you heal yourself so quickly? And how did you end up in the Titan Armory in a pool of your own ichor blood, with a sickle protruding from your torso—"

Ouranos whipped his head around. His eyes narrowed and a scowl wrinkled his face. "Clearly. I. Am. Not. Injured." He said with gravelly staccato through clenched teeth. "Now, if that's all—"

"But, you gasped your last breath," Hera said more insistently. "Right in front of Shade, Zeus, Metis, and myself. Your body turned to cosmic dust and became the Sky. How did you come back to life?"

I stepped forward.

"Don't you move," Ouranos said with his hands raised. His blue-eyed gaze shifted unpredictably over my shoulders.

"Fine," I said. Ouranos becoming particles of light definitely meant he was real. And this imposter was fake. And if I could shift into a dragon, then anyone could shift into anyone. But who would benefit from all this upheaval? Metis said that Kronos was behind her entire plan of deceit. And in the armory, Ouranos said, *"F-f-find K-Kronosss … "*

"But you know what I think … " I stepped forward again, risking all. "You're not Ouranos at all." More gasps rang out. "You're Kronos!"

Then right before our eyes he shapeshifted back into dark-haired and goateed Kronos, complete with eyebrows as big as ferrets. A chorus of exclamations rang out.

"You animal!" Don yelled. "Wait 'till I get my hands on you—"

"Yeah?" Kronos smirked. "How'd that work out for you last time we saw one another?"

"Rotten bastard!" Don lunged forward, but was frozen by Kronos' peculiar deity magic, telekinesis and energy manipulation. Don's arms were outstretched, his hands tightening into fists.

"Watch your tongue, boy," Kronos said. "Mind you, this is no admission of guilt. I can shift into Ouranos because our blood is the same. He's my father. We share many similarities."

Metis stepped forward. "What you don't know, Headmaster, is that I know all the details of your entire plan."

Kronos' face faltered, but then he recovered composure. "You know less than nothing!" Kronos laughed wickedly. "Girl, you're in the Phlegethon without a paddle."

"So is your little girlfriend, Campe!" I snarled, walking forward.

"Impressive. But you have no idea what you're facing right now."

"I have a bone to pick with you, Kronos." My hands tingled and ached fiercely as they summoned energy. I continued to stalk toward him.

"Is that some new trick you learned?" He pointed to my illuminated hands.

I took a step forward, but Kronos held his hand up. I met stiff resistance in the air around me. Kronos' hand produced some manner of force field, against which I now struggled to walk. I took another labored step forward. But it felt like my feet slogged through thickest mud. Yet, I continued to take steps.

"I can manipulate time," Kronos said, pulsing his hand toward me. "Stop it. Speed it up. Slow it down. I can bend energy. Whatever you are doing with your hands will never touch me."

And still, I continued to walk. Either his power had weakened or mine had grown beyond measure.

"Don't let him touch the Hurler!" Don said. "We'll never find him."

I ducked and rolled my left arm over the energy field Kronos had cast toward me like it was a rope. Then I grabbed hold of the energy rope, pulling myself closer to Kronos with each step. Kronos jerked toward me and then yanked himself backward.

"Kronos!" Rhea yelled. "You filthy—"

"Hush your fuss, pussy cat."

"That's lioness to you. You may have been involved in Ouranos' death, but you'll not harm my cubs." She pulled Metis back and stepped before all of us.

"Check that." We formed a semi-circle around Rhea. "This pride will protect our own."

"That figures," Kronos said, "Given that she is your mother, after all."

"Whose mother?" Don stood beside me. "My parents are on the island of Rhodes."

"And mine are on Samos," Hera chimed. So what are you talking about?"

"Go ahead. Ask Rhea, since she's so good at hiding things. Duplicitous wench." Kronos pointed to us; Don, Shade, Meter, Tia, Hera, and Me. "The entire stinking litter, right here. But I guess mama lion forgot to tell you that little tidbit. Only Nyx knows who your father is."

I reflexively stepped backward. I gazed at Rhea like I'd never known her, like it was our first meeting all over again. I wondered how I could both know someone and not know her at the same time? And wondered if I knew anything at all.

"*You're* my moth—" My mind raced in reconciliation of memory after revelation after deceit after surprise and I was afraid if I said any more, I would sob. One crushing blow after another. Rhea's eyes softened and tears perched at the edges of her lids.

I gasped, unable to utter a single syllable. Pressure built in my nostrils. Shallow breaths fought their way through my constricted throat. I choked back the hot tears that threatened to flood my cheeks as my entire life rushed through my mind in an assault of images and memories. Rhea held me close. The energy flushed through me with effervescence I couldn't explain.

As jarring and simultaneously soothing as that news was, it all made sense. Everything. I turned to Rhea, whose eyes had glossed over again. She cupped her mouth with her hand.

My lip quivered. All this time, my mother had been right under my nose. She'd greeted me at the base of the mountain, showed me around campus, cared for me. "You *knew* that I wanted to find my real mother," I said to Rhea.

Shade threw his hands in the air. "I'm lost!"

Rhea gazed into my eyes. "I wanted to tell you, all of you. I just couldn't. Not yet. The Oracles decreed that the day would come where Kronos would attempt to slay his six children. And I simply could not allow that to happen."

"Wait ... " Tia clapped loudly. "That means Kronos is—"

"Damn!" Hera said. "That's deep."

"So you hid us in plain sight," Meter said. "That's brilliant. But I still want to vomit."

For the first time, Kronos threatened to become unglued. "Rhea!" He roared, pointing to himself. "You mean I am the father? Of these six? You told me our children died at birth. You lied to me. I should strangle—"

In blinding fashion, the Khaos Council descended from the heavens in their signature shafts of energy. Once Erebus, Eros, and Phanes formulated fully, Kronos pointed to us.

"Those four were the last to persons to see Ouranos alive," Kronos yelled. "Apprehend them!"

"Our investigation took longer than normal," Golden-skinned Phanes said. "But, we've finally shed light on this dark set of events."

"Great," Kronos blared. "Get them."

"Kronos," Eros said, "the Council is hereby taking you in to custody."

"What did I do?" Kronos said.

"What didn't you do?" Don, Tia, and Meter yelled at the same time.

"Step away from the Hurler," Erebus ordered. "I'll not ask you again."

Kronos shook his head. "I can't do that." He reached for the Hurler.

A dark rope appeared in Erebus' palms. Before Kronos could raise his hands, Erebus' rope had bound Kronos' wrists and covered his hands in a black fog.

Eros said, "Time's up."

CHAPTER FORTY-SIX

Kronos' eyes darkened as the rope slithered around his mouth, rendering him mute. I seethed with unspent rage. Knowing he'd be in custody was satisfying, but not as satisfying as wrapping my hands around his throat. Or hitting him in the temple with a hot bolt of energy.

"Easy, Zeus," Eros said. "He'll not bother you all again. We have enough evidence to hold him in Tartarus where he will await his trial before Gaia in the High Court. And I apologize about the accusations earlier, but we had to make Kronos comfortable enough to think we weren't on to him."

"We also know about the spear now," Erebus said. "Its shaft is comprised of Dark Matter, a substance more powerful than cosmic dust, which Hestia, I believe, was on her way to discovering."

"That explains a lot," Tia said.

Erebus tugged on the dark rope that shackled Kronos. "Much of my own body is composed of Dark Matter and Dark Energy, which is why Kronos is powerless against the lasso I've produced."

Golden-skinned Phanes said, "As you can see, we already knew about Dark Matter's existence, but had neglected to inform students about it. Obviously, if this substance falls into the wrong hands, it could have disastrous ramifications. At least it won't be Kronos. We're not exactly sure how the weapon was formed, however, given that neither Kronos nor Hyperion are craftsmen. But I'm sure that will come out at trial."

"Again, I apologize for having to take such a hard line with you all," Eros said. "But Khaos business is always serious. That said, allow me to express my deepest condolences to you, Rhea, and to this school. I have love for you all and wish you the best moving forward."

I sighed. "What about Hyperion?"

Kronos grunted, struggling unsuccessfully against his constraints.

"Hyperion offered to turn on Kronos in return for amnesty," Phanes said. "I'm not sure I can trust his motivations. His testimony regarding Crete was that all injuries were your fault, not his. Pallas and Perses threw wildly wayward spears. The one that killed your friend ricocheted off your shield. The one that hit the lady, you pushed her into its path." His lips tightened into a line. "In any case, he's being detained, awaiting trial."

My mind reeled back to the attack as a boulder-sized lump of nausea formed in my gut. I wiped at the perspiration that suddenly formed on my brow.

"So, who's hauling the sun?" Meter asked.

"His son Helios has assumed the sun chariot duties," Phanes answered.

"Good. 'Cause a girl needs her daily dose of sunlight."

"We still have the matter of the empty Throne to consider," Erebus said. "We will return to help steward you through the transition."

The council members surrounded Kronos and then in an instant, they all vanished.

Rhea hugged me despite my foul, tattered clothes and Acheron odor. Soothing calm permeated me. She shushed me mentally while holding me tight. My muscles thawed. Tension fell away.

"Now you see why Professor Phoebe told you that shapeshifting into another person is grievously unforgivable, for so many reasons." Meter said.

"And now that the lion is out of the sack, I will discuss and reconcile everyone's origins very soon. You've been given way too much to digest for one day."

"So—" Meter's voice quivered. "I'm confused. Ouranos is … *dead*? Like, for real?" She covered her mouth with her hand. Tia hugged her probably as much for Meter as for herself.

Hera's voice was solemn. "We know what we saw in the armory. It took all my strength not to unravel."

"Never thought I'd see the day when … " Tia's voice trailed off. "And now you tell us that that ogre of a man Kronos is actually our father?" She knelt to one knee. "I'm going to need a stiff goblet of nectar."

My mind frayed. I wanted to chase after Kronos. Wanted to kill him with my bare hands. Wanted to hug Metis and talk about the dizzying conversation we'd begun in Tartarus. Wanted to hug Hera and share a gyro and talk world domination strategies.

Most of all, I had so many questions for Rhea that I didn't know where to begin. I desperately wanted to see Tos again. Wanted to go home. I missed my mother.

"Um, we all need some quality time in the bathhouses before we go *anywhere*." Hera pinched her nose.

Meter threw her arm around me. "Stinky or not, I can't thank you enough. The Underworld is an unforgiving place." The gold flecks in her eyes were still mesmerizing.

"Hey, I was on the rescue team too, you know," Shade said as he slid next to Meter. Meter's smile bloomed as she looped her arm through his.

"And don't forget Metis and Hera." I said.

Rhea smiled. "After you wash up, I want you all to join me in the

Headmaster's office."

Meter turned to Hera, Metis, and Tia. "Ladies, I think it's time for some balneotherapy and spa pampering."

Hera raised both hands. "Girl, after our little adventure, I'm gonna need about two days of therapy."

Everyone turned toward the bathhouses in silence. I think the day had been too much for all of us. I finished bathing before Don and Shade. My hands trembled with nervous energy about what Rhea had to tell us. I dressed quickly and then closed my eyes for several long moments on my bed.

Some time later, a knock at my door brought my attention back. Shade peeked his head around my door. His black tunic had returned, along with his black arm cuffs. "Are you ready? We're going to walk in together."

I rose to my feet and joined Shade and Don outside on the path down the hill from the housing area. All aglow, Hera, Meter, Tia, and Metis padded down the walkway and assembled with us. Together we trekked to Headmaster's office. Sadly, Rhea now reigned as sole headmistress.

Don announced our arrival by the lion's head doorknocker.

"Come in," Rhea called out.

We entered and arranged ourselves around the giant marble slab that had been Ouranos' desk.

"Recent events have been nearly too much for me to grapple with … partly because I knew what you didn't."

"That you were our mother?" Tia asked with a shaky voice.

Rhea nodded. She gazed at Tia. "I gave birth to you near a roaring hearth fire on the island of Kerkyra. You were the first. I cried ugly tears when I had to leave you. But I knew you were in very good care."

She ambled around the desk and held Don's hand next. "You were my only water birth, the biggest of all of my children. I delivered you to Arne among a flock of lambs on the island of Euboea."

Don wiped his eyes.

Rhea turned toward Hades. She cradled his chin in her palm. "My second born. I spawned you in the mouth of the volcano on Limnos, swallowed by shadows and the safety of darkness. I knew you'd be safe there."

Rhea then sat on the edge of the desk near Meter. "Demeter, you were my most difficult labor. You simply refused to come out. Water didn't work. Darkness didn't work. Finally, exhausted, I lay down in a field of high grasses on northern Kithira. It had been cloudy all day, but a strong ray of sunshine shot through the clouds and you were born right into it."

Meter covered her mouth with her right hand. Hera held her left hand.

"And Hera, you actually were my easiest childbirth. You seemed to be in such a hurry. It was a bright, sunny day on the shores of the river Imvrassos on Samos. I knew you'd fare well there." Rhea rifled her fingers through Hera's dark curly locks.

"And lastly ... " Rhea turned to me, "You, the baby brother to all of your older siblings, were of course born on Crete in the cave on Mount Ida. Amalthea and Adamanthea nursed you to be the strong young man you are today. And there was another newborn, Anytos, that I was certain would grow to be one of your best friends."

Hot, fresh tears emerged as memories leaked from my eyes. Metis eased to my side and embraced me tightly.

Rhea shook out her hands, clenched and stretched her fingers. "I am so sorry for any undue agony I have caused you. Please accept my apology. I felt like this was the correct moment to underscore your similarities instead of your differences. As we move forward, rebuilding this school and toward Kronos' trial, you all will need to be tighter than ever. Do you understand?"

We all nodded.

Don stepped into the middle of us. "I am blown away that we're all siblings. This is amazing and scary. It's a lot to digest."

"Exactly," Tia offered. "I mean, it's not a bad thing ... but every memory I've ever had now has to be threaded into a new narrative. A much larger tapestry."

"I don't know." Meter paced back and forth. "This actually makes perfect sense now. It totally explains why we fought like stags and goats."

"Whatev ... " Hera folded her arms. "I'm just glad we're all here together right now to enjoy this revelation." She propped herself against the side of the marble desk. "Samos was a fine beginning to my life. And yes, I now have a bit of context ... but don't think it's going to alter my world domination plans."

"Well, I still want to go back to Crete to see Amalthea," I said. "To make sure she's all right."

Rhea smiled. "I'd be upset if you didn't go. I owe her so much. Take everyone with you. She'll want to meet them—"

"Deal!" I said before she'd finished.

"We'd never dream of letting him go alone," Don said, beating his chest. "Mu Omega Pi. The six of us will be fine, together," Don said. "Especially with the deity magic that Zeus, Hera, and Shade have."

"I am itching to get some of that cosmic dust," Tia announced. "It just occurred to me ... Kronos stole my research. What a ride that was! Attacked by Kronos in the Observatory. Epic fight between him and Ouranos, let me tell you. Tables flying. Air bending. If it weren't so terrifying, it would've been amazing." Tia was definitely back to her true chatterbox form.

"We figured as much," I said. "But, we did find something helpful that you'll want to see."

"The scroll," Shade and Hera said at the same time.

Meter laughed. "Are you two friends now?"

Hera wrinkled her nose. "Girl, stress and a common enemy will work wonders. And, he did save my ass down there." She pointed to the ground and smiled. "No one is all bad. But don't get the wrong idea. I'm still all business."

Shade smiled and put his arm around Hera while shooting a glance at Meter. "Well, Meter, I just don't think things are gonna work out between us, being siblings and all."

Meter threw her head back and cackled. "Way to let a girl down easy." She winked at Shade. "Somehow, I'll live." She paused and smiled. "We both will. Come over here and give your little sister a hug."

Shade closed the distance between him and Meter. Their embrace was sweet and supportive. And perfect.

"After we grab something to eat, let's hurry to the Cloudwell," I said.

Don smiled. "Look at you. You've gone from tiny twig to full grown tree in one term."

"I guess I have."

"Every being goes through an incubation period," Rhea said. "And when the time comes for them to emerge into the world ... it happens, whether they're ready for it or not. Consider this your coming out party."

"Do you remember our earlier conversation ... about life and opposition?" Rhea asked me.

I nodded.

She smiled the warmest smile I'd seen from her yet. Her eyes welled with tears again. She sniffled and wiped her eyes. Her voice cracked. "Way to grab those reins."

$$\Sigma$$

After eating, I walked to the Cloudwell with my brothers and sisters and Metis. Bright pinks and oranges streaked through lapis across the western sky, while indigo darkened the east.

My heart ached for Rhea ... and for Amalthea ... but especially for Tos, that he would never meet my real mother, or these great siblings of mine. He could never see what I'd become, or the power I wielded. Then, I realized that perhaps everything happened exactly how it was supposed to happen, not necessarily how I wanted. But, all the events had fallen into place as the cosmos had designed them. My existence was part of a larger, more complex mosaic, where if I drew close, I could only see my tile. However, if I stepped back, I could see the entire vision. But, I still missed my friend. I palmed my chest where his wound had been.

Once I reached the Hurler, Metis brushed my shoulder and said, "You know, the thing I've always loved about sunsets is the interplay of dark and light colors. Lines blurred. No ending. No beginning."

I'd recently been so caught up with Hyperion's relationship to the sunrise and sunset that I hadn't stopped to simply admire them for what they were. Beautiful. I appreciated Metis' refreshing ability to do that, to remind me of life's beauty.

"All right—" I interrupted my own thoughts. "Are we all ready?"

They nodded and placed their hands atop the Hurler.

"When we get back, we're going to need to design some killer weapons to protect us against future threats," I said. "So be thinking about what kind of signature weapon you want to make. And Hera, we definitely need to get you a better weapon than just your mind."

She smiled. "There is no greater weapon."

I held my hand in the air. A sphere of yellowish-white energy strings crackled, pulsing around my closed fist. "I beg to differ."

ACKNOWLEDGEMENTS

As always, I thank my loving family for supporting me through teeth gnashing and hand wringing, the late, late nights and the up way too early's that it takes to realize a dream.

The saying, "It takes a village…" definitely applies to this novel's journey. I first conceived this story in 2011 at the SCBWI International Conference in New York, fittingly under the watchful eye and powerful scepter of Hermes who stands high above Grand Central Station. SCBWI, is a village all by itself, an ultra supportive community of like minded writers and artists. I'm so glad I joined.

I then joined forces with the best critique group ever from NV SCBWI. CRITERATI, we called ourselves. And it was in this group of awesomeness that The Sky Throne took its first baby steps as I sent out chapter by chapter every two weeks to get torn apart. I then got accepted to the world renowned NV SCBWI Mentor Program, where I was mentored by Suzanne Morgan Williams.

Additionally, I want to recognize all the critique partners, BETA readers, and others who ever helped on the story: Heather Petty, Tracy Clark, Ellen Hopkins, Dawn Callahan, Temoca Dixon, Jenny MacKay, Julie Dillard, Caryn Neidhold, Kim Harnes, Naomi Canale, Lisa Marcusson, Stacey Rice, Amanda Tremblay, Joel Pettipiece, Amy Cook, Jason Roer, Nikki Mann, Marissa Graff, Martina Boone, Melpomene Selemidis, Maria Bitar, Ella Kennen, my editors, Laura Whitaker and Michelle Millet, and finally Georgia McBride. Thank you so much.

CHRIS LEDBETTER

Chris Ledbetter grew up in Durham, NC before moving to Charlottesville, VA in 11th grade. After high school, he attended Hampton University where he promptly "walked-on" to the best drum line in the conference without any prior percussion experience. He carried the bass drum for four years, something his back is not very happy about now.

After a change of heart and major, he enrolled in Old Dominion University and earned his degree in Business Administration. He's worked in various managerial and marketing capacities throughout his life. He taught high school for six years in Culpeper, VA, and also coached football.

He has walked the streets of Los Angeles and New York City, waded in the waters of the Atlantic and Pacific oceans, and climbed Diamond Head crater on Hawaii and rang in the New Year in Tokyo, Japan. But he dreams of one day visiting Greece and Italy.

His writing awards include: Evernight Publishing Readers Choice: Best YA Book of the Year 2015, Library of Clean Reads Best Reads of 2015, USA Today HEA Blog Must-Read Romance 2015.

OTHER MONTH9BOOKS TITLES YOU MIGHT LIKE

INTO THE DARK
SERPENTINE
EMERGE

Find more books like this at http://www.Month9Books.com

Connect with Month9Books online:
Facebook: www.Facebook.com/Month9Books
Twitter: https://twitter.com/Month9Books
You Tube: www.youtube.com/user/Month9Books
Tumblr: http://month9books.tumblr.com/
Instagram: https://instagram.com/month9books

Stuck in her best friend's body, only one can survive.

INTO THE DARK

CAROLINE T. PATTI

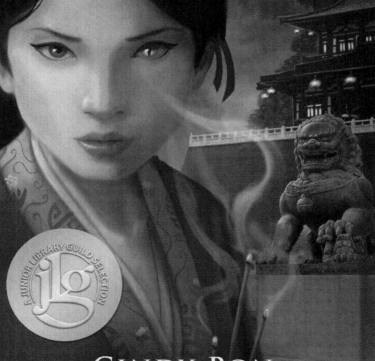

SERPENTINE

"Unique and surprising, with a beautifully-drawn fantasy world that sucked me right in!" — **Kristin Cashore**, *New York Times* bestselling author of **BITTERBLUE**

CINDY PON

MER CHRONICLES
BOOK 1
She will risk everything to stop him from falling in love with the wrong girl.
Emerge
TOBIE EASTON
"The most fun I've had reading in a long time!" —Wendy Higgins, *New York Times* bestselling author of the *Sweet Evil* series